Rewriting December

Rewriting December

Nicole Crystal

Nicole Crystal

Rewriting December

BY NICOLE CRYSTAL

Copyright © 2024 by Nicole Crystal
Library of Congress Cataloging-in-Publication Data
Names: Crystal, Nicole, author.
Title: Rewriting December
Description: First Edition
Revised Version
ISBN: 9798990286603 (trade paperback) |
ISBN: 9798990286627 (trade hardback) |
ISBN: 9798990286610 (ebook)

For Stephanie,
Thank you for all your support
and encouragement.
May I always be your Arden.
Love you, Sis!
♥

This story contains themes and situations that may be distressing for some readers. These include:

- Depictions of car accidents and related trauma
- Loss of family members
- Infidelity in relationships
- Alcohol abuse and addiction
- References to sexual assault (non-graphic)
- Mental health issues, including depression
- Toxic relationship dynamics
- Self-destructive behavior

While these themes are handled with care and are part of the characters' growth journeys, reader discretion is advised. If you are sensitive to any of these topics, please proceed with caution or consider whether this story is right for you at this time.

Prologue

Jake

December 13ᵗʰ, Six Years Ago

They say your life flashes before your eyes when you're about to die. For me, it was just a pair of amber eyes, flecked with stardust.

I'm pinned to my seat, the taste of blood and airbag dust thick in my throat. Through the cracked windshield, snowflakes mock me, each one a ticking second off my life.

Then she's there, this girl with fire in her eyes and determination set in her jaw. She's kicking at my windshield like it personally offended her, and I want to tell her to save herself, that I'm not worth it.

But she grabs my face, forcing me to look at her. "Promise you'll stay with me," she demands, her voice steel wrapped in velvet.

I can't speak, can barely breathe, but I manage a nod. Because how can I say no to an angel?

Blood runs down her wrists as she struggles with my seatbelt. When it finally gives, my chest heaves. She tugs at me, her slight frame straining against my dead weight. Somehow, between her determination and my desperate will to live, we manage to get me partway through the shattered windshield. Pain sears through every nerve, but I cling to those eyes. They're my lifeline, my reason to keep fighting.

"You're going to be okay!" she calls as paramedics pull her away, and I believe her. I have to.

I try to call out, to ask her name, but my voice fails me. As darkness creeps in, I make a silent promise: I'll find her again. My starry-eyed angel. My savior.

1

∽

Cora

November 27th

I stare at the final page on my screen, cringing as the protagonists ride off into the sunset for their happily ever after. If only editing romance novels aligned with reality—an epic love story that explodes like an overstuffed pillow.

No. The stories I'm assigned don't conclude with their sister, husband in tow, picking them up outside their apartment with only two suitcases and a box of tear-soaked tissues after discovering their fiancé had been cheating on them for months.

Bing!

I tap the notification without thinking. Logan's name mocks me from the tiny screen, my personal reminder why love isn't enough. And despite my best efforts, the tears fall as that familiar cocktail of humiliation, grief, and exhaustion hits once again.

Three damn weeks of this. Three weeks since I stormed out, leaving Logan silhouetted in the doorway, his tattered excuses echoing down the hall. How long until that image becomes a distant memory instead of the picture burned into my brain?

My sister appears in the doorway, interrupting my spiral. "Another bad day?"

"If, by bad, you mean I'm fresh out of wine and dignity? Then absolutely," I respond, bitterness seeping into my voice as I toss the phone out of view.

Arden winces, but her voice remains calm like always. *She's going to make an excellent mother.* "It's only been twenty days, hon. Go easy on yourself. You'll be back on your feet in no time."

I snort. Back on my feet? I'm holed up in my sister's guest room, and I've barely left it since I got here. I even skipped Thanksgiving last week just to cozy up under the covers solo. I'd be thrilled to 'see the light of day' at this rate.

As if reading my mind, Arden tugs at my arm. "Come on. We're going downstairs to the coffee shop. You need to get out of this apartment."

"Arden, no—" I start to protest, but she's already pulling me towards the door.

"Grab your computer. There's some nice space to work down there," she insists. "Consider this sisterly intervention."

Ten minutes later, I'm reluctantly perched on a stool at The Daily Grind, nursing a cappuccino I didn't really want. The cheerful jingle of bells every time the door opens feels like a personal attack on my fragile emotional state.

"See? Isn't this better than wallowing in that empty room?" Arden asks, her early pregnancy glow making me feel even more like a human dumpster fire by comparison.

"Jury's still out," I mutter. But I have to admit, the rich aroma of coffee and the gentle hum of conversation is not terrible.

"Get used to it," Arden says firmly. "I'm now requiring at least thirty minutes of playtime a day. Consider this your personal playground."

"Should I go back to calling you 'mom' like when we were

teenagers, too?" I tease, trying to suppress a smirk as I eye her over my mug.

"Guess all that practice will come in handy soon enough," she says with a shrug, placing her hand over her not-at-all-showing stomach. Then again, she is only nine weeks along.

I look around the small café, taking in the faux fireplace and shelves of books. There are worse places I could be. Like with Logan.

"So, this will be my mandatory outing, huh?" I quip. Might need to brush up on my conversation skills because the only people I've spoken to in the last three weeks are the fictional characters in the books I'm reading.

My gaze wanders to the counter, where a barista is chatting with a customer. Was he here when we walked in? He's scruffy, with an unkempt beard and messy hair that looks like it hasn't seen a comb in days. But there's something about him—maybe the way his eyes crinkle when he smiles, or the easy grace of his movements—that catches my attention.

Arden follows my line of sight and lets out a bark of laughter. "See something you like?"

"Are you kidding?" I bite back. "I'm pretty sure the last thing I need right now is some hot, scruffy barista who will break my heart another six ways to Sunday."

"Hot and scruffy, huh? Sounds like progress," Arden teases. "Don't let Jake's appearance fool you. He can be a gentleman when he wants to be."

There's something in her tone—a hint of familiarity that goes beyond just knowing her local barista—but before I can question it, Jake looks our way. His eyes meet mine briefly, and I quickly refocus on the cappuccino, feeling my cheeks burn.

"The only progress I'm interested in is progressing back to your guest room and my date with a pint of ice cream," I reassure her. But as I peek over the rim of my mug, I catch Jake glancing our way again.

This time, he offers a small, crooked smile that makes my heart do an unexpected flip.

Not your type, girl, I remind myself. Though I'm already involuntarily analyzing him for manuscript inspiration. With a hint of a tattoo showing on his bicep and killer waves, he's giving major wounded bad-boy character vibes. And God knows readers eat up that plotline—some inked hottie healing a broken heroine's ravaged heart, finding true love and blah blah blah.

My phone chimes mid-assessment, and I glance down, seeing Alyssa's name flash.

Alyssa: *Still on for our standard Monday happy hour? Or are you ditching me again for more Hallmark movies?*

I groan, not sure whether I should appreciate the one friend I'd managed to keep during my Logan-hazed relationship or keep pushing her away now that he's gone.

Arden glances at my phone with a raised brow. "Don't you dare cancel again," she warns. "You need this, Co. Besides, Alyssa's probably the only person who can match your cynicism about romance right now."

I sigh. "I'm not exactly in the mood for anything called 'happy hour.'"

Arden starts to argue, but she's cut off by the ringtone from her phone. She glances at the screen and grimaces. "It's work. I have to take this." She stands, gathering her things. "You'll be okay here for a bit?"

"Go. I'll just sit here in my 'personal playground' judging people's coffee order until I hit my required thirty minutes."

As Arden leaves, I pull out my laptop, figuring I might as well get some work done. You know, being Monday and all. I'm deep in the throes of editing a particularly cringe-worthy love scene when a voice startles me.

"Refill?"

I look up to find Jake standing there, coffee pot in hand, his blue eyes twinkling with amusement. Up close, his scruffiness is even more apparent, but somehow it works for him. I realize I've been staring without answering and quickly nod, pushing my mug towards him.

"Thanks," I manage, trying not to notice how his hands dwarf the coffee pot. "I'm going to need all the caffeine I can get to make it through this... literary masterpiece."

Jake's eyebrow quirks up. "Literary masterpiece, huh? Reading it for fun or..."

"Work," I finish. "I'm an associate editor. And let's just say if this is what passes for romance these days, I'm glad I'm swearing off men."

Jake's eyes widen slightly, and I feel my face heat up. *Great. Not only am I the creepy girl staring at the hot barista, but now I'm the bitter, man-hating creepy girl.*

But then Jake's lips twitch into a grin. "Well, on behalf of my gender, I apologize for whatever crime against literature you're suffering through."

A laugh escapes for the first time since... well, since before I called Arden that night. "Trust me, this goes way beyond a simple apology. We're talking reparations on a global scale."

Jake leans against the table, his eyes dancing. "That serious, huh? Maybe I should be taking notes. You know, in case I ever decide to pursue a career in terrible romance writing."

"Oh God, please don't," I groan, but I'm smiling despite myself. "The world can only handle so many 'throbbing members' and 'heaving bosoms.'"

Jake lets out a surprised bark of laughter, drawing curious glances from nearby tables. "Duly noted. I'll stick to coffee for now."

"I'm Cora, by the way," I say, meeting those piercing blues that look like they've already lived a lifetime.

"Jake," he says with a smile. "And you're Arden's..."

"Sister," I finish when he trails off. "I'm staying with her for a few weeks." *Or months*, I add silently. *However long it takes for me to reestablish how to function on my own again.*

"Well, nice to meet you, Cora."

There's a moment where we're just grinning at each other, and I feel something warm unfurl in my chest. *Am I... attracted to a man again?*

The spell is broken by another customer calling for Jake's attention. He straightens up, looking almost reluctant. "Duty calls. But, uh, let me know if you need anything else. To get through your literary ordeal."

I watch him go, my heart fluttering when he glances back and catches me looking. I shake my head, trying to clear it.

What am I doing? I'm not ready for... whatever this is. I have a pity party for one scheduled with Alyssa later, and the last thing I need is to complicate things with some espresso-slinging bad-boy type, no matter how cute or funny he might be.

Still, I'm smiling as I turn back to my laptop. Maybe getting out of the apartment wasn't such a bad idea after all.

Several hours and countless stolen glances later, I reluctantly pack up my laptop. As much as I'd like to camp out in this coffee shop forever (for purely professional reasons, of course), it's time to face the music. Or in this case, face Alyssa and her inevitable inquisition.

I give Jake a small wave as I leave, earning another one of those crooked smiles that does funny things to my insides. *Stop, Cora. He's just the first guy to show you attention after Logan. It means nothing*, I chastise myself as I drop off my computer and head out into the chilly, late November air.

The bar Alyssa chose is already crowded when I arrive, the

after-work crowd in full swing. I spot her at a high top, already nursing what I'm sure isn't her first cocktail of the night.

"Well," Alyssa drawls as I slide onto the stool across from her. "If it isn't the elusive Cora Cooper, finally emerging from her cave of misery and Ben & Jerry's."

"Hello to you too, Lys."

She signals the waiter. "Two dirty martinis, extra olives. We're drowning sorrows tonight."

"I don't have any sorrows to drown," I protest weakly.

Alyssa fixes me with a look. "Honey, you've been wearing the same leggings for a week, and I'm pretty sure that hoodie has seen better days. Trust me, you've got sorrows."

I glance down at my outfit and wince. She's not wrong.

"So," Alyssa leans in, her eyes gleaming with a mix of concern and mischief, "tell me. How bad is it really?"

I take a long sip of the martini, letting the alcohol burn a path down my throat. "On a scale of one to 'contemplating joining a convent?' I'd say I'm hovering around 'seriously considering adopting seventeen cats.'"

Alyssa laughs. "Please. You're allergic to cats. Try again."

I sigh, fiddling with my olive skewer. "It's... it's bad, Lys. I keep thinking I'm over it, that I'm moving on, and then bam! I'll see something that reminds me of him, or I'll have a moment of weakness and check his Instagram, and it's like I'm right back where I started."

"Tell me you haven't been drunk texting him," Alyssa says, narrowing her eyes.

"No!" I exclaim, then pause. "Well, maybe a few times. Arden confiscates my phone most nights now." *Especially after Logan begged for me to come back and I started to pack my bags.* But I don't tell Alyssa that.

"Smart woman, your sister," Alyssa says approvingly. "Unlike that idiot ex of yours. God, I still can't believe he had the balls to cheat on you with a co-worker. Talk about a walking cliché."

I wince at the blunt reminder. "Yeah, well, apparently I have a type–'emotionally unavailable man-children with a desire to destroy my self-esteem.'"

"Screw that," Alyssa declares, signaling for another round. "Your type from now on is 'hot, emotionally stable men who worship the ground you walk on.' Or, you know, just 'hot.' We can work on the rest later."

I laugh into my glass. "Is that your type these days?"

Alyssa grins wickedly. "Honey, my type is 'breathing and between the ages of 25 and 45.' I'm an equal opportunity enjoyer of the male form."

"You're incorrigible," I say, shaking my head.

"And you love me for it," she retorts. "Now, enough sulking. We're going to find you a rebound tonight if it kills me."

I nearly choke on my olive. "What? No, absolutely not. I am not ready for... that."

Alyssa waves dismissively. "Nonsense. The best way to get over someone is to get under someone else. Trust me, I'm practically a doctor in this field."

"I think I'll stick to my ice cream therapy, thanks," I mutter.

"Suit yourself. But don't come crying to me when you've forgotten how to flirt. Speaking of which..." Her eyes focus on something over my shoulder, a predatory grin spreading across her face. "Don't look now, but there's an extremely fuckable specimen at 3 o'clock who's been checking you out for the last five minutes."

Despite my protests, I find myself turning slightly, curiosity getting the better of me. Looky there, she's right again. The guy is hot, all sandy hair and tanned skin. But it only makes me picture another guy with dirty blonde hair who asked me to marry him two months ago, only to cheat on me weeks later.

"To Logan-ish," I murmur, taking another long sip of the drink to rid myself of the memory.

"Oh! I've got it!" Her eyes light up with an idea that I'm sure I'm going to hate. "How comfortable would you be with a blind date?"

"Lys, no. I can barely handle talking to men I know right now, let alone strangers."

"Hear me out," she insists. "I know this guy, Baker. He's cute, he's funny, and most importantly, he's nothing like Logan. It could be just what you need to remind yourself that not all men are lying, cheating scumbags."

I eye her skeptically. "I don't know..."

"Come on, Co," Alyssa pleads. "One date. If it's terrible, I'll personally buy you a year's supply of ice cream and swear off matchmaking forever."

"That's a pretty big promise."

"That's how confident I am," she says with a grin. "Besides, what's the worst that could happen?"

I raise an eyebrow. "Do you want that list alphabetically or chronologically?"

Alyssa rolls her eyes. "Okay, drama queen. But what else are you gonna do this weekend? Mope around your sister's apartment? Come on. You know you want to have a little fun! And trust me, this guy will knock your socks off."

I chew on my lip, considering. Maybe Alyssa has a point. If nothing else, it evens the score, right? Lord knows Logan's probably out galivanting around despite his phone calls begging for me to come home.

"Fine," I sigh, already regretting my decision. "One date. But if he turns out to be a serial killer, you're testifying at the trial."

Alyssa squeals, clapping her hands together. "You won't regret this. Now, let's talk outfits. You can't meet your potential future husband in leggings and a ratty hoodie."

As Alyssa launches into a detailed analysis of my wardrobe (or lack thereof), I wonder what I've gotten myself into. But beneath the anxiety, there's a tiny spark of something else. Hope, maybe? Or at least the possibility of it.

Because my life, right now, needs more than a light edit—it needs a complete rewrite.

2

∽

Jake

November 29ᵗʰ

I stare at my reflection in the coffee shop window, barely recognizing the guy looking back at me. Unkempt beard, hair that hasn't seen a comb in days, dark circles under eyes that have seen too much. I look like hell. But then again, I feel like it, too. Just another day in the life of Jake Rhoades, professional screwup.

With a sigh, I slink into the coffee shop a solid fifteen minutes before my shift starts. Judging by the way my manager's eyes nearly pop out of her skull, she's probably wondering if I'm still riding the drunk train from last night's bender. But for once, I went to bed stone-cold sober.

I do a sweep of the room, finding her immediately. Cora. My guardian angel. My used-to-be best friend's sister-in-law. It's been two days since she first stumbled into the shop with Arden, and I still can't believe it's really her.

Slipping on my apron, I shake my head at the irony of it all. Six years ago, I was in a car wreck. Now? I'm a human coffee dispenser for the girl who saved my sorry ass—twice—and can't even pick me out of a lineup. It's like a cosmic joke without a punchline. Or maybe it's the greatest hit I'll never write.

The café's mind-numbing rhythm takes over. Grind, tamp, brew. Repeat. It's about as exciting as watching paint dry, but hey, at least paint doesn't have to think.

I glance up, catching another glimpse of her. Her honey-colored hair is lit up like a halo, and suddenly I'm back in that car. The acrid smell of burning rubber, blood seeping into the steering wheel, the pain in my shoulder causing me to lose consciousness for a second time. Then her. My personal action hero with eyes that could melt steel.

I shake it off, trying to focus on the here and now. But those amber eyes are suddenly right in front of me, clearing their throat like they're about to deliver a sermon. They're the same eyes that kept me tethered to this body that night, the ones that haunted my morphine-addled dreams in the hospital, and–who am I kidding–the same ones I pictured this morning while brushing my teeth.

"Welcome back, Cora," I manage, plastering on a grin that feels about as genuine as a three-dollar bill. And damn, if those eyes aren't even more stunning up close.

"Morning, Jake," Cora responds, "Large coffee, please. Black."

"Rough night?" I ask casually, sneaking glances at her as I pour. *Rough night? Smooth, bud!* I'm acting like I've never talked to a woman. Then again, I've never really talked to this one before.

A wry smile twists on Cora's lips. Not that I'm looking at them. "More like a rough month. Or year. Take your pick," she says with a hint of bitterness.

I chuckle, the sound rusty from disuse. "I hear you. Life has a way of kicking you when you're down, doesn't it?" *I should know, I'm practically on a first-name basis with rock bottom at this point.*

"You have no idea," Cora sighs, then seems to catch herself. "Sorry, I'm sure you don't need to hear my sob story when you first get in."

I shrug, sliding her coffee across the counter. "Hey, misery loves company, right? Besides, I'm told I'm a pretty good listener." *Which is rich, coming from the guy who's spent the last five years avoiding any meaningful conversation.*

Those amber eyes tick up to mine, and I swear I see a flicker of recognition. I want to say something, to thank her, to ask her where she's been all these years. But that would mean answering where I've been. And, well, I already know how that would end.

I hold my breath, waiting for... I don't know what. A miracle, maybe?

Cora blinks, and just like that, the moment's gone. "Thanks," she says, taking the mug.

"Yeah, no problem."

Not like my world isn't suddenly upside down by her sudden reappearance or anything.

As she returns to her table, my phone buzzes in my pocket. I pull it out to see a text from Lindsey, asking if I'm free tonight. Disappointment curdles at her misguided belief that we share some "friends with benefits" arrangement. Why'd I think getting involved with a twenty-one-year-old was a good idea? Then again, when do I ever think about anything I do?

With a shake of my head, I pocket my phone without responding. I've got work to do, followed by a long shift at Sadie's tonight.

My eyes land on Cora again, all furrowed brow and intense concentration. No. I can't afford to get distracted. Not even by ghosts from my past. Even if those ghosts have eyes I could drown in and a smile that makes me forget how to breathe.

Still, I keep glancing at Cora's table. Each look lifts the fog a bit, makes things seem almost... okay. Until I remember that guys like me don't get second chances. We get to pour drinks, sling coffee, and pretend we're not one depressing power ballad away from totally losing our shit.

When she approaches the counter again later that afternoon, I nearly jump out of my skin.

"Hey," she says, sliding her mug across. "Me again. Could I get another refill? And maybe a muffin? Apparently, caffeine isn't a suitable replacement for actual food. Who knew?"

I chuckle, grabbing the pot. "Arden giving you a hard time about your eating habits?"

Cora's eyebrows shoot up. "You and her are on a first-name basis, huh?"

Shit. She doesn't know Arden and I have history. Backpedal, backpedal! "Oh, you know. She's a regular. You pick things up."

She eyes me curiously, but mercifully lets it slide. "Right. Well, thanks for the coffee. And the muffin."

As she turns to go, my mouth decides to stage a coup against my brain. "I'm here most weekdays."

She pauses, a hint of a smile on her lips. "So I've been told. By Arden."

And then she's gone, leaving me to wonder what else Arden might have said. Clearly, not that we were roommates for a short stint. You know, before life changed.

The rest of my shift crawls by slower than a snail on sedatives. By the time I drag myself into Sadie's that evening, I'm ready to perform a trust fall into the beer taps.

"Whoa there, sunshine," Natalie says as I slump against the bar. "Who pissed in your cornflakes this morning?"

I manage a grunt. "Just living the dream, Nat. One soul-crushing shift at a time."

Like always, Natalie sees through my bullshit. After more than five years, she might know me better than I know myself.

"Seriously, Jake. What's up? You look like you've seen a ghost."

If only she knew how close to the truth that was.

"You ever have someone from your past show up out of nowhere and turn your whole world upside down?" I ask with a sigh.

Nat's eyebrows shoot up. "Honey, that's the plot of every second chance rom-com ever made. But coming from you? This I gotta hear."

I give her the cliff notes version as we set up for the night. No way I'm sharing everything. The less she knows, the better.

"Let me get this straight," she says, hands on her hips. "The girl who saved your life six years ago just waltzed back into your life, and you're what? Scared?"

Put like that, it sounds ridiculous. But then again, my whole life is pretty ridiculous at this point. "It's not that simple, Nat."

"Seems pretty simple to me. Girl saves boy. Boy's now pining for girl. Girl comes back. Cue happily ever after."

"Because my life is just one big fairy tale, right?" I add sarcastically. "In case you haven't noticed, I'm not exactly Prince Charming material."

Nat's expression softens and I already know where this is going. "Jake, you've got to forgive yourself for what happened. You couldn't have known..."

Yeah, and I couldn't have known I'd be living the glamorous life of a bartender with a side of crippling guilt, but here we are.

Before I can dive headfirst into my pity party, the first customers start trickling in. And because the universe loves a good joke, Lindsey's among them, all tight clothes and shark-like smile. Fuck. I should've texted her back. Maybe then I could've avoided this train wreck in stilettos.

"Hey there, handsome," Lindsey purrs, leaning over the bar. "You never responded earlier."

I manage a weak smile. "Yeah, sorry about that. Got caught up with... stuff."

She pouts, but I can see the calculation behind her eyes. "Well, maybe we can make up for lost time later?"

For a hot second, I'm tempted. It'd be so easy to fall back into old habits, to lose myself in the familiar haze of booze and bad decisions. But then Cora's face flashes in my mind, and suddenly, I'm not so keen on my usual brand of self-destruction.

"Not tonight, Linds. I've got band practice in the morning."

It's not a lie. Owen nearly bit my head off last week when I showed up an hour late, reeking of strawberries and regret. The joys of sorority bathrooms.

Still, Thursdays? They're my lifeline. For a few hours, I get to shed this skin of surly, damaged bartender and become someone else. Someone who isn't drowning in a sea of grief and Jack Daniels. Because when I'm on that stage with Owen and Chris, I'm the Jake I used to be—before Tessa and Thomas, before my life became a country song minus the pickup truck.

Lindsey huffs, clearly not used to rejection. Join the club, sweetheart. I've been rejected by life itself.

The rest of the night passes in a blur of drink orders and forced smiles. Six years of this, and I've got the act down pat. Oscar-worthy performance, really.

By last call, I'm running on fumes and considering the sweet embrace of my old friend, Mr. Whiskey. But instead of reaching for the bottle, I find myself thinking of amber eyes and second chances. What the hell?

Natalie's jaw drops like she's watching a pig sprout wings. "Wow, Jake, this girl really has your head spinning, huh?"

"Yeah, or maybe I've finally pickled my brain with all this booze," I reply with a small laugh. *Or maybe it's my savior showing up five days before the worst month of the year.*

When I finally stumble back to my apartment, I grab my guitar, hoping music might keep the nightmares at bay. But as I settle onto the couch, something weird happens. My fingers start moving, coaxing out a melody that doesn't sound like it was born in the bottom of a whiskey bottle.

Before I know it, I'm scribbling lyrics like a man possessed. And here's the kicker–they're not my usual doom and gloom greatest hits. They're... hopeful? Christ, I must be losing it.

But as I stare at the words, I can't help but think maybe, just maybe, my guardian angel's back for round three. And this time, hopefully, I'll give her something better to remember me by.

3

Cora

December 1st

I stare out the window of the highrise apartment that no longer feels like home, watching snowflakes drift toward the streets below. It's December first. The kick-off to the worst month possible. That special time of year when my life inevitably turns into a dumpster fire. If I could skip the entire thirty-one days, I'd do it in a heartbeat.

Welcome to Cora Cooper's Annual December Disaster™.

The accident. Sam. The wedding. And now this. Filling another suitcase at my used-to-be home for a blind date I should have never agreed to.

Why'd I think Logan telling me he loved me in December was the cure to my curse? I close my eyes, the memory flooding back. His apartment. New Year's Eve. Three years ago.

Emotions burn hotter. Bitterness. Grief. Exhaustion. The unholy trinity of post-break-up blues.

Am I really ready for a date?

Alyssa's friendly reminder text flashes mockingly on my phone screen.

Alyssa: *Did Baker text you about tonight, yet? You're going to love him, Co!*

Love him? Ha.

Note to self, liquid courage fuels bad decisions and boosts sucker tendencies. Because, somehow, after three martinis, Alyssa made rebound dating sound like a stroke of brilliance. Now, sober and standing in the gray light of my former bedroom, apprehension hits like a freight train. I'm about as ready for this date as I am to run a marathon in stilettos.

I could cancel—blame the fresh snowfall—but defeated looks terrible on me lately. Besides, I've already used up my quota of pathetic for the month, and it's only day one. I might as well get this over with and play nice for Alyssa.

I zip the bag shut with a vengeful finality, my eyes catching on our engagement photo. Our frozen smiles mock me, like characters in a badly-written romance novel where the 'happily ever after' got scrapped in the final edit.

Logan wants me to forgive him. After finding out he'd been having an affair for months? Please. It left me wondering if his proposal was just some last-ditch effort to throw me off the trail of suspicious crumbs I'd found.

The kicker? It worked. For those blissful weeks of engagement, I actually bought into the fantasy—we were that college couple again. Inseparable. In love. Living our own personal fairy tale.

I squeeze my eyes shut, willing my inner editor to redline that tiny, traitorous voice whispering, "Maybe he'll change!" Time to vacate this former life before I start romanticizing our 'good times' and conveniently forget why I left in the first place.

Been there, done that, got the emotional whiplash to prove it.

As I trudge toward Arden's apartment complex, my reflection in the glass door reads like a rough draft of myself. Hair? A veritable bird's nest of tangled storylines. Eyes? Raccoon-ringed with yesterday's mascara. And—fantastic—my shirt's inside out. At least that's an apt metaphor for my life right now.

Nailed it, Cooper. You're a walking rejection letter.

The cheerful chime of The Daily Grind's door catches my attention. I pause, one foot on the sidewalk, one in snow-slush purgatory. A strong coffee sounds heavenly, but do I really want Jake to see me in my "I've given up on life and fashion" ensemble?

Not that I actually want anything to happen with Coffee Shop Jake. He's just... intriguing. In a totally-not-my-type, walking-red-flag kind of way that has my inner editor itching to rewrite his story.

Oh, what the hell. It's December. Looking like a disaster is practically mandatory. Besides, might be good for him to see me at my worst. Less chance of bad ideas. And given how this month is starting up, I need all the help I can get in the bad idea prevention department.

I push through the door, the rich aroma of coffee hitting me like a caffeinated hug. Worth it.

As expected, Jake's at the counter. What's not expected is how my stomach does a little flip when he glances my way. Damn him and those R-rated fantasies he starred in Wednesday night.

Then again, I'll take "inappropriate daydreams about the hot barista" over "wallowing in ex-fiancé misery" any day of the week. Small victories.

"Cora, I wasn't expecting to see you today," Jake says. There's an edge to his voice he didn't have before. Is he... nervous? The idea sends a thrill through me.

And just like that, my "I don't care what I look like" bravado evaporates faster than my last paycheck. "Yeah, I, uh... needed a caffeine boost." I tuck a wayward strand behind my ear, noticing how Jake's gaze follows the movement. Great. He's probably wondering if I've heard of this revolutionary invention called a hairbrush.

Jake clears his throat, a slight tremor in his hands as he sets down the mug he's holding. "Another rough morning?"

I give a brittle laugh. "Is it that obvious? And here I thought I was nailing the 'effortlessly disheveled' look."

"Nah," he waves, his charming tone returning, "you just look like you could use a pick-me-up after your trip."

Trip? I follow his gaze to where I'm death-gripping my suitcase handle. Shit. Forgot I was still carting around my baggage–literal and emotional.

"Just... spring cleaning. In December," I say, aiming for casual and hoping it doesn't sound like a cry for help.

"Ah, yes. The traditional December purge," he muses, lips twitching.

I roll my eyes, but I'm smiling despite myself. "Okay, smart guy. How about less sass, more caffeine?"

"Coming right up, oh purger of seasons."

As Jake turns to the espresso machine, I catch myself admiring the way his shoulders move. Down, girl. This is not the time for a romance novel moment. Even if he does fill out that t-shirt like it's his job.

"So," Jake says over his shoulder, voice casual but with an undercurrent of... something. "Any exciting plans for the weekend?"

The blind date flashes into my mind like a horror movie trailer. "Oh, you know. Just... existing. Maybe alphabetizing my regrets."

Jake turns back, espresso in hand and a half-smile that's warm and rich, like the coffee he serves, but with an aftertaste of... something else. "Existing is good. Harder than it sounds some days."

Our fingers brush as he hands me the cup, and I swear I feel a spark. Or maybe I've just been statically charging myself on this sweater all morning.

"Thanks," I murmur, reluctantly pulling my hand away before I do something stupid. Like ask if his hands are free later for more existing.

Am I starving for a man's touch? When did that become a thing?

My inner monologue kicks into overdrive, speed-writing potential conversation starters. But before I can hit 'publish' on any of them, Arden's voice cuts through the café's background chatter, "Coco! I thought that was you!"

I wince at the nickname. Nothing says 'desirable adult woman' quite like sounding like a small, yappy dog.

"Coco?" Jake repeats, his eyebrow raising.

"Family nickname," I mutter, shooting Arden a look that could curdle milk. "Just Cora to everyone else. You know, people I don't share DNA with."

Jake nods, his gaze drifting back to my suitcase. "So, you're still at Arden's for a bit longer, then?"

I fidget with my coffee cup, remembering my previous admission, Arden's ascending presence, and the fact that I probably look like I've been beta-reading tear-jerkers all night. "Yeah, just for a bit. Still workshopping my next chapter, you know?"

Jake's lips quirk in a half-smile. "Well, if you need a change of scenery again for your... editing, The Daily Grind's got some great corners for people-watching. Or, you know, hiding from overenthusiastic sisters."

The editor part of my brain goes into overdrive, parsing his words for subtext. Is Jake offering me an escape route or angling for more face time? And why do I hope it's the latter?

"I might just take you up on that," I say, surprising myself with how much I'm looking forward to it.

Arden's gaze ping-pongs between us, her grin spreading like a gossip wildfire. "Am I interrupting something?"

"Nope," I say too quickly. "Just chatting about... existing."

Arden's drawn-out "Sure" is so loaded it could sink a battleship. I'm positive my neck is now a shade of red undiscovered by science.

Jake's not faring much better, looking like he wants the espresso machine to swallow him whole.

Desperate to change the subject before Arden starts planning our wedding, I turn to her. "Did you need something?" *Or are you just here to ruin my chances at inappropriate flirting with attractive baristas?*

Arden's expression shifts, becoming more serious. "Just wanted to check how things went at the apartment. Any unexpected visitors?"

I force a smile, acutely aware of Jake standing on the other side of the counter. "No, thankfully. A December miracle."

Arden nods, glancing between Jake and me again. "Well, I was just about to head up. Are you staying down here, or..."

Stay and marinate in this new nervous energy? Tempting, but...

"I'll be right behind you," I respond. Might as well get this dress hung up before I have to add ironing to my list of to-do's prior to tonight's disaster—I mean, date.

"Great, I'll grab my things," Arden says, already heading back in the direction she came from.

Just like that, I'm alone with Jake. The silence stretches between us like a rubber band, ready to snap. Do I have to explain the suitcase now?

"December," I sigh, almost to myself, like the month is a personal affront. Jake's knowing laugh has me intrigued. "I take it you're not a fan either?"

His laugh fades, replaced by a smile that doesn't quite reach his eyes. "Let's just say, the holidays and I have a... complicated relationship. But hey, January's just around the corner, right?"

"It can't come soon enough," I murmur.

Our eyes engage in a wordless dialogue, exchanging volumes in the space between blinks. It's like I'm seeing him clearly for the first time. There's something achingly familiar about his gaze, a shared connection that feels like both a lifeline and a live wire. I'm tempted to dive in, to lose myself in the narrative of what-ifs and maybes—

"Alright, got everything," Arden announces, her voice yanking me back to reality. She materializes at my side, computer bag slung over her shoulder like a punctuation mark ending our moment.

"Jake," she says, her tone warm and familiar—too familiar. "Don't be a stranger, okay? And let's not wait so long to catch up next time."

I look between them, frantically searching for context clues. Why do I get the feeling I'm missing something here?

As we head to the elevator, I can't help but look back. Jake's already with another customer, but I catch him sneaking a glance my way. It's a fleeting moment, barely a footnote. Still, it sends my pulse racing.

What is it about him...?

The elevator doors close, and Arden waits approximately 0.2 seconds before pouncing. "So," she says, her voice dripping with faux-casualness, "that was some intense coffee ordering back there. Do you always stare soulfully into baristas' eyes, or is Jake special?"

I roll my eyes so hard I'm surprised they don't fall out. "Oh please, I was just being friendly to your barista BFF." I parry her question with one of my own, determined to shift the narrative focus. "If any-one should be on trial for questioning, it's you. Since when are you besties with the local coffee slinger?"

Arden gasps dramatically. "You caught me. Jake and I have been running an underground coffee cartel. Very hush-hush. We call it 'Beans and Dreams.'"

I snort despite myself. "Seriously, though, what's the deal?"

"What? I can't have friends you don't know about?" Arden quirks an eyebrow. "And don't change the subject, missy. You were totally flirting."

"What? No," I sputter. "I was just... getting some much-needed caffeine."

"Is that what the kids are calling it these days?" Arden smirks.

The elevator dings, saving me from having to respond. Thank you, elevator gods.

Arden heads for the apartment door, her voice softening. "Whatever it was, it was good to see you smiling again. Even if it was at my 'BFF,' as you so eloquently put it."

"Yeah, well, don't get too excited," I reply, hauling my emotional baggage–and my suitcase–inside. "I've still got a blind date to survive tonight. Emphasis on survive."

Arden shakes her head. "I still can't believe you let Alyssa talk you into this."

I let out a soft laugh, heading toward my bedroom. "Aren't older sisters supposed to protect their siblings from bad decisions, not encourage them?"

"Maybe when they haven't put themselves on house arrest for a month," Arden winks. "Now, let's see the dress you picked for this disaster... I mean, date."

As I pull out the dress, I wonder if I'm making a huge mistake. But then again, it's December. Mistakes are practically mandatory.

* * *

The afternoon slips through my fingers like loose pages, my mind a chaotic first draft alternating between Jake's smile and tonight's looming blind date. Productivity? Please. At this rate, I'll be demoted to editing grocery lists.

As 9 PM approaches, I'm wrangling my hair into submission for the third time. Nothing screams "totally over my ex" like waging war on every rebellious curl.

"You sure about this?" Arden asks, eyeing me like I'm on the verge of spontaneous combustion.

I think about the Logan-shaped hole in my chest. "I need to start somewhere," I say, addressing my reflection more than Arden. "Besides, my hermit application was rejected on a technicality."

Arden squeezes my shoulder, her expression a mash-up of concern and amusement. "Just remember, I'm one SOS text away from staging a daring rescue."

With a deep breath that does absolutely nothing to steady my nerves, I give myself a final once-over and head downstairs. While waiting for my ride, I mindlessly scroll through social media—and there he is. Logan, grinning next to some Stepford-wife-in-training. Caption: "New beginnings ❤"

Well, if that isn't the plot twist from hell. So much for his heartbroken text last night.

I close the app, slide into the Uber, and banish my phone to the depths of my purse like it's committed a cardinal sin. And let's be honest, hasn't it? Because if this is what moving on looks like—forcing myself into uncomfortable situations while my ex is tagged in photos from his next prize—I'm not sure I'll survive.

Don't go there, Cora. You deserve better than what Logan gave you.

When the driver approaches the restaurant (or is it a bar?) I glance up at the name, checking that it matches the text Baker sent. Sadie's.

Sadie's... Why does that sound so familiar?

Suddenly, it hits me—a flash of déjà vu as vivid as red ink on a white page. This was where Logan and I were supposed to meet Arden three New Year's Eves ago. The night Arden would finally meet the man I thought was my happily ever after.

A snowstorm changed our plans that night. Instead of venturing into the city, we ended up at a friend's party. Before the clock struck midnight, Logan whispered those three little words that seemed to break my December curse.

Or so I thought.

I shake my head, willing the memory to dissolve like sugar in bitter coffee. As if I needed another Logan-shaped thought tonight. At this rate, I could start a drinking game—a shot for every ex-related flash-back. On second thought, better not. I'd be passed out before the appetizers arrived.

Forcing down the lingering ache, I push open the door. Sadie's isn't the intimate setting I'd imagined for a blind date—it's all crowded spaces, dim lighting, and pulsing music. Then again, this whole scenario is Alyssa's brainchild. I shouldn't be surprised if the evening reads like a rom-com with a touch of chaos theory.

You've got this, Cooper. Time to start a new chapter.

Minutes after I claim one of the high-tops, a charismatic redhead approaches with a smile. "What can I grab for you, hon?"

"Light beer. Whatever's on draft." I glance at the empty seat across from me, fidgeting. "I'm meeting someone. A blind date." *Way to broadcast your desperation.*

Her lips quirk. "How about a shot to accompany that beer? On the house." She spins around, tossing a glance over her shoulder. "I'm Natalie, by the way. If you need anything, just holler."

Fantastic. The waitress's sympathetic glance might as well be a neon sign flashing "Recently Dumped, Approach with Caution." I resist the urge to check if I've accidentally pinned that label to my dress.

By 9:15, my impatience morphs into dread. My phone screen re-mains stubbornly blank, no explanatory text in sight. I fire off a quick "Did I get the day wrong?" message, but it doesn't stop the knots tightening in my stomach with each passing minute.

Natalie, bless her, appears with another round. I down the second shot, hoping liquid courage might lessen the growing anxiety. Then, just as I'm contemplating closing my tab, my phone buzzes.

Baker: *I'm just running late. Be there in an hour!*

An hour? Really? Who does this guy think he is? Clearly, not the reliable, on-time type.

I let out a sigh, weighing my options. Do I cut my losses and make a run for it, or tolerate another hour of side-eyed pity from the Friday night crowd?

As if on cue, the door swings open, and I swear time slows down. Because there, in all his infuriatingly handsome glory, is Logan. And wrapped around his arm like a designer accessory is the blonde from his social media post.

You've got to be kidding me.

Shock and nausea boil over as I watch them saunter in, Lost in their own little world of new romance bliss. Any remaining composure shatters instantly at how he cozies up to his latest prop, oblivious to my horrified presence.

CHECK PLEASE! Now!

I can practically hear Alyssa's smug commentary: "Told you rebound insta-lust would cure the December curse, babe! Too bad the universe heard Insta-Ex Karma instead."

I can handle an hour alone. But Logan smirking in my periphery while I await Blind Guy's grand entrance with tequila coursing through my veins? Nope. I need an escape, like yesterday. But Natalie's nowhere in sight.

I sink lower in my seat, praying Logan doesn't look this way. If I can just survive a few more excruciating lines of this romance-turned-horror story.

4

Jake

Another Friday night at Sadie's, another blur of faces and drinks. The bass thrums through the floorboards, matching the dull ache behind my eyes. I've been on autopilot for hours, my hands moving with practiced efficiency while my thoughts drift elsewhere.

"Hey, Casanova," Natalie calls, sliding a tray toward me. "I know we're taking it easy on you, being your birthday and all, but think you could drop this off at eight for me? Poor girl looks like she could use another one and I've got to get these shots to a rowdy bachelorette party."

I'm about to tell her exactly where she can shove her charity case when I glance up, noticing the 'poor girl' she's referring to.

Holy mother of... I have to do a double take, my jaw practically hitting the floor. There, looking like she just stepped out of one of my more vivid fantasies, is Cora.

The soft curls framing her face, the subtle makeup, and the way that backless dress hugs every dangerous curve hidden beneath those baggy sweatshirts she's been sporting lately—it's enough to make a grown man weak in the knees.

My grip on the bar tightens, knuckles turning white as my mind wanders to thoughts of peeling that sinful lace creation off her body, inch by tantalizing inch. *Christ, get it together, Rhoades.*

As I study her more closely, I realize how alone and entirely out of her element she looks. What's she doing here?

"Still on planet Earth, birthday boy?" Nat says, breaking through my trance. "You gonna take that tray or what?"

I blink, realizing I've been staring. "Yeah, I've got it."

She raises an eyebrow. "You know her or something?"

"Or something," I mutter, already reaching for the tray. Before she can ask any more questions, I'm making my way across the crowded room, heart pounding in a way it hasn't in years.

"Need anything else, miss?" I ask gently, setting the shot on the table.

"Not unless you want to be my date for the evening," she replies dryly, still staring at the screen of her phone.

She doesn't know it's me yet. I can work with that.

I lean in, channeling my best smooth operator voice. "Well, my shift ends at three. If you're not opposed to a little late-night romance..."

"I didn't...that wasn't..." She huffs, her gaze slowly dragging up to meet mine. The instant recognition dawns on her, her entire body goes rigid. "Jake? Coffee shop Jake? What are you doing here?"

"Coffee shop Jake?" I smirk, oddly pleased by the nickname. "That's all I am to you? I thought we had something special."

Her cheeks flush, and those parted lips are doing dangerous things to my self-control. I gesture at my work shirt. "I work here. Gotta pay bills somehow." I slide into the open chair, leaning closer. "Now, the better question is, what brought you here? Assuming you're not just here to admire the view."

Cora lets out an exaggerated sigh, those mesmerizing orange-flecked eyes rolling skyward. "Oh, you know, just living out my own personal romantic comedy. Emphasis on the comedy, less on the romantic."

"Sounds riveting," I say, settling in. "I've got time for a feature-length story if you're up for sharing."

She eyes me skeptically. "Don't you have, I don't know, actual work to do?"

I wave dismissively. "Nothing that can't wait. Besides, I'm excellent at multitasking. I can listen and judge other people's drink choices simultaneously."

That gets a laugh out of her. "Alright, then. Brace yourself for the tragic tale of Cora's love life." She takes a generous swig of her drink. "Four weeks ago, I left my fiancé. Turns out he'd been auditioning replacements since before he even proposed. Hence the whole staying at my sister's sub-plot."

"Ouch," I wince, genuine sympathy coursing through me. *Cheating.* The one thing I'll never get over. Or understand.

"It gets better," she continues, a wry grin twisting her lips. "Tonight, my well-meaning but clearly delusional BFF set me up on a blind date to help me 'get my groove back.'" She uses air quotes, rolling her eyes again. "Shockingly, Prince Charming stood me up. And that—" she tilts her head towards a table across the way, "—is my supposed-to-be heartbroken ex, looking anything but devastated."

She slumps back, chuckling humorlessly. "So much for a distracting romantic meet-cute, huh?" Those starry eyes capture mine again, a mix of hurt and self-deprecating humor shining in their depths. "God, why am I even telling you all this? You probably think I'm pathetic."

I reach across, squeezing her hand before I can stop myself. "Not pathetic, trust me. It's his loss, one hundred percent. That woman can't hold a candle to you, not even if she was dipped in wax and set on fire."

Cora's lips twitch, fighting a smile. "Quite the poet, aren't you?"

"What can I say? I'm a man of many talents," I quip, relieved to see a hint of genuine amusement in her eyes. "Seriously though, anything I can do to help? I make a mean Molotov cocktail if you're interested in a little petty arson."

She laughs, the sound warming me from the inside out. "Tempting, but I think I'll pass on the felony charges. Pretty sure this night is beyond salvaging. Unless you've got a time machine hidden somewhere?"

I pretend to check my pockets. "Fresh out of time machines, I'm afraid. But..." I hesitate, weighing my options. "If you want, I could help make him jealous. Be your stand-in, save the night, that sort of thing."

My fingers graze her wrist as I speak, and I freeze when I notice the scar just below her right palm. A vivid memory of the accident flashes through my mind—Cora clutching her hand, glass shards embedded in her skin. Reflexively, my shoulder twitches, a phantom pain resurfacing.

Cora, oblivious to my momentary lapse, places her other hand over mine. The touch sends a jolt through me. "That's sweet, Jake, but I can't ask you to do that." Her smile falters then, and she gently withdraws her hand. "I think I've had enough drama for one night. I'm going to call it quits before he notices me."

As she starts to gather her things, an unfamiliar panic sets in. I can't let her walk away, not again. Not after this morning's almost-maybe-something.

"Hey, Cora," I croak as those amber eyes snag mine. "Look, I know tonight's been a trainwreck, but... maybe we could grab a drink sometime? Without the ex-fiancé dramatics."

She hesitates, and I can practically hear the gears turning in her head. "Jake, I—"

"Just as friends," I add quickly, not ready to hear whatever dismissal she was about to use. I haven't asked a girl out since... Yeah, not going there tonight. "No pressure, no expectations. Just two people who apparently keep running into each other."

"Friends, huh?" she repeats. A small smile tugs at her lips as she pulls out her phone. "I guess I could get your number. Figure out a time for something purely platonic."

I laugh, feeling more like my old self than I have in years as I type in my contact info. When I hand it back, our fingers brush, and it's like hitting the perfect chord.

"Reach out anytime," I say, then glance over at the asshole ex. "And Cora? You deserve someone who sees how amazing you are. Don't let anyone make you feel otherwise."

Her smile grows, even as she tries to suppress it. "Jake, you barely know me."

I know you better than you might think. The thought catches me off guard, and I push it away.

"But thank you," she adds. "For listening, for the offer. It means more than you know."

As she walks away, I'm left with a mix of hope and terror. I've just opened a door I swore I'd keep shut. But as I watch her go, I can't bring myself to regret it. Not yet, anyway.

I head back to the bar, reaching for the next drink ticket when a flash of movement catches my eye. Cora's ex is on his feet, his gaze fixed on the exit where Cora just disappeared. There's something in his expression that sets off every nerve ending.

"Shit," I mutter, already in motion before my brain can catch up with my feet.

"Jake? What the hell?" Natalie's voice slices through the noise, but it's background static now.

"Emergency. Cover for me," I toss over my shoulder, shouldering my way through the crowd.

Without waiting for a response, I'm out the door, my protective instincts kicking into overdrive. Five years of keeping the world at arm's length, and suddenly I'm racing headlong into someone else's drama. But this isn't just anyone. This is my angel. And right now, she's the one who might need saving for once.

5

Cora

There are moments in life when you realize you're standing at a cross-roads, pen poised over the page, ready to write the next chapter of your story. Tonight, as I step out of Sadie's into the crisp December air, I'm hit with the overwhelming certainty that this is one of those moments.

The smart move would be to go home, curl up with a pint of ice cream, and continue nursing my broken heart. That's what the protagonist in any respectable romance novel would do after being semi-stood up on a blind date, only to run into her cheating ex.

But then again, no editor worth their salt would let their heroine off that easy.

As if on cue, a familiar voice calls out behind me, "Cora, wait!"

I turn, my heart performing the literary equivalent of a page-turner's cliffhanger. Because there he is. Logan. My ex-fiancé—all tousled sandy hair and sea-green eyes that once upon a time made me weak at the knees. Even now, a traitorous part of me wants to lose myself in the warmth of his gaze, to believe in the happily-ever-after we'd planned. But I've read this story before. I know how it ends.

"Can we talk for a sec?" Logan asks, his voice softening. He takes a step closer, and I catch a whiff of his cologne—a scent that brings back a flood of memories. Laughter-filled dinners in the city, lazy Sunday mornings in bed, the way he'd wrap his arms around me when he got home from the office...

I shake my head, banishing the thoughts. Those memories are just ghost text now, words that no longer belong in my story.

"What else do you need to say?" I ask, hating the way my voice wavers.

He runs a hand through his hair—a nervous tick I once found endearing. Now it just seems calculated, like everything else about him. "It's not what you think, Cor. She's... she's nothing to me."

A bitter laugh bubbles up. "Really? That's the line you're going with?"

Confusion flickers across his face, quickly replaced by that earnest look he gets when he's trying to convince me of something. It's the same look he wore when he convinced me to move in together, to get that bedroom set we couldn't afford, to say yes when he proposed...

"I know I messed up," he says, taking another step closer. "But what we had—what we have—it's worth fighting for. You're my best friend, Cora. My partner. Remember that weekend we spent at that little B&B out East? How we talked about our future, our dreams?"

Instantly, I'm transported back, wrapped in Logan's arms as we planned out our lives together. The memory is so visceral I can almost smell the musty pages of the ancient books lining the shelves, feel the warmth of Logan's smile as he described the home we'd build together.

I squeeze my eyes shut, willing away the tears threatening to fall. When I open them again, I meet Logan's gaze head-on. "I remember, Logan. I also remember finding another woman's earring in our bed. Funny how those dreams you talked about didn't include fidelity."

Logan flinches as if I've physically struck him. Good. Let him feel a fraction of the pain I've been carrying.

"Cora, please," he says, his voice cracking. "I made a mistake. A huge, unforgivable mistake. But I love you. Doesn't that count for something?"

Love? Is that what he was feeling with the blonde inside?

As I picture what I just witnessed, my thoughts shift to Jake—to his understanding eyes and the way he saw right through my facade. Of how, in just a few short interactions, he made me feel more seen than Logan had in months.

"It counted for everything, Logan," I say softly. "Until you proved it didn't mean anything at all."

I turn to leave, my heart pounding with the finality of a book snapping shut.

"Cora, wait, " Logan says, his hand closing around my wrist.

The door to Sadie's swings open, and there, like a genre-defying hero, stands Jake. My breath catches as he strides forward, his expression a perfect blend of brooding antihero and knight in shining armor.

Jake's stormy eyes flick between us, reading the scene. Then, without a word, he slides an arm around me, his touch igniting a warmth that could thaw the iciest of plotlines.

"Hey, babe," Jake murmurs, his gravelly voice sending tingles to my toes. "Thanks again for visiting me tonight."

It takes me a moment to catch up, as his words from earlier return. This is about making Logan jealous. Being "the stand-in." I nod almost imperceptibly, accepting my role.

Jake's eyes lock with mine, a flicker of vulnerability showing beneath his otherwise cocky exterior. A silent question asking, "Is this okay?" as he leans closer. In answer, I meet him halfway. And when our lips touch, it's like the first line of a perfect novel—electric, promising, hinting at depths yet to be explored. The kiss is softer than expected, a gentle press that contrasts sharply with Jake's rough appearance. It's not the passionate, all-consuming kiss of fairy tales, but something more real, more honest.

I gravitate closer, my fingers tangling in his shirt. Jake responds by turning up the heat on our little improv scene, his tongue sliding against mine, the warmth contrasting with the cold December air. It's a slow burn rather than a raging fire, but no less potent.

A voice in my head screams caution. It's too soon, too raw after Logan to feel this kind of spark. But another part of me argues that this—whatever it is with Jake—feels more real than anything I've experienced in months.

When we part, I'm left searching for the perfect prose to describe the indescribable. Jake's eyes, dark and focused, linger on mine like an unspoken 'to be continued' that has me dizzy, caught between fear and exhilaration.

"You good?" Jake asks softly, his tone carrying more meaning than the simple question implies.

I nod, not trusting my voice. Because how do I even explain what that was? What I'm feeling? Confused, like a heroine who just realized she's in a different story than she thought.

Jake turns to Logan, his posture protective but not possessive. "I didn't mean to interrupt. Just wanted to say goodnight to Cora one final time."

Logan's face is a study in conflicting emotions—anger, confusion, and something that looks suspiciously like regret.

"Who are you?" Logan demands, his polished facade cracking.

"Jake Rhoades," Jake replies simply, offering his hand. The gesture's polite, but there's a challenge in his eyes.

Logan hesitates before shaking Jake's hand, his knuckles white. "Logan McAllister," he grits out. "Cora's fiancé."

I cringe. "Ex-fiancé," I correct firmly, finding my voice at last. "I thought I made that pretty damn clear when I left, Logan."

Jake's lip twitches, suppressing a smile. He leans in close, his breath warm against my ear. "I can stay if you need me to," he murmurs, low enough for only me to hear.

His offer is tempting—oh, so tempting—but I shake my head. This is a confrontation I need to face on my own.

"You've done plenty."

Jake nods, understanding without me having to explain. He presses a soft kiss to my temple—a gesture that feels far too intimate for our supposed act—before stepping back.

"Text me when you're home safe, Coco baby," he says, loud enough for Logan to hear.

Coco baby? He's getting far too good at this performance.

As Jake walks away, I turn back to Logan, ready to face whatever he's about to throw my way.

"Who the hell was that?" Logan asks before the warmth from Jake's touch has even worn off.

I straighten my spine. "Not you. And we're not engaged anymore. How dare you introduce yourself that way."

Logan runs another hand through his hair, glancing back at the bar. "Come on, Cora. If I had known you'd be here—"

"You'd what?" I interrupt, my voice sharp. "You'd have hidden your date better? Made sure I didn't see so you could pretend to still be heartbroken?"

He flinches, a flicker of genuine remorse in his eyes. "That's not... Cora, please. Can we talk about this? Really talk? I'll meet you anywhere, anytime."

I pause, considering. Part of me wants to hear him out, to understand why he threw away everything we had. But a stronger part knows where that talk would lead. And it's time to close this chapter of my life.

"You know how to reach me, Logan," I say firmly. "But I'm not making any promises."

Without waiting for a response, I turn and walk away, my heels clicking against the pavement in a steady rhythm. Each step feels like progress, moving me further from the pain and closer to... something new.

As I round the corner, I pull out my phone, smiling at Jake's contact name: "Coffee Shop Jake." My fingers hover over the keys for a moment before I type:

Me: *Quite the bold move back there* ☺ *Do you perform these stand-ins often?*

I don't have to hold my breath too long, as he replies almost instantaneously.

Jake: *You're the first. Though I might need some convincing it was just a stand-in. Was that your tongue in my mouth?* 😛

My skin heats up despite the cold temperatures. But then my phone chimes again.

Jake: *In all seriousness, please text me when you get home. I'm worried about you walking back in that dress.*
Me: *You weren't joking. I really do have to convince you it was pretend, huh? And if memory serves correctly, it was actually your tongue in my mouth.*
Jake: *Semantics*
Me: *Regardless, thank you for the assist tonight.*
Jake: *Anytime, Cora. Sweet dreams.*

I tuck my phone away, still smiling as I begin to analyze the evening's events. Jake's unexpected appearance, the electric moment we shared, the look in Logan's eyes... It's all swirling in my mind, begging to be sorted and understood.

But for once, I resist the urge to edit and scrutinize. Instead, I let myself enjoy the moment, the possibility, the potential of a new story unfolding.

Maybe this December won't be a disaster after all. Or maybe it will be, in the most thrilling way possible. Either way, I'm ready to find out.

6

∽

Jake

December 2ⁿᵈ

The silence of my apartment is deafening after the chaotic symphony of the bar. I collapse onto the couch, guitar in hand, my fingers finding familiar chords before my brain can catch up. The melody comes easier than breathing, but the words... they're like trying to grab smoke.

I strum the same progression for the hundredth time, willing the lyrics to materialize. But all I can think about is her. Cora. The girl who's rewriting my carefully constructed solo into a duet I'm not sure I'm ready to perform.

Her last text glows on my phone screen: *Home safe. Thanks again for the rescue, Coffee Shop Jake.*

I snort. Coffee Shop Jake. If she only knew.

My fingers move of their own accord, plucking out a softer tune that somehow captures the warmth in her eyes, the curve of her smile. Damn it. This isn't what I do anymore. I don't write love songs. I don't fall for girls with autumn-fire eyes and smiles that could melt permafrost.

And yet...

I grab my notebook, pen hovering over the blank page. The words start to flow, unbidden:

I'm chaos, I'm damage
Shrapnel lodged too deep to extract
I'll slice and scar all that I touch
But your palms heal wounds unseen
Your joy makes destruction pause
Your light shines bright in my darkness

I touch my lips, last night replaying on a loop. Kissing her. Touching her. The way she felt in my arms, like she belonged there.

Fuck.

I promised myself I wouldn't fall again... not after Tessa, not after the damage of shredded hopes and dreams. No relationship. No expectations. No desire to relinquish that faultless control over my life I've attempted to regain.

Until her.

Everything about Cora has me questioning the fortress I've built around my heart. Her shy warmth and those eyes that can see right through me. And against all reason, I want to let her in.

Could I? Or would I just let her down? I'm too broken inside to love right. I should save her the excruciating disappointment and pull away before this fragile, foolish flame between us fully sparks to life.

But damn it, if I can't be better than that prick she was engaged to.

The memory of him sauntering back into the bar, smirking as he left with his date, makes my blood boil. I channel that anger into the music, the chords growing harder, more aggressive.

You see the man I lost years ago
Somehow you resurrect buried hope
I'm both saved and condemned by your faith
Your lips on mine, Your heart in mine,
Can I keep it safe? Can I love you enough?

I stare at what I've scribbled, a mix of hope and terror coursing through me. It's been years since I've written like this. And after Wednesday's random writing spree, I'm on a roll.

A harsh laugh escapes. Some birthday present this is turning out to be. Here I am, twenty-nine, writing love songs like a teenager with his first crush.

But as I play through the song one more time, I can't deny the truth staring me in the face. Whether I'm ready for it or not, Cora Cooper has found her way under my skin.

And God help me, I don't know if I want her out.

What will happen when she finally realizes who you are, a voice whispers. *When she discovers the truth about how you found out it was her?*

I exhale, setting the guitar aside. Do I want her to find out? To know the kind of person I really am?

The digital clock on my nightstand blinks an accusatory 8:47 AM. Another night of insomnia courtesy of ghosts I can't seem to shake.

Just as I'm contemplating the merits of a morning run, there's a pounding at my door that could wake the dead. Or at least the neighbors.

"What the hell?" I mutter, stumbling to the door. I yank it open, ready to tear into whoever decided 9 AM on a Saturday was an appropriate time for a social call.

Owen bounds in, vibrating with a restless energy that I haven't seen in years. Not since... before.

"You're not going to believe this!" he calls, pacing the space between the kitchen and living area like a caged animal.

I grunt, shuffling to the kitchen to start the coffee. If I'm going to deal with my brother's manic energy, I'm going to need caffeine. "You could've called first," I grumble.

"Do you want to hear the news or not?" He bounces on his toes, still moving in circles. "Happy belated birthday, by the way. Hope you did something fun."

"I worked until four," I say dryly, fiddling with the coffee machine. "How are we even related?"

"I ask myself that all the time," he answers, laughing. He pauses when he spots the guitar and open notebook on the couch. His eyes widen. "Holy shit. Are you writing again?"

I scratch the back of my neck, suddenly feeling exposed. "Not sure what's come over me."

Lie. I know precisely what's happened. Her.

The coffee machine beeps, saving me from further explanation. I pour two cups, sliding one across the counter to Owen. "So what's so urgent it couldn't wait until a decent hour?"

Owen's grin nearly splits his face as he shoves his phone under my nose. "We have an audition!"

Audition?

I read the email once, twice, hoping the words would rearrange into something logical. This has to be a joke.

"But...the song..." I grasp for words, flabbergasted. "I only just wrote it... You recorded it? When we played it Thursday?"

Owen's hand lands heavily on my shoulder, joy radiating from his touch. "I made it into a demo. Sent it out to a few places yesterday afternoon and got this reply first thing this morning. You did it, little brother. I told you that song was special!"

I choke on my coffee. Shit.

"Dude, I haven't written in over five years. Of course, you'd like it. I didn't realize anyone else would."

"It's good, Jake. Really good." He lets out a short laugh before continuing to explain the details. "The audition is Wednesday. Four songs."

I stare down at the coffee mug, dread pooling in my stomach. "Owen, we have one song."

His mouth falls to a hard line. "We have over thirty."

My head snaps up, jaw clenched. No way. He can't seriously mean...

"He would've wanted us to use them," Owen continues, holding my gaze unflinchingly.

He. Thomas. Our younger brother. Even the thought of exhuming those songs, soaked in memories of him, makes me sick to my stomach. Each chord, each lyric, a reminder of what we lost. What *I* lost.

Owen scrubs a hand down his face when I remain mute. "It's been five years. I thought you said you were ready," he challenges quietly. "What's the point otherwise?"

"It's..." I falter, at a loss. How can I explain? That I'll never be prepared to revisit the ghost of Thomas, of Tessa? That those wounds will never close, always remaining just below the surface of my carefully constructed guise?

Owen's expression softens. He slowly slides my notebook across the counter, the words from this morning taunting me. "What about all those dreams we had as kids?"

I scoff. Our ambitious thoughts as teenagers, the desire to make it big—dreams I've been too fucked up to even think about until now.

"It's only four songs, Jake," he coaxes gently. "Just think about it?"

My thoughts are as jumbled as every nerve in my body. All I've done the last five years is waste time. Groaning, I ask, "What does Chris think?"

"I haven't told him yet." He brings the cup to his mouth, taking a quick sip. "I didn't want to get him excited if you weren't gonna do it."

I pinch the back of my neck, tilting my head, as I consider the options. "You really think the song is that good?"

He nods slightly while grinning. "Jake, it's incredible."

Admiration. Something I haven't seen from him in a long time.

I suck in a ragged breath, my carefully constructed walls crumbling.

Tessa. Thomas. The fact there's only one new song. The small detail that the song is about Cora.

It all means moving forward, and I'm not sure I know how.

Finally, I meet Owen's hopeful stare and nod jerkily. "One step at a time," I rasp, thoughts already churning around lyrics I thought I'd never sing again. "I'll switch days at the coffee shop. We'll do the audition and then go from there."

As Owen whoops and pulls me into a bear hug, I can't help but wonder if I've just made the biggest mistake of my life. Or maybe it's the first step toward redemption.

7

Jake

The neon sign of Sadie's flickers like a faulty metronome, setting an erratic rhythm to match my mood. I pause outside, the weight of Owen's words from this morning still sitting heavy on my shoulders. Four songs. Four chances to prove we've still got it. Four opportunities to royally fuck everything up.

I push through the door, the familiar sound of clinking glasses and drunken laughter washing over me. It's a concert I know by heart, one I've been performing for years now. But tonight, there's a harsh note in the air. Change is coming, whether I'm ready for it or not.

"Well, well, look what the cat dragged in," Natalie calls over the noise. "You're early. Should I be worried?"

I grunt, tying my apron with practiced ease. "Bite me, Nat. I'm allowed to be punctual once in a while."

She eyes me, her gaze sharp enough to cut glass. "Uh-huh. This wouldn't have anything to do with your coffee shop girl showing up last night, would it? You two seemed pretty cozy."

I freeze for a split second before forcing a casual shrug. "Don't know what you're talking about."

Natalie laughs. "Please. I haven't seen you look at anyone like that in years. Did something else happen with Miss Damsel in Distress?"

For a split second, I consider telling her the rest of the story. About the second time I saw Cora. About what I felt when I kissed her last night. But old habits die hard, and deflection has always been my strongest suit.

"Just what you saw last night," I mutter, grabbing a ticket and mixing a drink. "Besides, she's Mark's sister-in-law. End of story."

Natalie's eyebrows shoot up. "Oh, honey. You don't do anything by halves, do you?"

I shoot her a glare. "Drop it, Nat."

She holds up her hands in mock surrender, but I can see the wheels turning behind her eyes. That's the thing about Natalie—she always knows when to push and when to back off. It's why we've worked so well together all these years.

"Fine. But just so you know, I'm here if you want to talk about it. Or anything else that's got you looking like you're carrying the weight of the world on those shoulders of yours."

I manage a half-smile. "Thanks, Nat. I'll keep that in mind."

As the night wears on, I fall into the familiar rhythm of pouring drinks and dodging advances from tipsy patrons. But my mind keeps drifting back to the notebook sitting in my apartment, filled with lyrics I thought I'd buried years ago. And to Cora, her smile haunting me like a melody I can't shake.

The Saturday night rush presses around me, clamoring bodies shouting drink orders that keep my hands occupied and mind blissfully numb, at least for a while. But as I slide another finished cocktail down the bar, boisterous laughter catches my attention.

I glance up to see Owen and Mark weaving their way towards two vacant seats, appearing extremely out of place amidst the frenzied crowd. Unease flickers through me. They never drop by on DJ nights anymore. Not since...well.

"Great to see you, too. Poker night get canceled or something?" I ask lightly with a raised brow.

Owen holds my gaze, a hint of something I can't completely place. "Wanted to check in and see how the evening is treating our rising rockstar."

I force a sarcastic laugh. "Rockstar? Last I checked, I was still playing bartender for tips."

"Gotta start somewhere," Mark chimes in, motioning to a group of giggling women. "I mean, it's how you've built your fanbase, right?"

I shrug. The easy back-and-forth feels like an old song we used to know, but the rhythm is off.

Mark's expression suddenly shifts from playful to serious. My stomach drops like a bad bass line. "So, heard you ran into Arden's sister last night."

Shit. Is that why he's here? He heard about me and Cora? I freeze, searching for an escape route and coming up empty. "Yeah, briefly. I was working." Keep it vague, Rhoades. No way I'm admitting to that kiss if he doesn't know.

Mark's eyes narrow, but he just nods. "Heard her ex showed up too. Must've been quite the show."

I breathe, relief washing over me. He doesn't know the details. "Yeah, guy's a real piece of work."

"Next time, knock that fucker out," Mark grunts.

With pleasure, I think, remembering Logan's smug face.

Mark takes a drink, eyeing me curiously. "You would've stepped in if things got ugly, right?"

I nod, maybe too quickly. "Of course. She's your sister-in-law." An image of Cora's lips flashes through my mind. I shove it away before Mark can read it on my face. After two years as roommates, the guy can read me like sheet music.

"Good," Mark says, still watching me closely. "So, what exactly went down? Arden was pretty vague."

My cue to exit.

"Just your typical 'he tried, she said no' drama. Nothing major," I offer, thankful when I spot a group of women heading toward the bar. "Sorry, gentlemen. Gotta run. Duty calls."

I mix their drinks, but my mind's in overdrive. There's no doubt Mark caught my unguarded reaction about Cora. The question is, what's he going to do about it? And more importantly, what am I going to do about this growing, impossible attraction to her?

I'm about to refill some glasses when I notice Mark and Owen leaving. *Leaving? Am I in the clear?* Mark pauses, calling over the bar.

"Hey, Jake. Having some guys over Monday for the game. You should come by."

The invitation hits me like an unexpected key change. I haven't set foot in that apartment in years. I was ready for him to tear into me about Cora, maybe even take a swing. Lord knows he's been waiting for an opportunity. But a casual invite? It's throwing me for a loop.

If this is Mark extending an olive branch, I can't turn it down.

I meet his gaze, fear and hope strangling my voice. "Wouldn't miss it."

Mark's smile doesn't quite reach his eyes, but it thaws something long frozen inside me.

It's not until they leave that the full weight of what I've agreed to hits me. I'm going to Mark's apartment. Where Cora's staying. The girl who saved my life... twice. The one who might be here to do it again.

Am I ready for that?

* * *

The night spirals into chaos when one of the servers bails due to a family emergency. Natalie and I divide and conquer, juggling the bar and extra tables like we're in some twisted circus act. I'm so caught up in the frenzy that I barely have time to breathe, let alone think about Owen's bombshell or Mark's olive branch.

Then, like the opening chords of a song I can't forget, I hear her voice.

"Do I need to file a formal complaint about the service here?"

My head snaps up. Cora. Looking like a perfect melody in a world of discordant noise. And despite the voice whispering she's a complication I can't afford right now, I'm already moving toward her like she's got me on a string.

"Cover for me," I mutter at the nearest server, practically shoving the tray into their hands.

Cora's watching me approach, a hint of a smile showing. "Fancy seeing you here. Again."

I lean against the bar. "Already back for an encore, huh? Didn't get enough drama last night?"

She laughs, the sound hitting me like a shot of top-shelf whiskey. "It was Arden's idea. Girl's night out and all. But I'm a sucker for a good performance."

"Well, stick around. I might just put on a show for you." The words are out before I can stop them, loaded with more subtext than a Dylan song. *God, I'm hopeless.*

Cora's eyebrow arches. "Oh? And what kind of show did you have in mind?"

I'm treading dangerous waters here, but I can't seem to stop myself. "Depends. What are you in the mood for? Comedy? Tragedy? Romance?"

"Hmm," she pretends to consider, leaning in closer. "How about a mystery? I'm still trying to figure you out, Jake Rhoades."

Her proximity is intoxicating. I grip the edge of the bar, anchoring myself. "Trust me, I'm not that complicated."

"I don't buy that for a second," she says, her voice low and thrumming with intensity. Her eyes are searching mine like they're lyrics she's desperate to understand.

Suddenly, I'm out of my element. Do I lean in and kiss her? Does she want me to? I'm about to say something—probably something monumentally stupid—when a shrill voice breaks through the moment like feedback from a blown amp.

"Jake! Babe! We need shots over here!"

I close my eyes briefly, cursing under my breath. Lindsey. Of all the goddamn timing.

When I look back at Cora, her expression has cooled considerably. "Sounds like you're needed elsewhere, *babe*," she says, her tone clipped. "Don't let me keep you from your adoring fans."

No doubt Cora thinks Lindsey is someone special. If she only knew.

"Cora, it's not—" I start, but she's already turning away.

"Have a good night," she tosses over her shoulder, disappearing into the crowd.

I stand there, feeling like I've just watched my last chance at happiness hop on the express train to Anywhere-But-Here. Fan-fucking-tastic.

Slapping on a grin that feels about as genuine as a lip-synced concert, I turn back to Lindsey and her giggling entourage. As I pour their shots, I catch Lindsey eyeing me like I'm the last piece of gear at a fire-sale. Christ, I've seen that look before. It's the precursor to drama I definitely don't need.

She leans in, her whisper hot against my ear. "We need to talk, Jake. About us."

I jerk back. Us? There is no "us," sweetheart. But something tells me Lindsey's not reading from the same songsheet.

This is what happens when you think with your dick instead of your brain, genius, my inner voice sneers.

As soon as I can break away, I escape to the storage room, desperate for a moment to get my head on straight. I lean my forehead against the cool metal shelving, closing my eyes. But all I can think about is tracking down Cora and explaining... what, exactly? That I'm a mess? That I'm not worth her time? That despite all that, she's the only melody I can't get out of my head?

Yeah, that'll go over real well.

When I finally emerge, the bar's chaos has died down to a dull roar, but the tension inside me is still at a fever pitch. Then, like the sign I've been waiting for, I spot Cora only a few feet away.

Before my brain can veto the idea, my feet are already moving. "Cora, hold up!"

She spins around, eyebrow cocked. "Stalking me now?"

I press a palm to the wall behind her, hovering close but not daring to touch. "In my defense, you show up at my bar. Twice."

"Fair," she replies with a small shrug. "And there's no sign of an ex tonight."

"Nope," I whisper. "Just you."

Our gazes collide, and the world around us fades to background noise. Those amber eyes of hers are like a spotlight, and I'm center stage with no setlist. My mind wanders to dangerous territory—tangling my fingers in her hair, tasting those lips until we're both gasping for air.

But this time, it wouldn't be for show. It'd be all too real.

Then reality slams into me like a missed chord. She's Mark's sister-in-law. Way out of my league.

"So, uh, where's Arden?" I ask awkwardly, shifting back.

Confusion flickers across Cora's face. "Last I saw, she was tearing up the dance floor. Why?"

I shrug. "Thought you ladies always traveled in packs for bathroom runs."

"Some of us can pee solo, believe it or not," she retorts, her eyes raking over me in a way I shouldn't enjoy this much. "So... You and my sister. What's the story there? Seems like you're more than just her go-to barista."

I chuckle, the sound coming out more strained than I'd like. "Trust me, it's not what you're thinking."

"Oh?" Her eyebrow arches. "And what am I thinking, Jake?"

I run a hand through my hair, buying time. "I don't know. Ex-lovers? Coffee shop romance gone wrong?"

She laughs, the sound warming me like a perfect melody. "Quite the imagination you've got there. So, if it's none of those things, why'd you look like you were about to bolt when you brought her up?"

Because you make me want things I shouldn't. Because Mark would kill me if I tried something. But I can't tell her any of that, so instead I go with, "It's complicated."

"Isn't everything?" she says softly, inching closer. And fuck if I'm not leaning in.

I swallow. Hard. "Cora, I—"

"It's okay," she interrupts, a sad smile playing on her lips. "You don't have to explain. I get it. You're not the sharing type."

Her words sting because they're true. I've spent years building these walls, and now, faced with someone who makes me want to tear them down, I'm paralyzed.

She's close now, close enough that I can smell her perfume. Her fingers reach out, almost touching my shirt before pulling back. "You know," she murmurs, "for such a mystery, you're surprisingly easy to read sometimes."

"Oh yeah?" I manage thickly. "What are you reading right now?"

Her eyes meet mine, and I swear the temperature in the room spikes. "A touch of horror. That this—whatever this is—is probably a bad idea."

I let out a shaky breath. "Definitely a bad idea," I agree, even as every fiber of my being screams to close the distance between us.

"And yet," she whispers, "here we are."

We stand there, caught in a moment that feels both endless and far too brief. I want to touch her, to pull her close, but I know if I do, there's no going back.

"There's so much you don't know about me, Cora," I finally say, my voice barely above a whisper. "So many reasons why you should run the other way."

She pulls back slightly, her eyes searching mine. "Well, when you're ready to let someone in on the great Jake Rhoades mystery... you know where to find me."

I summon every ounce of willpower I possess to take a step back. "Get home safe, Coco baby."

She smiles, a mix of understanding and something else I can't quite name. "Goodnight, Jake."

I watch her walk away, desire thrumming through me like an unfinished song. As I slump against the wall, the day's events crash over me—Owen's audition news, Mark's olive branch, and now this electric encounter with Cora. It's all pushing me out of the carefully constructed comfort zone I've called home for years.

I pull out my phone, staring at the blank screen. Part of me wants to text her, to keep this connection alive. But another part, the part that's been running scared for five years, holds me back.

As I make my way back to the bar, Natalie gives me a knowing look. "You okay there?"

I grunt noncommittally, but my mind is already racing ahead. To Wednesday's audition. To Monday's game at Mark's. To the next time I'll see Cora.

I pull out my songwriting notebook, jotting down a few lines that have been bouncing around my head.

Comfort's a cage I've called home
But your touch is the key to the lock
Do I dare step into the unknown?
Or stay safe in this familiar block?

As I process the words, I realize I'm at the bridge. Keep the safe, numbing routine I've clung to, or face the terrifying, exhilarating possibility of something more.

The choice, it seems, is mine to make.

8

Cora

December 3ʳᵈ

Sunday morning greets me with a pounding headache and a flood of memories from last night. Jake's intense blue eyes, his breath hot on my skin, the sparks between us... I groan, burying my face in my pillow. What was I thinking?

My phone buzzes, and for a heart-stopping moment, I think it might be Jake. But it's just my mom. Again. I briefly consider letting it go to voicemail. But avoidance has never been my strong suit.

"Hey, Mom," I answer, my voice flat as I brace myself for the conversation ahead.

"Cora." Her crisp tone betrays no emotion. "I wanted to check in. See if you were reconsidering your rash decision regarding Logan?"

I pinch the bridge of my nose, fighting a sigh. *He's managed to captivate her, too.* "There's nothing to reconsider. Logan and I are done."

"Don't be foolish. Logan has an excellent career trajectory. You'd be smart to consider it."

I bite back a sarcastic retort. If only she knew about the bartender

I'd nearly kissed last night. "He cheated on me. Multiple times. His 'potential' doesn't change that fact."

"Affairs happen, Cora," she says dismissively. "What matters is the stability and future he offers. Your little editing job won't sustain the lifestyle you're accustomed to."

Her words hit me like a slap. I've managed to avoid this conversation since graduation solely because of Logan's *potential*. But now that she brought it up... I'm about to unleash a scathing rebuttal when there's a knock at the door. Mark and Arden are out, probably off being disgustingly happy somewhere. Should I answer it? Or pretend I've suddenly developed a severe case of door-phobia?

Then again, it's an excuse to get off this call.

"I have to go, Mom. Someone's at the door."

"Think about what I've said, Cora. Don't throw away a promising future over something that can be worked through. Logan called me yesterday, and he sounds committed to making things right."

I end the call, my mother's cold pragmatism clinging to me like a toxic cloud. As I move to answer the door, I wonder how Arden and I turned out so different from our parents.

Speaking of the devil...

"Logan," I manage, swinging the door open.

He stands there, looking like he stepped out of a J.Crew catalog, all tousled hair and apologetic eyes.

"Cora," he replies, his voice softer than the cashmere sweater he's wearing. "Can we talk?"

I hesitate, torn between slamming the door and... well, slamming the door harder. The memory of Jake's almost-kiss flashes through my mind, making me feel guilty for reasons I can't quite explain. Because apparently, my love life wasn't complicated enough already.

Where the hell is Mark when I need him? He'd be all too happy to play the overprotective brother-in-law right about now.

"Please," Logan adds, his eyes pleading. "I want to make things right. After seeing you at the bar on Friday... I realized how much I've lost."

I raise an eyebrow. "You mean when you were there with another woman?"

Logan has the decency to look ashamed. "That was... I was trying to move on. But seeing you there, Cora... it hit me how much I still love you."

Damn my romantic heart and its traitorous soft spot for second chances. "You have five minutes," I say, crossing my arms over my chest like a shield.

Logan nods, relief flooding his face. "I know I messed up. These past few weeks without you... I'm lost, Cora. No one gets me the way you do. I've been going to therapy, trying to understand why I did what I did."

My resolve wavers, and I hate myself for it. This is the man who betrayed me, who shattered my trust. So why does part of me still want to hear him out?

"I got these," Logan continues, pulling out an envelope. "I thought maybe we could start over?"

I take the envelope, my heart sinking as I see what's inside. Tickets to see Stuffed Olives, my favorite band, next Saturday.

"When did you get these?"

"Months ago," he admits. "Before... everything. I thought maybe we could go together. One night, no strings attached. Just to talk."

I stare at the tickets, my mind a whirlwind of conflicting emotions. "I can't, Logan," I say finally, handing the tickets back. "It's not that simple."

He nods, looking defeated but not surprised. "I understand. But I'll be there. If you change your mind..."

As he turns to leave, the weight of our shared history crashes over me. This isn't just about us anymore. It's about untangling our lives, our shared apartment, our intertwined families.

I close the door, leaning against it with a heavy sigh. Despite the lingering affection, I know I'm not the same Cora who fell in love with Logan. That Cora wouldn't have felt a spark with a blue-eyed bartender. That Cora wouldn't be dreaming of a fresh start.

Realization washes over me: I need space entirely on my own, void of pressure or expectations. I need my own apartment.

I head back into my room, my manuscript from Friday staring up at me from the make-shift desk. I can't help but see the parallels from the story to my own. Like the protagonist, I'm at a crossroads. But unlike her, I don't have the luxury of an author guiding me towards a predetermined happy ending.

With a surge of determination, I open my laptop and dive into apartment listings. It's time to start writing my own story, typos and plot holes included.

* * *

Alyssa and I hurry toward the bar Monday evening, braving the city's icy wind. Confidence still surges from my decisions in the last twenty-four hours. After Logan's abrupt appearance yesterday, I visited several apartments this morning and signed a lease for a cozy one-bedroom. The first step of my new solo chapter.

Even the thought of officially meeting Baker during my weekly happy hour with Alyssa doesn't have me anxious. For the first time in forever, I feel in control.

"I still can't believe you signed on the spot," Alyssa remarks, opening the door to the bar.

"I know. But it just felt right, you know?" I answer casually, thoughts shifting to the homey twelve-suite complex. "Like it could be home. And having it already available for occupancy? It's like it was fate."

"I get it. It's just... quick," Alyssa says, her attention already drifting to a group in the corner. "Did you call Logan yet?"

I wrinkle my nose like I've just smelled month-old milk. "Let me bask in my independence for a hot minute before I deal with that particular plot twist, okay?"

Alyssa's focus snaps back to me, a mischievous glint in her eye that makes me instantly wary. "Speaking of twists, ready to meet Baker?"

Ah yes, the infamous Baker. Alyssa's perfect antidote to my Logan-induced heartache. Because clearly, the best way to get over someone is to throw yourself at the nearest available man. What could possibly go wrong?

"Lead the way," I sigh, mentally preparing myself for an evening of awkward small talk and forced laughter.

Baker turns out to be... well, let's just say if disappointment had a poster child, he'd be it. Tall? Check. Dark? Check. Handsome? If you're into the "I use more product in my hair than most people use toothpaste in a year" look. As we exchange pleasantries, I realize I've misjudged him entirely. He's not the protein-shake-chugging gym rat I'd anticipated. Oh no, he's a DJ.

This is who Alyssa thought could be my happily ever after? Then again, I did ask for someone who wasn't Logan.

"So, Cora," Baker says, leaning in so close I can smell his overpriced cologne, "Alyssa tells me you're in publishing. That must be exciting. Bet you've read some pretty steamy stuff, huh?"

I take a large gulp of wine, wishing it was something stronger. "Oh yeah, nothing gets the blood pumping like correcting grammar and debating the Oxford comma."

Baker laughs like I've just delivered the punchline of the century. "Well, if you ever want to live out some of those fantasies, I've got a pretty impressive... sound system at my place."

I nearly choke on my drink. If subtlety were a language, Baker would be functionally illiterate.

As he launches into a story about his latest gig—complete with far too many name-drops and thinly veiled innuendos—I find myself playing a mental game of "Would You Rather." Would I rather listen to Baker's "sick beats" or endure another awkward encounter with Logan? Would I rather attempt to decipher Baker's DJ lingo or try to unravel the enigma that is Jake?

Jake. The name alone sends my thoughts spiraling. Intense blue eyes, a crooked smile that could melt glaciers, and enough emotional baggage to fill a cargo plane. Yet, somehow, I'd take his complicated silences over Baker's non-stop chatter any day.

"Earth to Cora," Alyssa's voice shatters my Jake-induced daydream. "You still with us?"

I plaster on a smile that feels about as genuine as Baker's tan. "Sorry, just lost in thought. Baker was just telling me about... um..."

"My killer set at Club Euphoria last weekend," Baker supplies, winking. Actually winking. "I had the place going wild. You should come check me out sometime, Cora. I'll put you on the VIP list."

"Tempting," I lie, wondering if it's too early to fake a medical emergency.

Alyssa shoots me a look that clearly says "play nice." I sigh internally. I know she means well. She's been a good friend these past few years, especially with Logan's... everything. But sitting here listening to Baker's not-so-subtle attempts to get me back to his place isn't exactly healing my broken heart.

"I need another drink," I announce, standing abruptly. "Anyone else? No? Great."

I scan the bar, half-hoping to see a familiar face behind the counter. Maybe Jake has a third job I'm not aware of. But he's nowhere to be seen, and I'm not sure if I'm relieved or disappointed.

When I return to the table, Alyssa is chatting with a sandy-haired guy I vaguely recognize. Chris, I think? A musician, if I remember correctly. Meanwhile, Baker has apparently taken my absence as an invitation to prepare his grand finale.

"So, Cora," he says, his voice dropping to what I assume he thinks is his sexy DJ voice, "how about we get out of here? I've got some sick tracks I've been working on. I could give you a... private listening session."

I glance at my watch, thanking the literary gods for this perfect excuse. "Oh, would you look at the time? I completely forgot I have an early meeting with a very important... book. Raincheck?"

Baker's face falls faster than the bass at one of his gigs, but he recovers quickly. "Sure thing, babe. How about this weekend? I've got a set at Pulse, and—"

"I'll have to check my schedule," I interrupt, already gathering my things. "You know how it is. Books to edit, commas to obsess over."

I mouth "I'll call you later" to Alyssa as I make my escape, silently promising her a full review of DJ Disaster tomorrow.

The crisp night air hits me like a wake-up call, leaving behind the stuffy atmosphere and Baker's even stuffier cologne. Freedom has never smelled so sweet.

As I wait for my Uber, my fingers hover over Jake's name in my contacts. Is it too soon to reach out after Saturday night? My inner editor wages war with my impulsive side, but for once, impulse wins out.

Me: *Finally met the guy who didn't show up on time last Friday. Pretty sure I've had more chemistry with my coffee maker. Please tell me your night involves fewer terrible pick-up lines and more actual human interaction.*

I hit send, immediately second-guessing myself. Great job, Cooper. Nothing says "I'm totally over my ex" like telling the guy you're crushing on about your awful blind date.

As I slide into the Uber, my phone chimes. But it's not Jake's reply. It's Arden.

Arden: *Don't forget Mark's hosting game night. Warning you in case you leave happy hour expecting solitude.*

I groan. A house full of rowdy sports fans sounds about as appealing as another hour of Baker's DJ exploits. I'm about to change my plans and head to the nearest bookstore when my phone buzzes again. Jake's name flashes on the screen, and suddenly, my heart's doing a gymnastics routine worthy of the Olympics.

Jake: *Sounds like a rough night. I'd offer to rescue you, but I'm stuck at Mark's game night. Rain check on that human interaction?*

Jake's at Mark's house? Jake knows Mark? Why am I just learning about this now? I think about the cryptic conversations we've had about how Jake knows Arden. What else don't I know about this man?

My fingers hover over the keyboard, a dozen questions fighting to be typed out. But instead, I opt for casual.

Me: *Small world. Didn't realize you knew Mark. Was that on purpose?*

As the Uber navigates through the city streets, my mind races. Jake and Mark. Jake and Arden. How many other connections am I missing? It's like I'm editing a story with crucial pages missing, and Jake holds all the missing pieces.

I lean back, a mix of curiosity and anticipation swirling in my chest. Something tells me this night is about to take an unexpected turn. But this time, I'm not sure if I'm the author or just another character in this unfolding plot.

9

∽

Jake

December 4ᵗʰ

The reflection mocking me in the elevator glare is a stranger. Gone is the shaggy beard and unkempt hair, replaced by a clean-shaven jaw and a haircut that wouldn't look out of place in a boy band. Christ, what was I thinking?

Oh, right. Audition. Fresh start. All that bullshit.

The doors slide open, and I walk toward Mark's apartment. My hand hovers over the 3C marker, caught between the urge to bolt and the nagging voice in my head telling me to man up. It's just a few hours of watching sports with the guys. No big deal. Except it is, because I haven't done this in years. Not since...

Yeah, still not going there.

I exhale, forcing down the anxiety bubbling in my gut. This is what normal people do, right? Watch games with friends, drink beer, pretend the world doesn't have it out for you?

Before I can chicken out, I knock. The door swings open, and there's Mark, beer in hand, looking like he's seen a ghost.

"Jake?" he stammers, eyes wide. "That really you, man?"

I resist the urge to check behind me. "Last time I checked. Unless my evil twin finally decided to make an appearance."

Mark blinks, then cracks a grin. "Holy shit, dude. You look... different."

"Gee, thanks. Just what every guy wants to hear," I deadpan. "You gonna let me in, or should I start growing the beard back right now?"

He steps aside, chuckling. "Get in here, smartass. Beer's in the fridge."

But despite the easy banter, I can feel the tension just below the surface. Our history hangs between us like a broken guitar string—that disaster of a bachelor party, me bailing as best man, skipping the wedding entirely. I was too busy wallowing in my own angsty solo to show up for his big duet.

Mark grabs a beer from the fridge and tosses it my way. "So, what's with the extreme makeover? Auditioning for a boy band or something?"

I catch the bottle and take a long pull, buying time. How do I explain that seeing Cora at the bar on Saturday night sparked something in me? That for the first time in years, I actually give a damn about how I look?

"Nah," I say instead. "Just figured it was time for a change. Got that audition coming up, you know?"

Mark's eyebrows do a little dance. "Right, the audition. How's that coming along? Nailed down your setlist?"

I shrug, aiming for casual but probably hitting somewhere around 'trying too hard.' "Still fine-tuning it. You know how it goes."

He nods, a hint of pride in his eyes. "That's great, man. Really."

Before I can respond, Arden appears in the doorway, doing a double-take when she spots me. "Jake? Is that really you?"

I manage a sheepish grin. "In the flesh. Heard there was free food."

Arden rolls her eyes, but there's a warmth there. "Some things never change. The new look suits you, though."

As we settle into the living room with a few faces I don't recognize, I can't help but glance around, half-hoping to catch a glimpse of Cora. Mark notices, his eyes narrowing slightly.

"Looking for someone?" he asks, his tone casual but with an undercurrent of concern.

I shake my head, trying to play it cool. "Nah, just taking in the changes. It's been a while since I've been here."

Mark nods, but I can see he's not buying it. "I heard the girls showed up at the bar after we left. Must've been some weekend, huh?"

I tense, waiting for the other shoe to drop. "Yeah, Cora mentioned it was girls' night out or something."

Arden jumps in, her hand on Mark's thigh. "It was nothing, honey. We went to dance. Jake was just being a good bartender, right?"

I nod, grateful for the lifeline. "Just doing my job."

Mark leans in, his voice low. "Look, Jake, I know we talked Saturday, but... Cora's been through a lot lately. She's in a vulnerable spot."

"Mark," Arden warns, but he presses on.

"I'm just saying, maybe now's not the best time for... whatever this is." He gestures at my new look.

Irritation flares, but I tamp it down. "Relax, man. I'm not looking to complicate things." What else am I supposed to say to that? *No plans to date your sister-in-law yet, but ask me again tomorrow.* Because I'm not convinced, I wouldn't go out with her given the opportunity. Even if I know she should stay the hell away from the broken version of who I've become.

Mark holds my gaze, then nods. "Alright. I just don't want to see her get hurt. Or you, if this goes sideways." *Like last time* suspending, unspoken between us.

The conversation shifts to safer topics, but Mark's words keep playing in my head. A gentle reminder that when I inevitably fuck this up, it's him I'll have to answer to. I force my eyes on the screen, determined not to let them wander to the door or my phone. But my mind's playing its own game, wondering where Cora is, who she's with. So much for not wanting to complicate things...

It's nearly halftime when my phone buzzes. Cora.

A grin spreads across my face before I can stop it at her comments, but it's quickly replaced by a sour realization. She was on a date. Which means she wants to date. And I haven't dated since... Tessa.

All the reasons she should stay far away from me return with a vengeance. What the hell was I thinking? That hanging out with Cora would magically heal me? That I'd suddenly remember how to play the role of a decent guy?

Better she learns the truth sooner rather than later. Starting with where I am.

Me: *Sounds like a rough night. I'd offer to rescue you, but I'm stuck at Mark's game night. Rain check on that human interaction?*

She responds right away. Because, of course, I just totally confused her.

Cora: *Small world. Didn't realize you knew Mark. Was that on purpose?*

I wait for more questions, but nothing else comes. Is she upset? Disappointed I haven't mentioned that Mark and I used to be best friends?

The minutes tick by agonizingly slow. I'm halfway through convincing myself she'll never talk to me again when the sound of the apartment door opening cuts through the noise in my head.

And there she stands. My angel in the flesh.

Cora's eyes lock with mine, and I see the puzzle falling into place. She knows. It was me in that accident. Her lips part in a silent gasp, her eyes widening with a mixture of shock and disbelief.

"Jake?" she breathes, her voice barely audible.

I give an almost imperceptible nod, my heart racing. The carefully constructed walls I've built, the secrets I've kept–they're all about to come crashing down. And the scariest part? A part of me is relieved.

"Cora? Everything okay?" Arden asks from somewhere nearby.

Cora startles, as if suddenly remembering we're not alone. She blinks rapidly, composing herself with visible effort. "Fine." She forces a smile, gaze remaining on me. "I didn't know Jake would be here."

She takes one step closer, motioning toward the hallway. "Since you are, maybe you could help me with something? In the other room?"

I don't hesitate, desperate to tell her. To explain as much as I can. I know I'll have to answer to Mark later, but I'm not even sure what'd I say right now. *Remember that crash senior year? Yeah, it was your sister-in-law that saved me.*

He'd wonder why I never said anything. But I have my own reasons. Reasons I'm not ready for anyone to know. Not yet.

As soon as we're out of sight, Cora grabs my wrist, pulling me into the nearest room. She closes the door behind us, leaning against it as if to physically hold back the flood of questions I can see in her eyes.

"It was you," she whispers, her voice trembling. "All this time... how'd I miss it?"

I swallow hard, my throat suddenly dry. "Cora, I—"

"How long have you known it was me?" she interrupts.

The question I've been dreading. "Longer than I should admit," I confess, unable to meet her gaze. "I recognized you... a while back."

Her sharp intake of breath is like a knife to my gut. "A while back," she repeats. "And you never said anything? Never reached out? Do you know how many times I thought about you? Wondered what happened?"

I run a hand through my hair, frustration and shame warring

within me. "It's complicated, Cora. There are things... reasons I couldn't..."

"Couldn't what, Jake?" Her voice rises slightly, hurt and confusion evident in every word. "Tell me that you survived. Tell me you knew me."

I flinch, her words hitting too close to home. I want to tell her everything–about Tessa, about the day I saw her with Arden, about how she saved me without even knowing it. But the words stick in my throat, held back by years of survivor's guilt and self-loathing. Because I survived and they didn't.

"I wanted to. God, Cora, you have no idea how many times I almost reached out. But I... I wasn't in a good place. For a long time."

Cora's expression softens slightly, concern replacing some of the hurt. "What happened to you, Jake? After that night? I tried to look for you."

Instead of answering, I find myself reaching for the hem of my shirt. Before I can second-guess myself, I pull it over my head, turning slightly to reveal the angry scar that mars my left shoulder.

Her eyes widen, a small gasp escaping her lips. Hesitantly, she steps closer, her hand hovering just above my skin. "May I?" she asks softly.

I nod, not trusting my voice. Her fingers are warm as they trace the raised flesh, sending shivers down my spine.

"I thought you were dead," she murmurs, her touch feather-light. "When I pulled you out, you were so still..."

"I was in and out of consciousness for a few days, surgery after," I admit, picturing the image I woke up to. The blood on the steering wheel. The pain in my shoulder. The girl in the car pinned against mine. An eighteen-year-old version of Cora.

I turn to face her, catching her hand in mine. Gently, I turn it over, revealing the thin scar that runs along her wrist. "What happened to you?"

She shudders as my finger traces the outline of the jagged line.

"Broken wrist. Minor surgery and a month of having to stay with my parents in Florida while I went through physical therapy."

Unable to resist, I bring her wrist to my lips, placing a soft kiss on the mark. "Guess we both got battle scars that night."

Our eyes meet, and suddenly the air feels thick with unspoken words and shared pain. We're standing so close I can feel the warmth of her breath, see the flecks of gold in her amber eyes.

"Jake," she whispers, her free hand coming to rest on my chest, right over my thundering heart. "Why didn't you tell me last week?"

I close my eyes, leaning my forehead against hers. "Because I was afraid," I admit, the words barely audible. "Afraid of what you'd think of the man I've become. Afraid that knowing the whole truth would make you regret ever pulling me out of that car."

Cora pulls back slightly, her eyes searching mine.

I take a shaky breath, running a hand through my hair. "Cora, I... there's so much I want to tell you. But I don't even know where to start."

She reaches out, her fingers grazing my arm. The touch sends electricity coursing through me, and I have to resist the urge to pull her closer. "You don't have to say anything you don't want to," she offers softly. "We've got time."

Time. The word is full of promise and possibility. But also danger. Because time has a way of changing things, of revealing truths we might not be ready to face.

"It's just... December," I finally manage, my voice rough.

"Like something always goes wrong?" she adds, her eyes widening. "Like you're cursed?"

"Yeah," I confess, surprised by her understanding. Is that what she meant last week? In the coffee shop? "You too?"

She nods. "Every fucking December. I thought I was going crazy, but..."

"But you're not," I finish for her. Our eyes connect, and I'm back, drowning in the depths of her gaze.

Then reality comes crashing back as a cheer erupts from the living room. Cora jumps slightly, as if suddenly remembering where we are.

"We should probably..." she starts, gesturing toward the door.

"Yeah," I agree, hastily pulling my shirt back on, even as every fiber of my being screams to stay right here. In this moment. With her.

As we shift closer to the door, Cora stops, placing her hand on my arm. "Jake, I don't know how to process all of this."

I let out a shaky breath, my thumb instinctively grazing her scarred wrist. "Join the club. I've been trying to figure it out for years."

The words catch in my throat. She doesn't know the whole story. The real reason I never said anything. Would she be this kind, this vulnerable with me if she did? The thought makes my stomach churn.

Cora's eyes search mine, and for a heart-stopping moment, I wonder if she can see right through me. "Any luck?" she asks softly.

"Not until now," I admit, the honesty of it hitting me like a sucker punch. "But, Cora, I meant what I said Saturday. I've got skeletons. Lots of them."

She nods, a flicker of understanding in her eyes. "I think we both do, Jake."

And with that, she opens the door, stepping back into the noise and light of the party. I follow, my mind reeling. For the first time in years, I'm not looking for an escape route. Instead, I'm wondering if maybe, just maybe, I'm finally ready to face down my past in order to learn every note of hers.

As we rejoin the others, caught between Mark's suspicious glare and Arden's knowing smile, one thought echoes in my mind: This December could change everything. And I'm terrified of how much I want it to.

10

∽

Cora

You know those plot twists in romance novels that make you want to throw the book across the room because they're so outrageous? Well, apparently, the universe decided my life needed one of those, and it came in the form of a clean-shaven jaw and a haircut that screams "boy band nostalgia tour."

Jake. The man I hauled from twisted metal and shattered glass six years ago. The same Jake who's been fueling my caffeine addiction and my heart palpitations for the past week. How did I miss it? How did I not recognize those ocean-blue eyes that once stared at me like I was their only lifeline?

I'm perched on the edge of the couch, sipping water like it's the world's most fascinating beverage, pretending to be engrossed in a game I couldn't care less about. But let's be real, my attention is laser-focused on the walking, talking plot twist across the room.

My analytical brain is running wild, trying to reconcile the Jake I've barely glimpsed to know with the broken man all those years ago. Blurry visions of that day flash through my mind—the crash, seeing him lifeless against the steering wheel, his bruised and bloodied face when he finally turned my way.

The irony of it all isn't lost on me. I've spent six years trying to delete my "December curse" from my personal narrative, only to find its origin story lounging in Mark and Arden's living room like it belongs in the acknowledgments.

I sneak another glance at Jake, catching him mid-laugh at something Mark said. The sound tugs at something deep inside me, a bittersweet reminder of the carefree boy he must have been before whatever tragedy rewrote his story.

God, what I wouldn't give to edit out whatever pain he's been through.

But that's not how life works, is it? We can't just strike through the difficult chapters and hope for a better narrative. No, we have to live through every messy, complicated sentence.

Then again, my own life is proof of that. Because, let's face it, there's a reason I call it my December curse. The accident, what happened with Sam a year later, Mark and Arden's wedding the following year, and then Logan...

Could I have met Jake years before now? If I'd taken Arden up on her invite to visit? If I'd been half the sister to her that she's been to me?

She didn't even hesitate when I called her that night. When I broke things off with Logan. I never had to ask if I could stay here with her and Mark. They just let me cry, brought me back here, and made me feel like I belonged despite how I'd pushed her away for years.

I'm pulled from my spiral by the buzz of my phone. It's Jake, because of course it is.

Jake: *You're super interested in the game, huh?*

I can't help the sardonic smile that tugs at my lips. Even now, with the weight of our shared past hanging between us, he's trying to make me laugh. It's endearing and infuriating all at once.

I bite my lip, tapping out a reply.

Me: *Riveted. Go... team?*
Jake: *Nailed it. You're clearly a sports fanatic.*
Me: *Books are more my thing.*

Memories of Sunday afternoons with Logan flash unbidden. Him, watching whatever games were on, and me on the couch reading.

Jake: *What else is your thing?*

He really wants to know? Me?

Me: *Pretty much the cliché. Eats up romantic gestures, long walks on the beach over a picture-perfect sunset. Bubble baths, roses, and candle-lit dinners.*

Jake stares at my text for what feels like forever, and I wonder if I said too much. I was half-joking, but everything I put was also true. They are what I like. It's why I chose my career, rewriting stories to be less of the vanilla romance plot. And still, even after all that's happened, I still love the whole "ride off into the sunset happily ever after."

Well, maybe not "love" recently, more like appreciate.

Finally, my phone flashes again.

Jake: *Tell me something that isn't cliché. Something most people don't know. Aside from the fact that you're a walking, talking, breathing angel?*

My breath catches at that, and I glance up to see Jake smiling at me. But there's something else there, too. Hesitation maybe?

Me: *I never told Arden. Or anyone. About what else happened during the accident. About you.*

Jake: *Too humble?*

I meet his gaze, physically shrugging in response.

Me: *Your turn. What don't people know about you?*

I watch as he chews on his cheek before his fingers swipe his screen.

Jake: *A lot, Cora. And someday, I'd love to share it all. But for now, maybe we can start with how I got a pretty amazing birthday gift this year. It was last Friday.*

I shake my head in disbelief. Last Friday was his birthday? The night I ran into him at Sadie's? The night we kissed?

But that means...

Me: *Your birthday is on December 1ˢᵗ? Mines the 31ˢᵗ. The start and end of December. Do you find that as ironic as I do?*

Jake starts typing, then stops. Starts again. My heart races as I wait for his response. But before it comes, Mark jumps up, startling me. The rest of the living room follows suit. Something happened with the game, and Mark's chattering excitedly with the guys.

I slip my phone into my pocket, Jake's unfinished message burning a hole in my mind. Following Arden to the kitchen under the guise of helping her clean up, I try to focus on anything but the questions consuming me. Is there more to my December curse than I thought? And why is Jake here now?

I need a moment—or longer—to recalibrate my worldview.

"So," Arden drawls, sidling up next to me at the sink, "want to tell me what that whole secret room rendezvous was about?"

I nearly drop the plate I'm drying. "What? Nothing. We just talked."

Arden raises an eyebrow, looking unconvinced. "Uh-huh. And all those loaded looks you two keep sharing are..."

I feel the heat creeping up my neck. "I don't know what you're talking about."

"Oh please," Arden scoffs, bumping my hip with hers. "I haven't seen this much unresolved tension since that time you got locked in the supply closet with your high school crush."

I groan, remembering the mortifying incident. "Low blow, sis. Low blow."

"Hey, what are sisters for if not to bring up embarrassing memories at the most inopportune times?" She grins, clearly pleased with herself.

I'm saved from having to respond by the sound of approaching footsteps as people head out of the apartment. Jake and Mark enter the kitchen, and suddenly the room feels too small, too warm.

"Thanks for having me over," Jake says, his voice doing that low, gravelly thing that makes my insides turn to jelly.

Mark claps him on the shoulder, but his smile doesn't quite reach his eyes. "Any time, man. Don't be a stranger, yeah?"

Jake nods, his gaze flickering to mine before quickly looking away. "I should head out, too. Work tomorrow and all."

"Speaking of tomorrow," Arden pipes up, twirling a dish towel absently, "Jake, you're still off Tuesday nights, right?"

Jake's brow furrows slightly. "Yeah, why?"

Arden's eyes sparkle with that mischievous spark I know all too well. "Well, I was thinking... it's been ages since we had a movie night. You know, for old times' sake." She glances at Mark, a silent plea in her eyes.

Mark catches her look and sighs, a mix of exasperation and fondness. "What my wife is trying to say, in her oh-so-subtle way, is that we're free tomorrow night. If you wanted to join us for a movie, we'd love to have you."

Jake blinks, clearly caught off guard. His eyes flicker to me for a split second before he manages a nod. "Uh, yeah. Sure. That sounds... nice."

"Great," Mark says, clapping Jake on the shoulder. "I'll walk you out."

As they head towards the door, Jake's gaze finds mine one last time. There's a universe of unspoken words in that look, questions and answers swirling in those storm-blue eyes. Then he's gone, the soft click of the door echoing in the sudden silence.

I let out a breath I didn't know I was holding, my mind reeling from the evening's revelations.

"You okay?" Arden asks in a low voice, concern etched on her face. "I didn't mean to overstep—"

"No, it's fine," I say, perhaps a bit too quickly. Is it fine? I mean, I do want to see Jake again, but... My thoughts are interrupted when Mark reappears, closing the front door behind him.

Something clicks in my mind, and I turn to Arden, narrowing my eyes. "Hold up. Why did you really invite him over tomorrow? And what was that whole bookshelf thing about? What am I missing here?"

Arden chews her lower lip, shooting a glance at Mark, who's now looking at us with raised eyebrows. "Well," she starts, her voice hesitant, "he's been... different lately. In a good way."

She gestures towards Mark, almost pleadingly. "You saw him tonight, right? He looked like his old self again. Actually happy, even."

Mark lets out a long sigh, running a hand through his hair. "Arden, honey, you can't 'fix' Jake by setting him up with Cora. That's just asking for trouble."

"I know, but..." Arden begins, her voice trailing off.

"But what?" Mark counters. "You know as well as I do that the Jake we knew... he hasn't been the same since we lost them."

My mind reels, trying to piece together this puzzle I didn't even know existed.

"Whoa, wait a second," I interject, holding up my hands. "Lost who? And what exactly needs 'fixing' with Jake?"

Arden and Mark exchange a loaded look, having one of those wordless conversations that only longtime couples seem capable of. After a moment, Mark nods.

Arden turns to me, her expression grave. "Why don't we sit down for a bit, Co? There's... there's some stuff you should probably know."

My heart starts racing as I follow them to the living room, sinking into the couch. The atmosphere has shifted, heavy with unspoken words and hidden histories. Something in their expressions tells me I'm about to get answers to questions I didn't even know I had.

Mark clears his throat, his eyes fixed on a point somewhere over my left shoulder. "Jake and I... we grew up next door to each other. Practically brothers."

I furrow my brow, piecing together fragments of conversations I've overheard over the years. Something doesn't quite fit. "Wait, I thought Owen was your childhood neighbor? The best man from your wedding?"

Mark's jaw tenses, and suddenly, the rest of that memory clicks into place. Owen, opening up after a few beers, telling me about his younger brother. The one who was supposed to be Mark's best man before he backed out.

"Jake is Owen's brother," I say slowly, the picture forming. One I'm not sure I want to see.

Mark nods, his voice tight. "There were three of them. Owen, Jake, and Thomas Rhoades. Jake was a year younger than me in school, Owen a year older."

"And Thomas?" The words slip out before I can stop them. Immediately, I wish I could take them back. Both their faces fall, and Arden places a comforting hand over Mark's.

"Thomas passed away," Arden replies softly, her voice barely above a whisper. "Five years ago. There was a car accident." She visibly swallows, as if the words are physically painful. "Thomas and Jake's girlfriend, Tessa. They... they didn't make it."

Another car accident?

"But Jake survived?" I ask, not fully understanding.

Arden shakes her head, her eyes glistening. "He wasn't there. Thomas was taking Tessa to the airport. Something about a fight they'd gotten into that morning."

She looks over at Mark, who's visibly shaken, as if he's reliving that day. The pain etched on his face makes my heart ache.

"Jake... he wasn't the same after that," Mark adds harshly. "Blamed himself for not being the one driving that day."

The weight of that guilt... I can't even begin to imagine. Jake lost his brother and girlfriend in one brutal stroke. My mind flashes to Arden, to the guilt she carried after my accident. She was supposed to drive our parents that day. If I hadn't made it... God, she'd never have forgiven herself.

"He pushed everyone away," Arden continues, her hand finding Mark's. "We tried to help, but..."

But what? My brain is already filling in the blanks with scenarios that make my stomach churn. I think of my own struggles after the accident, the nightmares that plagued me for months. But I had my family, college. What did Jake have?

"Is that why he wasn't at the wedding?" I ask before realizing what I brought up. Memories of that night surface against my will. Drinking myself numb, strange arms guiding me upstairs when the spinning got out of control. I cringe internally. If Jake had been there... No, that's not a road worth traveling down.

Mark's voice pulls me from the dark spiral. "He said the pain was still too fresh. To be fair, it was pretty close to the one-year anniversary. I should've thought about that, but we'd already set the date before..."

"It was in December," I breathe, the realization hitting me like a punch to the gut. "When he lost them?"

Arden nods, not quite understanding the significance. But I do. Suddenly, Jake's words from earlier echo in my mind: "A lot, Cora. And someday, I'd love to share it all." Is this what he meant? This ocean of pain and loss he's been drowning in?

"I'm not pushing you toward him because I want you to date him," Arden clarifies, her voice gentle. "He's been through a lot. Just like you. And somehow, I don't know... you two around each other both seem... happy."

"Happy," I repeat, tasting the word. It's been so long since I've associated that with myself, let alone someone else. "That's why you invited him tomorrow? Because I make him happy?"

Arden's eyes soften. "I think you both deserve a second chance at happiness, Co. Whatever form that takes."

I stand to head to my room, my editor brain kicking into overdrive. Is this why I was drawn to Jake from the start? Some cosmic force bringing us back together, the girl who saved his life now destined to heal his heart like some "fated lovers reunited by tragedy" story?

I catch myself, realizing the dangerous territory my thoughts are wandering into. Haven't I been down this road before? With Sam, thinking I could fix him with enough care and understanding. Then with Logan, believing my love could make him a better man.

God, when did I become this person? This... fixer. Always trying to save everyone but myself. Better yet, at the expense of myself.

But Jake isn't a manuscript I can edit. He's a real person with real trauma. And me? I'm still navigating my own stormy waters.

The irony isn't lost on me. Here I am, contemplating how to

save someone else when I can barely keep myself afloat. Some savior I'd make.

I pause at my bedroom door, turning back to Arden and Mark. "Thank you for telling me. I... I need some time to process all this."

Arden nods, understanding in her eyes. "Take all the time you need, sweetie. We're here if you want to talk more."

I sink onto my bed, grabbing my phone almost unconsciously as I wrestle with the steady onslaught of conflicting emotions.

A new message flashes from Jake. I open it, unable to resist.

Jake: *Sorry If I made the rest of the night awkward for you*
Me: *It's okay. You're not in trouble.*
Jake: *Oh, I'm definitely in trouble, Cora.*

Me too, Jake, me too.

11

Jake

December 5th

The scent of buttered popcorn wafts through the air as I stand frozen outside Mark and Arden's apartment, my hand poised to knock. The muffled sound of laughter filters through the door, a stark contrast to the silence I've surrounded myself with for years. I take a deep breath, willing my racing heart to slow. It's just a movie night, for Christ's sake.

But as I think about Cora waiting on the other side, my palms start to sweat. Funny how facing a room full of drunk college kids at Sadie's is a breeze, but the thought of sitting next to her for two hours has me more nervous than my first time on stage.

I run a hand through my freshly trimmed hair, still not used to the shorter length. "You've faced worse, Rhoades," I mutter to myself. "Just channel your inner rock star and knock on the damn door."

Before I can talk myself out of it, I rap my knuckles against the wood. The door swings open, revealing Arden's beaming face.

"Jake! You made it!" She pulls me into a quick hug, the scent of her flowery perfume momentarily overwhelming me.

"Well, you're the ones who wanted to hang out with me two nights in a row," I say with a hint of sarcasm.

Arden rolls her eyes good-naturedly. "Come on in, everyone's waiting."

The lights are already turned down when I step inside, creating a more intimate atmosphere. It's both welcoming and slightly unsettling.

I glance across the space, seeing Mark sprawled on the larger couch, beer in hand. "Welcome back, Jay," he offers, raising his bottle in mock salute.

I nod, noticing Cora for the first time. She's curled up on the loveseat, but there's something off about her smile. It sets off warning bells, questions forming about what happened after I left last night. Did Mark warn her to stay away? Or worse, does she *want* to stay away?

I push the thought aside for now. "So, what cinematic masterpiece are we subjecting ourselves to tonight?" I ask, trying to keep my tone light as I make my way to the only open spot—next to Cora.

Arden grins, brandishing the remote like a weapon. "I managed to talk Mark out of his usual gore-fest. We're going with something a little more... festive."

I raise an eyebrow, glancing at Mark. "You're willingly giving up your horror movie night? Who are you and what have you done with my best friend?"

Mark groans dramatically. "Trust me, it wasn't willingly. I was outvoted. Apparently, 'tis the season for holiday cheer or some nonsense."

"It's called 'Let It Snow,'" Cora chimes in, her voice softer than usual. "Based on a John Green novel. It's got a bit of everything—mystery, romance, holiday magic."

"Sounds riveting," I deadpan, earning a small chuckle from Cora.

As Arden starts the movie, I can't help but remember how our tradition of college horror movie nights led to her and Mark getting together. The irony of it now sitting here, next to her sister, isn't lost on me.

"Think you can handle a little romance without falling asleep?" Cora whispers, a hint of her usual spark returning to her eyes.

I lean in closer, my voice low. "I don't know, depends on how good the soundtrack is. Music is more my *thing*."

She rolls her eyes, but I catch the slight upturn of her lips. "Music man, huh?" Her gaze trails my body before she adds, "I can see that."

I contemplate telling her about the audition tomorrow, about what it means, but the volume kicks up, signaling the opening scene.

I try to focus on the screen. I really do. But between the dim lighting and the warmth radiating from the woman next to me, she's all I can think about. My thoughts drift inevitably to the song for tomorrow. The one she inspired last week. *When I close my eyes, all I see is you.*

I sneak a glance at Mark and Arden, cuddled together on the other couch. They look so comfortable, so at ease with each other. For a moment, I let myself imagine what it would be like to have that kind of connection again. To let someone in past all my carefully constructed walls.

Just as I start to lean closer, Cora's phone lights up with a text. I catch Logan's name before she quickly turns it over and I'm reminded of all the reasons why that's a dangerous path to go down. We're both carrying baggage, both nursing wounds that haven't fully healed.

She shifts slightly, her knee brushing against mine. It's an innocent touch, but it sends a jolt through me that rivals any feedback from my guitar. I clear my throat, trying to dispel the tension.

"So, is this John Green guy always this..." I search for the right word, "...saccharine?"

Cora chuckles softly. "Not always. But I thought we could all use a little sweetness right now."

Her words hang in the air, loaded with meaning. I wonder if she's thinking about Logan, about the life she left behind. The thought sends a pang through my chest that I'm not ready to examine too closely.

"Sweetness, huh?" I mutter, more to myself than to her. "Been a while since I've had much of that in my life."

Cora turns to me, her eyes searching mine. "Jake, I—"

Her phone buzzes again, cutting off whatever she was about to say. I can't see the screen, but judging by the way her shoulders tense, I'd bet it's her ex again.

"Everything okay?" I ask, aiming for casual but probably hitting somewhere around 'nosy neighbor.'

Cora's smile is strained. "Yeah, it's just... Logan. He's having a hard time with me signing a lease for my own place."

Wait, what? She's moving out? The news hits me like an unexpected key change. Does that mean no more coffee shop encounters?

"He still thinks I'm dating you," she adds, filling the silence with a nervous laugh. "And, well, he's...persistent."

"Persistent is a nice way of putting it," I mutter, bitterness seeping into my voice. "Manipulative is probably more accurate."

Cora flinches, and I immediately regret my words. "I'm sorry, I shouldn't—"

"No," she interrupts, "you're right. It's just... complicated."

I laugh, but there's no humor in it. "Isn't it always?"

As the movie plays on, forgotten in the background, I can practically hear the gears turning in Cora's head. Part of me wants to pull her close, to promise her a happy ending. But I know better than anyone that some songs take time to compose.

"You know," I say, finally breaking the silence, "I've been thinking a lot lately. About second chances."

Cora turns to me, curiosity flickering in her eyes. "Yeah? What about them?"

I fidget with the hem of my shirt, searching for the right words. "They're... complicated. Part of me wants to believe in them, but another part..."

"Is terrified?" Cora finishes, her voice barely above a whisper.

I nod, meeting her gaze. "Exactly. It's like standing on the edge of a cliff. You know the view might be breathtaking, but the fall..."

"Could destroy you," she murmurs, understanding etched on her face.

When the credits roll, I realize we've been lost in our own world for who knows how long. I glance over to see Mark fast asleep, his head in Arden's lap. Arden catches my eye and gives an exaggerated eye roll.

"This," she mouths, she mouths, gesturing to her sleeping husband, "is married life." She gently coaxes Mark to his feet, guiding him towards their bedroom.

All at once, Cora and I are alone in the dimly lit room. The silence stretches between us, electric and fragile.

"So," Cora says, her voice soft, "glad you came?"

I slide closer, my arm finding its way to the back of the couch. Not quite touching her, but close enough to feel the heat radiating off her skin. "Glad doesn't begin to cover it," I murmur, my voice rough with unspoken want despite all the reasons I shouldn't.

Cora turns to me, those amber eyes searching mine. She bites her lip, and I swear I can hear the opening chords of a song I haven't written yet.

"Jake," she breathes, "what are we doing here?"

The question hangs in the air, heavy with possibility and fear. I swallow hard, buying time. "Well, I thought we were watching a movie, but clearly I missed something."

A smile tugs at her lips, but it doesn't reach her eyes. "You know what I mean. This... tension between us. It's not just in my head, is it?"

"No," I admit, the word feeling like both a confession and a surrender. "It's not just you. But Cora..." I trail off, struggling to find the right words.

She leans in, her fingers ghosting over my scar. Fire ignites under my skin at her touch. "But what, Jake?"

I close my eyes, overwhelmed by her nearness. "I'm not exactly boyfriend material. And you... you're still healing from your breakup."

"And you're still healing too," she counters softly. *So, she does know.* Somehow that makes it better and worse at the same time.

Her hand finds mine, our fingers intertwining. "We're both pretty messed up, huh?"

I open my eyes, finding her gaze. The understanding I see there threatens to undo me completely. "Yeah," I whisper, "we are."

"Maybe that's okay," Cora says, her voice barely above a whisper. "Being messed up together."

My heart thunders in my chest. I lean in, close enough to count the flecks of gold in her eyes. "Together, huh? That's a dangerous word, Cora."

She doesn't back away. Instead, her free hand comes up to rest on my chest, right over my racing heart. "I'm starting to think some dangers might be worth it."

I can't help the low groan that escapes me. "You don't know what you're asking for."

"Don't I?" Her eyes flick to my lips, then back to my eyes. "I'm not naive, Jake. I'm still getting over... But there's something about you, something I can't seem to stay away from."

My resolve crumbles. I cup her face in my hands, our foreheads touching. "God, Cora. You have no idea what you do to me."

She leans into my touch, her breath warm against my lips. "Then show me."

That's all it takes. I need this—need her—more than my next breath. I close the final distance between us, capturing her lips with mine. And when my tongue meets hers, it's like striking a match in a room full of gasoline. Everything explodes.

I kiss her like a dying man gasping for air. My hands roam her body, desperate to memorize every curve.

"Maybe just tonight," I pant against her neck, trailing hot kisses down to her collarbone.

"One time," she agrees, arching into me as my hands slip under her shirt.

We're a tangle of limbs and suppressed desire. I know we're making a colossal mistake, but I can't bring myself to care.

"Jake," Cora moans, and Christ, my name on her lips is the sweetest melody I've heard in years.

I pull back, struggling to catch my breath. "You're driving me crazy."

She grins, wild and reckless. "Good crazy or bad crazy?"

"Both," I admit, diving back in for another taste.

We're so lost in each other that we almost miss the creak of the floorboards. Arden's voice slices through our haze like a record scratch.

"Jesus Christ," she mutters, averting her eyes. "I just wanted some water, not a live show."

We spring apart, reality crashing back like a bucket of ice water. Cora looks thoroughly kissed and utterly mortified. I'm not faring much better, my heart pounding like I've just run a marathon.

Arden shakes her head, retreating to the kitchen. "Next time, use a bedroom. Preferably not in my house."

In the sudden silence, the weight of what just happened settles over us. This isn't just some hook-up. This is... everything.

I stare at her, wondering if this is it. If I can be *him* again. But then I see Cora's phone flash with Logan's name. Her words echo in my head, *"I'm still not over..."* Suddenly, I'm drowning in memories of

December's past. Tessa. The pain. The betrayal. The vow I made not to let anyone get that close again.

"I should go," I say, my voice rough with want and panic.

Cora nods, not quite meeting my eyes. "Yeah, that's... that's probably best." But her fingers twitch towards me, betraying her words.

I make it to the door before turning back. Cora's still on the couch, looking beautifully wrecked and utterly lost. It takes everything in me not to go back to her.

"Goodnight, Cora," I manage, before stepping out.

In the hallway, I lean against the wall, my head spinning. What am I doing? I'm a mess, a shell of who I used to be. And Cora... she's still untangling herself from Logan. We're both carrying so much baggage.

But God, the way she makes me feel...

I pull out my phone, thumb hovering over her name. I should text her, tell her this was a mistake. Or call her, hear her voice one more time. Instead, I pocket the phone, paralyzed by indecision.

Back in my apartment, the silence is deafening. My guitar sits in the corner, mocking me. Tomorrow's audition looms, reminding me of the song I wrote for Cora, and the ones I penned for Tessa.

I sink onto the couch, head in my hands. How did I let this get so complicated? When did I become this guy?

I can't keep playing this game. It's not fair to Cora, and it's tearing me apart. I need to make a decision—commit to whatever this is between us, or cut ties before we both get hurt. And fuck if that fallout isn't going to be absolute hell.

12

Jake

*December 7*th

The phantom taste of Cora's lips haunts me as I down another shot of whiskey. It's been two days since that night, and I can still feel the heat of her skin under my fingertips, hear the soft gasps she made as I kissed her neck. Christ, what I wouldn't give to go back to that moment, to lose myself in her again.

But reality's a cold bitch, isn't it?

I stare at my silent phone, Guns N' Roses wailing about Paradise City in the background. Paradise? Yeah, right. More like purgatory.

Cora's vague text from this morning mocks me: *Hope all is well.*

Well? I'm about as far from "well" as you can get without actually being six feet under. But hey, at least I haven't reached for anything stronger than whiskey. Small victories, right?

I knock back another shot, embracing the burn. It's a poor substitute for the fire Cora ignited in me, but it'll have to do. I've got a band rehearsal to get through, and I can't afford to be lost in thoughts of starry eyes and soft skin.

"Jake!" Owen's voice crashes my nightmare. "You planning on rejoining us anytime soon?"

I grunt, pushing away from the bar. "Yeah, yeah. Keep your pants on."

As I make my way back to our setup, my phone buzzes. For a split second, hope flares in my chest. Maybe it's her. Maybe she's thinking about me too, maybe she—

But it's not Cora. It's Lindsey. Again.

Lindsey: *Hey sexy, can't wait to see you perform later! Celebrate after?* ☺

I swallow a groan. This girl doesn't know how to take a hint. Or maybe I just suck at giving them. Story of my life.

"Everything okay?" Chris asks as I rejoin them, eyeing me warily.

"Peachy," I mutter, strapping on my guitar. The familiar weight grounds me, reminds me why I'm here. Music. It's always been my salvation, my escape. Maybe it can save me from myself one more time.

But even as I lose myself in our first song, a traitorous part of my mind wonders what Cora would think if she could see me now. Would she be impressed? Would she finally see past the screw-up bartender to the musician underneath? Does she even know there is a musician underneath?

Who am I kidding? She's probably too busy packing, getting ready to start her new life. A life that doesn't include me.

The song ends, and reality crashes back in. Owen's looking at me with a mix of concern and excitement. "Dude, that was intense. You okay?"

I force a grin, hoping it doesn't look as fake as it feels. "Never better. What's next?"

As Owen launches into our setlist, I try to focus. But Cora's still there, lingering at the edges of my mind like a bittersweet melody I can't shake.

Two days. It's only been two days, but it feels like a lifetime. And

I'm starting to wonder if I'll ever feel whole again without her. Maybe I should reach out and tell her how I actually feel. Except that would mean admitting feelings. Turning back into what? Who I used to be? Naïve and in love? What if Cora did the same thing?

A familiar ringtone cuts through the air, halting our jam session. Owen's eyes go wide as he fumbles for his phone.

"It's Alex Caine," he mouths, excitement and disbelief warring on his face.

My stomach drops. Alex Caine, the guy who could make or break our career. The same career I've been running from for years, drowning my potential in cheap whiskey and even cheaper hookups.

Owen puts the call on speaker, and Alex's voice fills the room. "Boys, I've got news. The promoters were super impressed with you all yesterday, and there was a last-minute cancellation for this Saturday. They want you. To open for Stuffed Olives."

Stuffed Olives? They're huge.

"This Saturday?" Chris echoes, his drumsticks frozen mid-twirl. "As in, two days from now?"

"I know it's insane timing," Alex says, "but the execs were adamant about locking you down. We can offer a decent payout and a guaranteed slot next month."

The room goes silent. I can feel Owen and Chris's eyes on me, waiting. They know my history, know how close I came to throwing it all away after Tessa. After Thomas.

For a moment, I'm back there. The conversation with Tessa. The argument with Thomas. Then the call from my mother later that evening and the crushing weight of guilt that's been my constant companion ever since.

But then I think of Cora. Of her smile, her laugh. The way she looks at me like I'm worth something. Hell, she saved me, so I better make myself worth something.

"We'll do it," I hear myself say, surprising even me.

Owen and Chris erupt in cheers, but I barely hear them. All I can think about is Cora in the crowd, watching me on stage. Maybe this is my chance to show her–to show myself–that I'm more than my mistakes.

As Owen wraps up the call, Chris claps me on the back. "You sure about this, man? It's a big step."

I nod, a wry smile tugging at my lips. "Yeah, well, gotta grow up sometime, right? Might as well be now."

We dive into planning mode, the energy in the room electric. But even as we hash out setlists and staging, my mind keeps drifting back to Cora. Before I can talk myself out of it, I pull out my phone.

Me: *Curious if you're free Saturday?*

Her response is almost immediate, but it's not what I hoped for.

Cora: *Packing. I move into the new apartment on Sunday.*

Of course. She's moving on, literally and figuratively. Why would she drop everything for a guy she barely knows?

I shove the phone back in my pocket, trying to ignore the ache in my chest. This gig, this chance–it's not about her. It can't be. It's about me, about the band, about finally facing the music I've been running from for far too long.

As we launch into our next song, I pour everything into it–the pain, the hope, the fear. For the first time in years, I let myself feel it all.

The rest of rehearsal flies by, full of chord progressions and lyric sheets. By the time we wrap up, the sun's setting, painting the sky in shades of amber that remind me too much of Cora's eyes. I shake off the thought. *Focus, Rhoades. You've got a gig to play.*

* * *

Playing Thursday nights at Sadie's has been our staple for the last six years, the one constant in a sea of chaos. When I step onto the familiar stage, the lights shining down, I wonder what it will feel like to play somewhere new, somewhere where memories of Tessa and Thomas don't haunt me. It's like the idea of playing the safe, monotonous bass line, or jumping into a wild solo that could either soar or crash spectacularly.

"You boys ready to give these folks a preview for Saturday?" Sadie calls from the side of the stage.

I give her a mock salute. "Yes, ma'am. Wouldn't want to disappoint our biggest fan." Because she has been. She's been with us through it all. Even gave me the full-time bartender job when I started to spiral, trying to "keep me out of trouble."

We launch into our set, and I feel the familiar rush of adrenaline. This is where I belong, where everything makes sense. For a few blissful hours, there's no Cora, no Tessa. There's just the music, raw and real and mine.

But reality has a way of crashing back in.

I'm barely off stage, sweat still cooling on my skin, when I spot a flash of platinum blonde. Ah, fuck. Here we go.

"Jake!" Lindsey's voice bulldozes my post-show buzz. "I heard the news! About Saturday at Joe's! Oh my God, I'm so excited for you."

Apparently, word has officially gotten out.

She launches herself at me, all fake tan and desperation. I catch her reflexively, but my skin crawls at the contact. This isn't what I want. This isn't who I want.

"Thanks, Lindsey," I mutter, gently but firmly setting her back on her feet. "We just got the call earlier today."

But Lindsey, bless her heart, has never been great at reading the room. She leans in, her perfume cloying in the air between us. "So, I was thinking... maybe we could celebrate your big break? My place is free tonight."

Nausea hits at the thought of *celebrating* with Lindsey tonight.

"Sorry, Lindsey," I say, surprised by how much I mean it. "I'm not interested."

Her face falls, a mix of confusion and hurt that makes me feel like the world's biggest asshole. "But... I thought we had something special?"

Christ. How do I even begin to unpack that?

I catch Natalie's eye as she sets down another tray of drinks. She mouths something that looks suspiciously like "your mess, Jake."

And fuck, what a mess I've made.

"Look," I start, running a hand through my hair. "What happened between us... I was drunk and lonely. You deserved better than that. You still do."

Lindsey's eyes narrow, hurt morphing into anger. "What are you saying, Jake? I'm not good enough now that you're playing some big show?"

I shake my head. When did my life become such a merry-go-round of regret piled upon regret?

"I'm saying there's someone else," I manage. It's not a lie. Not at all. I just don't know what happens when that "someone else" sees the real me—the broken, fucked-up mess beneath the surface.

"You're making a mistake," Lindsey spits, venom lacing her words. "You'll be back."

I watch her storm off, her words echoing in my head. *You'll be back.* How many times have I heard that before? How many times have I proved it true?

I slump against the bar, suddenly exhausted. Natalie slides a glass of water my way, her eyes full of concern and, yeah, pity.

"You okay there, Romeo?"

I let out a bitter laugh. "Just living the dream."

She doesn't buy it for a second. "You know, Jake, it's okay to want something more. Someone more."

Her words hit me like a sucker punch. Because isn't that what I'm afraid of? Wanting more, reaching for it, only to have it slip through my fingers like everything else?

I drain the water, wishing it was something stronger. "Maybe. But what if I'm not built for 'more,' Nat? What if this is all I'm good for?"

She shakes her head, disappointment clear on her face. "That's bullshit, and you know it. The Jake I know wouldn't give up without a fight."

As I push away from the bar, her words follow me. The Jake she knows. But which Jake is that? The one who lost everything five years ago? The one who's been sleepwalking through life ever since? Or the one who, for the first time in years, feels something real when he looks into Cora's eyes?

I step out into the night, the cool air a stark contrast to the heat of the bar. Saturday's show looms ahead, a beacon of possibility and potential disaster. And somewhere out there, Cora's packing up her old life, getting ready to start anew.

My phone feels heavy in my pocket, Cora's number just a few taps away. But as I stare up at the starless city sky, I realize something.

It's not just about Cora. It's not just about the band. It's about me. About who I want to be. About whether I'm ready to step out of the shadows of my past and into whatever light the future might hold.

As I walk home, a new melody starts to form in my head. It's raw, unfinished, but it's there. A song about second chances, about the courage to try again.

Maybe it's time to stop running. Maybe it's time to face the music.

Because if there's one thing I've learned, it's that in life, just like in music, the most beautiful harmonies often come after the harshest discords. And who knows? Maybe this time, I'll finally get it right.

13

∽

Cora

December 8ᵗʰ

Three nights ago, I sat frozen on Arden's couch, the ghost of Jake's kiss still burning on my lips. The silence he left behind was deafening.

"You okay?" Arden had asked, settling beside me.

I nodded mechanically, but my mind was racing. What just happened? How did I let myself get swept away like that?

"I think I made a mistake," I whispered, more to myself than Arden.

"Which part?" she asked. "The kissing, or letting him leave?"

I looked up, tears threatening to spill. "Both? Neither? I don't know, Arden. It's all happening so fast."

She wrapped an arm around me. "Sometimes fast isn't bad, Co. But only you can decide if it's worth the risk."

Now, three days later, I'm wandering through a furniture store in a daze, surrounded by bedroom sets that all blend into one beige blur. Talk about anticlimactic. This isn't how the protagonist in one of my novels would act. She'd be having some grand epiphany, making a bold decision, charging headfirst into her bright new future.

But this isn't a novel. This is my life, and I'm stuck overthinking every interaction, every touch, every loaded glance from that night, trying to convince myself that I'm making the right choice by maintaining distance. Because that's what mature, self-aware women do, right? They don't leap headfirst into the arms of brooding, emotionally unavailable men, no matter how electric their kisses might be.

I pause in front of a mirror, catching sight of my reflection. The woman staring back at me looks tired, conflicted, and annoyingly indecisive.

Get it together, Cooper. Take your time. You know you need to be on your own. To heal.

With a sigh, I turn my attention back to the task at hand. Furniture shopping. Another plot point in the 'Cora Starts Over' narrative. I settle on a decent-looking arrangement that can be delivered quickly and fits within the budget my parents gifted me. Their 'easy button' Christmas and apology-for-breaking-off-your-engagement gift. Not that I expected anything different. They've never been good at talking through feelings. Instead, they parent the only way they know how— by throwing money at it.

As I finalize the purchase, I glance at my phone, contemplating sending Jake another text. Because despite my attempt to "find myself" the last few days, I definitely broke down and stalked the coffee shop. Low and behold, no Jake. Either day. So, like an addict needing a fix, I sent some super-vague message yesterday.

And then he comes back asking if I'm busy Saturday?

God, am I making the right choice? Or am I just running away from something potentially amazing because I'm scared?

I breathe in the frigid December air and pull my coat tighter around me as I wander aimlessly down the row of shops. The streets are alive with holiday cheer, white lights twinkling in shop windows, scents of roasted chestnuts and peppermint flooding my senses. It's all so picture-perfect that it almost makes me believe in the magic of the season again.

Almost.

Because right then, I heard a familiar voice calling my name.

"Cora?"

I turn, my heart sinking as I see Logan's parents lighting up with gleeful waves. His mother pulls me into a crushing embrace that smells like Chanel No. 5 and sugar cookies. A harsh reminder of the life I left.

"Oh, Cora! So glad you were able to make it after all. We've missed you, dear!" Mrs. McAllister gushes.

Make it? My mind races, desperately trying to catch up with this unexpected narrative twist. "I'm sorry, Mrs. McAllister, I'm not sure—"

"Nonsense, dear," she interrupts, her enthusiasm bulldozing over my confusion. "Don't apologize. Updating the reservation to four won't be any trouble." She squeals, patting her husband's arm. "Such a treat. I can't wait to hear how the wedding plans are coming."

Wedding plans? Realization dawns with the subtlety of a neon sign: They don't know. Logan hasn't told them we broke up. They still think I'm going to be their daughter-in-law.

Before I can set the record straight, I spot him—Logan, his golden hair gleaming under the twinkling lights like some rom-com hero. His eyes catch mine, time briefly freezing. I half expect a voiceover to kick in, narrating my inner turmoil.

"Cora? What are you—"

"Isn't it obvious?" his mother interrupts, pulling him into a hug. "She came to surprise you, dear. Oh, you two are just the cutest."

Surprise him? A city of 2.7 million people, and I run into them... that's the fucking surprise.

His parents, blissfully oblivious to the tension, link arms and head toward the restaurant. "You kids coming?" Mrs. McAllister calls over her shoulder.

Logan drapes an arm over my shoulder, jerking me awkwardly to his side. "You both go ahead inside. I need a minute alone with Cora, if you don't mind."

"You've got to be kidding me," I mutter, feeling like I've stumbled into some twisted alternate reality.

As soon as his parents disappear from view, I shrug off Logan's arm. "What the hell, Logan?" I hiss. "Why are they acting like we're still together? Your mother asked me about our wedding plans, for Christ's sake."

Logan has the decency to look ashamed, color draining from his face. "It's complicated—"

"Complicated?" I interrupt, my voice dripping with sarcasm. "I left you because you were cheating on me. I'm moving this weekend. Sounds pretty cut and dry to me."

Logan drags a hand through his hair, frustration etched on his face. "Look, Cora, I was going to tell them. Tonight, actually. My dad... He was diagnosed with early onset dementia that Monday after you left. And I don't know. I just... couldn't."

The words hit me like a physical blow, momentarily silencing my anger. "What?"

"Mom's barely holding it together," Logan continues, his voice low and strained. "Our engagement... it was the one bright spot she kept clinging to. I couldn't bring myself to take that away from her, too."

I feel my resolve wavering, even as I mentally kick myself for it. This is classic Logan, tugging at my heartstrings. But the pain in his eyes looks genuine, and I do love his parents despite their son turning out to be a lying-cheater.

"And what about me, Logan?" I ask, my voice shaking slightly. "You destroyed my world, too, when you broke my trust. You don't get to play the victim here."

"I know," he says softly. "And I'm sorry. I should have told them, I just..." He trails off, looking lost. "Please, Cora. One dinner. I can't tell them now, not like this. Not when I can't predict how Mom will react."

I close my eyes, exhaling slowly. This is a terrible idea. Every romance novel cliché is screaming at me to walk away. But I think about Logan's mom, about his dad facing a terrifying diagnosis. About the family I thought I was going to be a part of.

"Fine," I concede, already questioning my decision. "One dinner. But after this, you tell them everything. And don't you dare try anything stupid."

Logan nods, relief washing over his features. "Thank you. I promise, after tonight, I'll make everything right."

Just like all the other promises he kept, I remind myself.

Still, I follow him inside and take a seat, feeling like I stepped into a surreal play where I'm woefully under-rehearsed. Logan's parents beam at us, their faces alight with an excitement that makes my stomach churn. If they only knew what was coming.

"So, Cora," Mrs. McAllister leans in, her eyes sparkling, "tell me everything. Have you set a date yet?"

I force a brittle laugh and lie through my teeth. "Oh, you know how it is. We're just... taking our time."

Logan squeezes my hand under the table, a gesture that once brought comfort but now feels like a carefully choreographed lie. I resist the urge to pull away, reminding myself why I'm here. One dinner, one last act of kindness. I can do this.

As the evening progresses, I find myself slipping into the role of doting fiancée with an ease that's both comforting and disturbing. Logan plays his part flawlessly, all charming smiles and loving glances. It's a masterclass in method acting, enough that I almost believe it myself.

But reality has a way of creeping in, doesn't it? With every fabricated wedding detail, every shared laugh over inside jokes, another crack forms in my carefully constructed facade. This isn't just dinner; it's a funeral for the future we'll never have.

"You two are just perfect together," Mrs. McAllister comments.

Perfect? If only she knew how far from perfect we really are.

"Thank you," I manage, the words tasting like ash in my mouth.

As dessert arrives–a decadent chocolate cake that Logan and I used to share on special occasions–I find myself drowning in memories. Weekend dates, late-night drinks, dreams whispered in the dark. It's all there, a highlight reel of a life I thought I wanted.

As we step out of the restaurant and say our goodbyes, the frigid air hits me like a wake-up call, clearing away the fog of our carefully crafted charade. The scent of snow and city streets mingles with the lingering notes of Logan's cologne, a bittersweet reminder of what once was home.

"Cora," Logan starts, his voice soft and achingly familiar. "Thank you for tonight. I know it wasn't easy—"

"Don't," I cut him off, weariness seeping into my bones. "Just... don't, Logan. You got your dinner. Your parents got their farewell performance. Now it's time for the curtain call."

He blinks, a flicker of hurt crossing his face. Something twinges in my chest–regret? Longing? I push it down, ignoring the traitorous voice in my head whispering of comfort and second chances.

"I'll be by the apartment tomorrow to pack," I continue, my words less certain than I'd like. "Then I'm... I'm gone."

I turn away, my steps faltering despite my best efforts. Behind me, I hear Logan call my name, his voice wrapping around me like a warm blanket on a cold night.

"Cora, please," he says softly. "Don't let this be the end."

I pause, torn between the urge to run and the pull of the familiar. "I think it has to be, Logan. I think I need to be on my own for a bit."

As I walk away, the city lights blur into a kaleidoscope of

confusion. Am I really doing the right thing? Am I ready for this? For goodbye?

Tomorrow looms ahead, a blank page waiting to be written, because sometimes, the happily ever after we imagined isn't the one we're meant to live. Then again, sometimes, we're not as ready to turn the page as we thought.

14

∽

Cora

December 9ᵗʰ

The elevator ride to Logan's floor feels like ascending toward my own personal purgatory. Each floor brings a new wave of memories—the day we moved in, our first big fight, the moment I started to suspect something was off, the night he proposed...

I clutch my bag like it can shield me from ghosts I'm not ready to face. Last night's dinner with Logan and his parents replays in my mind, a bittersweet reminder of what I'm leaving behind and why.

"You okay, Co?" Arden's voice cuts through my spiraling thoughts. Her concerned gaze meets mine in the mirrored walls of the elevator.

"All good," I say with a forced smile. "What about you? Still glad you gave up your anniversary to pack up the remnants of your little sister's failed relationship?"

Arden's frown deepens, but Mark lets out a bark of laughter. "At least you brought reinforcements this time," he says, trying to lighten the mood. "Though I still say we should've brought Jake along. Maybe seeing you with another guy would finally get it through Logan's thick skull that it's over."

Been there, tried that. I contemplate telling them about the night at Sadie's last week, but what's the point? And God, if they knew about last night's little charade...

"Yeah, because nothing says 'I'm over you' like parading a new guy around," I retort, aiming for sarcasm but probably hitting somewhere between 'mildly hysterical' and 'one comment away from a breakdown.'

The elevator doors slide open with a final, ominous ding. Suddenly, we're face to face with door 1204—my former apartment, my former life.

Logan opens the door before we knock, his eyes red-rimmed and hair disheveled. He looks like he hasn't slept, and a petty part of me hopes he's as haunted by last night's dinner as I am.

"Hey," he says, his voice gravelly as he takes in the 'reinforcements' I brought. "Come on in."

As I step over the threshold, the familiar scent of home—of us—hits me like a punch to the gut. For a moment, I'm suspended between two worlds: the comfort of the familiar and the promise of something new.

My eyes scan the apartment, seeing it with new clarity. The couch where I spent countless evenings reading while Logan watched TV, our silence growing louder with each passing day. The bed where goodnight kisses became a forgotten ritual. The kitchen where I'd dutifully prepare dinner, playing the role of the perfect future wife.

Each corner holds a memory, a reminder of the life I thought I wanted. But now, those memories feel like scenes from someone else's story.

"So," I say, aiming for casual, "where should we start?"

Logan gestures vaguely, not quite meeting my eyes. "Living room is almost done. Just some stuff in the bedroom, clothes mostly, and then your desk."

As we begin sorting through the remnants of our shared life, the weight of the past few weeks settles over me. How much has changed.

How much I've changed. I think about the job I love that Logan never quite understood, the nights out with friends he subtly discouraged, the dreams I had that never quite fit into his vision of our future.

The time away has been good. For me. For who I want to be.

Unbidden thoughts of Tuesday night with Jake surface. I know it's fast, but is Arden right? Am I refusing a possibility over some preconceived notion that I need to "find myself" first?

"Cora?" Arden's voice pulls me back to the present. "You want to keep this?"

I reach for the frame in her hands. It's a picture from our first vacation together, all sun-kissed skin and carefree smiles. A snapshot of a happier time, of a Cora I hardly recognize anymore.

"No," I say, my voice surprisingly steady as I place it in the 'donate' pile. "I think it's time to make some new memories."

Time ticks by, each box labeled in black permanence of the new future I'm writing. But, still, it hurts to know everything that happened here, every memory is just that. The Past. A different time starring two different people.

"Clothes are done," Arden calls from the bedroom, emerging with an assessing Mark at her side. "What else can we do?"

I catch the time. Five already.

"I can handle the rest," I say, motioning toward the desk I have yet to go through. "Why don't you two go? I know you have reservations for dinner, and you've already given up enough of your anniversary."

Arden watches me apprehensively, gaze darting to Logan before responding. "You sure that's a good idea, Co? We're happy to stay as long as you need us."

My confidence wavers momentarily before I put on my best poker face. "I'll be fine. Really. It shouldn't be much longer."

Arden glances at Mark, who shrugs. "If you're absolutely sure, okay."

Outward, I keep a reassuring grin, even as I falter internally. "Of course."

I'm stronger. I can handle the inevitable goodbye, can't I?

But when Mark and Arden leave, and the two of us are alone in the apartment for the first time since I walked out, the air feels thicker than I anticipated.

"I'll finish the bedroom," I whisper, desperate to maintain space.

I clear out my old nightstand, sighing when I find the letter. It's like stumbling upon the prologue of a story I thought I'd finished editing. Hands shaking, I read the words once golden with promise, now only ash. The note Logan wrote me a few weeks after our first date, when I first dared to dream he might be my happily ever after.

"Need any help?"

I startle as Logan enters, his features tense. I shove the letter away, trying to regain control of my rebellious emotions. "Almost done."

Logan scans the room, his eyes lingering on the packed boxes. "Seems like we moved in here yesterday, giddy as kids playing house," he sighs. "Now it feels like the setting of a post-apocalyptic novel."

I blink rapidly, fighting the sting of tears. This isn't the time for a dramatic finale. And since when does Logan know what a post-apocalyptic novel is?

Logan's voice drops, rough with emotion. "You were my everything, Cora. My inspiration, my joy, my entire goddamned world."

"Don't," I whisper, the word barely audible. "We're not characters in one of my romance novels, Logan. You can't change what happened to us."

His fingers graze mine, achingly familiar. Every bone and muscle aches with fatigue, yet adrenaline still spikes reflexively at his touch.

"What'd you decide for tonight?" he asks softly. "About the concert?"

Logan gently turns my hand, pressing the concert ticket into my palm. I stare until it finally comes into focus. Stuffed Olives. Tonight.

"Oh, Logan." I swallow hard, tasting the bitterness of missed opportunities. "I can't. Today's drained every ounce of energy I have. I just want to crawl into bed and pretend this is all a bad dream."

His face flickers with disappointment. "It's your favorite band, Cora."

I should hold firm. Say no. But as remorse clouds Logan's green eyes, my resolution wavers. "It is. But–"

"Just as friends," Logan adds sweetly. "It could take your mind off all this. Give you something else to remember us by."

My inner editor screams at me to say no, to stick to the plan. But for some reason, my tongue refuses to cooperate.

Logan glances at his watch. "Stuffed Olives won't go on until eight-thirty. We've got time."

"Even if I wanted to, I don't have anything to wear," I mutter, grasping at excuses like a writer trying to fix a plot hole.

Logan tilts his head toward the boxes of clothes. "I'm sure we can find something. Besides, I don't care what you're wearing. Just that you'd be there."

I hesitate, wondering why I'm even considering this. But then again, it is my favorite band. And maybe a tiny part of me wants to prove I can handle this, that I'm strong enough to spend time with him and not want more.

"Maybe just for a few songs." The words tumble out before I can stop them.

Hope lights up Logan's face. "That's my girl."

His girl. The phrase grates against my newfound independence like nails on a chalkboard. Had I really lost myself so much that I stopped being my own person?

As I ruffle through a box, my mind wanders through the gallery of faces that have shaped me. Brent, the off-and-on high school sweetheart. Sam, the college boyfriend who shattered my world and made me question my worth. And Logan, who was kind and patient, but slowly chipped away at my dreams until they fit into his vision of our future.

Each relationship taught me something, made me stronger. But they also made me lose sight of myself bit by bit.

Then Jake's face surfaces, bringing with it a rush of emotions I can't quite name. With Jake, I don't feel like a supporting character in someone else's story. I feel like... me. The eighteen-year-old version, unchanged by life who saved a complete stranger. The real me I'd almost forgotten existed.

I zip up my dress and pull out my phone, fingers hovering over Jake's name. What would I even say? That I'm ready to dive into the intense, dangerous connection we felt on Tuesday? I reread his last message. He'd asked what I was doing tonight. Was that his way of reaching out, of showing he's ready too?

I set the phone down, my reflection in the mirror catching my eye. The woman staring back at me looks different somehow. Stronger. More certain.

In that moment, I make a decision. Tonight, I'm going to this concert. Not for Logan, not even for Stuffed Olives, but for me. To say goodbye to the Cora who let others define her. To embrace the Cora who's ready to write her own story—plot twists, cliffhangers, and all.

And maybe, just maybe, a certain blue-eyed bartender could be more than a supporting character. But whether he is or isn't, this story—my story—is going to be uniquely, unequivocally mine.

15

Cora

The neon sign of Joe's flickers like a faulty plot device, casting an eerie glow over the queue of excited concertgoers. I tug at the hem of my dress, feeling a mix of determination and unease. This isn't how tonight was supposed to go. I should be nestled in my bed at Arden's with a good book, awaiting tomorrow's move and the promise of a fresh start. Instead, I'm here to prove to myself that I can face Logan without crumbling.

"Ready?" Logan's hand on the small of my back feels like an unwelcome reminder of our shared past.

I take a deep breath, reminding myself of the strength I felt earlier. "I'm ready," I say, more to myself than to Logan.

As we enter the smoky air filled with pulsing bass, I'm hit with a wave of nostalgia. How many nights did Logan and I spend in places like this, drunk on cheap beer and the hope of forever? I push the memories aside, focusing on why I'm really here—to close this chapter of my life on my own terms.

"I'll grab us some drinks," Logan shouts over the music, his lips brushing my ear. "Why don't you find us a place to sit?"

He disappears into the crowd, and I feel a flicker of doubt. Am I really strong enough for this? Or am I just playing into his game? I lean against the wall, trying to ground myself, when a familiar voice bellows from the speakers.

There's no way...

But as I glance at the stage, there's no mistaking him. It's like the universe is telling me something, reminding me what I stand to gain.

Jake.

The spotlight bathes him in a golden glow, transforming him from the brooding barista I know into something... more. His fingers dance across the guitar strings with a grace I never knew he possessed, his voice a warm caress that has tingles coursing down my skin.

Jake's in a band? He's playing here? Tonight?

My stomach lurches into my throat. Fragments of our conversations replay in my head, but nothing suggested... this. How many other layers are there to Jake that I've failed to see? To ask about?

The crowd's roar fades as Jake's voice, more confident than I've ever heard it, fills the venue. "Joe's, wow!" He grins, his blue eyes sparkling in the spotlight. "We want to thank you for welcoming us tonight. Before our last song, I've got to give a shout-out to some incredible band-mates."

My eyes widen as he introduces the band. "Our manager and bass player, Owen." Owen–from Mark and Arden's wedding. Jake's brother. The pieces start falling into place, a story I should have seen all along.

"We've got Chris on the drums." Chris? Alyssa's friend from the bar? Oh, God. All these connections I've been too blind to notice.

"I'm Jake, and we're All Rhoades," he continues, his fingers beginning to coax out a new melody from his guitar. "Stuffed Olives is about to hit the stage, but before they do, we want to share a brand new song with you. One I wrote less than two weeks ago. It's called 'All I See Is You.'"

He writes music, too. He wrote it less than two weeks ago. My heart races as I do the math. Two weeks ago... when we first met at the coffee shop?

As the other instruments join in, creating a tapestry of sound, I find myself moving closer to the stage, drawn by an invisible force. Jake's voice, raw and emotional, washes over me:

"I lost hope I could feel this way.
Lost the chance to love without fear or pain.
I walled off my battered heart for so long.
Then, in my darkness, an angel came."

The crowd parts before me like I'm Moses and they're the Red Sea. Suddenly, I'm at the edge of the stage, looking up at Jake as he pours his heart out through his music. His presence is magnetic. This isn't just talent or passion; this is Jake laying his soul bare for all to see.

"When I close my eyes, all I see is you. You.
Endlessly in my thoughts, but you don't know my name.
Drawn to take a risk, to let you in, still confused if I can
Is my heart brave enough to try again?"

As he sings, his eyes scan the crowd, eventually landing on mine. Recognition flashes across his face, followed quickly by shock, hope, and something else I can't quite name. In that instant, everything else fades away–the crowd, the music, every hesitation. It's just me and Jake, two lost souls recognizing each other across a sea of strangers.

This is the connection between us, I think to myself. What I couldn't describe earlier. A soul-deep connection that exists without even trying.

"You rescued me more than you could know.
My guardian even when you were far.

Though you linger in my dreams, your name remains unknown.
Will I dare drop my shield and show my scars?"

The lyrics hit me like a freight train. This song... it's about me. About us. About that night six years ago and everything that's happened since. I feel tears pricking at my eyes, overwhelmed by the depth of emotion in Jake's performance.

As he launches into the chorus again, his eyes never leaving mine, I'm overwhelmed by a sense of inevitability. This feels like fate, like every decision I've made has led me to this moment. It's terrifying and exhilarating all at once, like standing on the precipice of a great adventure.

My heart clutches as Jake croons the final lines, every word etching deeper into my soul:

"When I close my eyes, all I see is you.
Endlessly in my thoughts, but you don't know my name.
Is my heart brave enough to try again?"

The last note hangs in the air, leaving me in a sea of conflicting emotions. The beauty of his words. The challenge in my heart reflected like I'm looking in a mirror.

But the spell of his music is shattered by Logan's arms suddenly encircling my waist, his liquor-laced breath hot against my neck.

"There you are, baby," he whispers into my ear.

Baby? I am such an idiot.

I stiffen, my editor's brain kicking into overdrive. This isn't how this scene is supposed to play out. Because Logan's touch feels wrong and Jake suddenly feels inevitable.

"Logan, stop," I say, twisting out of his embrace. My eyes dart to the stage, where Jake's expression has morphed from passionate to devastated. The sight of it feels like a physical blow, knocking the air from my lungs. No, no, no. He thinks I'm back with Logan.

"Jake!" I call out, but my voice is swallowed by the roar of the crowd. He's already disappearing backstage, his shoulders slumped in defeat. The urge to follow him, to explain, is overwhelming.

Logan's laughter punctures my panic like a pick. "Oh shit, was that the bartender? The one from Sadie's?"

His amusement grates on my nerves, highlighting the stark difference between him and Jake. Where Jake's song laid bare his vulnerability, Logan's reaction feels callous, disconnected.

I move forward, drawn to where Jake vanished. Logan's hand closes around my wrist, yanking me back. "Cora? Where are you going?"

"To see him," I spit, shaking off his grip. The possessiveness in his touch feels suffocating now, so different from the electricity I felt when Jake held me.

Concern flickers across Logan's face, but it's tinged with something else. Jealousy? "Why? You clearly mean nothing to him if he didn't bother to tell you he'd be here."

"Didn't bother to—" I start, then shake my head. How can I explain the depth of connection I feel with Jake? It's not just about tonight. It's about years of intertwined fates that I'm only now beginning to understand.

"It doesn't matter," I say, more to myself than to Logan. "You wouldn't understand."

As I push through the crowd, revelations crash over me like waves. The accident six years ago. Mark and Arden's wedding. Sadie's bar. Even Chris. Jake has been there, on the periphery of my life, all this time. How did I not see it before?

Security blocks my path to the stage. "Please," I plead, desperation coloring my voice, "I need to get backstage."

"Cora!" Logan's voice pierces through the noise. He reaches for me again, his touch familiar but no longer comforting. "You can't just leave. What about us?"

Fury rises in me, hot and sudden. I wrench my arm free. "There is no us, Logan! God, I knew coming here was a mistake. Stupid December curse strikes again."

"December curse? What are you talking about?"

"Forget it," I snap, the weight of years of disappointment and heartbreak threatening to crush me. "I won't do this right now."

I shove past him, gulping in the cool night air as I exit. Leaning against the wall, I try to steady my racing heart. How do I fix this? How do I make Jake understand?

I pull out my phone, staring at Jake's last text. Saturday. He was talking about tonight. And I shot him down. The realization twists in my gut like a knife.

"Talk to me, Cora!" Logan's voice makes me jump.

I groan, running a hand through my hair. "Logan, there's nothing to talk about. This," I gesture between us, "was a mistake. I shouldn't have come here with you."

"Because of him?" Logan scoffs. "Come on, Cora. You didn't even know he'd be here. You don't even know him."

"You'd be surprised," I mutter, thinking of all the ways Jake and I are connected. Then, louder, "Look, it doesn't matter. The point is, we're over. We were over the moment you brought someone else into our bed. And I can't believe I fell for your manipulations again."

Logan's face falls, and for a moment, I see a glimpse of the man I used to love. But it's like looking at an old photograph—familiar, but no longer real.

"You'd rather fix things with him, than with me?" he asks quietly. "After everything we've been through? You're choosing him?"

Am I choosing Jake? Or for once am I simply choosing to react? To be?

"It's not about choosing him over you," I say, my voice softer but firm. "It's about choosing me. About knowing what I deserve. And it's not this, Logan. It's not the constant doubt, the manipulation, the broken trust. I'm sorry, but I won't keep doing this dance."

I walk away, finding solitude around the back of the building. As I slide down the wall, the cold pavement grounds me in reality. This isn't a romance novel where a grand gesture fixes everything. This is real life, messy and complicated.

But as I sit there, Jake's song echoes in my mind. The raw emotion, the vulnerability, the hope. It's everything Logan and I lost long ago. Everything I thought I'd never feel again.

I pull out my phone, my fingers hovering over Jake's name. I have no idea how to fix this, but I know I have to try. Because for the first time in years, I feel something worth fighting for.

Taking a deep breath, I start to type, hoping I'm not already too late.

16

Jake

I storm offstage, venom ready to spew. Him. After everything, she went back to him. The image of Cora in Logan's arms burns behind my eyelids, a cruel echo of another betrayal I thought I'd buried.

My hands clench at my sides, knuckles white with barely contained fury. What the fuck was I on Tuesday? Just a convenient distraction until she resumed her regularly scheduled programming? No wonder she's barely reached out since then. Couldn't meet me tonight.

I didn't mean a damn thing.

I grab the wall as agony rips through my core, the taste of bile bitter in my throat. How could I be so fucking stupid? Again. I should've known better than to believe I deserved more than cold beds and empty bottles. Guys like me don't get happy endings. We're the cautionary tales, the ones who end up alone.

Leaning heavily against the unforgiving concrete, I fight to slow my ragged breathing. But anger still simmers in my blood, a familiar friend. Because for an all-too-brief interlude, I forgot my place in this tragedy. Forgot who I am. What I am. And in my weakness, I pried open vaults of agony I can never fully lock away.

Tessa's face flashes in my mind, her lips curved in that secret smile I later realized wasn't meant for me. I shake my head violently, trying to dislodge the memory. Not now. I can't deal with ghosts from both past and present.

I shoulder open the dressing room door with unnecessary force, making a beeline for the amber liquid that's never failed me. Good old Jack, always there when everyone else leaves. I reach for the blissful numbness that will blunt the pieces shattering inside.

I swallow greedily, chasing sweet oblivion because old habits die hard, and they're all I have left when the world goes to shit.

"So... eventful night?"

The voice, silky and unfamiliar, cuts through my spiral. I look up to see a blonde watching me curiously, her red lips curled in an impish smile. Some groupie finding her way into our room already?

I grunt, throwing back the remainder of my drink. The liquid burns a blistering trail down my throat, a welcome distraction from the ache in my chest.

She sashays closer, toying idly with her necklace. Her icy blue eyes wander slowly over me, and I fight the urge to squirm under her gaze. "Chris said you were talented. I can see the appeal. It's Jake, right?"

"Yeah," I mutter, already reaching for the bottle again. "Who are you?"

"A friend of Chris." She grabs the bourbon before I can, pouring herself a glass. Her eyes never leave mine as she adds, "Your performance was amazing. Such a sexy, edgy vibe."

I clench my jaw, muscles screaming from the effort not to hurl my glass across the room. She knows how to poke my weakest spots, to re-break the bone before it's fully healed. Women like her always do. They see the cracks and think they can fill them, not realizing they're just widening the fissures.

"I just want to be alone right now," I manage, my voice raw.

"Lying doesn't suit you," she purrs, refilling my empty glass. She catches a drop of liquor on her fingertip, sucking it clean with deliberate slowness. My pulse quickens despite itself, a Pavlovian response to the promise of forgetting. "I can help take your mind off... things."

For a moment, I'm tempted. This is familiar territory, after all. This is who I am, isn't it? The guy who drowns his sorrows in whiskey and willing women, because feeling nothing is better than feeling everything.

But as she moves closer, her hand trailing along my jaw, my mind rebels. All I can see is Cora—her smile, her laugh, the way her eyes lit up when I was singing. The contrast is jarring, and suddenly I feel sick.

Goddamnit. What was I thinking? As if I could ever be worthy of someone like Cora.

The crash of the door jolts me back to reality. I jerk away from the blonde's touch as if burned, nearly stumbling in my haste. Owen's triumphant grin falters as he takes in the scene, his expression morphing into something between confusion and disappointment. Chris, oblivious, saunters in behind him.

My hands shake as I reach for the bottle, pouring another glass. Anything to distract from the shame crawling up my throat.

"Jake, you killed it out there!" Owen said, his hand landing on my shoulder.

I force a smile that feels more like a grimace. "Yeah, we did good." The comment tastes like ash in my mouth. The show was amazing— it's me that's the problem.

Chris approaches, the blonde at his side. "Hey guys, this is Alyssa. A friend of mine."

Fuck. Of course she's with Chris. And like the terrible friend I am, I was about to what? Let her kiss me? Seduce me?

My phone buzzes, Cora's name lighting up the screen. My stomach lurches. What now? Is she gloating about her reunion with Logan? Telling me I never stood a chance?

I want to ignore it, to hurl the phone across the room. But I keep my mask on, unlocking my screen.

Cora: *It's not what you think. Please, let me explain.*

I stare at the words, my vision blurring. Part of me wants to believe her, to give her a chance. But the cynical voice in my head, the one that's kept me safe for the past five years, sneers. Not what I think? It looked pretty damn clear from where I was standing.

Every ugly, insecure thought I've battled alone since Tessa screams for release. *I told you so. No one wants you. You're not enough.* I smash my fists onto my thighs, trying to breathe past the familiar panic threatening to suck me under.

I won't do this to myself again. Won't be the other man in this game.

"Jake?" Owen's voice sounds far away. "You okay, man?"

I look up, realizing I've been silent too long. Owen's concerned stare, Chris's confusion, Alyssa's curiosity—it's all too much. I need to get out of here before I completely lose it.

"I need some air," I mutter, already pushing past them towards the door.

As I stumble into the hallway, I can hear Owen following me. But all I can focus on is the pounding in my chest and the echo of Cora's words on my phone. It's not what you think.

But what if it is? What if this is just another reminder that guys like me don't get second chances?

"What's gotten into you?" Owen calls out. "Is it her? The girl from the show? The brunette you were staring at?"

He noticed. He always notices.

I look away, squeezing the back of my neck. "Doesn't matter. She's no one."

"Bullshit." Owen blocks my path, uncharacteristic heat in his expression. "I'm not blind, Jake. Who is she?"

I start pacing the hallway, unable to contain the emotions that hit. Cora. Tessa. Thomas. He doesn't understand. He can't understand. What I've battled since then.

"Look," I say, my voice strained, "I don't know what possessed me to write that song. But she doesn't mean anything." The lie tastes bitter on my tongue. "She can't mean anything. I won't do that to myself again."

Owen stands firm, arms crossed. "Playing martyr again? What'd she do to earn your self-righteous bullshit?"

I slam my palm against the wall, pain barely registering through the alcohol fog. "I said forget it!"

He starts to walk back toward the room but stops, spinning to face me. His eyes blaze with frustration and concern. "You know what? No. It's about time you stopped throwing your pity party and grow the fuck up. You weren't the only one who lost someone in that crash. We did, too."

His words hit me like a physical blow. I open my mouth to argue, but he presses on.

"You don't get a pass at life because you're still heartbroken. God-damn it, Jake. Didn't you feel something when we were out there? Why can't that be enough? What's gonna make you stop acting like the world owes you something? News flash: Bad things happen. But that doesn't mean you stop living."

I'm stunned into silence. Then, the anger bubbles up again. "You really don't get it. You don't know the whole story. You don't know what it's been like," I spew back, blood boiling.

Owen's brows knit together in curiosity. "Try me. Tell me what you're feeling. At least feeling something is better than the nothing I've seen from you the last five years."

But I can't. It's my burden. No one knows the entire story. Tonight won't be an exception.

"Just go," I rasp, staring unseeing into the shadows.

As Owen's silhouette fades back into the room, I'm left alone with my thoughts and the weight of Cora's unanswered message.

I pull out my phone again, thumbs hovering over the keyboard. What do I even say? No need to explain. You're better off staying away from my trust issues and self-loathing?

I pocket the device and head for the nearest bar. Maybe a few more drinks will dull the ache in my chest and quiet the voice in my head that keeps whispering Cora's name.

The bartender eyes me warily as I order another shot. "You sure about that, buddy? You've had quite a few already."

I glare at him, pushing my glass forward. "I'm sure. Just pour."

He shrugs, filling my glass. "Your funeral, man."

I down the shot, welcoming the burn. It's familiar, comforting even. Like an old friend who always shows up when you're at your lowest. The room starts to spin, but I don't care. At least when I'm drunk, I don't have to think about the never-ending spiral of guilt, shame, and anger. At them. At me. At her.

Time fades to nothingness. I vaguely remember stumbling back towards our dressing room, the figures inside hazy as they motion for me to go somewhere else. Outside maybe?

The frigid night air hits me like a slap to the face as I stumble out of the venue. The parking lot swims before my eyes, streetlights blurring into indistinct halos. My legs feel unsteady, and the world tilts dangerously as I try to make sense of my surroundings.

In the dim glow, I glimpse blonde hair and red lips. Alyssa? Or is my alcohol-soaked brain playing tricks on me? I move towards the figure, old habits kicking in before I can stop myself.

"There you are, rock star," the voice purrs, but it sounds distorted, like I'm underwater. "I was hoping I'd see you again."

I try to respond, but my tongue feels thick in my mouth. The world spins, and suddenly I'm reaching out, grasping for anything to keep me upright.

Hands trail down my chest, but I feel nothing but cold. Giggling morphs into mocking laughter, and I squeeze my eyes shut, trying to block it out. But the darkness only brings visions of cinnamon hair haloed in gold.

I jerk away, bile rising in my throat. "I can't... This isn't..."

The world tilts again, and I hear a gasp. A name, slicing through the fog, sharp and clear: "Cora?"

Cora? Why would anyone say Cora?

I spin around too quickly, and the parking lot becomes a dizzying blur of lights and shadows. I catch a glimpse of wide, hurt, amber eyes before the world goes dark.

17

∽

Cora

December 10th

I stare at my phone: 8:45 AM. The screen's reflection is a stark reminder of my sleepless night, spent mentally rewriting the disaster that was yesterday. If only life came with track changes and a delete button.

As I drag myself up the stairs to my new apartment, fragments of last night assault me. Jake on stage, his soul laid bare in lyrics that felt written just for me. The hurt in his eyes when he saw me with Logan. Then... the gut-wrenching sight of Jake with his lips on Alyssa's. The world tilting as I stumbled away, vision blurred by tears.

The rest of the night is hazy, clouded by emotion and the drinks Alyssa plied me with after I broke down and told her everything. God, the irony.

Damn, Jake, how'd we manage to hurt each other so spectacularly in the span of a few hours?

I want to be angry with him. I want to channel my inner scorned woman and vow never to think of him again. But for what? Getting drunk? Making assumptions? Being exactly who everyone warned me he was?

It's not like we were together. And the honest truth is, beneath the hurt and confusion, there's a part of me that understands. We're both so broken, so afraid of being hurt again, that we're experts at sabotaging ourselves.

I turn the key, pushing the sinking feeling that I've lost something I never fully grasped deep into my chest. The movers will be here soon. It's time to start this next chapter.

My phone buzzes. Logan's name flashes on the screen.

Logan: *Everything's picked up and on its way. How are you holding up?*

I hesitate, my thumb hovering over the reply button. I should ignore him. Cut all ties after the show he put on last night. I picture the smug look on his face when he saw it all go down. Jake with Alyssa. The "I told you so" etched into his expression.

And damn it, if the part of me that's raw and hurting isn't craving the familiarity he offers.

Before I can reply, there's a knock at the door. I open it to find two movers... and Logan, dark circles under his eyes mirroring my own.

He holds up a coffee cup, eyeing me warily. "I thought... maybe you could use this," he says, voice rough with fatigue.

The rich aroma of hazelnut wafts toward me. It's a peace offering, a white flag in our personal war. I contemplate refusing, clinging to my anger and hurt. But I'm too exhausted for grudges.

"Come to gloat?" I ask, accepting the cup and letting the warmth seep into my cold fingers.

"I wanted to check on you," he admits hesitantly. "And to apologize. For how everything went down."

I take a sip of the hot liquid. Logan got me my favorite. After three years, of course he knows how I drink my coffee. *So does Jake*, a small voice cries. I push that thought away, too.

"Well, I'm over it," I lie, the words tasting bitter. "Today's a new day."

Logan nods, but his eyes search my face, seeing more than I want him to. "You don't have to pretend with me, Cora. I know you're hurting."

I consider letting my guard down. It would be so easy to fall back into old patterns, to let Logan comfort me. But then I remember Jake's song, the raw emotion in his voice. The connection we shared, however briefly.

I straighten my spine. "I appreciate the coffee, Logan. But let's just focus on getting these boxes moved in, okay?"

As I direct the movers, I can feel Logan's eyes on me. I know I should send him away, make a clean break. But right now, his presence is the only thing keeping me from falling apart completely. And if that makes me weak, so be it. Today, I'll take comfort where I can find it.

The movers are already gone by the time Arden arrives, a bottle of celebratory wine (and grape juice for her) in her hand. Her eyes widen when she spots Logan, and I can practically see the gears turning in her head, formulating questions I'm not ready to answer.

God, there's so much that happened since she and Mark left last night. I'm not even sure where to start.

"Cora, why don't you show me around?" Arden asks, with a subtle nod toward my bedroom.

Ready or not, it's time to explain.

As we retreat to the relative privacy of the empty room, I can feel the weight of her unasked questions pressing down on me.

"The bed set doesn't come until next Friday," I offer, grasping at small talk like a drowning woman clutching at straws. "And I can't get Wi-Fi turned on until Wednesday, so I'm probably staying at your place for a few more days."

Arden nods slowly, her eyes never leaving mine. "You're welcome to stay as long as you need. But Cora, honey, what happened? Why is Logan here?"

The dam breaks, and suddenly I'm pouring out the whole sordid tale—the concert, Jake's song, Logan's ill-timed appearance, Jake with Alyssa. It comes out in a jumbled mess of run-on sentences and fragmented thoughts, like a first draft in desperate need of editing.

"Oh, Cora," Arden sighs, pulling me into a hug. "I can't believe Jake would... not on purpose."

"He was drunk. Destroyed," I mumble into her shoulder. "I did it... I destroyed him. Broke his trust. After Tuesday... I told him I wasn't over Logan. Then I showed up with... Jake thought... I'm an idiot."

Arden pulls back, her hands gripping my shoulders firmly. "Listen to me, Coraline Grace. The only idiots here are those two jackasses who threw away a rare gift because facing real intimacy terrifies them. Logan, I expected as much. Jake... well, he should've trusted you before making assumptions. I thought he'd changed."

"What if—"

"No 'what ifs,'" Arden says, cutting me off. "You have so much love and passion to give someone worthy, Co. Don't let them make you believe you won't get your happily ever after."

She's right. Of course she is. It's what I told myself last night. What I do next is my choice. This is my story, with or without either one of them.

"So, what now?" Arden asks, gesturing towards the other room where Logan waits.

Before I can answer, Alyssa's voice rings out from the living room, her tone sharp enough to cut through paper. "What the hell are you doing here?"

I hear Logan's snide response. "Helping Cora assemble her new place. Got a problem?"

I close my eyes, take a deep breath, and step out into the chaos.

The tension in the living room is thick enough to cut with one of the many kitchen knives still packed away in a box labeled "Miscellaneous."

Alyssa stands like an avenging angel, her glare fixed on Logan. "Considering you shredded her heart into confetti, I actually do have a problem with you being here," she spits.

"You're one to talk," Logan retorts, his words dripping with disdain.

Alyssa's apologies from last night replay in my mind. *"It meant nothing. I had no idea this was the mystery man you'd talked about. I'm so sorry."* It hurt, but not nearly as much as I expected it to.

"Enough!" I interject, my voice sharper than I intended. "I appreciate the protective She-Hulk routine, Lys, but I'd rather just move forward. No more blame games, please. We've all made mistakes."

The next few hours pass slower than I'd like. When the door finally clicks shut behind the last of my well-meaning but exhausting support crew, I lean against it, exhaling deeply.

Silence descends, broken only by the faint hum of the refrigerator. I wander through my new apartment, fingers trailing along the new spaces. It's sparse, but it's mine. A blank slate soon to be filled.

The setting sun paints the walls in warm hues as I collapse onto the one piece of furniture—the couch as my mind races. So much has changed in such a short time. Logan, Jake, this move... it's like I'm living in one of those romance novels I'm always editing, complete with misunderstandings and dramatic confrontations.

My phone buzzes, shattering my contemplation. Jake's name flashes across the screen and I hesitate. What could he possibly have to say after everything?

Is he still angry? Does he hate me now? Or is there a part of him who knows he messed up? And if so, am I ready to forgive his overreaction?

I close my eyes, wondering what I would advise the heroine to do if this were one my manuscripts. Face her fears? Take a chance on the emotionally unavailable man? Or play it safe and protect her heart?

Then again, it's Jake. The man who started to bare his scars to me—literally and figuratively. The man I still feel this soul-deep connection to, I can't begin to explain.

Taking a deep breath, I open the message.

18

Jake

Consciousness returns like a sledgehammer to the skull. I pry open my eyes, immediately regretting the decision as the world swims into painful focus. The familiar surroundings of Owen's living room mock me with their normalcy.

"Welcome back to the land of the living," Owen's voice drills through my brain like an ice pick. "How's the head?"

"Like I've been hit by a freight train," I rasp, my own words echoing uncomfortably in my pounding head. "What the hell happened last night?"

Owen's face hardens. "You mean after you nearly started a fight in the parking lot, or after you threw up on Chris's shoes?"

Fragments of memories assault me: the performance, the electric high of being on stage. Cora's face in the crowd, a beacon of hope. Then, seeing her with Logan, my world shattering. The blonde in the dressing room. Stumbling outside, the world spinning. Cora's wounded amber eyes cutting holes straight into my soul.

I lurch upright, fighting a wave of nausea. "Shit. I really fucked up, didn't I?"

"That's putting it mildly," Owen says, his voice a mix of concern and disappointment. "You're damned lucky Chris and I hauled your sorry ass out of there before security got involved."

My hand instinctively goes to my pocket, fishing out my phone. There's a missed text from Cora. As I read her words, what's left of my dignity crumbles to dust.

Cora: *I know you don't have to believe me, but I didn't come with Logan as a date. He's a manipulator. And like an idiot who should've known better, I gave in to his offer for one final goodbye before I move tomorrow. But, Jake, please believe me when I say that I don't want him. That song was beautiful. I want to try, too. I'm sorry it took me until tonight to realize it.*

The timestamp mocks me—fifteen minutes after her first message. Before she saw me, drunk and belligerent. Before I proved to her, and everyone else, that I'm exactly the screwup they think I am.

I barely make it to Owen's trash bin before last night's over-indulgences violently rush out. Eyes watering, I brace my shaky hands on the countertop.

"Jesus, Jake," Owen sighs, handing me a glass of water. "You really outdid yourself this time."

I rinse my mouth, avoiding Owen's gaze. "Yeah, well, it's what I do best, right? Fuck things up."

"If that was your goal, congratulations," Owen says, his voice sharp. "You managed to piss off Chris and probably scared off that girl you wrote the song about. What the hell happened out there?"

The harsh fluorescent lights of the kitchen feel like needles in my eyes. I squint, trying to piece together the fragments of last night. "I don't... It's all a blur, man."

"Try harder," Owen presses. "Because from where I was standing, it looked like you were hellbent on sabotaging everything good in your life. Again."

His words hit me like a sucker punch, bringing back flashes of the night before. The look in Cora's eyes when she saw me in the parking lot contrasting with the connection while I was on-stage. *Fuck.*

"I saw her with someone else," I mutter. "Her ex."

Owen's eyebrows shoot up. "So naturally, your response was to get wasted and make out with Chris's crush?"

"It wasn't like that," I snap, but even as the words leave my mouth, I know they're a lie. Isn't that exactly what I did?

"Then what was it like, Jake?" Owen's voice softens slightly. "Because I'm trying real hard to understand here."

I slump against the counter, suddenly exhausted. "I don't know. I just... I saw her with him and something in me just snapped. It was like... like..." *Like Tessa all over again. Feeling insignificant.*

Owen sighs, running a hand through his hair. "Jake, I know losing Tessa and Thomas wrecked you. Hell, it wrecked all of us. But you can't keep living like this. You can't keep pushing people away because you're afraid of getting hurt again."

His words hang in the air between us, heavy with unspoken truths. If only he knew the real reason behind my fear, my self-destruction. But even now, I can't bring myself to tell him.

"It's not that simple," I say, my voice barely above a whisper.

"No, it's not," Owen agrees. "But you know what? Last night, on that stage? For the first time in years, I saw my little brother again. The guy who loved music more than anything, who could light up a room with his smile. I miss that guy, Jake. And I think you do, too."

I think about the way I felt on stage, the connection with the audience, with the music. With Cora. For a brief moment, I'd felt alive. Really alive, not just going through the motions.

"I don't know if I know how to be him anymore," I admit, surprised by my own honesty.

Owen's hand lands on my shoulder, solid and reassuring. "Maybe it's time to find out. Because this version of you? The one who drinks himself stupid and pushes away anyone who might care about him? He's not doing you any favors."

His words hit me like a sucker punch, forcing me to confront the ugly truth I've been running from. For the first time in years, I let myself really hear what Owen's saying. Let myself feel the full weight of my actions, of the pain I've caused others and myself.

I close my eyes, memories flooding back. The hurt in Mom's voice every time I skipped a family dinner. The disappointment on Mark's face when I bailed on his wedding. And now, Cora's wounded expression when I didn't give her the chance to justify her actions.

The familiar urge to lash out, to deflect with sarcasm or anger, rises in my throat. But I'm so damn tired. Tired of running, tired of hiding, tired of being the screw-up everyone expects me to be.

"I don't..." I start, my voice cracking. I clear my throat and try again. "I don't want to be this person anymore." The admission costs me more than I thought possible, leaving me raw and exposed. "I just... I don't know how to change."

Owen squeezes my shoulder. "You start by trying, Jake. One day at a time. And maybe... maybe by letting people in. Even if it's scary as hell."

As I nod, the enormity of what lies ahead hits me. Changing isn't going to be easy. There's so much Owen doesn't know, so much I've kept buried. The thought of opening up, of being vulnerable, makes my skin crawl.

But then Cora's face flashes in my mind. Her smile, her warmth, the way she looks at me like I'm someone still worth saving. And for the first time in years, I feel a flicker of hope.

"Cora does mean something to me," I say, finally meeting Owen's eyes. "And I messed up. I don't know if I can fix it."

Owen's lips quirk into a small smile. "Well, little brother, I think you start with fixing you. And the first thing you should do is take a shower. You smell like a distillery."

Despite everything, I find myself chuckling. It's not much, but it's a start. A small step towards the person I want to be. The person Cora deserves.

* * *

Eventually, I stumble out of Owen's apartment smelling slightly better. The December air slaps me awake like my pissed-off brother should have done last night. My head's still pounding with a bad drum solo, but there's something else there, too. A weird clarity I can't quite place.

I'm so caught up in my own bullshit that I nearly face-plant into the welcome sign of my apartment complex. And then I see him—Cora's ex, stepping out of the entrance like he owns the place.

What the actual fuck?

We lock eyes, and suddenly I'm back at Joe's, watching him slide his arms around Cora, that familiar cocktail of jealousy and self-hatred burning my throat worse than cheap whiskey.

Before I can decide whether to bolt or throw up again, he's on me. His fist connects with my face, and I taste blood. Seriously, dude? Of all the people?

"Stay away from her," he spits, already backing off like the coward he is. "She deserves better than you."

As I watch his car peel out, I can't help but laugh. It's a bitter sound, more fitting for a dive bar at 2 AM than a parking lot on a Sunday afternoon. Because here's the kicker—the asshole's right. Cora does deserve better.

I drag myself up to my apartment, blood trailing behind me like a fucked-up Hansel and Gretel. In the bathroom mirror, I face my latest masterpiece: bloody nose, black eye, bruised ego. The Jake Rhoades special. Except this time, it wasn't some random asshole in a bar. It was her ex. Because the humiliation wasn't bad enough.

I grip the sink, knuckles white, staring down my reflection. This guy – this mess of a human – he's not me. Not anymore. Can't be. I'm done being Jake the Fuckup, the punchline to everyone's joke.

My phone feels like it weighs a ton as I pull up Cora's contact. Part of me wants to call her, spill my guts, promise her the moon and stars. But the words stick in my throat like bad lyrics.

Owen's right. I can't drag Cora into my shit show. Not until I sort myself out. Figure out who the hell I am when I'm not drowning in booze and self-pity. I need to be the guy who owned that stage last night, the one Cora saw something in. The one I used to be before I let grief and guilt twist me into this walking disaster.

I start typing, delete it all, try again. It's messy, it's raw, but so am I. And for once, that doesn't feel like the end of the world.

This is it. Time to prove Cora didn't pull my sorry ass out of that wreck for nothing. Time to be the man she deserves–the one I know is still in here somewhere, buried under years of bullshit.

I hit send before I can talk myself out of it. It's not much, but it's a start. And right now, that's all I've got.

19

Jake

December 13th

The morning sun filters through the blinds, casting striped shadows across my face as I stare at the ceiling. My head throbs. I reach up and touch the still-tender bruise from Sunday's confrontation with Logan. Three days and I'm not any closer to moving forward. Owen's words echo in my mind: "You start by trying. By letting people in."

Easier said than done, bro.

My phone buzzes, and I groan. It's my mom. Again. I've been dodging her calls since my birthday, but today... today feels different. Maybe it's the lasting effects of my talk with Owen, or the unexpected vote of confidence from Sadie about a potential promotion earlier this week. Whatever it is, I find myself answering.

"Jake?" Her voice is a mixture of surprise and hope. "I didn't think you'd pick up."

"Yeah, well," I mutter, running a hand through my hair. "Guess I'm full of surprises lately."

There's a pause, and I can practically hear her gathering her courage. "I wanted to call and see if... if you'll come out next week. For

Thomas. For the anniversary of..." She trails off, not wanting to say the rest. *For the anniversary of his death.*

My stomach twists into a knot tighter than my guitar strings. Images flash through my mind: Tessa crying in Thomas's bedroom. The silent drive back to campus. The admissions that came after. Then...

"Jake?" My mom's voice brings me back to the present. "Are you still there?"

I squeeze my eyes shut, my free hand clenching into a fist. Five years. It's been five fucking years, and I haven't been to his grave since the day we buried him. The thought of going back now... it's like willingly walking into a minefield.

But then I think about Cora. About the song I wrote for her. About the guy I want to be. The guy I used to be. The one who didn't run from his problems, drowning them in whiskey and self-loathing instead.

"Yeah, Mom," I finally say, my voice like sandpaper. "I'll be there."

The silence on the other end is deafening. When she speaks again, her voice is thick with unshed tears. "It means so much. We missed you at Thanksgiving, and we didn't get to see you for your birthday."

Each word is another stone added to the mountain of guilt I've been carrying. But for once, instead of letting it crush me, I feel a spark of... something. Determination, maybe? Or just the desperate need to stop being such a disappointment.

"I know, Mom. I'm sorry," I say, surprising myself with how much I mean it. "I've been... I've been dealing with some stuff. But I'm working on it."

"Oh, Jake," she sighs, and I can hear the years of worry in her voice. "We know. Whatever you need, we're here, okay?"

I do know. And all I've given them in response is radio silence and half-assed excuses. "I'm getting there," I say, surprising myself with how much I mean it. "Hey, I've got to get to work. Need to be at the coffee shop in thirty, and then Sadie's got me training some new bartenders tonight."

"Sadie? You're still at the bar?"

"Yeah," I respond, a small smile tugging at my lips as I think about Sadie's offer from yesterday. The two new bartenders she's hired. The mid-day shift she wants me to work so I can take on more gigs for the band. "Actually, she's talking about giving me more responsibilities. Kind of a promotion, I guess."

"That's wonderful, honey," she says, and I can hear the pride in her voice. It's so rare, I almost don't recognize the feeling it stirs in my chest.

When we hang up, I head toward the shower, the thought of going home next week... of going back to Thomas's grave swirling in my head. Am I ready for that?

As if the universe is trying to answer, I catch the date on my phone. December 13th. The day Cora saved my life six years ago. The day that changed everything.

Unbidden, the memory washes over me:

The screech of metal, the acrid smell of smoke. Pain, everywhere. Then, through the haze, a pair of determined amber eyes. A voice, steady despite the chaos: "Stay with me, okay? Help is coming."

Talk about cosmic irony. Here I am, agreeing to face one part of my past, on the anniversary of another life-changing event. An event that's somehow circled back around, bringing Cora into my life again. To save me again. Or at least this time, to help me save myself.

* * *

The afternoon rush at the coffee shop is in full swing when Arden walks in. She heads straight toward me, her gaze zeroing in on the fading bruise around my left eye. A memento from my encounter with Logan.

"I've got this one," I tell my co-worker, moving to the register. "Hey, Arden. The usual?"

She nods, her eyes never leaving my face. "You look like you've seen better days." Her tone is casual, but I can hear the undercurrent of disappointment.

Heat creeps up my neck at the memory I can't fully grasp, blurred by whiskey and unwarranted rage. "You must think I'm bad news for Cora after the scene I caused," I mutter, staring down at the cup in my hands.

Arden clicks her tongue. "Can't say I was impressed with how you handled yourself. But that text you sent her... that was a start."

I look up, surprised. "She told you about that?"

Arden nods. "She was touched, Jake. Confused, but touched. Your honesty meant a lot to her."

The memory of my text floods back. I'd poured my heart out, apologizing for my behavior and admitting I needed to work on myself. Cora's response had been cautiously optimistic, saying she appreciated my honesty and was willing to talk when I was ready.

"I'm trying," I admit. "But I'm scared, Arden. I don't know how to be someone... deserving."

Arden's eyes soften, and I see understanding dawn in them. "You're a good man, Jake. You've had a lot of shit happen, and you thought the answer was to keep everyone at arms length so they couldn't hurt you. Then, the first time you let someone in, it burned you. At least, you thought so. But don't push her away. However strange it sounds, I think you might need each other."

I swallow hard, shocked by how well she read the situation, how well she knows me after all this time. "It's not that simple. I can't just ask for her friendship back. For her to be patient with me."

"Why not?" Arden challenges. "Cora's not Tessa, Jake. You don't have to prove your worth to her. Just being the man I knew once upon a time is more than enough."

I'm stunned by Arden's perceptiveness. How does she know so much about my relationship with Tessa? Mark doesn't even know that much.

All at once memories flash—Tessa's disappointed looks, her constant critiques, the way I bent over backwards trying to make her happy. Was it that transparent? And is that my problem? I've been trained to think I have to be better to be accepted, to be loved?

"I screwed up, Arden. I got scared and I lashed out. How do I fix that?"

Arden's face softens. "By being honest. With Cora, and with yourself. Don't let fear cost you a chance with her. Figure out how to make it right."

As she takes her coffee and turns to leave, I find myself calling out, "Arden?"

She pauses, looking back at me.

"Thanks," I say, meaning it more than I have in years. "And... how did you know all that about Tessa and me?"

Arden's smile is tinged with sadness. "I watched you change, Jake. We all did. You don't have to do that with Cora. Let her see the real you."

I watch her leave, feeling a strange mix of terror and hope. *See the real me?* Do I even know who that guy is anymore?

The rest of my shift passes in a blur of steaming lattes and holiday cheer, but my mind keeps circling back to Arden's words and the significance of today's date.

As if summoned by my thoughts, I catch a glimpse of familiar cinnamon hair through the front window. Before I can think twice, I'm shouting to my coworker, "Cover for me!" and bolting out the door.

"Cora!" I call out, probably louder than necessary. She spins around, nearly dropping her phone.

"Jake?" Her eyes widen. "Geez, are you trying to give me a heart attack?"

I rub the back of my neck, suddenly feeling like an idiot. *Do I apologize again? Tell her I can't stop thinking about her?* "Sorry, I just... I saw you and... yeah."

Perfect, Rhoades. Exactly what you were going for.

Cora's lips twitch, fighting a smile. "Eloquent as ever, I see."

"Hey, you try forming coherent sentences after six hours of caffeine-fueled customer service," I shoot back, grinning despite myself.

She laughs, and damn if it isn't the best sound I've heard all day. "Fair point. So, um... how've you been?"

"Oh, you know. Living the dream, one latte at a time," I quip, then wince. *Why can't I just be normal for once?* "Actually, I... I've missed seeing you around."

Cora's expression softens. "Yeah?"

I nod, swallowing hard. "Look, about that text I sent... I meant it, Cora. Every word."

"I know," she says quietly. "I just... I thought you needed space."

"I'm an idiot," I blurt out. "I thought I did, but... turns out space kind of sucks when you're not around."

Her eyebrows shoot up. "Wow, that was almost romantic. Who are you and what have you done with the Jake I met a few weeks ago?"

I chuckle, feeling some of the tension ease. "He's still here. Just... trying to be better, I guess."

Cora's smile is gentle. "You don't have to be better, Jake. Just be you."

Her words hit me like a ton of bricks. Isn't that what Arden was trying to tell me?

"Even if 'me' is a disaster?" I ask, only half-joking.

"Hey, that disaster came to my rescue at Sadie's," she says, reaching out to touch my arm. "Don't be too hard on him, huh?"

God, what'd I do to deserve someone like her in my life?

I catch her hand before she can pull away. "I don't want to lose you, Cora. Even if it's just as friends. I... I think I might need you in my life."

She looks at our joined hands, then back up at me. "Well, lucky for you, I'm not going anywhere. Except maybe to get some Wi-Fi installed at my new apartment."

I laugh, feeling lighter than I have in weeks. "Look at you, adulting and all."

"I know, right? Next thing you know, I'll be eating vegetables voluntarily."

We stand there grinning at each other until Cora's phone chimes. She glances at it, then back at me apologetically. "I should probably..."

"Yeah, no, of course," I say quickly, reluctantly letting go of her hand. "But maybe we could talk more? Soon?"

Her smile is bright enough to power the whole damn city. "I'd like that, Jake. A lot."

As I watch her walk away, I feel like I can finally breathe again. For the first time in years, I'm not itching to drown my emotions in the bottom of a bottle. Instead, there's a spark of something I'd almost forgotten—hope.

I head back into the shop, my mind buzzing with possibilities. Arden's words echo in my head: "You don't have to prove your worth to her. Just being the man I knew once upon a time is more than enough."

Maybe she's right. Maybe I don't need to be better to be accepted, to be loved. Maybe I just need to be... me. The guy who loves music, who cares deeply even when it scares the hell out of him, who's been through shit but is still standing.

As I tie my apron back on, I realize something. Happiness may not be a promise—it's fleeting, unpredictable. But feeling something, anything, is better than the numb emptiness I've been living in. And Cora? She makes me feel everything.

Maybe it's time I finally embrace it.

20

∾

Cora

December 15th

I end the call with the furniture company, frustration bubbling in my chest. "Due to the unexpected snowstorm, we'll have to reschedule your delivery for Monday," they said. Amazing. I glance around my nearly empty apartment, save for the few pieces of furniture I brought from Logan's—the couch, my desk and a small table. So much for my grand plans of fully settling in this weekend.

Outside, the snow falls in thick, heavy flakes, blanketing the world in white. It's beautiful, in a lonely sort of way. I wrap my arms around myself, suddenly feeling very small in this big, empty space.

Maybe I could head back to Arden's once the snow lets up.

I glance down at my phone as it alarms with a weather alert: "Severe snowstorm warning. Residents advised to stay indoors."

Or not... Looks like it'll be the couch tonight.

Crap. Does that mean I can't go to the grocery store as planned, either?

As if on cue, my stomach growls. I rummage through the few boxes I've unpacked, hoping to find something edible. No such luck. My gaze catches the bottle of wine from Arden... That's calories, right?

Just as I'm contemplating the merits of wine-flavored snow cones, a muffled thud echoes from the neighboring apartment. Until now, I'd assumed the unit was vacant, or perhaps occupied by a snowbird escaping the harsh Chicago winter. But now I hear movement, followed by a string of colorful curses that would make a sailor blush.

My lips twitch, amused by the creative profanity. I'm about to return to my unpacking when an unexpected sound filters through the wall—the gentle strumming of a guitar.

Curiosity piqued, I find myself drifting towards the shared wall. The melody is hauntingly familiar, tugging at something in the back of my mind. I press my ear against the cool surface, feeling a bit like a child eavesdropping on adult conversations.

A voice joins in, low and husky, sending an involuntary shiver down my spine:

"When I close my eyes, all I see is you..."

My heart stutters, then races. That voice. I'd know it anywhere, even muffled through drywall and insulation. It can't be... can it?

Before I can talk myself out of it, I'm out my door, hand raised to knock on my neighbor's. The music stops abruptly, and I suddenly realize how crazy this is. What am I going to say? 'Hi, I was eavesdropping on your private concert?' 'Funny running into you here... in your own home?'

My heart pounds in my ears as footsteps approach. I consider bolting back to my apartment, but my feet seem rooted to the spot. The door swings open, and time does that weird thing where it slows down, like I'm suddenly underwater.

Because there, looking as shocked as I feel, is Jake. His blue eyes wide with disbelief.

Of course it's Jake. It's December, after all.

"Cora?" he breathes, my name a question and an exclamation all at once.

I open my mouth, but no words come out. How do you even

begin to explain this level of cosmic coincidence? A laugh bubbles up in my throat, half amused, half disbelieving. "Hi, neighbor," I finally manage. "I, uh... heard music."

Jake's lips quirk into that crooked smile that never fails to make my heart skip a beat. "Looks like the universe isn't done throwing us together yet."

"Apparently not," I say, unable to keep the smile from my face. "Is this what you meant by talking more soon?"

He chuckles, rubbing the back of his neck and I catch the faded black eye I noticed on Wednesday. "Not exactly, but I'll take it," he starts. "Sadie's is closed for the night. Snowstorm and all, so I'm free if you want to come in. I promise I won't serenade you... unless you ask nicely."

I hesitate, remembering our conversation at the coffee shop. We'd agreed to talk, to figure things out, but this feels... big. Intimate in a way I'm not sure I'm ready for. But then again, when has anything about us been conventional?

"I don't know," I tease, leaning against his doorframe. "I might require nourishment in exchange for such pleasant company. You wouldn't happen to have any gourmet cuisine hiding in that barren wasteland you call a kitchen, would you?"

Jake's eyes light up with amusement. "As a matter of fact, I was about to throw in a pizza. Gourmet enough for you?"

I hum, pretending to think about it. "I suppose I could grace you with my presence. But only because I'm worried you might burn the building down if left to your own devices. And I haven't even fully moved in, so..."

"Your altruism knows no bounds," Jake deadpans, ushering me inside with a flourish. "Welcome to Casa del Jake. Try not to trip over all the clutter."

As I step in, I can't help but gasp at the stark emptiness. While I've been frantically nesting like a caffeinated bird, Jake's apartment is almost monastically bare. A worn guitar in the corner and a few scattered sheets of paper are the only signs of life.

"Wow, when you commit to minimalism, you really commit, huh? And here I thought my place was giving off 'just robbed' vibes."

Jake shrugs, a flicker of something vulnerable crossing his face before his usual smirk returns. "What can I say? I'm a man of simple tastes."

"Simple tastes, my foot," I snort, gesturing to his guitar. "That's a Gibson, isn't it? Those things cost more than my entire IKEA haul."

His eyebrows shoot up. "Impressive. Didn't peg you for a guitar aficionado."

"There's a lot you don't know about me," I say, winking. "Like my throw pillow collection. I'm full of fun surprises."

"I bet you are," he murmurs, his voice dropping low in a way that sends shivers down my spine.

For a moment, we're caught in each other's gaze. Then Jake clears his throat, breaking the spell. "So, uh, pizza? I promise it's not poisoned."

"Gee, thanks for the reassurance," I laugh, following him to the kitchen. "Though I have to ask, is this how you usually woo women? With the promise of non-lethal food?"

Jake clutches his heart in mock offense. "I'll have you know my wooing skills are top-notch. I just... might be a little rusty."

"Well," I say, hopping onto a barstool, "lucky for you, I happen to be an expert in romantic gestures. Perks of the job and all that."

"Is that so?" Jake says, leaning across the counter towards me. "And what would the expert suggest for a guy trying to impress a beautiful, witty neighbor who's way out of his league?"

My heart does a little flip at his words, but I keep my tone light. "Oh, I don't know. Maybe actually owning some plates to eat said pizza on?"

Jake laughs, the sound warm and rich. "Touché. I'll add that to my shopping list, right after 'throw pillows' and 'basic human necessities.'"

As we fall into easy banter, I can feel the last of the tension melting away. This is a newer side of Jake—funny, charming, and just the right amount of self-deprecation. And I might have just fallen a little further.

As he moves around the kitchen, stealing glances at me when he thinks I'm not looking, I realize something. Maybe we're both a little rusty at this. Maybe we're both a little scared. But maybe that's okay. Because whatever this is between us, it feels real. It feels right.

After throwing in the pizza, Jake completely shocks me, pulling out a handful of vegetables. I try not to drool as his muscles bunch and flex when he chops them.

When he reaches up to grab a mixing bowl (yes, he actually has dishes), I notice the inked words on his bicep. *When the lights go down, and the crowd fades away.* I'd seen the tattoo before, but never had a chance to focus on it like this.

Jake catches me staring, and I flush, suddenly self-conscious of my obvious gawking. *Real subtle, Cora.*

"They're just some old lyrics," he mumbles, turning back to the cutting board. But I notice the way his shoulders tense, like he's bracing for judgment.

Curiosity gets the better of me, and I slide off my stool, moving closer. "Can I see the rest?"

He pauses, then nods, pulling up his sleeve. The rest of it comes into focus. *...It's just me and my guitar and the words I need to say.*

"Did you write these?" I ask, tracing the inked lines with a reverent finger. The intimacy of the gesture isn't lost on me, and I feel a jolt of electricity where my skin meets his.

Jake clears his throat, a faint flush creeping up his neck. "Yeah, it's from one of the first songs I ever wrote. Back when we were all just kids in the garage."

"They're beautiful," I whisper, and I mean it. There's a raw honesty in those words that tugs at something deep inside me.

I look up at him, suddenly aware of how close we are. His blue eyes are intense, searching. I notice the faint bruising around his left eye again. Without thinking, I reach up to touch the discolored skin. "What happened here?"

Jake tenses under my touch, a flicker of something–pain? shame?–crossing his face. He takes a step back, busying himself with the vegetables again. "It was your ex," he says softly. "Makes sense now why I ran into him in the parking lot last Sunday."

I gasp, putting it together. Sunday. When Logan was at my apartment. "Logan hit you? Because of me?"

Jake's laugh is bitter, lacking any real humor. "I had it coming, Cora. After how I acted at the concert..."

The mention of that night hangs heavy between us. Aside from our few texts, we haven't really talked about it.

"Jake," I start, not sure where I'm going with this. "That night... it wasn't what you thought. I mean, I know how it looked, but—"

"No," he cuts me off, his voice tight. "You don't owe me an explanation. We weren't... I mean, I had no right to..."

He trails off, frustration evident in the set of his jaw. I watch as he struggles with something, his knuckles white as he grips the edge of the counter.

"It's just," he finally continues, his voice barely above a whisper, "seeing you with him... it brought up some stuff. Old wounds, you know?"

I nod, even though I'm not sure I do know. There's so much about Jake's past that's still a mystery to me.

He takes a deep breath, like he's steeling himself for something. "I've got issues, Cora. Deep-rooted ones that mess with my head, that make me hesitant to trust... to let people close."

"You lost people you loved, Jake," I say softly. "That's enough to make anyone scared."

Jake watches me intently for a minute. It's the first time I've acknowledged that I knew, and I wonder if he's surprised. But then he exhales, his eyes burning with more than just grief. "There's more to that story. A lot more."

The air feels thick with anticipation, and I find myself holding my breath. This is Jake trying, I realize. Letting me in.

"I'm listening," I say softly, reaching out to take his hand. And as his fingers intertwine with mine, I realize how perfectly they fit together.

Jake's hand trembles slightly, and I resist the urge to pull him closer. Instead, I wait, giving him the space to find his words.

"That morning," he starts, his voice low and strained. "Before their accident... Tessa told me she'd fallen in love with someone else."

The revelation hits me like a physical blow, and suddenly, Jake's behavior at the concert makes a painful kind of sense. "Oh, Jake," I breathe, my heart aching for him.

He continues, the words tumbling out now as if a dam has broken. "That's why I didn't drive her to the airport. Why Thomas took her instead. Finding out I wasn't enough..." His voice cracks, and I can see years of pain etched into his features.

I want to reach for him, to comfort him, but I hold back. There's more here, I can feel it. So instead, I gently prompt, "What happened then?"

Jake's eyes meet mine, and the raw vulnerability I see there takes my breath away. He opens his mouth to say something, then shakes it away, trying again. "I got the call from my mom. There was a semi that changed lanes. And I was left with this... this guilt. This anger. I pushed everyone away because it was easier than dealing with the pain."

As he speaks, memories of our own shared history flash through my mind. The car accident six years ago, pulling Jake from the wreckage. Does that guilt haunt him, too? Surviving?

"Seeing you with Logan that night," Jake continues, unaware of my inner turmoil, "it was like history repeating itself. I reacted instead of listening. I thought you'd chosen him."

His words hang in the air between us, heavy with implication. I feel tears pricking at my eyes as I realize the depth of Jake's pain, the reason behind his guarded heart. But there's something else too—a growing awareness of just how complicated this thing between us really is.

"Jake, I had no idea," I whisper, my voice thick with emotion. "I'm so sorry."

"I've never told anyone that," he admits, a glimmer of hope breaking through. "Not even Owen. They all think I'm just... grieving."

"Thank you for trusting me with this," I say softly. "I know it doesn't change what happened, but I want you to know... you are enough, Jake. More than enough."

Jake's eyes search mine, and for a moment, I see the scared, heartbroken boy beneath the tough exterior. Then, slowly, he pulls me into his arms, burying his face in my hair.

As I lean into his embrace, I can't help but wonder what this means for us. Are we really ready for this? Can two broken people help each other heal, or are we just setting ourselves up for more pain?

"We're kind of a mess together," I admit softly, voicing my fears.

Jake's uneven exhale skims my lips, sending tingles down my back. "No, Cora. We're a mess when we're apart."

His words settle over me, warm and comforting.

He's right. Because deep down, I know this is just the beginning. Our stories are already intertwined in ways neither of us fully understands yet. And as terrifying as that is, there's a part of me that can't wait to unravel the mystery that is Jake Rhoades—even if it means risking my heart all over again.

For now, though, I let myself sink into the moment, savoring the warmth of Jake's embrace. Whatever tomorrow brings, tonight we're just two people finding comfort in each other's arms while the storm rages outside.

And somehow, that feels like enough.

21

Jake

December 16th

Pancakes. I smell pancakes.

I lift my head from the couch, neck protesting my contorted sleeping position. There, haloed by the light filtering through the window, stands Cora, messy bun and spatula in hand. For a split second, I think I'm dreaming—or worse, that last night's confessions scared her off and my brain's conjured up this domestic fantasy as a coping mechanism. I pinch my arm just to be sure.

Ow. Nope, definitely awake.

I drag a palm down my face, willing my brain to catch up with reality. Cora's changed since last night, which means she let herself back in. To make me breakfast. After I spilled my guts about Tessa. Christ, what kind of Twilight Zone episode am I starring in?

Memories of last night flood back, hitting me like a freight train of emotions I'm not equipped to handle before coffee. We ate together, sure, but then... We talked. Really talked. For hours. About everything.

The highway. Six years ago. Her pulling my sorry ass out of that wreck. Me, the world's biggest dick, missing Mark's wedding. My band. Her job. It's like someone took a sledgehammer to the walls I've spent years building, and I just... let it happen.

But then, like the universe wanted to reward me for finally opening up, Cora fell asleep. On my lap.

"Morning, sleepyhead," Cora chirps, far too chipper for... what time is it anyway? "Thought I'd repay you for dinner. And carrying me to bed. And the, you know, emotional unburdening."

I blink at her, still half-convinced I'm dreaming. Because there's no way someone like Cora—smart, beautiful, way too good for me Cora—should stick around after seeing the mess that is Jake Rhoades up close and personal.

But here she is, making me breakfast. Looking at me like I'm something worth waking up early for. And damn if that doesn't terrify me more than any hangover I've ever had.

I smooth my bedhead somewhat desperately before shuffling to the counter. "You don't have to repay me for any of that," I manage through a jaw-cracking yawn. "Though I gotta say, waking up to you in my kitchen? Definitely beats the 'oh-shit-what-did-I-reveal' panic I was bracing for."

Cora's laugh, warm and genuine, eases something in my chest I didn't even realize was tight. "Please, after our conversation and you willingly donating your bed for the night? Making breakfast is the least I could do."

I shrug, beyond touched, as she pushes a steaming plate toward me. "Yeah, well, figured I owed you the truth. Especially after the other week. And, for the record, I did have to carry you to bed. You fell asleep on my lap. And as much as I enjoyed watching you, my arms were going numb."

Unable to resist, I tuck an unruly strand behind her ear, letting my fingertips graze her cheek. Cora leans into my touch, just slightly, and suddenly the kitchen feels about ten degrees warmer.

"So..." I redirect, reaching for the syrup, before I get lost in those amber stars. "What's the weather verdict? Should I prep for another slumber party tonight?"

Cora fights a smile, losing adorably. "Nice try, but it seems you'll get your bed back tonight. Roads are relatively clear."

I abandon all pretense, openly ogling her with a smoldering look I usually save for closing time at the bar. "Well, you're welcome to sleep over anytime. In fact," I stroke my stubble contemplatively, "I'm closing at Sadie's all weekend. Since your furniture doesn't come in until Monday... There's no sense in you suffering on your couch when there's a perfectly good bed right here."

Cora's cheeks pinken even as she arches one brow. "Careful, Jake. A girl might think you're trying to lure her into some sort of sleepover trap."

"Would that be such a bad thing?" I hear myself say before my brain can hit the mute button. God, how'd I make it through the entire night without crawling into bed beside her?

Because I don't have that permission yet, I remind myself.

Cora's eyes widen slightly, and I'm terrified I've pushed too far. But then her lips curve into a slow, dangerous smile. "I don't know. Might depend on how good the company is."

And just like that, we're back in familiar territory–this delicious dance of flirtation and innuendo that we've perfected over the past few weeks. But now, with last night's revelations still fresh, it feels different. Heavier. More real.

"Eight. Two. Two. Four," I blurt out, immediately wanting to kick myself. *Way to come off desperate, Rhoades.*

Cora tilts her head, confusion clear on her face. "What?"

"The door code," I explain, feeling heat creep up my neck. "You know, in case you decide to take me up on the offer. Or if you just want to raid my fridge while I'm gone. I hear my pancake ingredients are pretty popular."

Her lips twitch, clearly fighting back a laugh. "Right. Because we're..."

"Neighbors," I offer with a shrug, trying to ignore the way my heart is doing somersaults in my chest.

"Gotcha," Cora nods, taking another bite of pancake with an assessing stare. "Friendly neighbors who have platonic sleepovers and share door codes. Totally normal."

Except there is nothing normal about this situation. Not in the way she makes me feel, or the way she looks at me, or the way I want to be so much more than her platonic friend.

Yeah, I want this. I want her. Even if it scares the hell out of me.

* * *

It's Sunday night at Sadie's, and the bar is buzzing with its usual weekend energy. I'm behind the counter, supposedly demonstrating proper glass polishing technique to Bailey, our newest hire. But my mind is elsewhere, replaying Cora's text from earlier.

Cora: *Furniture is supposed to show up early tomorrow. Is that invite to crash at your place still available?*

My heart does a little flip every time I think about it. After turning down my offer yesterday, I hadn't expected it. Now, I can't stop picturing her curled up in my sheets, waiting for me to come home.

"Still with me, rockstar?" Natalie's voice interrupts my daydream. I blink, realizing I've been polishing the same glass for who knows how long. Bailey's looking at me expectantly, clearly waiting for some sage bartending wisdom.

"Right, so, uh... circular motions," I mumble, demonstrating half-heartedly. Bailey nods, standing closer than I realized.

Natalie rolls her eyes, gently shooing a reluctant Bailey towards the other end of the bar. "Why don't you help Justin with those orders? I need to have a chat with our oh-so-focused manager here."

As Bailey scurries off, Natalie turns to me, arms crossed. "Alright, share. What's got you so distracted? Or should I say, who?"

I busy myself with wiping down the counter, avoiding her knowing gaze. "Don't know what you're talking about."

"Uh-huh," Natalie says, clearly not buying it. "This wouldn't have anything to do with that girl from the other week, would it? The one you were making heart eyes at during your show at Joe's?"

My head snaps up, heat crawling up my neck. "I wasn't—that's not—"

"Save it, Rhoades," Natalie laughs, cutting off my stammering. "I've known you too long. So, what's the deal? Did you finally ask her out?"

I sigh, knowing there's no point in denying it. "Turns out she's my new neighbor. And yeah, maybe I like her. A lot."

Natalie's eyebrows shoot up. "Angel turned neighbor, huh? That's... convenient."

"It's not like that," I protest, even as my mind wanders back to Cora. "We're just... figuring things out."

"Well, figure it out faster," Natalie says, nodding towards the growing crowd at the bar. "Because right now, you're about as useful as a screen door on a submarine. Justin's already closing on his own, and at this rate, Bailey's going to think polishing a single glass for ten minutes is standard procedure."

I groan, running a hand through my hair. "I know, I know. I'll focus. Promise."

Natalie's expression softens. "Look, I'm happy for you. Really. It's good to see you interested in someone again. But right now, we need Jake the bartender, not Jake the lovesick teenager. Think you can manage that?"

I push down the fear that hits at her words. I have a job to do. Straightening up and plastering on my best 'charming bartender,' I smile. "Yeah, I got this. Thanks, Nat."

As I turn to help a waiting customer, Natalie calls out, "Oh, and Jake? When this shift is over, you're telling me everything about this girl. No exceptions."

I laugh, shaking my head. As I mix drinks and chat with patrons, I can't help but count down the hours until I can go home. To Cora. The thought sends a thrill through me, equal parts excitement and terror.

It's going to be a long night.

Luckily the busyness has the rest of the shift passing quickly. I manage to keep my head in the game, even throwing in some actual useful tips for Bailey and Justin between customers. But as last call approaches, my mind starts to wander again.

"Alright, Romeo," Natalie says as she helps me wipe down the bar. "You're practically vibrating. Get out of here before you spontaneously combust."

I glance at the time, surprised to see it's already past midnight. "You sure? I can stay and help close up."

Natalie waves me off. "Please. You'd just slow us down with your puppy dog eyes and constant phone-checking. Besides, I'm out next week and you're running the show with these two. You can make it up to me after."

I don't need to be told twice. After a quick rundown with Justin about tomorrow's inventory and a reminder to Bailey about proper glass storage, I'm out the door, taking the stairs to my apartment two at a time.

My heart's pounding as I reach my floor, and not just from the climb. I pause outside my door, suddenly nervous. Is this weird? Should I knock? It is my apartment, after all. But Cora's in there, probably asleep, and the last thing I want to do is scare her.

Before I can overthink it any further, I take a deep breath and quietly let myself in. The apartment is dark, except for the soft glow of the TV. As my eyes adjust, I spot Cora curled up on the couch, fast asleep.

She looks so peaceful that for a moment I just stand there, drinking in the sight of her. I'm treading on dangerous ground, edging closer to the kind of domestic bliss I swore off years ago. But right now, I'm wondering what the hell I was thinking when I made that vow. Why wouldn't I want to come home to this every night?

As I move closer, the weight of the upcoming week settles heavily on my shoulders. Tuesday's visit to my parents, the anniversary, old wounds that never quite healed—it all looms ahead like a storm on the horizon. Can I balance this newfound happiness with the ghosts that have been my constant companions for so long?

But as I lean down, brushing Cora's hair from her face, I know I want to try.

I intend on carrying her to bed like the other night, when Cora stirs, her eyes fluttering open.

"Jake...?" she murmurs, voice husky with sleep.

"Hey," I whisper, my hand instinctively cupping her cheek. "Sorry, didn't mean to wake you."

Cora smiles sleepily, leaning into my touch. "S'okay. Was trying to wait up for you."

The simple admission sends a wave of warmth through me, chasing away some of the darkness that's been threatening to engulf me. For a moment, I let myself believe that maybe I can face whatever's coming as long as I have this to come home to.

"You didn't have to do that, Cora."

"Wanted to," she mumbles, sitting up and stretching. The movement causes her oversized t-shirt (my t-shirt, I realize with a smirk) to slip off one shoulder. I swallow hard, trying to keep my thoughts PG and failing miserably.

"You, uh, ready for bed?" I manage, my voice hitting notes I haven't reached since puberty.

Cora nods, a hint of mischief in her sleepy smile.

I try not to read too much into the way her hand finds mine as we make our way to the bedroom. *Is this still just friendly, or...?* My mind's racing, caught between 'holy shit, this is happening' and 'don't fuck this up, Rhoades.'

We reach the bed, both hesitating like we've forgotten how this works. I run a hand through my hair, suddenly feeling like a teenager again. "So, uh... do you have a preferred side?"

Cora laughs softly. "Look at you, being all considerate."

I roll my eyes, but I can't help grinning. "Hey, I can be a gentleman when I want to be."

"I'll believe it when I see it," she teases, but there's a softness in her eyes that makes my heart skip.

"I'll just..." I gesture vaguely towards the bathroom. "Be right back."

Once inside, I splash some cold water on my face, staring at my reflection. "Get it together, man," I mutter. "It's just Cora. Beautiful, amazing Cora who's seen you at your worst and is still here."

I strip off my bar-scented shirt, debating if I should put a fresh one on, then decide against it. It's my bed, after all. When I return, Cora's perched on the edge of the mattress, looking both nervous and determined.

"You okay?" I ask, moving closer. "We don't have to do this if you're uncomfortable. I can take the couch again."

Cora shakes her head, a small smile playing on her lips. "No. I'm good. Just... processing, I guess. It's been a while since I've done the whole sleepover thing. I mean aside from..." She trails off, not needing to finish. Aside from accidentally falling asleep here Friday night.

"Yeah," I agree, sitting next to her. Our shoulders brush, and I swear I can feel electricity crackling between us. "For what it's worth, I'm a little nervous too."

She looks at me, surprise evident in her expression. "You? Nervous? I thought you were Mr. Smooth."

I laugh, the sound a bit shakier than I'd like. "Only on stage, sweetheart. Off stage, I'm just a mess trying to figure things out."

Cora's hand finds mine, her touch sending warmth spreading through my chest. "Well, that makes two of us."

We sit in silence for a moment, the weight of everything unsaid hanging between us. Finally, I clear my throat. "So, why did you take me up on this offer? Not that I'm complaining, but..."

Cora bites her lip, looking thoughtful. "Honestly? I'm not sure. I just... I wanted to be here. With you." She pauses, then adds with a smirk, "Plus, your bed is way comfier than my couch."

I chuckle, grateful for her ability to lighten the mood. "Glad I could be of service."

We slide under the covers, and after a moment of awkward shuffling, Cora curls into my side. It feels right, like she belongs there.

"This okay?" she murmurs, her breath warm against my skin.

"More than okay," I whisper back, tightening my arm around her.

I close my eyes, trying to calm the storm raging inside me. Having Cora this close, her soft curves molded to my harder planes, is both heaven and hell. A reminder of what I stand to gain and lose wrapped into one.

"Jake?" Cora's voice is soft, sleepy.

"Yeah?"

"I'm glad I'm here."

The words resonate through me, sparking a warmth that spreads from my chest to my fingertips. It's a feeling I'd forgotten existed, one I never thought I'd experience again. "Me too, Cora. More than you know."

I press a soft kiss to the top of her head, breathing in the scent that's quickly becoming my favorite addiction. For years, I've been running from moments like this, afraid of what I might lose. But now, with Cora in my arms, I want to hold on with everything I've got.

For tonight, I'll let myself have this moment of happiness, this sense of belonging I'd thought was lost forever. And as the week looms ahead—family, memories, and all the ghosts of my past—I silently pray I can make it through without losing sight of what's possible. Of what Cora and I could be.

Because for the first time in years, I have something—someone—worth fighting for.

22

Cora

December 18th

I wake to the gentle rhythm of Jake's heartbeat, my cheek pressed against his chest. For a moment, I allow myself to bask in the warmth of his embrace, the solid presence of his arms around me a stark contrast to the empty bed I've had lately.

This is dangerous territory, Cooper. Abort mission. Retreat. Run for the hills.

My inner editor is working overtime, red-penning every romantic notion that dares to creep into my consciousness. But my traitorous body refuses to budge, savoring the warmth radiating from Jake's bare skin.

Yesterday, crashing at Jake's seemed like a brilliant idea—a way to test the waters of our evolving relationship after Saturday morning's flirtatious pancake extravaganza. Now, wrapped in his arms, I'm wishing his lips were brushing the back of my neck instead of just his breath, and I'm forced to confront the reality of my situation.

I'm falling for Jake Rhoades. Hard and fast. And it terrifies me.

It's been less than two months since Logan shattered my world. Two months since I swore off men and vowed to focus on myself. Yet here I am, in another man's bed, my heart doing somersaults at his mere proximity. What happened to taking things slow? To healing?

Arden's words from last night echo in my mind: "Sometimes, Cora, the best way to heal is to let someone in. Jake's not Logan. Give him a chance."

Easy for her to say. She's got the whole happily-ever-after thing down pat with Mark. But me? I'm the queen of disastrous December romances. Sam. Logan. And now Jake? It's like I'm caught in some cosmic joke where the universe decides to upend my life every time the calendar hits December 1st.

Then again, didn't it start with Jake? The more time we've spent together, the more convinced I'm becoming of its significance. I remember the vulnerability in Jake's eyes last night. The way he looked at me like I was something precious, something worth protecting. It's so different from how Logan looked at me, even in the beginning.

Maybe that's why I'm here, in Jake's bed, instead of back at Arden's. Because for the first time in a long time, I feel seen. Understood. Like maybe I'm worthy of the kind of love I've always written about but never truly believed I could have.

I inhale Jake's scent—that familiar woodsy cologne now mingled with the faint aroma of the bar. I can't deny the sense of rightness that washes over me. When did this man's presence become so essential? A craving I can't seem to shake?

I glance at the clock: 8:15. The furniture company will be arriving soon. I should leave before I lose all rational thought and throw myself at this dangerously addictive man. It's still soon. We're both still healing.

But as I start to slide out from beneath Jake's arm, he makes a grumpy noise that sends tingles down my spine.

"Five more minutes," he mumbles sleepily, tightening his arm around me. "You're too warm to let go."

I chuckle softly, even as I melt back into his embrace. "Says the human furnace. I'm pretty sure I'm going to spontaneously combust if I stay here much longer."

Jake's lips curve into a smile against my shoulder. "Wouldn't be the worst way to go, would it?"

His breath fans across my skin, and suddenly I'm hyper-aware of every point of contact between us. The solid warmth of his chest against my back, the weight of his arm draped over my waist, the way our legs are tangled together. It's intimate in a way I haven't experienced in... well, longer than I care to admit.

"Is this the way you seduce all your women?" I tease, my voice embarrassingly breathy.

Jake's chuckle is low and warm. "Just you."

Oh boy.

I turn in his arms, meeting his gaze. Those ocean-blue eyes, still hazy with sleep, hold a warmth that makes my heart stutter. It's a look I've read a thousand times, edited into countless manuscripts, but never truly experienced. Until now.

"You know," I say, aiming for lightness, "when I agreed to crash here, I didn't realize it came with such attentive room service."

Jake's lips quirk into that crooked smile that never fails to make my stomach flip. "What can I say? I aim to please."

His hand drifts to my waist, leaving a trail of goosebumps in its wake. The simple touch ignites a slow burn low in my belly, and suddenly I'm caught between wanting to fan the flames and douse them with a bucket of cold reality.

As if he can read my mind, he rests his forehead against mine, our breaths mingling. "Cora," he murmurs, a hint of wonder in his voice. "I'm not sure I remember how to do this. But being here with you... it feels right."

I can't help but smile, my fingers tracing the stubble along his jaw. "What, the whole 'waking up next to someone' thing? I hear it's like riding a bike."

Jake chuckles, the sound rumbling through his chest. "Yeah, if the bike's been rusting in a garage for five years."

"Well," I tease, "I'd say you're doing a pretty good job for a rusty bike."

His eyes meet mine, a vulnerability there that catches me off guard. "You make it easy," he admits softly. "Too easy, maybe."

I swallow hard, understanding the weight behind his words. "Jake, we don't have to—"

"No," he interrupts gently. "I want this. I want you. I'm just... not used to wanting anything anymore."

The honesty in his voice makes my heart ache. "Join the club," I whisper.

Jake's hand finds mine, our fingers intertwining. "Look at us," he says with a wry smile. "A couple of emotional wrecks trying to figure out how to be human again."

"Hey, speak for yourself. I'll have you know I'm a highly functioning emotional wreck, thank you very much."

"Oh yeah?" Jake's eyebrow quirks up. "Is that why you're in my bed, wearing my shirt?"

I feel my cheeks heat up. "It's comfortable," I defend weakly. "Besides, I didn't hear you complaining last night when you found me in it."

"Trust me," he growls playfully, his hand slipping under the hem of the shirt to rest on my bare waist, "I'm not complaining now."

The touch sends a shiver through me, and a small gasp escapes my throat. Jake's eyes darken at the sound, his gaze dropping to my lips.

"Cora," he murmurs, his voice rough. "I really want to kiss you right now."

My heart races, a mix of excitement and fear coursing through me. *This is it, Cooper. Last chance to bail before you're in too deep.*

But as I look into Jake's eyes, I realize it's already too late. I've been in too deep since I saw him in that coffee shop. Maybe since I pulled him from that wreck six years ago.

"What's stopping you?" I whisper, throwing caution to the wind.

For a heartbeat, neither of us moves. Then, slowly, Jake closes the distance between us.

The first brush of Jake's lips against mine is gentle, almost hesitant. It reminds me of that night at Sadie's, full of promise and possibility. But as I thread my fingers through his hair, pulling him closer, the kiss deepens. This isn't the frantic, desperate encounter from Arden's. No, this is slower, more deliberate. It feels like we're writing a new chapter, one neither of us is quite ready to title.

My head screams for caution, but my heart... It's ready to dive headfirst into the abyss.

Jake's hands explore my body with a reverence that makes my breath catch. His touch is both gentle and urgent, like he's trying to memorize every curve, every dip, every scar. When his fingers trace the outline of my hip bone, I arch into him, craving more.

"God, Cora," he breathes against my neck, his lips leaving a trail of fire along my collarbone. "You have no idea what you do to me."

I bite back a moan, my nails scraping lightly down his back. "Oh, I think I have some idea," I murmur, my voice husky with need. "Believe me, the feeling's mutual."

The confession ignites something primal in him as he shifts, hovering over me with an intensity that steals my breath. But even in this moment of passion, he pauses, his eyes searching mine. "Still okay?" he asks, ever the gentleman.

And wow, I didn't realize those two words could make me want him more, could make me fall for him more.

I nod, words suddenly escaping me. The vulnerability in Jake's eyes is quickly overtaken by desire as he slides his hands up my thighs, bunching the hem of his borrowed shirt and pulling it over my head.

"You're beautiful, Cora," he breathes, his gaze roaming over me like I'm some priceless work of art. His fingers trail down my shoulders, my arms, pausing at my wrists as his thumb brushes the scar on my right hand. "So perfect."

I lean forward, pressing my lips to the scar on his left shoulder. The reminder of the day that brought us together. "And you," I murmur, punctuating each word with a kiss along the jagged line, "are absolutely intoxicating."

Jake groans, the sound vibrating through me as I wrap my legs around him, urging him closer. "Fuck, babe," he pants, his hands tightening on my hips, "if you keep that up, this is going to be over embarrassingly fast."

A laugh bubbles up from somewhere deep inside me. When was the last time I felt this free? This alive? "We can't have that, can we?" I tease, rolling my hips against his just to watch his eyes roll back in pleasure.

The shrill ring of my cell phone cuts through our lust-haze like nails on a chalkboard. We both freeze, the spell momentarily broken.

"Ignore it," Jake pleads, his eyes dark with desire as he dips his head to my abdomen, his fingers making teasing patterns against my skin.

I'm tempted. So, so tempted. But as the ringing persists, reality starts to seep back in. "It could be the furniture company," I groan reluctantly.

Jake's lips curve into a mischievous smile against my skin. "Well, then by all means, answer it," he says, his tone deceptively innocent. "But don't think it means I'm stopping."

With a herculean effort, I reach for my phone, trying to steady my breathing. "H-hello?" I manage, my voice embarrassingly breathy. Jake, the beautiful devil, chooses this moment to press a slow, open-mouthed kiss just below my navel, his eyes locked on mine in a silent challenge.

I bite back a gasp, glaring at him even as heat pools low in my belly. "Y-yes, I'm here," I assure the caller.

As I struggle to focus on the caller's words, I can't help but marvel at the man in front of me. Jake Rhoades, with his crooked smile and haunted eyes, somehow managing to make me feel more in one morning than I have in years.

By some miracle, I conclude the call without betraying Jake's delicious distraction. Tossing the phone aside, I fix him with a mock glare, my body still thrumming with unfulfilled desire.

"You," I accuse, poking his chest, "are trouble."

Jake grins, unrepentant. "Guilty as charged." I stifle a moan as Jake's hands press against the inside of my thigh. "So, what's the verdict? Do we have time for me to finish what I started?" he continues.

Time? Oh, how I wish...

"They'll be here in five minutes," I admit reluctantly.

"Shit," Jake groans, burying his face in my neck. "Rain check then?"

I laugh, running my fingers through his hair. "Definitely."

We lie there for a moment longer, neither wanting to break whatever we've started. Finally, with a sigh, Jake rolls off me, but keeps me close.

"Later," he promises, the word full of meaning.

I lean in, pressing a soft kiss to his lips. "I'm home all day if you want to stop by after your shift at the café."

"I'll be there," he says, but there's a flicker of something in his eyes—a shadow that wasn't there a moment ago.

As I gather my things, I can feel Jake's gaze on me. There's heat there, yes, but also something deeper–a tenderness mixed with a hint of... fear? From what just almost happened? Or...?

"Hey," he calls softly as I reach the door. I turn back, my breath catching at the sight of him, all tousled hair and conflicted eyes. "Thanks for staying."

The simple words carry so much weight. I know he's not just

talking about last night. He's thanking me for seeing him, for not running away from his past, for being here in this moment.

"Anytime," I reply, meaning it more than I've meant anything in a long time.

As I close the door behind me, I can't shake the feeling that something's changed. Jake's words from Friday echo in my mind—about his past, about Tessa and Thomas. I wonder if I've unlocked something in him, something he's not quite ready to face.

A nagging doubt whispers, what will happen if he can't?

23

〜

Cora

I'm lost in a Jake-induced haze, reliving the electric moments from this morning, when an insistent knock jolts me back to reality. Jake? I glance at the time–it's too early for him to be off work, but maybe...

The smile on my lips vanishes as I peek through the peephole. Logan? What fresh hell is this?

Briefly, I consider pretending I'm not home. But as I watch him shift from foot to foot, a bouquet of roses clutched in his hand like some rom-com cliché, I know I can't avoid this confrontation forever. Whatever reason he's here, ignoring him won't make it go away. *Time to put on your big girl pants, Cooper.*

I steel myself, taking a deep breath before opening the door. "Logan," I say, my voice carefully neutral. "This is... unexpected."

His eyes roam over me, and I'm acutely aware that I'm still wearing Jake's shirt. A flash of hurt crosses Logan's face before he masks it with a practiced smile. "You look good, Cora. Really good."

The compliment, once so familiar, now feels hollow. I think of Jake's reverent gaze this morning, how he looked at me like I was the most beautiful thing he'd ever seen, and Logan's words pale in comparison.

Does that show healing or simply that I'm attention starved?

"Thanks," I reply, not bothering to return the sentiment. "What are you doing here, Logan?"

He holds out the roses, a peace offering I have no intention of accepting. "I found some more of your things at the apartment. Thought I'd drop them off." His eyes flick past me, into the apartment. "Can I come in? Just for a minute? I... I need to talk to you about something."

Every instinct screams at me to say no, to shut the door in his face and go back to my Jake-induced haze. But a small, traitorous part of me—the part that spent years loving this man—whispers that I owe him this much.

"Fine," I concede, stepping aside. "But make it quick. I have plans."

Logan picks up a box at his feet, brushing past me as his familiar cologne wafts through the air. For a split second, I'm transported back to our apartment, to a future I thought was certain. The whiplash of emotions leaves me dizzy.

"You've really made this place your own," Logan remarks, his eyes scanning the room. "Our apartment looks so empty in comparison."

Our?

"It's not our apartment anymore, Logan," I say, my voice soft but firm. "You made sure of that."

He flinches, guilt flashing across his face. "I know. I just... God, Cora, I've made such a mess of everything."

The raw honesty in his voice catches me off guard. This isn't the smooth, confident Logan I'm used to. He looks tired. Defeated.

"What's going on, Logan? Why are you really here?"

He runs a hand through his hair, a gesture so familiar it makes my heart ache. "I told my parents about us. About... what I did."

I raise an eyebrow, genuinely surprised. "All of it?"

Logan nods, sinking onto the couch. "Yeah. It was... it was rough. Mom cried. Dad didn't say much, but his disappointment was pretty clear."

I feel a flicker of sympathy. Then I remember the pain he caused me, and it hardens into something colder. "That must be hard for you," I say, not quite able to keep the edge out of my voice.

Logan looks up at me, his eyes pleading. "I know I screwed up, Cora. I know I hurt you, and I'll regret that for the rest of my life. But seeing you here, in this new place, looking so... happy. It just hit me how much I've lost. How much I threw away."

I cross my arms like a shield. "Logan..."

"No, please, let me finish," he interrupts, standing up. "I'm not here to beg for another chance. I know I don't deserve that. I just... I want you to know that I'm getting help. Therapy, to figure out why I did what I did. And I'm making changes at work, trying to find a better balance."

I blink, taken aback by his words. This is a side of Logan I've never seen before–vulnerable, introspective. But can I believe him? Believe he's genuinely trying to change? Or is this just some game? Another attempt to win me back?

"That's... good, Logan," I say carefully. "I hope it helps you."

He takes a step closer. "I know it's too late for us. But I just want you to be happy, Cora. Even if it's not with me. You deserve that."

The sincerity in his voice makes my throat tight. But before I can respond, another knock at the door interrupts us.

Time to put Logan's comment to the test.

My heart races, knowing instinctively who it is. I move to answer it, hyper-aware of Logan's eyes on me. *Here's hoping Jake can trust me this time. That he won't react on instinct.*

As I open the door, Jake's familiar form fills the frame. His smile, so warm and open this morning, falters as he takes in the scene behind me. The transformation is instant–gone is the playful, sweet Jake from this morning, replaced by a man whose walls are visibly slamming into place.

"Jake," I breathe, silently pleading, *please don't do this.* "I didn't expect you so soon."

His eyes meet mine, a storm of emotions swirling in their blue depths. "Clearly," he says, his voice low and controlled. "Should I come back later?"

His question is loaded with subtext. And for the first time, I wonder if this was a bad idea. Exploring this.

"No," I say firmly, reaching for Jake's hand. "Please, stay. Logan was just dropping off a few things. He was about to leave."

I tug Jake inside, desperate to bridge the sudden chasm between us. His hand is tense in mine, and I can feel the rigidity in his body. It's like he's bracing for impact, expecting the worst. The contrast to his openness this morning is stark and painful.

Logan clears his throat, drawing our attention. "So, you two made up, then?" His attempt at casual falls flat, the hurt evident in his voice.

Jake stiffens beside me. There's a darkness in his eyes I've only seen one other time. This is about to get ugly.

"Logan," I warn, my voice low. "Don't."

But Logan, never one to back down, presses on. "Seriously, Cora? After what happened at the concert?"

Jake's thumb strokes my hand, a small gesture that grounds me. When he speaks, his voice is deceptively calm. "You got something to say, man?"

Logan's eyes narrow. "Yeah, actually. How's the eye healing? Still tender?"

"It's fine," Jake replies, his voice tight. "Barely noticeable now. Cheap shot, by the way. But not bad for an accountant."

Logan flinches at the jab, his composure cracking. "At least I can provide for her. What are you gonna do, bartend for the rest of your life?"

"Logan!" I snap, my patience wearing thin. "That's enough. So much for all that 'as long as you're happy' line. You need to leave. Now."

But Jake surprises me, pulling me closer. His lips brush my cheek in a gesture that feels both protective and possessive. "It's okay, babe," he murmurs, his eyes never leaving Logan. "I think we're done here anyway."

Babe? What is this? Confirmation I'm choosing him, or machoism?

Logan's laugh is harsh and humorless. "Guess Cora's cool with you sticking your tongue wherever you please."

Jake goes rigid beside me, a muscle ticking in his jaw. For a moment, I think he might lash out, but then a cold smile spreads across his face. "Do you really want to know where my tongue's been, Logan?"

What the...?

"Okay, that's it," I interject, stepping between them. "Go, Logan."

Logan's face contorts with hurt and anger. "Whatever," he snarls, grabbing his coat. "Enjoy your rebound, Cora. I'll be here when he inevitably fucks up. Again."

As the door slams behind Logan, the silence that follows is deafening. Jake's shoulders slump, the fight draining out of him like air from a punctured balloon. He looks... lost. Scared, even. It's a jarring contrast to the cocky barista I first met.

"Well, that was a shitshow," I mutter.

Jake's laugh is hollow, his eyes fixed on the roses Logan left behind. "Yeah, you could say that." He looks up at me, his expression a mix of frustration and vulnerability. "I'm sorry, Cora. I just... I didn't expect to see him here."

I step closer, reaching for his hand. "I didn't know he was coming by, Jake. If I had, I would've given you a heads-up."

He nods, squeezing my hand before letting go. "I know. It's not your fault. It's just..." He trails off, his gaze distant.

"What is it?" I prompt gently, recognizing the internal struggle playing out on his face.

Jake takes a deep breath. "It's a lot, Cora. Seeing him here, the flowers, thinking about tomorrow... I'm not sure I know how to handle it all. How to be *that* guy to everyone I need to be."

Flowers? He's upset because Logan brought flowers? Wait...

"Tomorrow?" I repeat. "What's tomorrow?"

Jake meets my eyes, and the pain I see there takes my breath away. "It's the anniversary of Tessa and Thomas's... you know. My mom called earlier to remind me about the plans."

Understanding dawns, and my heart aches for him. "Oh, Jake. I'm so sorry. I didn't realize—"

"It's okay," he cuts me off, but his voice is strained. "I thought I could handle it, but now... I'm not so sure."

I reach for him again, but he takes a step back. The distance between us feels like miles.

"Jake," I say softly, "talk to me. Don't shut me out."

He laughs, but there's no humor in it. "Shut you out? Cora, I've barely let you in."

"That's not true," I counter, thinking about our conversation this morning, last Friday. "You've shared more with me than—"

"And maybe that was a mistake," Jake interrupts. The moment the words leave his mouth, I can see regret flash across his face. "No, that's not... fuck. I didn't mean it like that."

His comment stings, but I force myself to remain calm. "Then what did you mean?"

Jake runs both hands through his hair, frustration evident in every line of his body. "I don't know. I thought I was ready for this—for us. But with everything happening... I'm scared I'm going to mess it up. Mess us up."

His honesty catches me off guard. This is the Jake I've been hoping to see—vulnerable, open. I can see the anger simmering just below the surface, but he's trying to keep his composure.

"Jake," I say, taking a cautious step towards him. "Being scared is okay. This is new for both of us. But pushing me away isn't the answer."

He looks at me, conflict clear in his eyes. "I know. I just... I need some time to process. To figure out how to deal with tomorrow without losing sight of... this." He gestures between us. "To be able to separate it all."

Part of me wants to insist on staying, on helping him through this. But I remember my own journey, how sometimes space was what I needed most.

"Okay," I nod, even as my heart clenches. "Take the time you need. But Jake?" I wait until his eyes meet mine. "Remember you're not alone in this. When you're ready to talk, I'm here."

Relief washes over his face, mingled with something that looks a lot like affection. "Thank you, Cora. I... I'll call you later, okay?"

As he turns to leave, I can't help but add, "And Jake? You're stronger than you think. You've got this."

He pauses at the door, a small smile tugging at his lips. "You really are an angel. I hope you know that."

"I've just been through a lot of therapy," I admit, trying to lighten the mood.

Jake studies me for a long moment, his expression softening. He takes a step closer, then stops, as if caught between the desire to stay and the need to go. "I'm sorry I messed all this up today. I want to be better for you, Cora. I really do. But I need to sort through some things first. On my own."

I nod, understanding even as disappointment settles in my chest. "I get it. Just... don't forget I'm here, okay?"

"Trust me," Jake says, his voice rough with emotion, "that's not something I could ever forget."

He leans in, pressing a soft kiss to my forehead that lingers just a moment too long to be casual. "I'll call you," he murmurs against my skin before pulling away. He pauses as his hand reaches the doorknob again. "Cora, I..." he starts, then chews on his lip, seemingly at a loss for words.

"I know," I say, understanding the unspoken sentiment. "Me too."

With a final, intense look that says more than words ever could, Jake steps out, the door closing behind him with a soft click.

24

∽

Jake

December 19ᵗʰ

The cemetery gate creaks open, the sound grating against my already frayed nerves. I kill the engine but can't bring myself to exit the car just yet. My hands grip the steering wheel, knuckles white against the chill seeping through the windows.

How did I end up here? Not just in this graveyard, but in this mess of emotions?

Yesterday morning, I woke up with Cora in my arms, feeling hopeful for the first time in years. Now, barely twenty-four hours later, I'm right back where I started—alone, conflicted, and facing ghosts I thought I'd buried long ago.

I close my eyes, memories of yesterday flooding in like a badly mixed track: Cora's smile, soft and warm in the morning light. Owen's text about the band's social media. Opening the app and seeing those damn photos from five years ago. Graduation. All of us grinning like idiots. Me and Tessa.

If I'd only known what was about to happen. What was already happening.

Then fucking Logan, showing up at Cora's place, looking like he'd

"

stepped out of a fucking Forbes photo shoot. He was the cherry on my sabotage-sundae.

And just like the Jake I've come to know, I retreated into old habits, pushing Cora away instead of letting her in. But, fuck, if he didn't call me out on my inability to be deserving.

I cringe, remembering how close I came to reaching for a bottle. But Cora... she saw through my walls. Even after I acted like a complete ass, she still reached out. Still tried to understand. Still wanted to be the angel I've dreamed of.

Her unwavering support both comforts and terrifies me. What if I'm not the man she thinks I am? What if I can't be the person she deserves? The guy who brings flowers and plans dates. The man who doesn't run every time shit gets too real.

The snow crunches under my boots as I finally drag myself out of the car. Each step towards Thomas's grave feels heavier than the last, weighed down by memories and regrets I've carried for far too long.

I brush snowflakes off the headstone, revealing the stark reality carved in granite: Thomas James Rhoades. My brother. My best friend. The guy who stabbed me in the back and then died before I could...

Before I could what? Forgive him? Kill him myself?

"How could you do it?" The words tear from my throat, raw and ragged. "You knew what she meant to me. You knew how much I loved her. It fucking destroyed me. Why her? Why that night?"

My fingers claw at my scalp, tugging at my hair as if I could physically rip out the memories. But they keep coming, a greatest hits album of misery:

Staying up with Owen in the living room after the family party at my parents' house.

Tessa and Thomas going to bed early.

Waking up to find Tessa crying in Thomas's room.

The silent drive back to her dorm.

Her confession, shattering my world in five brutal minutes. She'd slept with Thomas. Fallen in love with him.

Punching Thomas. Telling him I never wanted to see his face again.

If I'd known it'd be the last time...

"Why couldn't you have just stayed the fuck away from her?" I scream at the unforgiving stone. "If you had just left her alone, maybe..." The rest catches in my throat, choking me.

Maybe you wouldn't have died.

Maybe I wouldn't still hate you.

All the fucking study groups they did together. All the rehearsals and performances she was at. Their internship out east the previous summer. I was so fucking clueless. The two people I trusted wholeheartedly tore me to shreds with one blow.

Tears blur my vision, hot trails of regret on my face. Five years of running, of drowning myself in booze and meaningless hookups. For what? To protect myself? To punish a dead man? To push away anyone that makes me happy? Anyone who makes me feel like, maybe, I'm not beyond saving?

The silence of the cemetery presses in, broken only by the occasional crunch of snow as I shift my weight. My breath fogs in the air, each exhale carrying the weight of words I can't bring myself to say. To Thomas. To Cora. To myself.

"I don't know how to do this, man," I mutter, my voice barely above a whisper. "How to forgive you. How to stop hating you. How to..." I trail off, choking on the truth. *How to live without you.*

The answer used to be simple: don't live. Just exist. Drift through life in a haze of alcohol and meaningless gigs. But now? Cora's back. And the thought of her makes everything so much more complicated.

"She makes me want to try, Thomas," I admit. "Said I was enough," I laugh, the sound harsh and bitter in the quiet cemetery. "Thinks I'm the guy you always said I could be. Isn't that fucked up?"

I close my eyes, memories washing over me. Thomas, Owen, and me, staying up late, dreaming about the future. About the band making it big. About changing the world with our music even though he had the brains to do so much more.

"Remember how you used to say our songs could save lives?" I ask the silent stone. "I never told you, but she saved mine. Not only during my accident. But the day you died. And I think... I think maybe she's here to do it again. I just don't know if I deserve it."

The guilt rises like bile in my throat. "Why'd you run to her after, man? Why'd you offer to drive her when you knew—" I swallow down the lump in my throat. "You knew how much it destroyed me."

A twig snaps behind me, the sound like a gunshot in the stillness. I whirl around, my heart leaping into my throat.

Mom.

Her face is a mirror of my own pain, eyes red-rimmed and puffy. How long has she been standing there? How much did she hear?

"Jacob," she whispers, her voice breaking on my name.

And suddenly, I'm not a 28-year-old man with a chip on my shoulder and guitar calluses. I'm that scared, angry kid again, desperate for someone to tell me it's all going to be okay.

"Mom," I choke out, and then she's there, arms wrapping around me, holding me together as I start to fall apart.

All the anger, all the pain, all the guilt I've been carrying for five long years comes pouring out in great, heaving sobs. I cling to her like a lifeline, face buried in her shoulder, breathing in the familiar scent of her perfume.

"I'm sorry," I gasp between sobs, not even sure what I'm apologizing for. For pushing her away? For not being there? For surviving when Thomas didn't?

"Shh," she soothes, running a hand through my hair like she did when I was little. "It's okay, Jake. It's okay."

But it's not okay. It hasn't been okay for five years. And as I pull back, meeting her tear-filled gaze, I see a flicker of something in her eyes. Something that makes my blood run cold.

Fear.

"Mom?" I ask, my voice barely above a whisper. "What is it?"

She takes a deep breath, her hands trembling as she reaches for mine. "There's something I need to tell you," she says, her voice quavering. "Something I should have told you a long time ago."

Bile rises in my throat as her lips part, the words that follow hitting me like a wrecking ball.

"I knew." Her whisper stops my world, the air suddenly too thick to breathe. "I knew about them, Jake. About everything. I didn't know if you did. I didn't want you to hate him."

No. This can't be happening.

I stumble backwards, shaking my head, as if I could physically reject her words. But they're already burrowing into my brain, poisonous and inescapable.

"You knew...?" The question claws its way out of my throat, each syllable more painful than the last. "All this time, you knew Tessa betrayed me? With him??"

I double over, a fresh wave of agony tearing through me. Somehow, this makes it infinitely worse and better at the same time. The permanent knot of guilt loosens around my throat, allowing me to breathe even as the ground crumbles beneath my feet.

Mom reaches for me, but I recoil violently, a tidal wave of bitterness and betrayal crashing over me. She knew! Every sleepless night I spent battling nightmares, every waking moment consumed by anguish—she remained silent!

"Don't push me away," she pleads, her voice breaking. "Don't think for a second this secret hasn't consumed me, too. I just... I couldn't lose you, too."

"How?" I manage to spit out, the single word dripping with five years of pent-up pain.

"He came to me," she sobs, the answer tumbling out in a rush. "That morning, after you left. He was so upset, Jake. He confessed everything. He wanted my advice on how to make things right. He didn't... he didn't feel the same way she did. He said it was a mistake."

He didn't feel the same way?

The revelation hits me like a freight train, derailing every assumption I've clung to for the past five years. I sink to my knees in the snow, my legs no longer able to support the weight of this new reality.

"I told him to go to her," Mom continues, her voice thick with tears. "To make it clear that it could never happen again. That his bond with you meant more than anything. I thought... if he set things straight... if Tessa understood the depth of the pain she caused... But then..."

She dissolves into heart-wrenching sobs, her body shaking uncontrollably. And suddenly, I see it—the guilt that's been eating her alive all these years. She blames herself.

"I told him he was dead to me," I choke out, the confession ripping from somewhere deep inside me. "Those were the last words I ever said to him, Mom. I wanted him to suffer the way I was suffering... I wanted him..."

"No, Jake. No," she cries, dropping to her knees beside me.

I lunge into her arms, desperate for something solid to cling to as the world spins off its axis. We hold each other tightly, united in our grief, staring down at the grave that lies between us.

Everything I thought I knew, every truth I held onto, is suddenly turned on its head. The anger that's fueled me for five years sputters and dies, leaving behind a yawning emptiness.

"Please don't hate him, Jake," Mom whispers, her tears soaking through my shirt. "He loved you more than anything."

He loved me... not her. But still, he made a choice. A choice that shattered our bond, a choice that led to his untimely end.

I don't know if I can ever fully forgive him for the role he played in this twisted tale. But here, cradled in my mother's embrace, her love and forgiveness washing over me, I begin to understand that holding onto blame and bitterness has only ever poisoned one soul—my own.

"I miss him," I finally confess, my gaze fixed on the cold granite of his headstone. The anger that once consumed me slowly gives way to a profound, aching sadness.

"Me too," Mom whispers, her eyes filled with a newfound understanding as she looks at me. She wipes at her tear-stained cheeks and exhales slowly, as if she's tucking away the emotions that have been laid bare, burying them deep within herself once more.

It makes me wonder how she's dealt with it all this time, how she's remained so strong despite her own guilt. Was it for me?

The thought brings an entirely different kind of guilt, shame at how selfish I've been, thinking I'm the only one who has been hurting, who lost something so precious.

As we stand, brushing snow from our clothes, I feel different. Not healed—not by a long shot—but... lighter. Like maybe, just maybe, there's a path forward through all this pain.

I think of Cora, of her unwavering belief in me. Of the way she makes me want to be better. And for the first time in five years, I feel a flicker of hope.

Maybe it's time to stop running from the ghosts of my past. To face them head-on, no matter how much it hurts. And maybe, someday, I'll find a way to forgive—not just Thomas, but myself as well.

When I reach my parents' driveway, I pull out my phone, bypassing Cora's name to scroll to another contact.

"Hey, it's Jake," I say when the line connects. "I think... I think I'm ready to talk about that therapist you mentioned."

It's a small step, but it's something. Because it's time I stop expecting someone else to save me and learn how to save myself.

25

∾

Cora

December 20ᵗʰ

I toss the manuscript onto my growing "reject" pile with a sigh. Another impossibly perfect meet-cute between two impossibly perfect people. If I have to read one more story about soulmates finding each other through the magic of hashtags and carefully curated Instagram feeds, I might hurl my laptop out the window.

Who am I kidding? My editor's paycheck depends on this fairy tale fodder. But after the rollercoaster of the past few days, these stories feel about as realistic as a unicorn prancing down Michigan Avenue.

Speaking of fairy tales gone sideways...

My eyes drift to my silent phone for the millionth time today. No missed calls. No texts. Radio silence from Jake since yesterday afternoon with a promise to "explain soon."

I've respected his need for space. Really, I have. But the urge to reach out, to make sure he's okay after facing such painful memories, gnaws at me like an over-caffeinated terrier.

Before I can talk myself out of it, I'm typing Jake's name into the search bar. It's not stalking if his profile is public, right? Just... thorough research. Yeah, that's it.

The Jake staring back at me from those early posts is a stranger. Bright-eyed and grinning, arms slung around a raven-haired beauty who must be Tessa. There he is again, sandwiched between Owen and a younger guy with the same ocean-blue eyes. Thomas. My heart clenches, knowing the tragedy that awaits this smiling trio.

I scroll faster, watching the transformation play out in pixels. The carefree college kid morphs into the brooding heartthrob, guitar in hand, eyes smoldering for the camera. It's like watching a butterfly fold itself back into a cocoon.

And then... nothing. For years. Just the occasional band update, devoid of personal content. Until a few weeks ago—a candid shot of Jake, mid-laugh behind the bar at Sadie's. Posted by the band's account, not Jake's. But still. It's the first glimpse of that unguarded smile I've seen in his entire feed.

Is it a coincidence that it's right around the time we reconnected?

I shake my head, banishing the thought. Don't go there, Cooper. You're not some magic fix-it fairy for Jake's demons.

But as I stare at that laughing photo, I hold onto hope that the carefree Jake could return.

I look down at my phone, feeling like some romance-novel-obsessed cyberstalker. What am I doing?

I need air. I need perspective. I need...

I glance at the screen. 8 PM on Wednesday. I need to not be that girl who shows up uninvited at her maybe-boyfriend's workplace.

But as I slip on my favorite college hoodie (bright orange, because subtlety is clearly my strong suit), I know exactly where my feet will take me.

Sorry, Jake. Sometimes a girl's gotta write her own story.

The crisp December air hits me like a wake-up call as I step outside. It's one of those rare mid-fifties days that make you question your entire Midwestern existence. Teenagers in shorts sprint past bundled-up tourists, and the streets buzz with pre-Christmas energy. I pop in my earbuds, hoping music will drown out the voice in my head screaming "bad idea" on repeat.

My treacherous feet carry me through the city, each step feeling like I'm wading deeper into questionable decision territory. Before I know it, I'm staring up at the neon sign of Sadie's, wondering if I've finally lost my romance-addled mind.

I hover outside, caught in a rom-com plot of my own making. Do I saunter in like I own the place? Pretend I just "happened" to be in the neighborhood? Or turn tail and run before I embarrass myself further?

The universe, ever helpful, makes the decision for me as a group of giggling women spill out the door. Their cloud of perfume and excitement washes over me, and suddenly I'm inside, blinking in the dim light like a mole thrust into daylight.

Reality check: I'm in a swanky bar on a Wednesday evening, wearing a hoodie that makes me look like a traffic cone with legs. *Smooth move, Cora.*

I scan the room, my heart doing a little flip when I spot Jake behind the bar. He's laughing at something a brunette in a skintight dress is saying, all easy charm and devastating smiles. Definitely not the depressed, brooding sight I expected to find after the silence.

He's working. He has to be personable. That's his job, dummy.

Before I can make my grand exit (or melt into a puddle of embarrassment on the floor), a slightly familiar voice breaks through the ambient chatter.

"Cora? Is that you?"

I turn to find Chris grinning at me, his sandy hair artfully tousled in that 'I woke up like this' way that probably took an hour to achieve.

"Chris! Hi!" My voice comes out unnaturally high. "Fancy meeting you here. In this bar. Do, uh, you work here, too?"

Chris's grin widens. "Nah. But I do perform here on Thursdays. With the band," he says casually, eyeing my decidedly un-bar-like attire. *Play here on Thursday?* "Just here with some friends. What about you?"

"Me?" I laugh nervously. "I was just... out for a walk. Thought I'd pop in for a quick drink."

"Interesting choice of venues," he muses. "But since you're here, I'll gladly buy you one. Maybe catch up."

Buy me a drink? Warning bells go off in my head. This is veering dangerously close to date territory, and the last thing I need is to complicate my already messy love life. But before I can formulate a graceful exit strategy, Chris's arm is around my shoulders, steering me towards the bar. Towards Jake, who's now chatting with the red-haired bartender.

Abort, Cora.

"You know, I actually forgot I need to, um... feed my cat." *My cat?*

Chris glances at me confused, but it's too late. Stormy blue eyes find mine, confusion quickly shifting to something more dangerous as he notices Chris's arm around me.

In the span of a heartbeat, Jake's out from behind the bar and in front of us.

"Jake, hey," Chris says coolly.

Jake's lips twitch, gaze trained on me. For a split second, I see a flicker of... something. Surprise? Anger? Before I can decipher it, his face smooths into a neutral mask.

"Cora," he says, his voice carefully controlled. "This is unexpected."

Unexpected that I'm here, or with Chris, I want to ask.

Chris, oblivious to the tension crackling between us, leans in conspiratorially. "I was just about to buy this lovely lady a drink. Any recommendations for someone with..." he pauses, giving me an obvious once-over, "...such unique taste?"

I bristle at the backhanded compliment, but Jake beats me to the punch.

"I'm gonna borrow this lovely lady for a moment," he says, his tone brooking no argument.

Chris looks between us, confusion evident on his face. "Uh, sure. I'll catch up with you later, Cora?"

As Chris retreats, Jake's eyes bore into mine. "We need to talk," he says quietly. "Now."

Jake steers me to a dimly lit corner, his hand burning a trail of electricity along my lower back. Great. Now I'm living out every cliché I've ever edited.

"What are you doing here, Cora?" Jake's voice is low, intense.

I laugh nervously, aiming for nonchalance and probably landing somewhere between 'mildly unhinged' and 'future restraining order recipient.' "Oh, you know. Just out for a casual stroll. In my favorite hoodie. Totally normal Wednesday behavior."

Jake's eyes narrow, not buying my act for a second. "Cora."

I deflate like a day-old birthday balloon. "Fine. I was worried about you, okay? After yesterday... I just wanted to make sure you were all right."

Something flickers in Jake's eyes that looks a lot like relief. *Relief?* "You came here for me? And Chris...?"

Is that the bigger issue? Chris?

"Chris is friends with Alyssa," I say matter-of-factly. "I ran into him when I was too nervous to come over and say hi. You know, giving you space and all."

When Jake simply tilts his head, I rush to add, "Look, this was clearly a mistake. I'll just go, and we can pretend this never–"

"Jake!" A high-pitched squeal crashes into our conversation.

I turn to see a blonde straight out of a Barbie factory catalog sashaying towards us, all legs and lip gloss and predatory intent.

"There you are!" she coos, completely ignoring my existence. "I've been looking everywhere for you, silly. Are we still on for tonight?"

Jake tenses beside me. "Lindsey," he says, his voice strained. "Now's not a good time."

Lindsey's eyes finally decide to acknowledge my presence, raking over me with the kind of disdain usually reserved for gum on designer shoes. "Oh," she says, her voice dripping with faux sweetness. "I didn't realize you were... busy. With the walking fashion disaster."

I feel Jake shift beside me, his arm snaking around my waist to pull me closer. "Actually," he says, his voice taking on warmth, "I'm very busy. With my girlfriend."

Girlfriend?

My brain short-circuits, leaving me gaping like a fish out of water. Jake's hand tightens on my hip, and déjà vu hits. Are we pretending?

"That's right," I hear myself say, snuggling closer to Jake. "So sorry to crash your plans, but you know how it is. Can't keep my hands off this one."

Lindsey's face contorts like she's just bitten into a lemon soaked in vinegar. "Whatever," she spits, turning on her impossibly high heels. "Enjoy your... downgrade."

As she storms off, I turn to Jake, my heart pounding a samba against my ribs. "Girlfriend, huh?"

Jake has the grace to look sheepish. "I panicked," he admits. "Lindsey's been... persistent. I thought maybe if she thought I was taken..."

"So I'm your human shield against overzealous groupies?" I ask, trying to keep my voice light despite the ache blooming in my chest. "Gee, every girl's dream."

Jake's eyes widen. "No! God, no. Cora, that's not..." He takes a deep breath, his gaze intense. "None of this with you has been an act. Not one second."

The sincerity in his voice makes my knees weak. Or maybe that's just the adrenaline crash. "Jake," I start, not even sure what I want to say.

"I know," he says softly. "I know I've been all over the place. Monday was a walk down memory lane. And yesterday was... more than I expected."

He runs a hand through his hair, a gesture I'm starting to recognize as his 'I'm about to bare my soul' tell. "I don't... I don't want to be a mystery to you. I should've been honest about what I was feeling Monday night. About what happened that night."

"Jake," I start, "I've told you from the beginning you don't have to say what you aren't ready to."

He reaches for my hand, twisting our fingers together. "That's just it. I'm ready. I want to, Cora. I... I needed to know that I was doing it for the right reasons. Not just because I needed someone to save me again."

"I never thought—"

Jake squeezes my hands, and I pause. "It was Thomas," he says softly. "Who Tessa fell in love with. Who she was cheating on me with."

His brother? And I thought Logan and his co-worker was terrible. But if it were Arden...? The thought alone makes me physically ill.

"Yesterday, at the cemetery, I thought I knew what I was facing. My guilt, my anger at Thomas. But then my mom showed up, and..."

Jake's voice cracks, and I resist the urge to wrap him in my arms. Instead, I wait, giving him the space to find his words.

"She knew, Cora. She knew about Thomas and Tessa. All this time, she's been carrying that secret, thinking she was protecting me." He laughs, but it's a hollow sound. "She told him to cut things off. Told me what happened between them was a mistake, a moment of weakness that spiraled out of control. That it was why he offered to drive..."

I blink, trying to process this bombshell. "Oh, Jake..."

His eyes find mine, and the vulnerability I see there takes my breath away. "When I left yesterday, I needed time to process. To figure out who I am without all that anger and guilt weighing me down. But then I saw you with Chris, and I just... I couldn't bear the thought of you thinking I didn't want you."

My heart does a little somersault. "You... want me?"

Jake's laugh is genuine this time. "Cora, I've wanted you since the moment you walked back into my life. Hell, maybe even since you pulled me out of that wreck six years ago. I just didn't think I deserved you."

"And now?" I ask, hardly daring to breathe.

"Now?" He steps closer, his hand coming up to cup my cheek. "Now, I still think I don't deserve you. But I want to try to be the kind of man who does. If you'll have me."

I can't help the snort that escapes me. "If I'll have you? Jake, I showed up at your workplace in a hoodie that makes me look like a sentient traffic cone. I think it's safe to say I'm all in."

His smile is like the sun breaking through clouds. "God, I've missed your snark."

"It's been less than two days," I point out.

"Two days too long," he murmurs, his thumb tracing my lower lip. "I'm sorry I didn't reach out. I just... I wanted to be sure. To know that when I came back to you, it was for real. No more running, no more hiding behind my past."

I nod, understanding dawning. "And are you? Sure, I mean?"

Jake's eyes never leave mine as he speaks. "I'm sure that you make me want to be the man I used to be. That when I'm with you, all the noise in my head quiets down. I'm sure that I want to see where this goes, even if it scares the hell out of me."

"It scares me, too," I admit. "I'm not exactly the poster child for healthy relationships."

Jake grins. "Then I guess we're a matching set of emotional baggage," he says, leaning in to brush his lips over mine. "My angel."

A laugh escapes. "An angel? In this getup? More like a crossing guard who raided a college student's laundry basket."

Jake's eyes crinkle with amusement as he takes a step back, his gaze sweeping over my less-than-stellar ensemble. "Hey, don't knock it. You're single-handedly bringing traffic cone chic to the masses."

"Oh good, I've always wanted to be a fashion icon," I deadpan. "Move over, Anna Wintour. There's a new sheriff in town, and she's dressed like a construction zone."

Jake's laugh is rich and warm, sending little sparks of joy through my chest. It's a sound I could get used to hearing. A lot.

Just then, a crash from the bar reminds us where we are. Jake winces, glancing over his shoulder. "I should probably..."

"Go," I nod, trying not to let disappointment seep into my voice. "You know, do your job. That thing they pay you for."

He turns back to me, hesitation clear in his eyes. "I don't want this to end," he admits softly.

Do I? Am I ready for whatever comes next after the emotional rollercoaster of the last few weeks? I think about our night together last weekend. Yeah, I'm willing to try.

"Well," I say, aiming for casual and probably landing somewhere between 'overeager teenager' and 'desperately trying to play it cool,' "I hear you bartenders work most nights. But rumor has it you get days off occasionally. You know, when the planets align and Mercury's in retrograde or whatever."

Jake's lips quirk up in a smirk. "Are you asking me out, Coco?"

"Me? Ask out the sexy bartender who just called me his girlfriend? Perish the thought," I retort, my cheeks flushing traitorously.

"Mmm," Jake hums, his eyes dancing with mischief. "And here I was, about to clear my incredibly busy schedule tomorrow afternoon just to spend time with a certain romance editor. But if you're not interested..."

My heart does a little jig in my chest. "Well, if you're offering, I suppose I could pencil you in."

Jake grins, pulling me close for one more quick kiss that leaves me dizzy. "It's a date. I've got rehearsal until four, but after that, I'm all yours. At least until we're on stage at nine."

Stage? Chris's comment from earlier resurfaces. *They play here. Thursdays.* Why was I never informed of this?

A thought strikes me, and before I can overthink it, I blurt out, "Can I come? To see you play, I mean. Here. Tomorrow."

Jake's eyes widen in surprise, then soften with something that looks suspiciously like adoration. "Yeah. Yeah, I'd like that a lot."

"Great," I beam, already mentally cataloging my closet for something that doesn't scream 'I dressed in the dark while battling a pack of rabid raccoons.' "It's a date. Two dates. We're overachievers."

Jake smiles, giving my hand one last squeeze before reluctantly stepping away. "I'll text you the details for tomorrow. And Cora?" He pauses, his gaze intense. "Thanks for showing up. Even if you did give me a minor heart attack in the process."

I offer a mock salute. "All in a day's work for your friendly neighborhood angel-slash-crossing guard."

As I watch Jake head back to the bar, a warm glow settling in my chest, I can't help but think that maybe–just maybe–I've stumbled into a love story even better than the ones I edit. It's messy and complicated and nothing like I imagined, but then again, aren't those the best kinds of tales?

26

∽

Jake

December 21ˢᵗ

The blank page stares back at me, mocking. I've been sitting here for an hour, pen-poised, waiting for inspiration to strike. But my mind's a broken record, skipping between memories of the past two days on repeat.

Thomas's grave. Mom's confession. Cora in that goddamn orange hoodie.

I close my eyes, but it only makes the images sharper. Cora's smile, the way her eyes light up when she laughs. The warmth of her body pressed against mine, her breathless whispers echoing in my ears.

Before I can overthink it, my pen starts moving:

Your lips on mine, a perfect fit

Two fractured souls uniting

With tender give and take, we'll build

The start of something truly right

I halt, pulse thundering. Christ, when did I turn into such a sap? But even as I cringe at my own corniness, I can't stop the flood of images. Every kiss we've shared. Cora's brilliance, inspiring lyrics I never thought I'd write again. A future I don't deserve but desperately want.

"Looks like someone's got it bad."

I nearly fall off my stool, clutching my notebook to my chest like a teenage girl with a diary. Owen's standing there, grinning like the cat that ate the canary.

"When the hell did you get here?" I growl, trying to slow my racing heart.

Owen's smirk widens. "Long enough to see you mooning over that notebook like it holds the secrets of the universe." He nods at the pages. "Can I see?"

I hesitate, then shrug. What the hell? I hand it over, watching as his eyes scan the words.

"Damn, little brother," he says softly. "She's really got you, doesn't she?"

I open my mouth to deny it, but what's the point? "Yeah," I admit. "She does."

Before Owen can respond, Chris appears, breaking the moment. But it's probably for the best. I'm not ready for a heart-to-heart about my feelings.

"Perfect timing," Owen says, clapping Chris on the shoulder. "I've got news. We just got asked to play the New Year's Eve countdown at Navy Pier!"

His sentence hits me like a shot of top-shelf whiskey, burning and breathtaking all at once. Navy Pier? New Year's Eve? Holy shit.

As Owen explains the logistics–two songs, tight schedule with our gig here–I'm already picturing it. The crowd, the energy, Cora watching from the sidelines...

"Think we can have that new song ready by then?" Owen asks, tapping my notebook.

I glance down at the lovesick scribbles, a mix of terror and determination coursing through me. Ten days? "Yeah," I hear myself say. "We can make it happen."

As the guys head to the stage, I find myself reaching for my phone, Cora's name glowing on the screen. Should I tell her about Navy Pier? Part of me wants to shout it from the rooftops, but another part–the part that's been burned before–whispers that it's too soon, that I'll jinx it somehow.

In the end, I settle for a text.

Me: *Can't wait to see you later. Dress warm. I've got a surprise.*

Cryptic? Maybe. But hey, a guy's gotta maintain some air of mystery, right?

The rest of rehearsal flies by in a blur of chord progressions and lyric sheets. By the time we wrap up, my fingers are aching and my throat's raw, but there's an energy thrumming through me that I haven't felt in years.

"Alright, boys," Owen says, clapping me on the back. "See you all in a few hours. And Jake? Try not to look so terrified. It's just a date."

I roll my eyes, but my stomach does a little flip. Just a date. Right.

Why the hell did I tell him?

As I make my way home, doubts start creeping in like uninvited guests at a party. What am I doing? I'm not boyfriend material. I'm barely functional adult material. And Cora? She deserves someone who's got their shit together, not a walking disaster with a guitar.

I pause outside my apartment, key in hand, contemplating calling the whole thing off. It'd be easier, right? Safer. For both of us.

But then I remember the way Cora looked at me in that ridiculous orange hoodie, like I was worth something. Like maybe I could be the guy she deserves.

And, damn, I want to be.

Fuck it. I'm doing this. Time to be the Jake I used to be.

I shower in record time, spending an embarrassing amount of time deciding what to wear. Since when did I start caring about this shit? When my starry-eyed angel showed back up and made me want to be someone worth saving, that's when.

I stand in front of the mirror, adjusting my shirt for the millionth time as a familiar voice in my head pipes up. *You're gonna screw this up, Rhoades. Just like you screw up everything else.*

I grip the edge of the sink, forcing myself to take a deep breath. No. Not this time. I'm not the same guy I was five years ago. Hell, I'm not even the same guy I was two weeks ago.

I grab the small gift bag from the counter, giving myself one last once-over. My palms are sweating like I'm about to play Madison Square Garden instead of taking a girl to see a Christmas tree. Christ, I'm a mess.

It's just a date, I remind myself. With the girl who's got you writing love songs for the first time in five years. With the girl who keeps saving you from yourself. No pressure.

I head for Cora's door, my heart pounding a rhythm that could rival any drum solo. Here goes nothing.

Or maybe everything.

Cora opens the door, and for a second, I forget how to breathe. She's traded in the traffic cone hoodie for a deep green sweater that makes her eyes pop like fireworks.

"Wow," I manage, eloquent as ever. "You look... not like a crossing guard."

She rolls her eyes, but I catch the hint of a smile. "Be still my beating heart. Such romance."

"Hey, I'm saving all my smooth moves for later," I grin, offering her the gift bag. "For you."

Cora's eyebrows shoot up as she pulls out a pair of earmuffs. "Um, thanks? I think?"

"Trust me," I say, taking them and gently placing them on her head. "You'll need these where we're going."

"Which is where, exactly?" she asks, adjusting the earmuffs.

I tap the side of my nose. "Then it wouldn't be a secret. Now, shall we?"

As we head to the L station, Cora keeps shooting me suspicious glances. "You know, in most of the books I edit, mysterious outings end with the heroine tied up in a basement."

I can't help but laugh. "Kinky. But I was thinking something a little more... festive."

"Because we both love this holiday so much," she deadpans.

I guide her toward the platform, grinning. "Maybe it's time we find a reason to."

The train ride is a comedy of errors. We're packed in like sardines, and every lurch of the car sends Cora stumbling into me. Not that I'm complaining, mind you.

"So," Cora says, her face mashed against my chest as we sway with the train's movement. "This is cozy."

"Just wait," I murmur into her hair. "The night's young."

When we finally reach our stop, I lead Cora out into the crisp night air, still scarcely believing she's giving me this opportunity.

"Soooo Miss Romance Queen," I drawl, bumping her shoulder. "How about a quick lesson on dating? What's your ideal date activity? You know, for future reference."

Cora pretends to think about it before answering, "Dancing. What about you? What would you choose to do?"

I shrug, not able to contain my smile. "Honestly, anything involving music. Dancing included."

As we round the corner, the Millennium Park Christmas tree comes into view, a towering giant dripping with lights.

Cora's gasp is audible even over the bustling crowd. "Oh, Jake," she breathes, her eyes wide with wonder. "It's beautiful."

I watch her face, mesmerized by the way the lights dance in her eyes. "Yeah," I say softly. "It is."

We spend the next hour wandering around the tree, Cora snapping photos and dragging me into selfies. I'd normally rather gargle glass than pose for pictures, but the joy on her face makes it impossible to say no.

"You know," Cora says as we start heading back to the station, her gloved hand warm in mine, "for a brooding musician, you're pretty good at this date thing."

I puff out my chest in mock pride. "I aim to please. But the night's not over yet, angel. You ready to see me in action?"

Cora's eyes gleam mischievously. "Depends. Are we talking about your musical skills or...?"

I nearly choke on air, heat rushing to my face. "Jesus, Cora. Warn a guy before you say shit like that."

Her laughter echoes through the night air as we board the train. Another packed ride with Cora pressed against me. Shucks.

"Have to admit," she murmurs, her breath warm against my neck, "thinking about you holding a guitar has my head spinning already."

I smirk, trying to keep my cool despite the electricity crackling between us. "That so? I should've invited you weeks ago, then."

The train ride passes in a daze of heated glances and not-so-accidental touches. By the time we stumble out at our stop, we're both a little breathless and more than a little worked up.

As we walk toward Sadie's, Cora nestles into my side, her pace slowing. "Hey, what are you doing for Christmas next week?" she asks, looking up at me through those killer lashes.

The question catches me off guard. Christmas. Right. That's a thing normal people do.

"I'm actually staying at my parents' place on Christmas Eve," I admit, the words feeling strange on my tongue. "It'll be the first time I've slept over since they moved."

Cora's eyes widen slightly, and I can practically see her biting back a dozen questions. But she just nods, a soft smile on her lips. "That's great, Jake. Really."

Is it, though? The thought of spending a whole night as a family makes my stomach churn. Will we go back to our old traditions? Will the memories be too much to handle? But after everything that happened at the cemetery, after Mom's confession... I knew it was time to stop running. From everything.

"Yeah, I guess it is," I say, more to convince myself than her. "It's just... it's been a long time, you know? Last time I was there for Christmas, Thomas was..." I trail off, the rest sticking in my throat.

Cora squeezes my hand, her touch grounding me. "It's okay to be nervous," she says softly. "But I'm proud of you for going."

Her words hit me like a sucker punch to the gut. Proud. When was the last time anyone said that to me?

"I don't know if I'm ready," I confess, the honesty surprising even me. "But I think... I think I want to be. Does that make sense?"

Cora nods, her eyes shining with something that looks a lot like understanding. "It makes perfect sense. And Jake? It's okay if it's not perfect. Just being there, trying... that's what matters."

I let out a breath I didn't know I was holding, feeling something loosen in my chest. Maybe this is what moving forward feels like.

"What about you?" I ask, suddenly desperate to change the subject. "Any big holiday plans?"

"Florida," she says, her breath fogging in the cold air. "I told you that, right?"

I shake my head, a knot forming in my stomach. "You're leaving? When? Why?"

She peers up at me, cheeks dimpling as she struggles to contain a smile. "My parents moved to Florida six years ago. Arden and I always go down to spend the holiday there. We fly out Saturday morning." Her eyes dance with mirth. "Gonna miss me or something?"

Fuck, yes. More than I probably should after such a short time. The thought of her being gone, even for a week, makes my chest tight. But it's also a relief, in a way. A chance to get my head on straight, to make sure I'm doing this for the right reasons.

I slide my hand across her cheek, tracing her jawline to her softly parted lips. "Absolutely," I say, meaning it more than I've meant anything in a long time.

Her lips part subtly, cheeks blooming pink. She sways closer as I trace their fullness, restraint hanging by an agonizing thread. "Maybe you could show me how much before I go?"

Desire rockets through me, but a glance at my watch brings me back to reality. "Soon," I vow. "Right now, I've got a show to put on. And you, angel, have a front-row seat."

As we push through the doors of Sadie's, the familiar cacophony washing over us, I can't shake the bittersweet knowledge that our time is limited. But maybe that's okay. Maybe it'll make every moment count that much more.

Time to show Cora Cooper exactly what she'd be missing in Florida. And hopefully, show myself that I'm capable of being more than the screw-up I've been for too many years.

27

∾

Cora

The final sultry note hangs in the air like a promise, and I swear the temperature in Sadie's just spiked ten degrees. I fan myself dramatically, torn between swooning and rolling my eyes at my own cliché reaction. Jake drops the mic with a smirk that should be illegal in at least forty-eight states.

Did my life just turn into a romance novel?

As Jake saunters towards me, all sweat-dampened and swaggering, I'm hit with the realization that this seductive musician version of him is even more potent than I remembered. It's like he's stepped right out of one of my manuscripts, but better–because he's real, and he's mine.

Mine? Is he fully mine? Am I ready for it if he is?

"Did you find that last one... inspiring, Coco?" Jake leans in, his voice a gravelly purr that does things to my insides that I'm pretty sure aren't medically possible.

I gulp as his hands–those ridiculously talented musician's hands–slide teasingly down my hips. Oh boy, I'm in trouble.

"Someone clearly has a high opinion of his talents tonight," I quip, aiming for breezy but probably landing closer to 'desperately trying not to jump him in public.'

Jake clicks his tongue, eyes dancing with mischief. "Not impressed? I could offer an exclusive encore performance at my place tonight."

Damn, is Jake smooth when he's trying. But I've edited enough romance novels to know how to play this game.

I tilt my chin, channeling every coy heroine I've ever rolled my eyes at. "Hmm, I suppose I could listen a little longer." I walk two fingers up his arm, thrilled when his breath catches. "Only because you've worked so hard today to prove there's more substance beneath all this rock star swagger."

Jake's laugh is low and rich, sending shivers down my spine. "The things you do to me, Cora Cooper." His fingers trail along my jaw, and I'm pretty sure I've forgotten how to breathe. "Give me fifteen minutes to wrap up, and then I'm all yours, 'kay?"

I nod, suddenly tongue-tied, as he strolls back toward his adoring fans. I watch him go, equal parts smitten and terrified. This perfectly imperfect man has me completely captivated, heart and soul. So much for my afternoon pep talk about taking things slow.

I'm still grinning into my cocktail, already envisioning a future of watching Jake perform weekly, when my phone vibrates against the table. The name on the screen hits me like a bucket of ice water.

Logan.

Logan: *Can we talk before you leave on Saturday?*

Logan: *I'm heading down to Florida this year, too. Would love to clear a few things up.*

What? Logan's family is hosting Christmas in Florida now? How perfectly inconvenient. When we were together, the fact that his aunt lived thirty minutes from my parents was a blessing. Now, it has me sick to my stomach, curious about what he's planning. Hopefully, it's not something stupid like showing up on Christmas morning.

Though protective, Big Brother Mark, might kill him if he tried. Especially since Jake and Mark are BFFs.

Maybe that'll work in my favor...

I slide my phone into my purse and head toward the bar. Logan's text can wait. No need to worry about what I can't control. I distract myself chatting with Natalie instead, waiting for Jake to finish up.

A few minutes later, an arm snakes around my stomach. "Ready to go home, babe?" Jake asks, warm breath fanning my ear.

I shiver, turning to meet Jake's overly eager gaze. My chest hurts from the joy radiating at the sight. He presses a soft kiss to my forehead, smirking, before glancing at Natalie. "Thanks for keeping her company, Nat. But if you don't mind, I'm gonna take her away now."

Natalie flashes a pleased grin. "Have fun, you two."

"Plan to," he responds, already tugging me—now beat red—away. "Night, Nat. See you tomorrow."

We walk toward the apartment, hand in hand, our leisure footsteps echoing on the empty sidewalks. Jake's more alive on the walk back than I've ever seen him. And when he swings up our linked hands with carefree rigor, happiness bubbles out before I can contain it.

Jake pauses beneath a lamp, head tilted curiously. "Are you laughing at me, Cora?"

"No." I flush, pressing fingers to my grinning lips. "I just don't think I've seen you like this before."

He smiles, raising a palm to my heated cheek. "Just a perfect day, I guess." He kisses my forehead, pulling me into our building. "Oh, and I forgot to tell you earlier, we got asked this morning to perform at Navy Pier for New Year's."

I halt mid-step. "Forgot? Jake, that's incredible!"

"Incredible?" His eyes twinkle with delight as he continues guiding me up the stairs. "It's only two songs, not like we're headlining."

Navy Pier. Just two songs.

Humble Jake.

Reaching the second floor, I grab his jacket collar and pull him closer. "I like the humility and all, but you totally could've scored bonus points leading with the fact that I was going out with some famous heartthrob tonight."

"Famous heartthrob?" Jake's laughter vibrates through me as we reach his door. "Maybe I wanted to make sure you liked the guy behind the guitar first."

As if that was a question.

He unlocks the door, stepping aside to let me in. The air feels charged, electric with possibility. I hover awkwardly in the entryway, suddenly unsure. This is usually the part in my novels where the heroine throws caution to the wind, swept away by passion. But real life is messier, isn't it?

And what if I can't...

Jake must sense my hesitation because his cocky grin softens into something more vulnerable. "Hey, no pressure, okay? We can just talk if you want. Or I could serenade you again. I know at least three more songs that aren't totally depressing."

Some of the tension eases from my shoulders. "Only three? I expected more from Chicago's next big rock star."

"I'll have you know I'm very versatile," Jake says, waggling his eyebrows suggestively. "I can even play 'Twinkle Twinkle Little Star' on demand."

"My idol," I tease, but I'm grinning like an idiot.

Jake's eyes crinkle at the corners, and I'm struck by how much I want this. Want him. But the little voice in my head–the one that sounds suspiciously like my inner editor–won't shut up. What if this changes things? What if I'm not enough? What if he realizes I'm too damaged?

"Cora?" Jake's voice pulls me back to the present. He's watching me with a mixture of concern and affection that makes my heart do somersaults. "Where'd you go just now?"

I take a deep breath, deciding to be honest. "Just... overthinking. It's kind of my superpower."

Jake steps closer, his hand coming up to cup my cheek. "Want to talk about it?"

I lean into his touch, marveling at how safe I feel with him. "It's silly. I just... I really like you. And maybe I'm terrified of messing this up, too."

"You won't," he says with a wry smile. "Because here's the thing I've realized tonight, Cora. I'd rather risk messing up with you than play it safe with anyone else."

Oh. Well, if that isn't the most swoon-worthy thing I've ever heard outside of a romance novel.

"Smooth talker," I murmur, but I'm smiling so wide my cheeks hurt.

Jake's eyes darken, his gaze dropping to my lips. "I could show you smooth," he says, his voice low and full of promise.

And just like that, the playful tension from earlier comes roaring back. I slide my hands up his chest, feeling his heart racing beneath my palm. "I don't know," I tease, even as I lean closer. "I think I might need that encore performance to be convinced."

Jake's grin is downright wicked as he reaches for his guitar. "Your wish is my command, Cora Cooper."

Jake's fingers dance over the strings, coaxing out a melody that wraps around me like a warm embrace. His voice, low and intimate in the quiet of his apartment, has goosebumps prickling. I inch closer, unable to resist the magnetic pull between us.

As the last note ends, Jake sets the guitar aside, his eyes never leaving mine. "So," he says, a hint of nervousness creeping into his cocky demeanor, "was that convincing enough?"

I pretend to consider, tapping my chin thoughtfully. "Hmm, I don't know. That was only one song. I might need another."

Jake's laugh is warm and rich. "You're really pushing the limits of this character's stamina."

"Just keeping you on your toes," I quip, my heart racing as he pulls me closer. "Can't have predictable plot development, can we?"

His hands settle on my waist, our playful atmosphere shifting into something more charged. "Cora," he murmurs, his breath warm against my cheek, "I need you to know that we don't have to do anything you're not comfortable with. I'm happy just being here with you."

When was the last time someone put my comfort first?

I answer by closing the distance between us, my lips meeting Jake's with a hunger that surprises us both. This isn't like our previous kisses—there's an urgency, a desperation that ignites every nerve ending in my body. Jake responds instantly, one hand cupping my face while the other splays across my lower back, pulling me flush against him.

His tongue sweeps into my mouth, and I lose myself in the taste of him—a heady mixture of mint and something uniquely Jake. My fingers tangle in his hair, tugging slightly, and the low groan that escapes him sends tingles, well, everywhere.

When we finally break apart, we're both breathing heavily. Jake's eyes are dark, stormy with desire, and I can see my own need reflected back at me. "Cora," he breathes, his voice low and intimate, "you're driving me crazy."

I can't help the mischievous smile that tugs at my lips. "Good crazy or bad crazy?" I tease, shifting slightly in his lap.

Jake's grip on my hips tightens, his fingers digging in deliciously. "Definitely good," he growls, before capturing my lips again in a searing kiss.

As things heat up, I feel a familiar anxiety creeping in. I pull back slightly, my heart racing for a different reason now. "Jake," I manage, my voice barely above a whisper, "there's something you should know."

Jake immediately stills, concern replacing the desire in his eyes. "What is it, sweetheart?"

I take a deep breath, steeling myself. "Intimacy... it can be... awkward for me. I don't always know how I'll react..."

Awkward? Who says that when they're making out with someone?

Jake's expression softens, and he brings a hand up to cup my cheek. "Hey," he murmurs, his thumb tracing my cheekbone. "We can take this as slow as you need."

His understanding, his patience, makes my heart swell. I lean into his touch, overcome with emotion. "How did I get so lucky?" I wonder aloud.

Jake's smile is tender, his eyes full of an emotion I'm not quite ready to name. "I ask myself the same thing every time I look at you," he says softly.

Emboldened by his words, I lean in, pressing a soft kiss to the corner of his mouth. "I want this, Jake," I whisper against his skin. "I want you."

A shudder runs through Jake at my words. He pulls back slightly, his gaze intense as it roams over my face. "Are you sure?" he asks, his voice hoarse with restrained desire.

In answer, I take his hand and guide it under my shirt, pressing it against my racing heart. "Promise."

Jake's eyes darken, and in one fluid motion, he stands, lifting me with him. I wrap my legs around his waist instinctively, a thrill running through me at this casual display of strength.

"Hold on tight, angel," he murmurs, his lips brushing my ear as he carries me towards the bedroom.

As he lays me gently on the bed, I'm struck by the tenderness in his touch, a stark contrast to the heated desire in his eyes. Jake hovers above me, his gaze roaming over me like he's committing every detail to memory.

"You're so beautiful," he whispers, reverence coloring his tone. "I want to worship every inch of you."

My heart races at his words, desire and anticipation coiling low in my belly. I reach for him, pulling him down into a kiss that's equal parts passion and promise. As clothes start to come off, I'm overwhelmed by how right this feels. Like every misstep, every heartbreak, every moment of doubt was leading us here, to this moment.

Jake's hands and mouth explore my body with a reverence that brings tears to my eyes. Every touch, every caress feels like he's writing a love song on my skin. And let me tell you, it's a chart-topper.

"Jake," I whisper, trembling, "please. I need you."

He enters me slowly, carefully, and it's like every piece of a puzzle I didn't know I was solving suddenly clicks into place. We move together, finding a rhythm as natural as breathing. It's not perfect–there's a moment where we bump heads and dissolve into giggles–but it's us. Real and raw and absolutely right.

As we chase our release, I'm overwhelmed by the emotion building in my chest. It's not just physical pleasure, though there's plenty of that. It's something deeper, more profound. Like my soul recognizes his, two parts of a whole finally reuniting.

"Cora," Jake groans, his forehead pressed against mine. "I'm close."

"Me too," I gasp, clinging to him like he's my lifeline. Maybe he is.

When we fall over the edge together, it's like every star in the universe explodes behind my eyelids. I cry out Jake's name like a prayer, and he answers with mine, a benediction on his lips.

When we come down from our high, Jake gathers me close, pressing soft kisses to my hair, my forehead, my lips. I've never felt so cherished, so... seen.

"That was..." He huffs an astonished laugh. "You're incredible. I don't deserve this. Don't deserve you."

I cradle his face between my palms, waiting until his gaze meets mine again, stripped bare and vulnerable. "Yes, you do, Jake," I vow fiercely. "We both do."

Jake searches my face like he's glimpsing sunlight after an endless winter night. Then he seals his mouth over mine, pouring out wordless gratitude and devotion until we're both breathless. Still intertwined, he manages to tug me under the sheets, tangling our sated bodies blissfully together as our heartbeats slowly sync.

"What are you thinking?" Jake asks softly, his fingers playing with my hair.

I prop myself up on an elbow, meeting his gaze. "I'm thinking that this December is not what I expected. You. This." I gesture vaguely between us, a small smile playing on my lips.

Jake's eyes crinkle at the corners, but there's a hint of uncertainty there. "Good unexpected, I hope?"

"The best kind," I assure him, leaning in to press a soft kiss to his lips.

As I pull back, I'm struck by the openness in Jake's expression, the vulnerability there. He's let me in. And it makes me want to do the same, to let him see all of me–even the parts I usually keep hidden.

I take a deep breath, steeling myself. "Saving you... that December. It started something. Something I spent a lot of time in therapy trying to figure out."

Jake's brow furrows slightly, but his hand never stops its soothing motion on my back. "I've been told therapy helps."

I nod, swallowing. "It does." I close my eyes, reliving so many conversations. Good and bad. "But there's still moments. When memories hit you unexpectedly, and you don't know how you'll react."

When I open my eyes, the blue ones staring back at me are full of understanding and patience. "As a newly minted patient, I'm told it helps to talk about it," he says softly. "And I'm here, Cora. Whatever you want to share, I'm listening."

New patient? Jake is going to therapy?

The realization fills me with more warmth than I expect. I nestle closer to him, drawing strength from his steady presence. "I mentioned that intimacy is hard for me," I start. "It, um... it started the year after our accident. The next December. I'd been dating this guy,

Sam." Even saying his name out loud has me fighting visions of that night. What he took from me.

"He was popular and charming, even had me convinced he loved me," I continue, squeezing my eyes shut as bitterness chokes me. "He got wasted at a party and wanted more than I was ready to give. He wouldn't stop..."

I shudder violently as phantom hands and slurred words assault me. Jake makes a wounded noise, crushing me fiercely against his chest. His steady heartbeat anchors me, even as I feel him trembling with barely contained rage.

"I left him. But at school, rumors spread. Painted me as frigid. A tease. I felt so dirty." My voice hitches as I force out the words. "It messed me up for a long time. I couldn't let anyone touch me after. Couldn't trust men."

Jake's muscles coil with tension, a quiet curse escaping his lips. When he speaks, his voice is gravelly with suppressed anger. "You faced the worst and came out stronger. That's real courage, Cora."

I draw strength from his words, continuing my story. I tell him about the next December at Arden's wedding, about drinking too much and sleeping with a married man, about waking up after taking a handful of pills the next morning. How Arden found me in the hotel room. Then I share about what happened between me and Logan. About the intimacy issues, and the fear I've had that it was somehow my fault he cheated. That I couldn't give him what he needed.

When I finish, silence hangs heavy between us. Then Jake cups my face, his eyes shining with unshed tears. "Cora, listen to me. None of that was your fault. You didn't deserve any of it. And you sure as hell didn't do anything to make Logan cheat. You're beautiful and perfect. Someone who believes in others despite the ugliness people have shown you. If Logan couldn't see that, shame on him."

His words wash over me like a balm, soothing wounds I didn't even know were still raw. "Thank you," I whisper, leaning into his touch.

Jake takes a deep breath, and I can see him wrestling with something. "There's something I need to tell you. Something I've wanted to tell you for a while, but I've been... I don't know, scared? About what you'd think of me."

My heart skips a beat. "You can tell me anything, Jake."

He swallows, and for the first time, I wonder if I can handle anything he'd tell me. If there's parts beneath the surface I can't understand.

"I knew who you were before Mark and Arden's wedding," he starts. I vaguely recall our conversations about him knowing it was me, but he'd never pinpointed when.

"I saw you. On December 19th. Five years ago," he continues, gaze not wavering from mine. "I'd just found out about Tessa and Thomas. I went back to the apartment... I didn't know what to do... I was angry. Broken. I grabbed a blade." He closes his eyes with a sigh, like he's reliving the moment. But when they open, they're clear. Blue. Honest.

"Then I saw you," he says softly. "You were standing in the parking lot, haloed in sunlight through the window of the apartment. Talking with Arden."

December 19th? Five years ago? I was with... Arden?

Jake brushes his lips over my forehead, regret and wonder mingling as fractured pieces start to align.

"You were there in my darkest hour. My starry-eyed angel still saving me even when you didn't know it."

Starry-eyed angel? Why does that sound familiar?

Synapses fire rapidly as puzzle pieces I didn't know existed fall into place. It was right after the night with Sam. I'd left school. Went to stay with Arden, desperate for an escape, but she was living with Mark at the time...

"Oh my God. You were Mark's roommate," I breathe, the

realization hitting me like a tidal wave. *How'd I miss it before?* "I slept in *your* room that night."

Jake nods, shame etched in his features for all the wrong reasons. "I'm sorry I didn't say anything that day... it's just... I was wrecked, baby. I couldn't let you see me like that. Not then. And after... God, I've wanted to tell you for so long."

As he speaks, memories flood back. The comfort I found in that room, surrounded by the essence of someone I didn't even know. *His room. Him. Jake.* The journal (was it a journal?) I read, filled with beautiful words about selfless love. Words that changed my life, that gave me hope when I needed it most.

That was Jake.

The man I'd saved.

My heart thunders in my chest as I realize the truth. He saved me, too. Without ever knowing it. His words, his essence, had been my lifeline on one of the darkest nights of my life.

And, oh no. The note. I left a note.

Did he see it? Surely not. I signed my name.

Jake brings his palm to my face, watching me intently as I spiral further. "Cora, if I'd known all you'd been through, how you'd understand..."

"Jake..." His name falls from my lips like a sigh, a whispered secret finally spoken aloud.

I can't tell him. Not yet. The weight of this revelation is too much, too precious to share right now. Instead, I pull Jake closer, pouring all the gratitude and love I feel into a deep, soul-searching kiss.

When we part, both breathless, Jake's eyes search mine, relief and wonder mingling in their depths. "You're not... upset?"

I shake my head, a soft smile on my lips. "How could I be? You've given me so much more than you know."

He pulls me close, burying his face in my hair. "Why couldn't I have found you sooner?"

"You found me now," I whisper fiercely.

As we lay there, limbs entwined, I'm struck by the incredible journey that's led us here. To this moment, in this bed, in each other's arms. Our lives have been intertwined in ways we're only beginning to understand, a tapestry of fate and choice woven together.

Maybe there is a bigger reason we're here. Together. Now. Maybe this is what breaking the December curse feels like. Or maybe this is simply another chapter, required to fully heal.

I begin to drift off to sleep in Jake's arms, but a nagging thought tugs at the edges of my consciousness. December isn't over yet. And if there's one thing I've learned, it's that this month always has one last surprise up its sleeve.

28

∽

Cora

December 22ⁿᵈ

I'm halfway through my third cup of coffee when my phone buzzes. My boss's name flashes on the screen, reminding me that I should be knee-deep in manuscript edits instead of daydreaming about last night.

Last night. The memory of Jake's confession, his touch, the way he looked at me like I hung the moon... it's enough to make my toes curl.

Focus, Cooper. You've got actual work to do.

I answer the call, wincing at my boss's chipper tone. "Morning, Cora! Just checking in before the holiday break. How's that romance manuscript coming along?"

"It's..." I trail off, glancing at the untouched pages on my desk. *Crap.* "It's progressing."

"Excellent! I knew I could count on you. Enjoy your holiday, and I'll see you in the new year!"

The call ends, leaving me staring at my reflection in the black screen. The woman looking back at me is flushed, bright-eyed, and completely unfocused on anything work-related. Who even am I right now?

Then again, it might be the best place I've been in since Arden picked me up from Logan's that first night. Still, it's so soon...

A soft knock at the door interrupts my identity crisis. I open it to find Jake, sleep-rumpled and gorgeous, holding up takeout bags like an offering.

"Breakfast?" he asks, a shy smile playing on his lips. "I had a craving and thought I'd repay the generous breakfast from last week."

My heart does a little flip. "My hero," I say, stepping aside to let him in. "I was just thinking about food. And... other things."

Jake's eyebrow quirks up as he sets the bags on the counter. "Other things, huh? Care to elaborate?"

Heat creeps up my neck. "Oh, you know. Work stuff. Manuscripts. Definitely not replaying last night in my head or anything."

Jake's laugh is warm and rich as he pulls me close. "Liar," he murmurs, his lips brushing my ear. "I bet you were missing me already."

I smack his chest playfully, even as I lean into his embrace. "Cocky much?"

"Only stating facts," he grins, pressing a kiss to my forehead. "Now, let's eat before it gets cold."

As we dig into the food, I realize how natural this feels. Like we've been doing this for years instead of days. Jake catches my eye, a lopsided grin spreading across his face. "What's got you smiling like that? Still thinking about last night?"

I roll my eyes, but can't stop the warmth that bubbles up. "Something like that."

Jake chuckles before pulling himself together. "So, about tomorrow... what time's your flight?"

"Eleven," I reply, suddenly very interested in my scrambled eggs. "Arden and Mark are on an earlier one."

"Oh?" Jake's voice is carefully neutral. "You're not flying to-gether?"

I sigh, finally meeting his gaze. "No, I... I booked this back in October. With Logan."

The memory has me thinking about Logan's text from last night. He's heading to Florida, too. Did he keep his ticket? On the same flight? Just like that, I'm not hungry anymore.

Understanding dawns in Jake's eyes. "Ah."

"Yeah." I push my food around the plate. "Arden and I weren't exactly close then."

I contemplate telling him about the text. About the possibility of Logan being on the same flight. But before I can say anything, Jake reaches across the table, his fingers brushing mine. "Hey, no judgment here. We've all got baggage. But if you want, I'd be happy to take you. To the airport."

His offer has my thoughts drifting elsewhere. To a realization that has me forgetting all about my ex, and to the man sitting in front of me. "Jake... you do realize what you're offering, right? Driving me to the airport... in December?"

He blinks, confusion clouding his features. "Yeah? Is that a problem?"

"It's just... the curse," I explain, feeling a bit foolish. "The whole December accident. On the way to the airport. And you... you're kind of at the center of it all."

Jake's brow furrows. "Me? Maybe the first one. But I wasn't even around for the rest."

"No, but... you could have been," I say softly. "You seeing me that day at the apartment, Mark and Arden's wedding. There's been a chance for us to connect every December for years now. And some-thing always got in the way."

Jake's quiet for a moment, his thumb tracing circles on my hand.

Then, he smiles–a slow, warm thing that makes my heart stutter. "That sounds less like a curse, and more like fate."

"Fate?" I echo, the word feeling strange on my tongue.

"Think about it," Jake continues, his eyes bright with something like wonder. "All those near misses, all those almost moments... they were just leading us here. To now."

I stare at him, speechless. How can he be so calm about this?

Jake must see the panic in my eyes because he squeezes my hand gently. "Hey, I get it. It's a lot. But Cora... I'm not scared of some curse. I just want to enjoy this. Being with you."

His words hit me like a freight train, leaving me breathless. "Jake..."

"Look," he says, his voice low and earnest. "I haven't let anyone in... like this... in years. But with you, it's different. It feels right. And yeah, maybe it's happening fast, but... I don't want to waste any more time."

My heart swells, even as a nagging voice in my head warns me about moving too fast. But looking at Jake, seeing the hope and fear warring in his eyes, I realize playing it safe might be overrated.

Whatever this is between us–fate, destiny, or just dumb luck–I want to see where it leads.

"Okay," I whisper, a smile tugging at my lips. "But if we end up in a ditch on the way to the airport, I reserve the right to say, 'I told you so.'"

Jake laughs, the sound warming me from the inside out. "I'll take my chances."

As we fall back into easy conversation, I can't shake the feeling that we've just turned a page to a new chapter. We haven't officially titled this story yet, but we've both acknowledged that we're co-authors in something. Something beautiful, messy, and incredibly fragile.

"So," I begin, aiming for casual as we clean up the kitchen, "what's your schedule like tonight?"

Jake glances over, a smirk playing at his lips. "Why, are you already missing me?"

I roll my eyes, swatting him playfully, but he just pulls me closer, nuzzling into my hair.

"If you must know," he murmurs against my ear, "I'm only at Sadie's until midnight. Perks of the new gig."

I pull back slightly, curiosity piqued. "New gig?"

"Kind of a promotion," Jake shrugs, but I catch a hint of pride in his voice. "Means fewer late nights." He pauses, then adds, "Actually, if you're free, you should stop by. We've got a new DJ tonight."

"Really?" I blink, surprised by the invitation. "You sure I won't be in the way?"

Jake's grin turns mischievous. "Trust me, you're the kind of distraction I'd welcome any night."

I feel a smile tugging at my lips. "Well, in that case... I'll try to swing by. If I can wrestle this manuscript into submission for my boss."

He leans in, brushing a kiss that tastes of coffee and unwritten possibilities. "It'd make my night," he murmurs.

Glancing at the clock, he grimaces. "Shit, I've gotta run. Coffee shop calls." He steals another not-at-all-quick kiss. "Text me later?"

As he heads out, I'm left reeling once again. Yes, this plot is developing faster than a pulp fiction novel. But Jake's right—it all feels like a story that was meant to be written.

29

Jake

December 23ʳᵈ

I wake before the alarm, Cora's warmth beside me like a drug I can't get enough of. Maybe that's why I'm up before 8 AM for the first time in forever. Christ, the way this woman's changing me.

Last night at Sadie's plays through my mind like a highlight reel. Cora, perched at the bar, those amber eyes following my every move. The way my stomach flipped every time our gazes met across the crowded room. It was different, having her there in my world, outside the cocoon of our apartments.

Even though Alyssa was there, making subtle comments about my history to Cora, it didn't seem to matter. Still, it had me anxious. Knowing Alyssa doesn't think I'm good enough. And watching other guys eye her like she was the last cold beer on a hot day... yeah, that didn't sit well either. But then Cora would look at me, and everything else faded away.

It was just the two of us again, in our own world.

And yeah, maybe I showed off a little. Flipped a few bottles, mixed some fancy cocktails. The women who usually flirt shamelessly seemed to get the message pretty quick when they saw how I kept glancing Cora's way.

I pull her closer, burying my nose in her hair. Bringing her home last night, knowing our time was limited... fuck, it was intense. Every touch, every kiss felt amplified. Like we were trying to memorize each other before she left.

The alarm's shrill cry cuts through the quiet, and I silence it quickly. Not ready to face reality just yet.

"Morning, beautiful," I murmur, pressing a kiss to her forehead.

Cora blinks up at me, a slow smile spreading across her face. "Mm, morning," she mumbles, voice thick with sleep. "What time is it?"

"Time to get up, unfortunately," I whisper. "Your flight's in a few hours."

She groans, burying her face in my chest. "Five more minutes?"

I chuckle, running my hand down her back. "As tempting as that is, I don't think your parents would appreciate me making you miss your flight."

Cora lifts her head, grinning. "I don't know, it might be worth it. I can think of a few ways to pass the time."

Her hand trails down my abs, and I catch it, bringing it to my lips. "Careful, Coco. Keep that up, and we definitely won't make it to the airport."

She laughs, the sound doing things to me I can't even explain. "Promise?"

I roll us over, pinning her beneath me. "You're playing with fire, babe," I growl playfully, nipping at her neck.

Cora arches into me, her breath hitching. "Maybe I like getting burned."

I'm tempted to say screw it and keep her here. But I know how important this trip is to her, even if the thought of her leaving makes my chest tight.

I press a kiss to her lips before reluctantly pulling away. "Come on, time to get up. I'll make coffee while you get ready."

Cora grins, tugging me back toward her. "I have a better idea. How about you open your Christmas gift?"

I don't bother hiding the surprise in my expression. "You got me a gift?"

She nods, a soft smile playing on her lips. "Of course. I hope that's okay."

I lean in, peppering her face with light kisses. "More than okay. But you didn't have to. You're gift enough." *Yup, I'm corny as hell. Ask me if I care.*

Cora giggles as my fingers find her ticklish spots. "I wanted to," she manages between laughs. "Now stop that and let me up! Otherwise I really will miss my flight."

She playfully pushes me away and slips out of bed, throwing on one of my t-shirts. The sight of her standing there, cinnamon hair tumbling over her shoulders and amber eyes sparkling, takes my breath away.

"You know," I drawl, propping myself up on one elbow, "if that gift is anything less than a life-size portrait of you just like this, I'm going to be sorely disappointed."

Cora rolls her eyes, but I catch the blush creeping up her cheeks. "You're ridiculous. Now get that fine ass of yours out of bed and come see what I got you."

I laugh, swinging my legs over the side of the bed. "Yes ma'am," I salute, grabbing a pair of pants. "Lead the way."

As I follow her into the living room, Cora reaches behind the couch and pulls out a large, wrapped package. My eyebrows shoot up in surprise. "Wow, you've been holding out on me. When did you sneak that in here?"

Cora just winks, a secretive smile on her face. "A girl's got to have some mysteries, doesn't she?"

"Mystery isn't always a bad thing," I whisper, guiding her mouth to mine one more time before tearing into the perfectly wrapped package. Inside are three canvases. All the same photo—my guitar—in different hues. They're perfect. Just like her.

I trace the image of one, looking up at her. "These are amazing, Cora. When? How?"

She tucks a lock of hair behind her ear, seeming nervous. "It was the only personal item in the apartment, so I thought," she motions uncertainly to the bare wall behind us, "they could maybe help make this place feel more like home?"

I tug her closer to me, wanting to show her exactly how much they mean to me. How much she means to me. When I pull back, I cup her cheek. "You're constantly surprising me. In ways I never thought possible."

When she smiles, I break away, finding my jacket. "Ready for yours?"

Cora's eyes widen as I pull out a small, wrapped box. "Jake, you didn't—"

I silence her with a quick kiss, my heart racing. "Just open it, angel."

She tears into the wrapping, gasping as she lifts out a delicate necklace. The tiny book pendant catches the light, and I swear my pulse skips along with it.

"It's beautiful," she breathes, fingers tracing the blue stone.

"Blue topaz," I explain, gently taking the necklace to clasp it around her neck. "For my December girl."

Cora's hand flies to the pendant, her eyes misty. "You remembered."

"I remember everything about you, Cora." I cup her face, thumbs stroking her cheeks. "Merry early Christmas."

She pulls me in for a kiss that makes me forget my own name. When we part, she glances at the clock and groans. "Unfortunately, we need to get moving, babe."

I tighten my arms around her, not ready to let go. "Five more minutes?"

"Jake," she warns, but I can see her resolve wavering.

"I'll make it worth your while," I murmur, trailing kisses down her neck.

Cora shivers, then playfully pushes me away. "Down, boy. Save that for when I get back."

I waggle my eyebrows as images of Cora pressed against the shower wall last night, water cascading down us as I kissed her throat... *Not going down anytime soon.* "Is that a promise?" I tease lightly.

"It's a guarantee," she winks, heading toward her suitcase.

When we're finally heading to the car, I can't resist one last quip. "You know, if you miss this flight, I could always give you a private encore of last night's performance."

Cora swats my arm, laughing. "Behave, Mr. About-to-play-Navy-Pier."

"With you? Never."

As I load the luggage, I catch Cora eyeing the car nervously. "Having second thoughts, babe?"

She takes a deep breath. "Just... are you sure this is a good idea? Us driving to the airport together?"

I grin confidently, bringing her wrist to my lips and kissing the scar there. "It'll be fine. No snow in the forecast."

Cora freezes in my arms, her smile fading. I can practically see the gears turning in her head, old fears battling with new trust.

"Cora, we're both gonna be just fine," I reassure her, guiding her gently to the idling car. "We're together this time."

As we settle in, I hand her my phone. "Why don't you pick out some music?"

She scrolls through my playlists, a soft smile playing on her lips when she spots the one titled "Cora." Yeah, I'm in deep.

"You have a playlist for me?" she asks, sounding almost shy.

I grin, tapping the list wordlessly. As the music fills the car, Cora melts into my shoulder. I exhale softly, savoring the moment. It's crazy how quickly she's become essential to me. The thought of a week apart... it shouldn't feel this hard, right?

As we hit the highway, I capture her hand, thumb tracing over her scar. "So, what big plans do you have for the week? Beaches and sunbathing?"

Cora laughs, the sound easing some of the tension in my chest. "Still December, so not exactly swimming weather. But there's usually some type of boating involved. Otherwise, some family events for the holidays." She pauses, then adds, "How about you? You mentioned your parents' house. Anything else?"

I keep my eyes on the road, trying to sort through the mess of emotions her question stirs up. "Mostly working. Nat's taking the week to spend with her son, so I'm closing most nights. Though we are playing at Sadie's on Christmas night for the first time ever." I glance over at her, steeling myself. "Assuming I make it through Christmas Eve first, I guess."

Cora squeezes my hand gently. "You said this is the first time you've stayed at their new house. How are you feeling about it?"

I exhale slowly, memories flickering behind my eyes. "Honestly? I'm not sure. It's been so long since I've done the whole family holiday thing."

Since Thomas. Since everything fell apart.

Cora stays quiet, giving me space to continue. "We used to have this whole Christmas Eve routine," I find myself saying. "Dinner, church service—my parents were always part of the music program. Some years, Owen and I would join in." A bittersweet smile tugs at my lips. "Then we'd head home, make enough popcorn to feed an army, and watch cheesy holiday movies. We'd take turns picking our childhood favorites."

Scratching out the words, I add, "It's going to be... different. Especially after everything that happened last week."

Cora's gaze doesn't leave mine, even as mine stays glued to the road in front of us. "Hey, if you need a lifeline, I'm just a phone call away. Day or night, okay?"

"Thanks, Cora. That means more than you know."

Wanting to shift to lighter topics, I ask, "So, you're still coming to the New Year's show at Sadie's, right? Even though it's your birthday?"

Cora's eyes sparkle with amusement. "Wouldn't miss it. Arden would never let me hear the end of it if I bailed again."

She pauses, then adds hesitantly, "What about the Navy Pier gig? Is that a closed event, or...?"

"Are you kidding?" I grin. "I want you there front and center. Consider this your official VIP invitation."

Cora's smile is radiant. "Look at you, Mr. Rock Star. Two shows in one night? I must be special."

I tug her closer, my voice low and sincere. "You have no idea how special you are, Cora Cooper."

As we approach the departure drop-off, reality starts to set in. I help Cora with her luggage, my movements slowing as if I can somehow delay the inevitable.

"So, I'll see you Saturday?" I ask, hating how uncertain I sound.

Cora nods, her eyes shining with emotion. I pull her into my arms, pouring everything I feel into one last kiss. It's deeper, more intense than our others—a promise and a plea rolled into one.

When we part, both slightly breathless, I rest my forehead against hers. "Have a safe flight, okay?"

"I will," Cora whispers. "Try not to miss me too much."

I laugh softly. "No promises there, sweetheart." Reluctantly, I take a step back. "Have a great Christmas with your family."

As Cora backs away, I can still feel the pull between us. Watching her go, I'm hit with the realization that what we've started is bigger than anything I've experienced before. It's amazing and scary as hell.

I stand there long after she's disappeared into the terminal, the memory of her kiss still tingling on my lips. A week. I can do this. We can do this.

But as I climb back into my car, the silence feels deafening. It's going to be a long seven days.

30

〰

Cora

Of course, airport security takes twice as long since it's the most hectic travel day of the year. But not even screaming toddlers or grumpy TSA agents can dampen my elated mood as the taste of Jake's good-bye kiss lingers.

I sprint through the terminal, weaving around travelers, and make it to my gate just as attendants start boarding. Catching my breath, I fire off a quick text to Jake.

Me: *Made it! About to board. Miss you already.*

His response is almost immediate.

Jake: *Miss you too, babe. Be safe. I'm just a call away if you need me.*
Me: *Same goes for you, rock star.*
Jake: *I might have to start calling you that after last night*
Me: XOXO

As I run my boarding pass, the agent stops me abruptly. "Just a minute, it seems you've been upgraded," she explains, tapping her fingers rapidly on the keyboard.

My stomach drops. "Upgraded?"

The warmth from Jake's words turn into a chill of dread. I'd hoped Logan hadn't kept his ticket, but...

The agent nods, handing me over a new ticket. "Yes, to first class. Seat 2A."

I should've known Logan wouldn't let me escape that easily.

I board the plane, steeling myself for what's to come. And there he is in 2B, looking as polished and put-together as ever.

Fucking December.

But I'm not the same person I was. Just a month ago, his presence would have left me a nervous wreck, questioning every decision I'd made. Now? There's a strength in me that wasn't there before. I touch the book pendant at my throat, thinking of Jake, of the person I'm becoming. Whatever Logan throws at me, I can handle it.

"Hello, gorgeous," Logan says, standing up with that familiar smirk. "Fancy meeting you here."

I force a neutral expression. "Logan. What a surprise."

He gestures to my seat. "I hope you don't mind the upgrade. I thought we could use the time to talk."

"That's presumptuous of you," I reply, stowing my bag. "Did it occur to you that I might not want to talk?"

Logan's smile falters for a moment. "Come on, Cora. We're going to be stuck together for the next few hours. We might as well make the best of it."

"I brought a book." I sit down, purposely angling my body away from him. At least he had the decency to remember I like the window seat. Or maybe he just wanted me to feel trapped.

As we take off, I try to lose myself in my novel, but Logan's presence is like a persistent itch I can't scratch. I can feel his eyes on me, waiting for an opening.

Finally, he breaks the silence. "Can I get you a drink?"

I hesitate. Part of me wants to refuse on principle, but another part whispers that a little liquid courage might help me get through this flight. "Fine. Vodka tonic."

Logan signals the flight attendant, and soon we both have drinks in hand. I take a sip, the familiar burn a welcome distraction.

"So," Logan starts, his voice softening. "How have you been?"

I turn to him, raising an eyebrow. "Really? Small talk?"

He shrugs. "I'm trying here, Cora."

"Trying what, exactly? To manipulate me? To guilt me into coming back?"

Logan flinches. "That's not fair. I made a mistake, I know that. But we were together three years. What we had... it was real. You can't just throw that away."

I take another sip of my drink, buying time. How do I make him understand? "Logan, it wasn't just one mistake. Our relationship was broken long before you cheated."

"What are you talking about? We were happy."

I let out a bitter laugh. "Were we? Because I remember feeling lonely, overlooked, like I was just another box for you to check off on your perfect life checklist."

Logan's brow furrows. "I never meant to make you feel that way."

"But you did," I say softly. "And the worst part is, I let you. I twisted myself into knots trying to be what you wanted, and I lost myself in the process."

"Cora, I-"

"No, let me finish," I interrupt, surprising myself with my firmness. "Do you know what I've realized since we broke up? I like dancing. I enjoy going out with friends. I love my job, even if you think it's frivolous. I'm not the perfect, polished girlfriend you tried to mold me into, and I don't want to be."

Logan stares at me, stunned. "Why didn't you ever say anything?"

"I shouldn't have had to," I reply. "The person who loves me should see me, really see me, without me having to spell it out."

A heavy silence falls between us. I pull out my phone, needing an anchor to reality.

Me: *Wishing you were here.*

Jake responds quicker than I expect.

Jake: *Want me to hijack a plane and stage a mid-air rescue? I've always wanted to be a sky pirate.*

A laugh bursts free, warmth spreading through my chest. I'm about to tell him about my current situation, but I hesitate. Would knowing I'm sitting next to Logan have him reacting like last time?

A throat clears next to me before I can make up my mind.

"That the boyfriend?"

I look up to find Logan watching me, his expression a mix of hurt and anger.

"It's none of your business," I say, putting my phone away.

Logan's jaw clenches. "If it's still that bartender, I have to say that I'm surprised he hasn't ruined it yet. Then again, you did take him back after he made out with your best friend, so the bar's pretty low."

Anger flares in my chest. "First off, you don't get to know why I decide to see anyone. Second, Jake and I weren't together at that concert. And, yeah, he sees me for who I am, not who he wants me to be."

"Well, I hope 'Jake' knows what he's getting into then," Logan says coldly. "You're not exactly easy to love, Cora."

I blink back tears, refusing to let him see how much he's hurt me. "I think this conversation is over."

I turn away, staring out the window as the coastline comes into view. We're almost there. I've almost made it.

As we start our descent, Logan touches my arm. "Cora, I'm sorry. That was out of line."

I look at him, really look at him, and for the first time, I see the cracks in his perfect facade. The desperation in his eyes, the slight tremor in his hand. He's scared, I realize. Scared of losing control.

"Logan," I say softly, "we're done. Whatever we had, it's over. I've moved on, and you need to, too."

"Moved on? It's been a month, sweetheart. You're just in a rebound. The sooner you realize that, the better."

I cross my arms. Because some things never change.

"Look," Logan says, his tone softening. "I know I hurt you. But I still care about you, Cora. I want you to know that."

He reaches into his carry-on and pulls out a small blue box. My stomach drops. "Logan, don't—"

"Just hear me out," he says, opening the box to reveal a pair of diamond earrings. "I got these for you. A diamond for each year we were together."

I stare at the earrings, their sparkle seeming cold and impersonal. All I can think about is the necklace Jake gave me, the tiny book pendant that showed he really knew me, really saw me.

"Logan," I say, my voice barely above a whisper, "do you even know my favorite book?"

He blinks, caught off guard. "What?"

"My favorite book. Do you know what it is?"

Logan's silence is answer enough.

"This is exactly what I'm talking about," I explain. "You buy expensive gifts, thinking that's what love is. But you never took the time to really know me."

Logan's face falls, his hand closing around the jewelry box. "Cora, I—"

"I can't accept those," I say firmly. "We're over, Logan. Please understand that."

He nods slowly, tucking the box away. For a moment, I see genuine hurt in his eyes, and despite everything, I feel a pang of sympathy.

As we stand to deplane, Logan stops me. "One last thing before you go? For old times' sake?"

Before I can react, he's holding up his phone, snapping a photo of us. I'm caught off guard, a reflexive smile on my face before I can stop it.

Logan grins, showing me the picture. "See? We still look good together."

I shake my head, but can't help a small, sad laugh. "Goodbye, Logan."

Walking away, I can feel his eyes on me. But for the first time, I don't feel the urge to look back. My future is ahead of me, and this time, I won't get caught up in what's behind me.

31

∽

Jake

December 24ᵗʰ

2:31 AM. Is it too late to text Cora? I run a hand through my hair, tugging at the roots. Owen's words from earlier keep bouncing around my skull like a bad hangover.

"You're in deep, little brother," he'd said, eyeing me over his coffee. "Never seen you like this over a girl before. You sure you're ready for all this?"

Ready? Christ, I don't even know what "all this" means. Cora sent a quick "landed safely" text, and I replied with… what? A thumbs up emoji and a call later? Was that enough?

I'm a goddamn mess. One minute I'm on top of the world, re-membering Cora's taste, her body against mine. The next, I'm spiral-ing, terrified I'll mess it all up. Because that's what I do, right? I break things. I run. And every time I think I'm better, something happens that makes me wonder if I'm kidding myself.

"Whatcha doin', Jake?" Bailey says, nearly making me drop my phone like some fumbling teenager.

Shit. I'm supposed to be training her with Natalie gone for the week, not mooning over my... what? Girlfriend? Can I even call Cora that?

I shove my phone away, grasping for something work-related to say. What comes out is: "Are you dating anyone, Bailey?"

Fuck me. Real professional, asshole.

I backpedal hard. "Sorry, that was... let's just get back to work, yeah?"

But Bailey's already leaning in, a predatory glare in her eye that sets off all my alarms. "Oh, I don't mind talking about personal stuff," she purrs. "I'm not seeing anyone serious. What about you, Jake? Got a special someone?"

The way she's eyeing me makes me want to crawl out of my skin. I take a step back, searching for an escape route. "I, uh... yeah?"

"Sounds complicated," Bailey replies. *Understatement of the century.*

Her hand lands on my arm, and it takes everything in me not to flinch. "Let me guess, she's just getting over someone?" she presumes. "And you're not sure if you're just a rebound?"

What? How'd she...

"I'm not judging, but you don't seem the type to be someone's bounce back," she continues, voice dripping honey. "Maybe we could talk about it. Grab a drink. Off the clock, of course."

My face burns, guilt churning in my gut. It's like I can feel Cora's eyes on me, even from a thousand miles away. "Thanks, but no," I say, probably too harshly. *Is she just being nice, or...?* Unsure, I soften my tone. "We need to keep things professional. I'm your boss, Bailey."

Bailey's smile flickers, but she recovers fast. "Of course."

I'm saved from this awkward conversation by a customer calling for another round. I bolt to fill the order, my mind a warzone of conflicting thoughts. *What the hell just happened? And how do I shut this down without making the next few days a special kind of hell?*

I shake my head, trying to focus on pouring without spilling.

But Cora's face keeps flashing behind my eyes, and I can't shake the thought: what would she think of all this? And when did her opinion start mattering so damn much?

Just when I think the night can't get any worse, in struts Lindsey, looking like she's won the lottery and wants everyone to know it.

"Where's your girlfriend tonight?" she chirps, sidling up to the bar with a smile that's all teeth.

I bite back a groan, bracing for another tantrum. But Lindsey's attention is already elsewhere, focused on some poor sap who's looking at her like she hung the moon.

"You hurt my feelings the other night," she pouts, running her claws up New Guy's arm. "But that's okay. I've already found a replacement."

Is this supposed to bother me? Hell, it's the best news I've had all night.

"Happy for you," I say, not even having to fake the relief in my voice.

They proceed to suck face while I finish last call, torn between amusement and pity for the poor bastard who doesn't know what he's in for.

As I'm wiping down the bar, my phone buzzes. For a split second, hope flares in my chest. But it's not Cora.

Owen: *How's it going, little brother? Surviving night #1 without your girl?*

I roll my eyes despite the smile tugging at my lips.

Me: *Fuck off. I'm fine.*
Owen: *Sure you are. That's why you've been moping around like someone stole your puppy.*
Me: *I don't mope.*

At least, not over women… Normally.

Owen: *Keep telling yourself that. Look, all I'm saying is, it's okay to miss her. It's okay to want something real for once. See you tomorrow night at Mom and Dad's.*

I contemplate telling him just how real what I feel for Cora is. But then Bailey's voice rings out again. "Everything okay? You seem… intense."

I look up to find her leaning across the bar, concern etched on her face. But there's something else there too, a glimmer of opportunity that sets me on edge.

"I'm fine," I say, probably too quickly. "Just… family stuff."

Bailey nods, her expression softening. "I get it. Family can be tough. Especially this time of year."

She has no idea how right her comment is, but I won't let her know that. I barely know this girl.

"Speaking of, we should probably get back to closing, huh?" I say, deflecting.

She nods. "Right. Off tomorrow. Any big plans to unwind tonight?"

What the actual fuck? Is this for real? How'd Natalie forget to warn me?

I force an easy chuckle to cover the defenses rising. "A coma. Didn't get much sleep last night."

It's almost four by the time I actually unlock my apartment, feeling like I've gone ten rounds with my own fucked-up psyche. I flop onto the bed, inhaling Cora's scent still lingering on my pillow. It's like a hit of the sweetest drug, and I'm already jonesing for more.

My phone buzzes against my chest, and again, hope flares. But it's just Bailey. Again.

Bailey: *Sorry if I made things weird earlier. I just really enjoy working with you.*

I cringe. This girl clearly doesn't know how to take a hint. I'd ignore it if I didn't need her to show up for the rest of the week while Natalie's gone.

Me: *Don't worry about it. We're cool. Thanks for stepping in for Nat tonight.*

I toss the phone aside, my gut churning. There's something off about Bailey, something I can't quite put my finger on. And the last thing I need is more complications in my life.

Still, her words from earlier return in full force. Rebound. That's not what Cora and I have, right? She's over her ex? Mostly, at least?

Before I can talk myself out of it, I grab my phone again and text the one person who's been on my mind all night. For reassurance or just to see her contact info, I don't know. Don't care.

Me: *You awake yet? Just got into bed, and my pillow smells like you. Missing those perfect for cuddling curves.*

Her response comes quickly, sending a jolt through me.

Cora: *I was still sleeping until SOMEONE texted me awake* ☺ *But if you want to head down here, I'll gladly take your hot body around me... even if you'll have me sweating all night.*

A grin splits my face in the dark. Cora wants me there. She's thinking of me, too. Yeah, this is fast. And I know I'm not ready. But I don't want to slow this down. Not when it feels this good.

Me: *You make that sound way too tempting.*

She sends a screenshot of flights from Chicago, and suddenly I'm imagining her there, all sleep-tousled and sexy in some old hoodie. The longing hits me like a freight train, leaving me breathless.

Cora: *Maybe my favorite bartender can mix me up some sex on the beach?*
Me: *Are you trying to torture me?*
Cora: *Always. But get some sleep—I know you didn't get much last night.*
Me: *Totally worth it. Merry Christmas Eve, Cora. Call me later?*
Cora: *It's a date. Merry Christmas Eve, Jake. Sweet dreams! XOXO*

I stare at the screen long after it goes dark, my mind a whirlwind of emotions. Cora's sweet goodnight text lingers in my thoughts, a beacon of hope in the storm of my anxieties.

It's Christmas Eve. The first one I'll spend with my family in years. The thought sends a shiver down my spine–equal parts dread and anticipation. What if I can't be the son they remember? What if the weight of the past is too heavy to bear?

And then there's Cora. Sweet, understanding Cora, who somehow sees past all my bullshit. What happens when she comes back and real life kicks in? Can I be the man she deserves while juggling the bar, the band, and my own demons?

I shake my head, trying to quiet the doubts. This is why I've kept people at arm's length for so long. It's safer. Simpler. But for Cora... For Cora, I'd brave a thousand uncomfortable family dinners. For the chance at a future with her, I'd face down every demon in my closet.

So bring it on Christmas Eve. I'm ready for whatever you've got.

<h1 style="text-align:center">32</h1>

ᴄᴡ

Jake

December 24th

I pull up to my parents' house around five. It's a newer build, unlike the four-bedroom 1960s house I grew up in. But I understand. This is how my parents ran from their grief. It's no different than how I left Mark's apartment after. Or how I pushed everyone away, throwing myself into multiple jobs, performing, and any other escape I could find.

I follow my mom upstairs, footsteps echoing oddly in the unfamiliar hallway. Trailing my fingers along the immaculate eggshell walls, I notice the absence of scuffs and scratches. It's more like walking through a model house than coming home.

"We just finished putting the third bedroom together since you were both staying tonight," Mom says over her shoulder, flashing a smile. Her brown eyes shine with the pleasure of having us both here again.

She nudges an anonymous door, revealing a bland, beige guest room. Gone is my light blue, poster and clutter filled, childhood one, replaced by something resembling a hotel room. Tidy and transient.

I set my bag on the edge of the mattress, trying not to let the unfamiliar comforter print unsettle me further. I can handle this for one night.

"What's this?" I ask, poking at a box with my name on it.

Mom leans against the door frame, watching me curiously. "Something I found in the basement. I think it was from when you moved out of Mark's. I didn't want to throw anything out without having you take a look." Her smile dims faintly. "It's good to have you here, Jake. Your dad and I... well, we've missed having you around."

I hear what she's not saying: It feels like getting a piece of you back again. It's a reminder that my absence at holidays and milestones hasn't just affected me. As shame and sadness hit, I scrub a hand over the scruff on my jaw. But Mom merely gives my shoulder a little squeeze before stepping back out into the hall.

"Dinner's in fifteen. The candlelight service is at seven if you'd like to join," she says softly. "Let me know if you need anything else, okay?"

I nod mutely, still shocked by the strangeness.

When she leaves, I eye the mystery box like it might explode. *From when I moved out of Mark's apartment.* My fingers twitch with the urge to both open it and chuck it out the window.

Screw it. If I'm gonna move forward, I can't keep running from the past.

Taking a deep breath, I peel back the flaps of the worn cardboard. It's like opening a time capsule to a life I barely recognize anymore.

The first thing I pull out is a framed photo of the four of us—me, Owen, Thomas, and Chris—on stage from one of our earliest gigs. Christ, we look so young, so clueless about what life was gonna throw at us. My chest tightens, a familiar ache of survivor's guilt threatening to swallow me whole. But there's something else now, too. A bittersweet pride in what we had, what we were.

I set it aside, only to be sucker-punched by the next photo. Tessa and me at North Avenue Beach, all sun-kissed and disgustingly in love. Still, the rage and betrayal that used to consume me when I'd see a picture of her… it's not gone, but it's different now. Muted. Like an old scar that's finally starting to fade.

Tessa's voice echoes in my head, clear as if she were right here. "Do you believe that there's only one person for everyone?"

There was a time I did. Back when I was so obsessed with Tessa, so convinced she was "the one," that I let our relationship consume me. I ditched the band, ignored my friends, even took an extra semester— all for her.

But now? Now I'm realizing we both liked the idea of "us" more than the daily reality. It wasn't the forever kind of love. It was bound to fail.

I think about the conversation with Mom after dinner last week, the word forgiveness echoing in my head. Is that how she got through all this? Letting it all go, knowing some things aren't meant to be understood?

I close my eyes, letting my imagination wander. If Thomas and Tessa were still alive, where would we all be now? I probably would've moved on from Tessa eventually. Found someone else. Hell, I might have even realized how unhealthy our relationship was. How she wasn't the everything I assumed she was when we were twenty. Or even twenty-three.

Thomas and I… we would've made up. He would've met someone else. He'd be here with us tonight, probably cracking jokes and hogging the popcorn during our nightly movie tradition.

The realization hits me like a ton of bricks. I can be disappointed in their choices, but still miss them. Still love them.

Tessa can be in my heart, but she doesn't have to own it. There's room for more.

The thought settles over me like a warm blanket. I can forgive her, even if I can't ever forget. And maybe… maybe that's enough.

I set the photo aside, my eyes landing on a stack of notebooks. My old song journals. I haven't looked at these since... well, since that day.

I grab the black and blue one I was working on that last winter, my fingers trembling as I flip through pages of lovesick ballads and angsty anthems. Reading them now is like reading a stranger's diary. Then I spot it—the last song I wrote before I locked all these memories away.

"My Starry-Eyed Angel," dated December 13th. One year after the accident with Cora.

I skim the lyrics, a weird mix of embarrassment and nostalgia washing over me. It's cheesy as hell, but there's something... genuine about it.

"My starry-eyed angel with a mysterious smile..."

Did I know even then that Tessa wasn't the one? That there was something pure and beautiful about the girl fate thrust into my life?

"You appeared when I needed a friend, my whole world was ready to end..."

Christ, how true that was. And still is.

"Someday, I'll find you and finally see, the face of the angel who rescued me."

I run a hand through my hair, kicking myself for waiting so long. I could've found her so many times before—Mark's wedding, social media stalking. Hell, I could've just talked to Arden. But maybe we were supposed to wait. To find each other now.

As inspiration strikes, I grab a pen from my bag and flip the page. But it's not blank like I expect. A handwritten letter I've never seen before fills the page.

Holy fucking shit.

It's a letter. From Cora. My brain short-circuits as I read her words, penned by a younger, vulnerable version of the woman I'm falling for.

Hi! You don't know me, and you probably never will. I'm Arden's sister, and I'm sleeping in your room tonight. I should start by apologizing that I read this, but insomnia and emotions made me desperate for a distraction. And somehow, these poems gave me hope and clarity when I couldn't find any.

I haven't even told Arden this, but I came here tonight to escape school.... escape my boyfriend. Well, ex-boyfriend now. He betrayed something precious. He took advantage of me last night in a way I wasn't ready for, and it got ugly, violent even. I thought I loved him, but at nineteen, I'm not sure I know what love means. I started to think I'd overreacted. That I was wrong. That if I really cared about him, I should give him what he wanted. Be the kind of girl he wanted me to be.

But reading this, I realized what I did was right. Love isn't just giving blindly. You write of selfless devotion, of finding joy in another's happiness before your own. Of gentle care instead of manipulation or force. Maybe I've misunderstood love. I was going to give up my values just to be wanted. That's not love, it's manipulation.

Whoever these songs are about, you clearly love her. I pray she cherishes that devotion, realizing how rare it is to find. You would do anything for her happiness, prioritizing her needs over yours. You wouldn't force her to do something she's not ready for just because it's what you want. You'd be patient. That's what it should be, selfless. Two people who make each other better by being together—freely and without condition.

Thank you for stopping me from making a huge mistake, for saving me from whatever could've happened. Maybe someday we'll meet under happier circumstances. I'll likely be an embarrassed fangirl if you connect me back to this note, but I thought you should know what you did for me.

I only hope that one day, I can find someone who will love me like the words in this book.

Cora.

I saved her?

I squeeze my eyes shut against the burn of emotion. How did I miss this note before? How did I miss this connection for so long? She's been right here. All along.

My hands shake as I re-read the letter, once, twice, a dozen times. Pieces start clicking into place—Cora's whispered words from Thursday night return, "You've given me so much more than you know." She didn't know I was Mark's roommate. Until three days ago.

She never knew this was my notebook.

Not that she knew the connection when she wrote this.

Our tangled history twists even deeper than I understood.

Cora's right.

Love is selfless.

Selfless, like Cora saving me in that accident. Selfless like my fierce, tenacious girl who still believes in goodness and fairy tales and happily ever after's despite all she's been through.

I flip back through all the songs, rereading the lyrics. Something swells hot and urgent in my chest, unfamiliar after so many numb years. Because I know now, without a doubt, I'm completely in love with her. Not the idealized version of her I've built up in my head, but the real her. The one who's seen me at my worst and still believes in me. The one who's just as broken and beautiful as I am.

I've probably loved her since that day in the wreckage, even if I was too blind to see it.

My phone buzzes, jerking me out of my revelation. It's Cora, because of-fucking-course it is.

"Hey beautiful," I answer, my voice thick. "Were your ears burning? Was just thinking about you."

Her laugh sends warmth spreading through me. "Oh, were you now? Anything interesting you'd care to share?"

Yeah, just that I'm completely, irrevocably in love with you. The words stick in my throat, too big, too new to voice just yet. But soon. God, soon.

As Cora chatters about her day, I can't help but smile. This is it. This is what I've been missing all these years. Not some idealized "soulmate," but a real connection with someone who gets me, flaws and all.

For the first time in forever, I'm not dreading the future. I'm looking forward to it. Because whatever comes next, I know I want to face it with Cora by my side.

* * *

When I end the call with Cora, a stupid grin plastered on my face, Mom's voice drifts up from downstairs. "Jake! Owen! Dinner's ready!"

I bound down the stairs, feeling lighter than I have in years. The dining room's decked out in all its Christmas Eve glory—Mom's good china, the fancy tablecloth, the works. It's like stepping into a time warp, except I'm not the same sullen kid I used to be.

"Well, look who decided to grace us with his presence," Owen quips as I slide into my seat.

I flip him off, but there's no heat behind it. "Missed you too, asshole."

Dad clears his throat, eyebrow raised. "Language, boys. Your mother worked hard on this dinner."

"Sorry, Mom," we chorus, like we're teenagers again.

Mom just shakes her head, a smile playing at her lips. "Some things never change. Now, who wants to say grace?"

There's a beat of awkward silence. We haven't done this in years, not since... well, not since Thomas. I take a deep breath and meet her gaze. "I'll do it."

Owen's fork clatters to his plate in shock. Mom's eyes go wide, and Dad... Dad just nods, a look of pride on his face that makes my chest tight.

I clear my throat, suddenly nervous. "Uh, thanks for this food and for... for family. And second chances. And sometimes third and fourth ones as well. Amen."

It's short, awkward, and probably the worst grace ever said, but Mom's eyes are shining, and even Owen looks touched.

"Well said, son," Dad says softly.

We dig in, and for a while, it's just the sounds of eating and murmured compliments to the chef. Then Mom breaks the ice.

"So, Jake, how's the bar? You mentioned a promotion the other week?"

I nod, swallowing a mouthful of mashed potatoes. "Yeah, more responsibility, better hours. Though it might just be so Sadie doesn't have to keep changing the schedule when we get band gigs."

"Speaking of," Mom starts, beaming, "I hear you boys have some big show for New Year's."

I shoot Owen a look, but he just shrugs innocently. At least one of us is keeping Mom updated. "Yeah, we're playing Navy Pier. It's... it's a pretty big deal."

"No shit?" Dad says, earning a swat from Mom for his language. "Sorry, but boys, that's fantastic. We're so proud of you."

The warmth in his voice catches me off guard.

"Thanks," I mumble, suddenly finding my green beans fascinating. "It's not a big deal, really."

"Like hell it isn't," Owen chimes in. "It's all that song you wrote, Jake. The songs you're writing."

As Owen launches into the most recent band details, I catch Dad's eye across the table. He gives me a nod, a silent "well done," and for once, I don't feel the need to deflect or run. I'm... I'm okay. More than okay.

After dinner and the candlelight service, we pile into Dad's car.

The familiar scent of pine air freshener and old leather seats brings back a flood of memories.

"You boys up for a movie?" Dad asks from the driver's seat.

I feel Owen's eyes on me, waiting. Ready to make an excuse if I need an out. But I don't. Not tonight.

"I think I'd like that," I say, surprising even myself.

Owen's jaw practically hits the floor before he recovers, grinning. "Jake, you pick the movie this year, then."

Back home, Mom and Dad head to the kitchen for popcorn duty, while Owen and I set up in the family room. It's so normal, so routine, that it almost hurts. "I think I'd like that," I respond.

"I started seeing someone," Owen says, slinking into the recliner, a sly smile crossing his face.

Oh. New news.

I raise an eyebrow. "Yeah? She coming by tomorrow or what?"

"Nah, not quite there yet. Might bring her to the New Year's gig though." His eyes glint mischievously. "What about you? Did you survive your second day without Cora? Or are you planning some grand gesture?"

Before I can answer, Mom and Dad walk in, arms laden with popcorn and drinks. Mom's ears practically perk up. "Cora? Who's Cora?"

"A girl Jake can't get enough of," Owen adds with a smirk.

Mom's jaw drops. I guess I should've expected the shock after five years without a love life update. "You're seeing someone, Jake?"

I shoot Owen a death glare. Traitor. "Uh, yeah. It's still new." *And I love her so much it scares the hell out of me.*

"New, my ass. You should've seen their googly eyes at the show Thursday night," Owen says, digging the hole deeper. "Turns out she's his neighbor."

Mom practically swoons. "Oh, how serendipitous!"

If Mom thinks neighbors are serendipitous, she'd squeal over the truth.

Dad, bless him, tries to save me. "Let's leave the boy alone. He'll tell us more when he's ready."

Thank God someone understands me. Except before I can change the subject, Owen drops another bomb. "Fun fact, Cora is Arden's sister!"

Mom's eyes light up like it's Christmas. *Oh, wait.* "Wouldn't it be perfect if—"

"Seriously?" I mutter, wishing the couch would swallow me whole. "We've been on one date." And where that's true, it doesn't bring justice to what's really between me and Cora. To the nights she's stayed over. The wordless conversations we've had. The connection that seems to transcend time.

Dad chuckles, clapping me on the back. "All right, that's enough. We want him to come back. Right, Ruth?"

They all quiet as the movie starts, but I can't wipe the smile from my face. A month ago, this would've been my personal hell. Now? It feels like... home. Like I'm finally becoming the person I was meant to be all along.

My phone buzzes, and I sneak a glance. It's Cora, of course.

Cora: *So, confession. I've been keeping something from you. Arden's pregnant! Just told the family. Wish you could've seen their faces!*

Well, shit. My eyes go wide, a grin spreading across my face like wildfire. Arden and Mark, having a kid. I'm gonna be an uncle. Sort of.

Me: *Holy shit! That's incredible. Tell Arden congrats from her favorite brother-in-law.*

I hit send, then cringe. Brother-in-law? Too much? Probably.

Me: *Also, I forgot to send this earlier.*

I attach the photo of her canvases hung up in my apartment.

Cora: ♥ *I didn't think my night could improve, but it just did.*
Me: *I'd be better if I could kiss you right now.*

Christ, I'm gone for this girl. But I don't care. It's Cora. And after my discovery tonight, I have a feeling my sappiness is about to hit a new level.

Cora: *Only a kiss? It's Christmas, so I'm in a VERY generous mood.*

Heat rockets through me, and I shift on the couch before anyone sees my obvious reaction. No, fuck it. This is too much fun.

Me: *Save that attitude for next Saturday night?*
Cora: *Or a video call later? XO*

Damn, this woman.

Cora: *And Arden says thank you... Also, you're sworn to secrecy until they tell Mark's family.*

I grin like an idiot, my chest about to burst. I glance around the room, and suddenly everything shifts into focus. Owen, snoring in his chair. Mom and Dad, cuddled up like teenagers. Me, sitting here, part of it all again.

And now Arden and Mark, starting their own family. A whole

new chapter, a fresh start for all of us. It's like the universe is giving us all a second chance, you know?

I think about the notebook upstairs, about Cora's letter. About how our lives have been tangled up for years without us even knowing it. And now here we are, on the brink of something I can't explain. But it feels big. Important.

The movie's still playing, but I couldn't tell you what's happening if my life depended on it. All I can think about is Cora. Her smile, her laugh, the way she looks at me like I'm worth something.

I've got a week of family stuff and work ahead of me before I see her again. A week that's gonna feel like a fucking eternity. But for once, I'm not dreading it. I'm... excited? Is that what this feeling is?

Because I know that at the end of it all, Cora's waiting. And whatever comes next—the band, this thing with us, all of it—I want to face it head-on. No more running. No more hiding. It's time I become the man I used to be. The man they all think I can be again.

Yeah, this feeling? This sense of belonging, of hope, of... love? This is what I've been missing all along. And I'll be damned if I let it slip away again.

33

Jake

December 25th

Christmas night at Sadie's, and I'm riding the high of our best show yet. Who knew opening the bar would have such an incredible turnout? I'm not sure if I should be thankful Sadie liked the idea, or amazed I came up with something that worked so well. The crowd has incredible energy, the band's tight as hell, and for once, I'm not drowning in holiday misery.

Last night with the family was... well, not terrible. Mom cried when I hugged her goodbye this morning, like I was shipping off to war instead of heading back to my apartment. But it felt good. Like maybe we're finally piecing our broken family back together.

I've been sneaking glances at my phone all night, hoping for a text from Cora. But it's Christmas. She's with family. I get it. Doesn't stop me from missing her like crazy, though.

We're packing up after the final set when Bailey taps me on the shoulder, face all serious. "We have a problem."

I turn, annoyed at the interruption. She's gripping her phone like it's a lifeline, knuckles white.

"Can it wait?" I ask, motioning to Owen and Chris hovering nearby. "I'm kinda in the middle of something here."

Bailey huffs, tapping her phone screen. "It's important. About your girlfriend."

My girlfriend? That's her problem.

I rake a hand through my hair, nerves skyrocketing. But I force patience into my tone. "I'm sure it's nothing that can't hold for a bit. Just give me, like, an hour to finish up?"

"Fine," she snaps. "But don't say I didn't try to warn you."

She stalks off, and I let out a breath. Part of me wonders if I'll regret brushing her off, but I can't deal with cryptic girl drama right now. It's Christmas.

Owen claps my shoulder. "Everything okay there?"

"Yeah, yeah," I mutter, scrubbing my face. Exhaustion's hitting hard now that the adrenaline's wearing off. "You're apparently not the only one involving themselves in my relationship status."

Owen laughs, but there's a hint of concern in his eyes. "Jealousy there, then?"

I shrug, trying to play it cool. "Not sure. I've only worked with her a few times, but there's something unsettling for sure."

Chris glances back toward Bailey. "From that girl? I'd say your gut is probably right."

That's what I'm afraid of.

We hang around for another half hour, recapping the night and finalizing New Year's plans. But my mind's not really in it. I keep thinking about Bailey's warning, about Cora, about how quickly things can go to shit.

Finally, Owen and Chris head out, leaving me to start the closing procedures. I'm halfway through inventory when the stockroom door opens, and Bailey walks in.

Here's hoping I'm wrong and she just has one of those personalities...

"Justin sent me to help with the refill list," Bailey says, all innocence and big eyes.

Yeah, right. I force my voice to stay casual. "Sure, take whatever you need."

She steps closer, fingers trailing over bottles like she's shopping for trouble. "So, I noticed your 'special someone' didn't show up tonight. Trouble in paradise? Or did you realize I was right the other night?"

I swallow the bitter taste in my mouth, every instinct screaming danger. "It's Christmas, Bailey. She's with family."

Bailey hums, her fingers dancing over the bottles. "Family, huh? Interesting choice of words."

My hackles rise. "What's that supposed to mean?"

"Oh, nothing," she says, her tone too practiced. "Just... well, I guess 'family' can mean different things to different people."

She pulls out her phone, thumbs tapping away. I try to focus on inventory, but my skin's crawling.

"You know," Bailey says casually, "I always wondered what it'd be like to date a musician. All that passion, those talented hands..."

I nearly drop the vodka I'm holding. "Bailey, that's not—"

"I mean," she continues, stepping closer, "take tonight. All those girls throwing themselves at you. How do you resist?"

I back up, my spine hitting the shelf. "I don't—I mean, I'm with Cora."

Bailey's eyes flare. "Right. Cora. The 'it's complicated' girl who's with family right now."

She holds up her phone, and my world tilts. There's Cora, smiling next to her douchebag ex on a goddamn airplane. First class.

"Sorry to say that I told you so," Bailey whispers.

What the fuck? I snatch the phone from her, zooming in. This can't be real, can it? I think back to breakfast the other morning. Cora telling me she booked the flight when she and Logan were together.

She would have told me if he was on the plane with her, right? But her cryptic text message... And fuck, she's wearing the necklace. The one I'd given her that morning.

Her comment from last week echoes. *You have to trust me, Jake, or this can never work.*

"Where did you get this?" I demand, my voice like sandpaper.

"Instagram," Bailey replies with a shrug. "Something about excitement to spend the holiday with his girl again."

She slowly pulls the phone from my hand and they clench involuntarily. My nails dig into my palms, but the pain grounds me, keeps me from losing it completely.

"There's gotta be more to this," I mutter, more to myself than Bailey. I think of the playfulness in our video call last night, the things she said. It doesn't add up.

Bailey laughs, but it's all wrong. "More to it? God, you're even more pathetic than Lo—" She cuts herself off, eyes widening.

I freeze, every muscle in my body tensing. *Of course. She knows him.* "Than who? Logan?"

Bailey's face goes blank, too quickly. "I didn't say that."

"But you meant it," I growl, stepping closer. The festive Christmas music filtering in from the bar feels like a twisted joke now. "What the fuck does he have to do with this? Did the two of you plan this?"

Bailey's composure cracks for a split second before she rallies. "No. I just... I've heard things, okay? About you. About her. I'm trying to help you see what's right in front of you."

I laugh, but there's no humor in it. "Sorry to disappoint, sweetheart, but I'm not that guy anymore." I think of Cora, of the promise I made to be better. For her. For myself.

"No?" Bailey presses closer, her voice dropping low. "Then prove it. Show me you don't care about her. About that photo."

Before I can react, she grabs my shirt and yanks me into a kiss. For a split second, I'm too shocked to move. Then I shove her away, hard, disgust rolling through me.

"What the actual fuck?!"

Bailey just smirks, motioning to her phone on the shelf. "There. Now you're even."

I stagger back, bile rising in my throat. "Is this all some sick joke to you?"

"It's not a joke, Jake," Bailey says, pocketing her phone. "Just admit it feels good to get back at her. To be better than some rebound."

"Fuck no." I point to the door, my voice deadly calm despite the storm raging inside me. "Get out. You're fired."

Bailey blinks, clearly not expecting this reaction. "You can't just—"

"Try me." My tone could freeze hell over. "Get off this property before I call the cops."

She hovers for a moment, then spins on her heel, spewing threats. But they wash over me like white noise.

As the door slams behind her, I slide down the wall, my head in my hands. What the hell just happened? What do I do now?

I pull out my phone, thumb hovering over Cora's name. I want to call her, hear her voice, let her explain. But doubt gnaws at me. What if Bailey's right? What if I'm just being played again?

It's Cora, my head screams. Cora. Not Tessa. The woman who showed up at the bar to see you when you couldn't face her.

Still, it's 2 AM on Christmas. This isn't a conversation for now. But I can't just sit here, drowning in my own thoughts.

I scroll through my contacts, pausing on another name. Someone who might actually have some answers.

I hit call, praying he picks up.

34

∽

Cora

December 26th

The Florida sun streams through the kitchen window, warming my face as I nurse my third cup of coffee. It's been three days since I landed here, three days of forced holiday cheer and dodging my mother's not-so-subtle inquiries about my love life. *Since when does she care so much?*

I trace the delicate book pendant hanging around my neck, a bittersweet smile tugging at my lips as I think about Jake's video call on Christmas Eve. Wow, am I in deep.

"Still in a daze from all that spiked eggnog yesterday?" Arden asks, cutting through my daydream. "I asked if you told Jake about Logan being on the plane?"

I blink, focusing on my sister's too-innocent expression. "What? No. Why would I?" *Not with how he's reacted every other time I've been around Logan,* I think to myself. Better to tell him in person. Especially since it meant absolutely nothing.

Arden shrugs, buttering her toast with exaggerated care. "Oh, I don't know. Because he's your boyfriend?"

I nearly choke on my coffee. "Boyfriend? We haven't exactly had the 'define the relationship' talk, Arden."

"Well, maybe you should," she replies, her tone just a touch too casual. "I mean, from what you shared last night…"

My cheeks heat up as I recall my drunk ramblings after the family Christmas party yesterday. Did I really tell her about what happened after the bar last Friday?

Still, she knows it's only been a week. What's she fishing for?

Before I can press, Mom breezes into the kitchen, zeroing in on our conversation like a heat-seeking missile.

"Who shared what last night?" she repeats.

Arden smirks. *Shit.* "Cora told me about a guy she started seeing," she replies.

"A guy she's seeing?" Mom echoes, her voice sharp enough to cut glass. "Cora, you're dating someone new? You and Logan just broke up."

I shoot Arden a glare that could melt steel. So much for sisterly solidarity. "It's… complicated," I hedge, already bracing for the inquisition.

Mom launches into a rapid-fire series of questions about Jake's job, background, and life goals, comparing each of my answers to Logan's. Because I haven't gotten enough of that already. From Logan.

I think about his behavior on the plane. It was odd. Almost desperate. Then again, all of our interactions since I walked out have shown a new side to him. It's so at odds with the polished version of him I knew intimately.

The doorbell's sharp ring cuts through Mom's interrogation like a lifeline. "I'll get it!" I practically shout, bolting from the kitchen before anyone can stop me.

I wrench open the front door, a snarky greeting for the unfortunate mailman dying on my lips as I come face-to-face with Logan himself.

You've got to be kidding me.

"Hey, gorgeous," he says, flashing that megawatt smile that used to make my heart flutter. Now it just makes my stomach churn.

"Logan?" I manage, my voice embarrassingly squeaky. "What are you doing here?"

He runs a hand through his artfully tousled hair, the picture of casual confidence. But there's an edge to his smile, a tightness around his eyes that sets off alarm bells in my head.

"Can't a guy check in on his girl?" he asks, taking a step closer.

I instinctively back up, my spine stiffening. "I'm not your girl anymore, Logan. We've been over this. Or did you miss my reminder on the plane?"

His smile falters for a split second before returning full force. "Come on, Cora. You can't tell me you're still dodging me because of that bartender. You deserve better than him."

"We're over because I don't trust you," I snap, anger flaring hot and bright in my chest. "And if you knew what I deserved, you wouldn't be trying to win me back like I was some prize."

Logan's facade cracks, desperation bleeding through. "Cora, please. I want another chance. To prove I can be the man you fell in love with. I gave you time to get whatever fling you needed out of your system. Now, can we pretend you're not going throw away our three years together for some guy who probably won't even remember your name in a month?"

I flinch, his words hitting too close to the doubts I've been trying to squash. But then I think of Jake–of his quiet intensity, the recent interactions where I've glimpsed a different side of him, the way he looks at me like I'm something precious.

Then again, this isn't about me and Jake. This is about me finally standing up for myself.

"Maybe," I say, my voice low but steady. "Or maybe he'll be the man you could never be."

Logan's eyes narrow, a calculating gleam replacing the desperation. "Really? You honestly believe he's better? Because I saw something this morning that makes me think your perfect bartender isn't as devoted as you think."

My heart stutters, even as my mind rebels against the insinuation. "Saw something? You don't even know him."

"I know more than you might think," he insists, pulling out his phone. "Maybe we should talk privately. You might not want an audience for this."

I cross my arms, planting my feet firmly. "Anything you have to say, you can say right here."

Logan hesitates, his eyes flicking past me to where I know Arden is hovering in the living room. Something passes between them—a silent challenge that ratchets up the tension in the air.

"Fine," he says finally, his tone clipped. "But don't say I didn't warn you."

Logan's thumb hovers over his phone screen, a mix of triumph and hesitation in his eyes. Just as he's about to reveal whatever "evidence" he thinks he has, Arden's voice breaks the tension.

"Oh, for heaven's sake," she sighs, stepping into view. "Logan, don't you think this has gone on long enough?"

Logan's head snaps up, confusion flickering across his face. "What are you talking about?"

I glance between them, the pieces slowly clicking into place. Arden's odd behavior this morning, her pointed questions about Jake... she knows something.

"Arden?" I ask, my voice low. "What's going on?"

My sister's eyes soften as she looks at me. "I'm sorry, Co. We didn't want you to find out like this. I was hoping Mark would get back before I had to explain."

"Mark?" I echo, just as a car pulls into the driveway. "What does Mark have to do with this?"

"Jake called him last night," she explains, smiling as she follows my gaze out front. "Something happened at Sadie's."

Something happened? At Sadie's?

I watch as Mark exits the driver's side of the car, my heart nearly stopping when the passenger door swings open. Jake? His eyes meet mine, exhausted but determined. Jake is *here*?

Logan tenses beside me, his grip on his phone turning white-knuckled. "What the hell is he doing here?"

"Oh, you didn't know?" Arden answers with an obvious smirk. "Jake is one of Mark's closest friends."

Jake approaches slowly, his eyes never leaving mine. "Hey, beautiful," he says softly, the corners of his mouth lifting in a tentative smile. "Sorry for dropping in unannounced."

"You're here," I breathe, still trying to process.

Jake takes another step closer, a question in his gaze that seems to say 'there's nowhere else I want to be,' and 'we should talk' all at once.

My feet move of their own accord, closing the distance between us. His arms open instinctively, and I crash into him, breathing in the scent of the bar and Jake all rolled into one. It's as if he came straight here from work. *Wait. Did he?*

I pull back just enough to look into his eyes, finding a storm of emotions swirling in their blue depths. Without thinking, I rise on my tiptoes, pressing my lips to his. Jake responds with the urgency of a writer racing against a deadline, his hand cradling my face as he deepens the kiss. Every unspoken word between us is suddenly translated into this wordless exchange, a flurry of sensations more eloquent than any dialogue.

For a heartbeat, the world around us fades like an inconsequential backstory. There's only Jake's warmth, his steadying presence, the way our bodies align like perfectly balanced prose. It's as if we've stumbled upon the most satisfying denouement, a resolution that feels both unexpected and inevitable.

A pointed cough breaks through our bubble, and reality comes crashing back. Logan's here. To show me something about Jake. Something that happened at Sadie's? Is that why he came?

I step back, glancing at our audience. Logan stands frozen, a mix of hurt and anger etched on his face. Arden watches with a knowing smirk, while Mark looks torn between amusement and concern.

"As touching as this reunion is," Logan bites out, "I think we have more pressing matters to discuss."

Jake's arm slides protectively around my waist, and I lean into him, drawing strength from his presence. "Right," Jake says, his voice rougher than usual. "Let's talk about those 'pressing matters,' shall we?"

I look up at him, concern replacing the giddy warmth of moments ago. "What happened, Jake? Arden said something about Sadie's..."

Jake's blue eyes meet mine, open and vulnerable. "I know I haven't fully earned your trust, Cora. But I want to," he whispers. Then he turns to Logan, his voice hardening. "And I didn't realize I'd get to hear from the source what the grand plan really was. To prove I'd what? Sleep with a co-worker?" Jake gives a humorless laugh. "Picked the wrong guy, Logan. I can't stand cheaters."

Logan's eyes widen before he collects himself. "Grand plan? I have no idea—"

"Save it," Arden interjects. "We know Bailey's your cousin. Know you put her up to it."

"Put her up to what?" I press, frustration mounting. I place a hand on Jake's chest, feeling his rapid heartbeat beneath my palm. "Can someone please explain what's going on?"

Mark steps forward, his calm demeanor a stark contrast to the crackling tension. "Jake called me last night, pretty shaken up. Seems Bailey–who, by the way, just started working at Sadie's–showed him a photo of you and Logan on the plane. Along with some post Logan made about spending Christmas with you."

I whirl on Logan, fury building. "You posted about us? After I explicitly told you we were done?"

Logan has the grace to look ashamed, but there's a defiant set to his jaw. "I thought if I could just remind you of what we had…"

"What we had," I spit, "was a lie. And this? This is low even for you. I don't even know who you are anymore."

Jake's arm flex around me, and I feel him take a steadying breath. "There's more," he says quietly, his voice rumbling through me where we're pressed together. "After Bailey showed me the photo, she… she kissed me."

The ground goes soft beneath my feet. I turn in Jake's arms, searching his face. "Did you…?"

"No," he says firmly, his eyes never leaving mine. His hands come up to frame my face, thumbs stroking my cheeks. "Never. I pushed her away immediately. But she got a picture of it. I'm guessing it's what Logan is trying to show you."

Relief floods through me, followed quickly by a wave of anger. I spin back to Logan, disgust churning in my gut. "Is that true? You set this whole thing up?"

Logan's facade crumbles, desperation etching lines into his face. "I didn't… it wasn't supposed to go this far. I just wanted to prove he wasn't the guy you thought he was."

"So you thought hurting me first was the solution?" I ask, incredulous.

"I thought I was protecting you!" Logan explodes. "This guy, he's got a reputation. I couldn't stand the thought of him using you and tossing you aside."

Jake tenses beside me, but his voice remains steady. "You don't know anything about me, or what Cora means to me."

"Oh yeah?" Logan challenges. "Then why'd you fly all the way down here instead of just calling her? Guilty conscience?"

Jake's eyes flash, but before he can respond, Arden steps between them. "Enough," she says firmly. "Logan, I think it's time for you to leave."

For a moment, it looks like Logan might argue. But then his shoulders slump, defeat written in every line of his body. "Cora, I'm sorry. I never meant..."

"Just go," I say, suddenly exhausted. "Please."

As Logan's car disappears down the driveway, I turn to Jake, a thousand questions burning on my tongue. But the vulnerability in his eyes stops me short.

"I'm so sorry," he says, his voice thick with emotion. "I should have trusted you. Should have called you the moment Bailey showed me that photo. But I panicked, and then I couldn't bear the thought of you thinking I'd betrayed you, so I just..."

"Hopped on a plane to Florida?" I finish, a small smile tugging at my lips despite everything.

Jake nods, a hint of his usual wry humor returning. "Not my smoothest move, I'll admit."

I step closer, my hand finding his. "I don't know, I think it's pretty romantic. In a slightly insane, grand gesture kind of way."

He laughs, the sound warming me from the inside out. "Yeah?"

"Yeah," I confirm, sliding my arms around his waist. "But next time, maybe just call first?"

Jake's arms tighten around me, his chin resting on top of my head. "Deal."

35

Cora

"So," Arden drawls, settling onto the couch, "are we going to talk about the fact that Jake flew over a thousand miles just to kiss you senseless on our front lawn?"

We're all sprawled across the living room, the adrenaline from Logan's dramatic exit finally wearing off.

"I mean, it wasn't just for the kissing," Jake quips, his signature smirk back in place. "Though it was definitely a highlight."

Mark snorts from his perch on the armchair. "At least you had the sense to call me first this time. Though I gotta admit, I didn't expect you to hop on a plane right after."

Jake shrugs, but I feel him relax slightly beside me. "What can I say? I'm full of surprises."

That he is. Because two weeks ago, that's not what happened. Heck, a week ago that wasn't even how he responded. This time was different. Is that progress?

I turn to face him, cupping his face. "Really, though, thank you for coming. For trusting me enough to show up."

Jake's eyes soften, his hand covering mine. "I'm done running from my past, Cora. I'm just sorry it took me some time to realize it."

"Okay, okay, enough with the googly eyes," Arden interrupts, though her tone is fond. "We still need to figure out what we're telling Mom and Dad. And by 'we,' I mean you two," she adds, pointing at me and Jake. "Luckily, we teed it up that you're seeing someone new."

That was the act this morning? It all makes sense now. Why she told Mom. She knew Jake was coming.

"Speaking of," Mark says, glancing towards the kitchen, "we should probably brace ourselves. Mom's bound to come investigate all the commotion any minute now."

As if on cue, we hear footsteps approaching. I give Jake's hand a reassuring squeeze.

"Cora? Arden?" Mom's voice calls out. "What's going on out here? Who was at the door?"

I take a deep breath, steeling myself. "In here, Mom," I call back, shooting Jake an apologetic look. "We, uh, have a visitor."

Mom appears in the doorway, her eyes widening as she takes in the scene before her. Her gaze collides with Jake, and I can practically see the gears turning in her head.

"Is this the musician I just heard about?" she asks, her voice deceptively calm.

I stand, pulling Jake up with me. "Yeah, Mom, this is Jake. Jake Rhoades."

Jake, bless him, reads the room and steps forward, extending his hand. "It's a pleasure to meet you, Mrs. Cooper. Apologies for dropping in. Just wanted to surprise everyone being the holiday and all."

Mom's eyebrow arches so high it nearly disappears into her hairline. "Quite the surprise, flying all the way down here. But I suppose it is Christmastime." She turns to me, her expression showing both confusion and amusement. "I suppose I'll let your father know we'll have another guest joining us for sailing. Assuming he's sticking around."

I glance at Jake, having no clue how long he's even in town for.

"That would be lovely," Jake replies. "I have to get back to Chicago tomorrow. But if you'd allow, I'd enjoy spending the day with you all."

Mom nods slowly, her gaze sweeping over Jake once more, taking in his slightly rumpled appearance. "Well then," she says, her tone clipped, "why don't you all get changed, and I'll update your father."

Once she's out of earshot, Jake lets out a shaky breath. "So, on a scale of one to 'facing down a dragon,' how was that?"

The three of us laugh, the tension breaking slightly.

"Oh, sweetie," I say, patting his chest, "that was just the warm-up round. You haven't even met my dad yet."

Jake's eyes widen comically. "Should I be worried?"

I stand on my tiptoes to press a quick kiss to his cheek. "Nah, you'll be fine. Probably." I tug him towards the stairs. "Come on, let's get you changed. Can't get on the boat looking like you just rolled out of a bar."

As we head upstairs, I think about the turn my life has taken. A month ago, I was nursing a broken heart and dreading another disastrous December. Now? Now I'm leading a gorgeous, kind-hearted man to a bedroom at my parents' place, about to introduce him to them as my...what? Boyfriend? Is that what he is?

"Hey," Jake says softly as I close the door. He pulls me close, his forehead resting against mine. "Are you okay with this? Me staying here? Meeting your family? I know it's soon—"

"It's fine," I interrupt. "But, Jake, are you? I don't want to push—"

"I want to, Cora." Jake's smile is soft and sure. "I meant what I said earlier. I want to be in your story for more than just a chapter."

My heart soars. "Good," I whisper, brushing my lips against his. "Because I think we're just getting to the good part."

Jake's laugh is warm and rich, a sound I'm quickly becoming addicted to. "Well then, angel, I can't wait to see what happens next."

His hands wrap around my waist, pulling me flush against him as his mouth finds mine once more. And damn it, if I'm not desperately wanting to skip the boat and spend the entire day tangled up together in this room. Especially when Jake backs me up to the mattress, gently lowering me down without taking his lips from mine.

A knock on the door forces us to separate, both trying to appear terribly inconspicuous as Mark peeks his head into the room. "Shit. Sorry!" He backs out hastily, eyes comically wide.

I roll my eyes, stifling a giggle. "It's fine, Mark. Come in."

He re-enters gingerly, gaze darting between us. Jake runs a hand through his recently ruffled hair, trying and failing to look nonchalant.

"Could be worse," I whisper, elbowing Jake. "Imagine if it was my dad."

Jake's exaggerated shudder makes me snort. Mark just shakes his head, tossing a bundle of clothes at Jake.

"Probably won't be swimming, but thought you could use these for the trip. Got an extra pair of sandals, too, Casanova."

Jake catches the swim trunks, grinning. "Thanks. I owe you." His face turns more serious as he adds, "For a lot."

Mark simply nods, and I can see the years of regret and apologies passing wordlessly between them. I realize that I'm not the only one benefiting from this recent change in Jake.

After reluctantly breaking apart to get ready, Jake settles next to me, appearing more relaxed and refreshed.

"So, anything you want to share about your parents before throwing me to the wolves?" he teases, tucking a rouge strand of hair behind my ear.

"Well, they're both retired corporate lawyers turned venture capitalists. They still believe I'm going to change my mind and do something more 'worthwhile—'" I use air quotes for emphasis, "—with my life than reading trashy novels, and they're big on things like first impressions and proper etiquette."

Jake nods. "Got it. Probably screwed already." He leans in closer, his lips fanning my neck. "But for the record, do you like what you do?"

"I get to read and get paid for it," I say, slightly breathless. "Kind of like getting paid to play the guitar and sing."

I can feel Jake's smile against my skin. "Touché. Just wanted to know how much I'm supposed to stand up for your career."

"I'd stay away from that topic if I were you," I warn.

Jake pulls back to look at me. "We'll see. Any other topics I should avoid?"

I adjust the collar of his shirt absently. "Hmm, let's see. Politics, religion, your opinions on the judicial system, and definitely don't mention that time you got arrested for public intoxication."

Jake freezes. "How did you know about that?"

I smirk, patting his chest. "I didn't. But thanks for confirming my suspicions."

He groans, dropping his head to my shoulder. "I walked right into that one, didn't I?"

"Yep," I say, popping the 'p'. "Don't worry, your secret's safe with me. For now."

Jake lifts his head, his eyes meeting mine with an intensity that makes my breath catch. "You know, for someone who believes in romance, you can be pretty devious."

I shrug, trying to ignore the way my heart races at his proximity. "What can I say? I like to keep things interesting."

"Mission accomplished," Jake murmurs, leaning in for a kiss that threatens to derail our entire plan.

I reluctantly pull away, smoothing his shirt one last time. "Ready to face the firing squad?"

Jake takes a deep breath, squaring his shoulders. "As I'll ever be. Lead the way, Coco baby."

The interrogation—I mean, introduction—goes about as well as expected. Mom's pursed lips could curdle milk, while Dad's handshake seems designed to test Jake's pain threshold. But my bartender-turned-boyfriend takes it all in stride, answering their rapid-fire questions with a charm that would make Mr. Darcy jealous.

As we follow my parents toward the dock, Jake leans in close. "Thoughts?"

I give a small smile. "You did great. Really. I think Dad might even like you."

"And your mom?"

I wince. "Well, Rome wasn't built in a day."

The boat trip goes surprisingly well, all things considered. Jake manages to impress Dad with his knowledge of nautical terms (who knew all those sailor-themed drinking songs would come in handy?), and even Mom seems to thaw slightly when Jake offers to help with the rigging.

As the sun begins to set, painting the sky in brilliant oranges and pinks, I find myself leaning against the railing, Jake's arms wrapped around me from behind. It's a scene straight out of a romance novel cover, and for once, I'm not itching to edit a thing.

"Care to share what's going on in that mind of yours?" Jake murmurs, his breath warm against my ear.

I lean back into him, sighing contentedly. "Just thinking about how this December is turning out nothing like I expected."

"Good different or bad different?"

I turn in his arms, meeting his gaze. "Definitely good. Though, I'm still waiting for the other shoe to drop. Old habits die hard, I guess."

Jake's expression softens. "Hey, no more curse talk, remember? From now on, it's all smooth sailing."

I groan at the pun, even as I laugh. "That was terrible."

"You love it," he teases, leaning in for a kiss that makes me forget all about curses and shoes dropping.

We're interrupted by Arden's voice, calling from the dock. "If you two lovebirds are done reenacting Titanic, we've got plans!"

I pull away slowly, rolling my eyes at my sister's antics. "Right, the Beachside Bar. You up for it?" I ask Jake.

His eyes light up. "Absolutely. I hear there might be some embarrassing Cora stories in it for me."

I swat at him playfully. "Don't you dare."

* * *

The Beachside Bar is exactly as I remember it from my summers working here during college—a perfect blend of tacky beach decor and nostalgic charm. As we settle into a booth, the familiar scent of salt air and fried food washing over us, I'm struck by how seamlessly Jake fits into this scene from my past.

"Alright," Arden announces, a mischievous glint in her eye. "Who's ready for some Cora Cooper: The Early Years?"

I groan, burying my face in my hands. "Do we have to?"

Jake pulls me closer, his grin wide and eager. "Oh, we absolutely have to."

As the night wears on, the embarrassing stories give way to a comfortable lull in conversation. I'm nestled against Jake, his warmth a constant reminder of how much has changed in such a short time.

Arden breaks the silence, a faraway look in her eye. "You know, it's kinda funny when you think about it," she muses.

I tilt my head, curiosity piqued. "What's funny?"

"If you two hadn't been in the hospital that winter, I might never have reconnected with Mark," she answers, a slow smile spreading across her face.

I blink, struggling to connect the dots. "Wait, what? You two started dating because of the hospital? I thought you met in college."

"Technically, we met in college but didn't stay in touch," Arden explains. "Then he approached me in the cafeteria and suckered me back in." She casts a soppy gaze at Mark, who puffs up under the attention. "He fell in love as I bawled into his shirt."

I gape at them, gobsmacked by this latest twist of fate. It's like the universe has been playing an elaborate game of six degrees of separation, and we're only now seeing the connections.

Mark glances longingly at Arden, oblivious. "I'm just sorry it took Jake almost dying for me to reach out to you. I'll apologize for it the rest of my life."

My gaze bounces between the two of them and Jake. "Hold up, Jake, did you know they met because of our accident?"

Jake's grip tightens around me as he looks at me curiously. "Well, yeah. I knew they reconnected at the hospital. But I had no idea it was you Arden was there to see. Then, anyway."

I don't realize everything Jake admitted until I notice the way Mark and Arden are staring at us.

Mark leans forward, something appearing to click into place. "Wait. You two knew each other? Before now?"

Jake's other hand finds mine beneath the table. Our eyes meet, both thinking the same thing. It's time.

"Funny story," I start, my voice barely above a whisper, "we, uh, kinda met during that accident."

"Noooo," Mark says slowly, shaking his head. He looks pointedly at Jake, disbelief coloring his features. "This is her? The girl who saved your life? This whole time, it was Cora?"

Arden's brow furrows. "What are you talking about? Saved his life?"

I take a deep breath, squeezing Jake's hand for support. "Well, our cars—" I nod toward Jake, "—were pinned together. And Jake…" I trail off, images of seeing Jake lifeless against the steering wheel flashing like scenes from a nightmare.

"I was in and out of consciousness," Jake finishes. "So, Cora here busted into my car and saved my life." He glances my way with a look of gratitude that takes my breath away. "She kicked through the windshield and got me out."

"Just before it caught fire," Mark adds, his jaw still open.

I whip my head around to Jake, shock coursing through me. "Fire? You never told me—"

"I didn't want to worry you," Jake says softly, his thumb tracing soothing circles on my hand. "You'd already done so much."

The gravity of what could have been hits me like a tidal wave. I clutch Jake's hand tighter, anchoring myself in the present, in the reality where he's here, safe and whole beside me.

"So all this time," Arden says slowly, "you two have been connected without even knowing it?"

I nod, still reeling. "Talk about a slow-burn romance," I quip weakly, falling back on humor to process the enormity of it all.

Jake chuckles, pressing a kiss to my temple. "I'd say it was worth the wait."

As we fill Mark and Arden in on the details, I'm struck by the intricate web of coincidences and choices that led us to this moment. It's like we've been characters in some grand, cosmic story, our paths intersecting and diverging only to come back together in the most unexpected ways.

"It's like the universe kept trying to push you two together," Arden muses, her eyes shining. "And you kept missing each other by inches."

"Until now," Jake adds softly, his gaze meeting mine with an intensity that makes my breath catch.

I think about all the Decembers that came before this one—the accidents, the heartbreaks, the near-misses. Each one a stepping stone, leading us here, to this moment.

"Maybe," I say, surprising myself with the certainty in my voice, "this is exactly where we were always meant to end up."

Jake holds me tighter, and I lean into him, savoring the rightness of it all. The four of us, all here by some strange circumstance. Call it fate, destiny, or coincidence. Whatever the reason, it doesn't matter. Because for the first time in a long time, I'm not scared of what December might bring. I'm right where I should be—wrapped securely in Jake's arms.

36

Jake

"Alright, enough sappiness, Cora," I say, slowly extracting my arms from around her. "We're doing karaoke."

I'm bone-tired, but there's no way in hell I'm calling it quits early. Not when every moment with her feels like borrowed time.

Cora gives a mirthless laugh. "Uh, no. You can. I don't sing."

I kiss her temple before flashing her a teasing grin. "Come on, I promise not to upstage you too badly with my angelic voice."

"Please, you just want an excuse to show off," she snorts.

I gasp dramatically. "Are you accusing me of being a boastful, attention-seeking performer?" At her pointed look, I drop the act with a chuckle. "Alright, guilty as charged. But admit it, you love my singing."

I punctuate this by serenading her loudly and off-key. Cora dissolves into giggles that warms me to my core. It's a sound I could get used to hearing every day. And isn't that a terrifying thought?

Taking advantage, I sling an arm around her shoulders, coaxing her gently. "One duet, that's all I ask. Then pick any song under the sun for your brother-in-law and me to perform after." I wink across the table, where Mark is suddenly very interested in his drink.

"And what do I get out of this deal?" Cora asks, failing to hide her smile.

So many options flash through my mind, each more tempting than the last.

"Don't answer that," Arden snares, apparently reading my gutter-filled mind. "As much as I love you, Jake, she's still my baby sister."

"Fine, say yes, and we all get a fun night out," I offer, smiling in Arden's direction with my G-rated answer. But beneath the table, I trace delicate patterns over Cora's thigh, alluding to more promises later.

Damn, I can't get enough of this girl. It's different from anything I've felt before. With Tessa, everything was a competition, a constant struggle to prove myself. But with Cora? It's easy. Natural. Like coming home after years of wandering.

"Okay, fine, one song," Cora finally answers, eyes sparkling. "But you better bring your A-game, rock star."

"Wait a minute, what about me?" Mark questions. "I didn't say I'd do it."

"You were just to sweeten the deal. I'll go solo," I admit as Mark mumbles a "thank you" beneath his breath. I squeeze Cora's leg, basking in her happy grin. "Pick anything you want, babe."

Cora and Arden are lost in the song list, cackling like they've found comedy gold in the karaoke tracks. It's then that the absurdity of my life hits me like a surprise drum solo. Last month, I was the poster child for brooding bartenders anonymous. Now? I'm in a tacky Florida bar, with people who seem to think I'm worth a damn, and a woman who makes me want to dust off my rusty 'decent human being' skills.

"Sure you won't regret this?" Cora teases, sliding off my lap and scooting closer to Arden as she submits their choice.

"Nah," I reply. Because with her smiling? I don't think I could regret a damn thing.

I guide her to the stage when our names are called, keeping her close as I sense her anxiety rising. It's funny how quickly I've learned to read her, like she's a song I've known all my life but am just now learning to play.

"Nervous?" I ask as we grab the microphones.

She simply smirks, smoothing down her skirt. "You're loving this, aren't you?"

"Being on stage with you by my side? Absolutely." *And isn't that the truth.*

I tuck a strand of hair behind her ears, watching her calm. It's a simple gesture, but it feels more intimate than any hookup I've had in the past five years.

I can scarcely tear my gaze from Cora as the opening lyrics to "Timber" by Pitbull and Kesha echo through the speakers. She brings the mic to her lips, swaying gently, a vision bathed under the rainbow lights shining on the stage. Then, I catch her gaze, the chaos around us fading.

Cora shocks me by nailing the opening, nerves vanishing. Her voice entwines flawlessly with mine until I nearly fumble the chorus, drunk less on karaoke courage than on her.

We build steadily in confidence and momentum as the song crests. Cora tosses her head back, lost in delighted abandonment, and I fall harder still. No glitzy stadium of adoring fans could ever compare to this view. To her. I capture the image mentally, praying Arden is videoing this.

As the music winds down, I reel Cora against me, never wanting this night to end. She fits effortlessly in my arms, cheek pressed to my racing pulse. It's like we were made for each other, two broken pieces finally finding their match.

"So, you do this often?" I tease when I remember how words work.

Cora's answering laugh thrums through me. "Only when I have a partner that can keep up."

My grin threatens to split my face. Dipping my face closer until our noses brush, I murmur low for her ears alone. "Careful, Coco, you'll make me believe I stand a chance at keeping an angel like you."

Cora stills before surging to her tiptoes and kissing me for the entire bar to see.

And suddenly, I want to blurt out that I love her. That I can't picture any night without her. That she's changed everything, made me want to be the man I used to be before grief and guilt turned me into a shell of myself.

But this is too new. So, instead, I bite my tongue and wait for the right time.

"Your turn, *babe*," Cora mocks, pulling back from my embrace.

She slinks off the stage, putting her hands together in the shape of a heart.

I burst into laughter as the Spice Girls' opening strains of "Wannabe" sound through the speakers.

She thinks this will... humiliate me? Not even close. I'm not even disappointed that I know all the words without reading the screen. If she only knew how many times Owen and I belted this out in our parents' garage...

I chance a peek at Cora, who watches eagerly, radiating joy. And in that moment, I know I'd do anything to keep that smile on her face.

Squaring my shoulders, I channel any mortification into pompous showmanship. If she wants a spectacle, who am I to deny her? I prance theatrically across the stage, belting into the mic with an exaggerated flair. I would sing anything she wanted me to if it meant seeing her this happy. Being the reason she's this content.

As the final notes fade, I surface from daydreams of a future world to the bright stage lights, lungs burning. I find Cora again, still gazing with adoration from below. She yells, "Impressive," as I scramble off the stage, sweeping her into a crushing embrace. Her laughter echoes into my chest as she relaxes into me.

Over her shoulder, Mark's knowing smirk barely registers. He mouths something suspiciously like "goner" before dodging Arden's swat. But I'm past denial now—no matter what the future holds, my life will never be the same now that I've had her in it.

"You know what they say about paybacks," I whisper jokingly on our walk back to the table.

"Show me, please," she pleads alluringly.

I contemplate tossing her onto the table and climbing on top of her, showing her exactly what I mean. But given that her sister and brother-in-law are sitting there, it might be frowned upon. So, I settle for pulling her back onto my lap and wrapping my arms around her possessively.

"Think I found my new permanent karaoke partner," I tease, nipping below her ear.

Cora giggles, leaning in closer. "Better duet with me again soon, then."

"Maybe next time without an audience so I can focus on making you hit all the high notes," I whisper, filling my lungs with her scent— that flowery number still covering my pillowcase.

"Looking forward to it."

And damn, holding her right now, I realize there isn't a price I wouldn't have paid to be here. To have this second chance. To be the man she deserves.

I straighten self-consciously as an unfamiliar man approaches our table, his curious gaze ping-ponging between me and Cora.

"Cora Cooper? Is that you?" he questions.

"Gram? Oh gosh. Are you still working here? I had no idea." Cora leans forward, simultaneously twisting her fingers into mine and squeezing. Already knowing what I need. Reassurance.

"Yeah. I manage the events here now," Gram answers, running a casual hand through his hair.

"Told you there'd still be people you knew here," Arden mumbles beside us.

After an agonizing second, Cora's bright stare connects with mine. Her lips curve encouragingly. "Gram, this is my boyfriend, Jake."

Boyfriend. The label sends an illicit thrill through me even as I paste on a polite smile. I'm her boyfriend. It means she's my girlfriend.

"Jake manages events for a bar up in Chicago," Cora adds with a sweet tone.

Gram's attention turns to me, reaching out a hand. "Hey, man. Nice job with the karaoke." He pauses, staring at me like he's trying to place me. "Chicago? Funny. I just came back from there this morning. One of my good friends wanted me to catch a performance up there. It's probably a long shot, but any chance you've heard of the place? Sadie's?"

I can't see Cora's expression, but I can feel her practically buzzing in my lap.

"That's the bar he works at!" she chimes enthusiastically, glancing back at me with a strange adoration. "His band plays there, too."

"No way," Gram starts. "That's why you look familiar. You're Jake from All Rhoades? Shit. Here?" He grabs the open seat, joining our foursome. "I saw your show last night. A buddy of mine has been trying to get me up there to see it, but it's hard with the shifts I work."

I know the feeling.

I hesitate momentarily under the attention. Playing to crowds is second nature after so many years of performing. But something about Cora proudly claiming me—boyfriend, manager, musician— has warmth spreading down my limbs like liquid gold.

"We're still experimenting with blending covers and originals," I explain, unable to restrain a grin. "But I'm glad you liked it. It's the first time we've done a Christmas show there."

"It was fucking awesome." Gram pauses, glancing between me and Cora. "Do you travel? We'd love to host you here sometime."

Cora latches on to my arm, beaming. "You should see the crowds he pulls in Chicago. I swear Jake has a cult following."

A laugh escapes before I can downplay Cora's praise. But the joy sparkling in her expression cuts off any self-deprecation. I glance up, meeting Gram's gaze. "We'd be thrilled to come down. Just say when."

"I'll send you his contact info," Cora adds. The smile she flips me promises all the reward I'll ever need.

Gram stands back up, tapping the table. "That'd be awesome, Cora. Maybe I can, uh, grab another round for the table? On the house."

"Dude, you've got fans everywhere," Mark comments with minimal mockery as Gram saunters back toward the bar.

"I only need one tonight," I reply, wrapping my arms tighter around Cora.

Mark makes a sarcastic comment, but I don't hear it over Cora's whisper in my ear. "I've been your fangirl for longer than you know."

Oh, I think I know now, I think to myself, leaning back to meet her blazing amber eyes. But instead of blurting out what I uncovered this week, I simply say, "You're amazing, you know that?"

"You are too, Jake." Her lips find my jaw as I bask in her open admiration, the sounds of the bar fading around us.

And here, in her arms, I might finally believe I can be enough.

37

∽

Jake

December 27th

I pry one eye open to the lazy morning sunshine, a contented sigh escaping my lips. Another follows as soft kisses dust across my jaw and down my neck. I slide my arms around Cora's waist, a smile tugging my mouth before our lips meet.

Several minutes pass, lost in soft caresses and mingled breath. Eventually, I pull back to admire her, utterly captivating in the glow of the bright sunshine.

"How is it possible for you to look even more beautiful first thing in the morning?" I say, twisting a golden strand of hair around my fingers.

Cora smiles, a subtle blush staining her cheeks that I can't resist kissing. "How are you awake? I expected you to be a zombie after a day of zero sleep and then... well, everything last night."

My chuckle morphs into a groan as her lips find the sensitive spot below my ear. I drag her closer, our bodies molding together like two puzzle pieces.

From the hallway, Arden's voice slices through our heated exchange. "Rise and shine, you two! Breakfast."

Cora attempts an innocent expression that might actually convince someone she didn't just have her tongue down my throat. "We'll be right there! I just need to...make myself presentable."

I prop myself up on one elbow, letting my heated gaze trail the length of her. "Presentable?" I tease. "I find your just-woke-up appearance extremely sexy."

With a strangled squeak, she smacks me with a pillow, only enhancing her dishevelment. "You're insatiable!" But her scolding lacks any real malice, her sunrise-colored eyes dancing.

I could totally wake up like this every morning for the rest of...forever. The thought should scare me, but it doesn't. Not anymore.

Minutes later, Cora's tugging me down the stairs, practically bouncing into the kitchen. "Morning, everyone!" she offers with a smile that radiates 'I just got laid.' With one glance at her father, I know he can see it, too.

Fuck. This ought to be an interesting breakfast.

I glance around at the group seated at the table. Cora's parents—formal and stiff with their phones out and coffee mugs in hand. Mark and Arden—huddled together, talking in hushed tones. The interactions contrast with one another. And I wonder how Arden and Cora ended up so different, so down to earth.

I hang back a bit, suddenly feeling like an intruder in this family scene. Cora, sensing my hesitation, reaches back and laces her fingers through mine, giving me an encouraging smile. It's a small gesture, but it grounds me, reminding me that I belong here. With her.

Her dad peers up from his phone, his gaze landing on our joined hands before meeting my eyes. I swallow, taking my seat. Can he see in my expression how I defiled his daughter last night? Does he own a shotgun?

The charged moment stretches. I resist wiping my suddenly clammy palms on my jeans, contemplating fleeing outside if only to get some fresh air. *Get it together, Rhoades. You were both cool last night. Act natural.*

When I'm about to say something—anything to lessen the tension—a woman I've never seen enters the room with a loaded plate. "Morning Cooper's! Anyone want banana pancakes? I've got another plate following this one."

She sets the plate on the table, and it's like someone hit the play button on a paused scene. The pressure releases, and sound returns to normal levels. As we pass around syrup and orange juice, Cora's hand slides comfortingly over my thigh under the table, and I finally relax.

"So, Jake," Mrs. Cooper begins, her tone carefully neutral. "Cora tells us you're quite the musician."

I nearly choke on my coffee. *Quite the musician?* That's a far cry from the disdain in her voice yesterday when she called me a bartender. I shoot a glance at Cora, who's suddenly very interested in buttering her pancakes.

"Oh, uh, I don't know about that," I stammer, rubbing the back of my neck. "I just enjoy playing, you know?"

"Don't be modest," Cora chimes in, giving me a playful nudge. "Tell them about your gig on New Year's Eve."

All eyes turn to me, and I feel my face heating up. "It's not a big deal, really. Just a small set at Navy Pier."

"Navy Pier?" Mr. Cooper repeats, his eyebrows rising. "That's quite impressive."

I shrug, uncomfortable with the attention. "We got lucky, I guess. Right place, right time."

"Luck had nothing to do with it," Cora insists, her eyes shining with pride. "You guys are talented. They'd be crazy not to want you."

Her unwavering support leaves me breathless, wondering how I go so lucky.

"Well," Mrs. Cooper says, a hint of a smile playing at her lips. "Perhaps we'll have to come up and see you perform sometime."

I blink, surprised by the offer. "That... that would be great," I manage, a warmth spreading through my chest.

The conversation flows more easily after that, the initial awkwardness melting away. As I listen to Cora and Arden banter about childhood memories, I'm hit with a memory of Christmas morning at my parents' house two days ago. The way the four of us got along, despite the absence we all felt. It was nice. Comforting in a way I didn't realize I needed.

"Hey, Jake," Mark calls, grabbing my attention from across the table. "Talking about New Year's Eve made me remember, are you free that afternoon? Before your big show?"

I think about the crazy schedule Owen sent us, planned out to the minute. "Um, maybe until five or so, why?"

Mark looks to Arden, who simply nods encouragingly. "Well, Arden's making me tell my parents. About the baby."

"Making you?" Arden repeats. "Don't you think they're going to be happy for you?"

Mark shrugs, glancing back at me. "Anyway, we thought it might be nice if you and Owen were there. Your parents, too. You know, since you all are more family than my own in some ways."

The invitation hits me like a sucker punch to the gut. *More family than his own.* This is another olive branch. Mark, welcoming me back into the fold. After everything that's happened, after all the years I pushed him away... it means more than I can express.

"Wouldn't miss it, bud," my voice betraying me, coming out all gravel and grit.

Mark nods, a small smile flashing. "It'll be like old times."

Old times. The phrase echoes in my head, bringing with it a flood of memories. Sleepovers, New Year's Eve parties in our old basement, Thomas always trying to keep up with us.

"Just promise me one thing," Arden pipes up, breaking through my daydream. "No recreating the Great Eggnog Incident of 2015."

I can't help but laugh, the tension in my chest easing. "Hey, that was all Owen's fault. I told him not to spike the punch bowl."

"And yet, somehow, you were the one who ended up singing 'All I Want for Christmas Is You' on the roof," Mark chuckles.

"In my defense," I say, holding up my hands, "I make an excellent Mariah Carey."

The table erupts in laughter, and for a moment, everything feels right in the world. I catch Cora's eye, her smile soft and understanding. This—this warmth, this sense of belonging—is what I've been missing all these years.

As everyone quiets and plates are cleared, reality starts to creep back in. My flight. Chicago. Leaving Cora. The thought sits like a lead weight in my stomach.

"I should get going soon," I say reluctantly, already missing the warmth of this makeshift family gathering. "Don't want to miss my flight."

Cora's face falls for a split second before she masks it with a smile that doesn't quite reach her eyes. "Of course. I can take you, if Mark doesn't mind."

"Not at all," Mark says, standing. "I'll help Jake grab his stuff from upstairs."

When we reach the guest room, Mark clears his throat. "Really great having you here, man. Missed this…"

The confession hangs between us, heavy with years of unspoken regrets and missed opportunities. "Me too, Mark," I manage. "Seriously, I can't thank you enough."

Before I can spiral into a pit of self-loathing, Mark yanks me into a crushing hug. It's forgiveness and understanding and brotherhood all rolled into one, and damn if it doesn't nearly break me.

We separate with watery laughs, emotions settling like dust after a storm. Without another word, Mark grabs my bag, and we head downstairs where goodbyes wait.

The ride to the airport is quiet at first, the weight of my imminent departure pressing down on us. Cora's knuckles are white on the steering wheel, and I want nothing more than to smooth away the tension I see in the set of her shoulders.

"So," I start, aiming for casual and probably missing by a mile, "what time do you get back Saturday?"

"Not until after six," she answers, a wobbly almost smile teasing her lips.

I nod, mind already racing ahead. "I'm working that night, but maybe you could stop by Sadie's after you land? If you wanted to, I mean. No pressure."

Cora's quiet for a moment, and I'm kicking myself for pushing too hard when she speaks. "Are you sure? I don't want to overwhelm you if you want to take this slow."

I laugh, the sound bursting out of me like a dam breaking. "Babe, I asked you. If you think it's too much, tell me. But honestly? By Saturday, I might be going through withdrawals."

Her lips quirk up in a smile. "Jake, I..." She pauses, biting her lip in a way that already drives me crazy. "My only speed with you seems to be zero to sixty."

Relief and joy explode in my chest. "Thank God," I breathe, reaching for her hand. "I was worried it was just me."

We're pulling into the airport now, reality looming large. I don't want to go. I want to stay in this bubble where everything makes sense, where I'm not Jake the screw-up, but Jake the guy who might actually deserve someone like Cora.

"These last two days," I start, turning to face her fully. "It's been... I don't even have words, Cora. You've turned my whole world upside down, you know that?"

She smiles, soft and a little sad. "You've done the same to mine."

"I know it's fast," I continue, the words tumbling out now. "And

I know we've got a lot to figure out. But I want this, Cora. I want us. Whatever that looks like."

Cora's eyes are shining now, and I want to kick myself for making her cry. But then she's leaning in, pressing her lips to mine in a kiss that tastes like promises and possibilities.

"I want that too," she whispers against my lips.

I rest my forehead against hers, breathing her in. "So we'll figure it out?"

She nods, her fingers threading through mine. "We'll figure it out."

Eventually, I pull away, grabbing my bag from the backseat. I know there's still uncertainty ahead—navigating our schedules, the band's future, the messy history between us. But there's no one else I'd rather have by my side.

"I'll see you Saturday, then," I say, unable to keep the grin off my face.

"Saturday," she confirms, her smile matching mine.

As I walk into the airport, I glance back one last time. Cora's still there, watching me go. And I know: this is only the beginning. Our beginning. And damn if I'm not ready for every single chapter.

38

Jake

December 31ˢᵗ

Waking up next to Cora is like hearing the perfect chord progression for the first time. It's familiar yet surprising, comforting yet exhilarating. Her wild hair forms a halo on the pillow, and her soft breaths create a rhythm I could write songs to for days. Four days apart felt like an eternity, but having her here now? It's like time stood still.

I trace the curve of her shoulder, fighting the urge to hum the melody that's been forming in my head since she walked into the bar last night. Memories replay in tantalizing visions. Her body pressed tightly to mine as we snuck dances at the bar. Her nails raking deliciously into my skin as we stumbled into her apartment, fused lip to lip. Her ankles crossed around my back as I laid her on this bed.

Cora stirs, mumbling something about five more minutes, and I can't help but grin. Damn, I love her.

"Sorry, Sleeping Beauty, but it's already past ten," I murmur, pressing a kiss to her forehead. "Though I gotta say, you make a compelling case for playing hooky."

She bolts upright, eyes wide. "Ten? Oh God, Jake, your family lunch!"

I trail kisses along her neck, reveling in the way she melts against me. "Relax, babe. Mark will forgive me if I'm fashionably late. Besides," I add with a smirk, "it's your birthday. Pretty sure there's a law against rushing the birthday girl."

Cora swats at me, but I catch her hand, bringing it to my lips. "Nice try, superstar, but your charm won't work on me."

"No?" I raise an eyebrow, pulling her closer. "What about my irresistible musical talents? I could serenade you right here..."

She laughs, the sound more beautiful than any song I've ever written. "As tempting as that is, I don't think Mark or Arden would appreciate you missing their announcement for an impromptu concert."

I sigh dramatically, flopping back onto the pillows. "Fine, fine. But first..." I hesitate, my heart suddenly pounding a rapid beat in my chest. "What do you say about joining me? At the Bell's, I mean."

Cora's eyes widen. "Join you? Like, meet your family?"

The words rush out like an overeager opening act. "Yeah, I mean, if you want to. There's this place I want to take you first, for your birthday, and I just thought..." I trail off, suddenly unsure. Am I pushing too fast? The idea of Cora meeting my family sounded great last night, but now...

Cora's lips meet mine, soft and sure. "I'd love to," she whispers.

My relieved laughter scatters any remaining doubt as I gently tug her off the bed. "Come on, then. Time to shower."

Cora laughs, twining her arms around my neck. "A shower, huh?"

I dip my head, nuzzling her ear. "Can't have you smelling like sin when you meet my saintly mother."

"Yeah, because I'm sure showering together will definitely keep things pure and innocent," she teases.

"Glad we're on the same page," I wink, pulling her into the steamy room and kicking the door shut.

Perfect start to the day. Perfect ending to December. And if I have my way, it's just the beginning of our forever.

* * *

I park the car on the main strip, and we walk hand-in-hand to Pen and Parchment. A local bookstore in my childhood hometown.

My pulse kicks up as we approach the weathered storefront, memories flooding back. The scents of musty paper and fresh ink embrace me—a portal to carefree boyhood afternoons buried in comics or discs while Mom worked.

"A bookstore?" Cora asks, almost giddy as she stares at the window display of new releases. She breathes in deeply, something about it signaling that paper and ink are some of her favorite fragrances.

"Thought we could do something for you since the rest of the day is my agenda." I squeeze Cora's hand, affection and nostalgia swelling in my throat. "A blend of your world and mine. My mom used to run the register here on weekends when I was a kid," I offer.

I point toward a far corner with a faded green armchair. "There's a music collection toward the back, so I spent a lot of time on that chair."

"Show me. All of it. Where you spent your time. What you listened to," Cora says, her delighted smile making my heart flutter wildly.

I swallow, burying the sudden urge to drop to one knee as I lead her through the store. Because every minute with her undoes another thread I've tied the last five years—every fear, every emotion I assumed was destroyed, everything I never thought I'd want again.

I'm disappointed today is planned to the minute, so we only have an hour. We make a few selections, and by "a few," I mean we leave with no less than six books, finishing the drive to Mark's parents' house. My pulse increases the minute we hit the stop sign at Central and Brown. Years of memories flood all at once—good and bad. Nights of ding dong ditch. Scraped knees. Fights and life-changing conversations.

I'm about to expose Cora to all of this—to me, to the person I've hidden away, slowly making his way to the light, ready or not.

As we pull into the too-familiar driveway, my grip on the steering wheel tightens. I stare at the house next door, flashes of that awful morning running through my mind. Thomas's pleading eyes, Tessa storming out the door, the panic rising in my chest as I ran after her.

Cora notices me tense up and covers my hand with hers. "Hey," she says gently. "You okay?"

I let out a shaky breath, unable to tear my gaze away from the house. "Sorry. Just a lot of memories here."

She nods, stroking her thumb along the back of my hand. "Just tell me what you need, okay?"

"You. I just need you." I lift her hand, something catching my eye on her wrist—a snowflake next to her scar. *How'd I miss that earlier?* "Is that a tattoo?"

Cora blushes, smiling. "Yeah, I got it on Friday. It's a little birthday gift to myself, my reminder of where it came from and what it represents."

"Which is..." I probe, examining the ink blending into her scar.

"The day that changed everything," she says softly.

A grin tugs at my lips as I repeat, "The day that changed everything."

Cora's amber eyes sparkle with a joy that takes my breath away. "Guess this was written in the stars, huh?"

"Don't go getting all poetic on me now, angel," I tease, but my voice is thick with emotion. "C'mon, let's head in before I start writing you a sappy love song right here in the driveway."

As we approach the door, a thought hits me like a missed chord. "Uh, slight confession," I mumble, rubbing the back of my neck.

"I may have forgotten to mention to my family that I was bringing a date. And, well… it's been a while since I've introduced anyone to them."

Cora's eyes widen comically. "Jake Rhoades, are you telling me they have no idea I'm coming?"

I shrug, unable to hide my amusement. "Hey, you didn't warn your family when I showed up. Thought I'd return the favor."

She swats my arm, but I can see the smile tugging at her lips. "Not fair! I didn't even know you were coming that day."

I cup her face gently, my thumb tracing her cheekbone. "Hey, don't stress. You look absolutely stunning," I murmur, lost in the sunset of her eyes. The words fly off my tongue like they've been waiting in the wings. "They're going to love you because I love—"

I snap my mouth shut, heat rushing to my face. Shit.

Cora goes still, her lips parted in shock. A blush blooms across her cheeks as my near-confession hangs in the air between us.

"Jake?" She breathes my name like the opening notes of a ballad.

I search her face, my chest pounding. "Um, can we just pretend I didn't almost say that, if I promise to explain it all later?"

Cora studies me for a long moment, her golden eyes probing mine. Slowly, a smile tugs at the corners of her mouth. "Okay," she whispers.

"Great," I exhale, relief and anticipation warring in my chest. "Now, can we please go inside before I blurt out something else I can't take back?"

But as I reach for the doorbell, I hesitate. This isn't how I planned it, but when has anything with Cora gone according to plan?

I turn to face her, taking both her hands in mine. "On second thought… I had this whole grand gesture planned for later, but I don't want you walking into this chaos without knowing how I feel."

I take a deep breath, my pulse a staccato beat. "Cora, being with you… it's like finding the perfect harmony I didn't even know I was missing. I know this has all happened fast, and I don't expect you to say anything back, but... yeah, I love you. I can explain it all later—"

Cora's lips capture mine, silencing my rambling. I pull her closer, melting into the kiss as her hands come up to frame my face. "I love you too, Jake," she whispers against my mouth.

Yeah, this is definitely the start of something beautiful. A little messy, a lot unexpected, but absolutely perfect in its own way. Just like the best songs always are.

I hit the doorbell, grinning like I've just nailed the perfect guitar solo. Whatever happens next, I've got Cora by my side. That's all the backup I need.

The door swings open, and Diane's there, crushing me in a hug before I can blink. "Jake! It's been too long!"

As she releases me, her eyes land on Cora. "And who's this lovely young lady?"

Wow, Mark's mom is acting different than I remember. But that's a question for another day. Instead, I clear my throat, suddenly feeling like I'm on stage without my guitar. "Mrs. Bell, meet Cora. My girlfriend."

Diane's eyes widen in recognition. "Cora? Arden's sister, Cora?"

As she ushers us inside it hits me, how much Cora was a part of my world without me fully realizing it. But Cora's right. Maybe there's a reason this is all happening now.

We step into the den, and it's like we're center stage. The whole family's there–Mark's dad in his chair that's probably older than me, Owen sprawled on the couch next to my dad, Mark on the floor by Arden's feet. All eyes on us.

"Hey, everyone," I greet, aiming for casual but probably hitting somewhere around 'lead singer who forgot the lyrics.' "Sorry we're late. You know, had to make a grand entrance and all that."

Mom's face lights up like I've just won a Grammy. "Jake, is this Cora? The one you told us about?" Before I can even answer, she's pulling Cora into a bear hug. "Oh, my, I didn't realize we'd get to meet you today."

I meet Cora's gaze over my mother's shoulder, unable to hide my grin. *Yes, I told my parents about you. Yes, last week.* And damn, she's beautiful when she's trying not to laugh at me.

The conversation flows around us, laughter and chatter filling the air, but a pang of guilt sneaks up on me. These people, my family, have been by my side through thick and thin, even when I pushed them away, too lost in my own grief and self-pity to see what was right in front of me. And yet, here they are—Mom chatting animatedly with Cora and Arden, Owen and Mark reminiscing about the good old days—still loving me despite everything.

Cora's hand finds mine, threading our fingers together like she can read my thoughts. I meet her glowing amber eyes again. Because however undeserved, I have a second chance here. At love, at life, at moving forward.

Sometime later, we're each handed a glass of champagne, and Mark and Arden make their announcement. Glasses clink, and the room erupts in congratulations. But I find myself rooted to the spot, blinking back tears I wasn't expecting.

I watch Mark and Arden, their faces glowing with happiness, and suddenly I'm transported back in time. Late nights spent laughing with Mark, sharing dreams and fears. The day he met Arden, the way his whole world shifted. And now, they're starting a family of their own.

My throat tightens. This is moving forward. Not without those we lost, but despite those we lost, carrying their memory with us as we go.

I feel a gentle touch on my arm and turn to find Cora watching me, her eyes soft with understanding. Without a word, she takes my hand, leading me away from the bustling kitchen to a quiet corner of the living room.

"You okay?" she asks softly, her fingers intertwining with mine.

I nod, swallowing hard. "Yeah, just... processing. It's a lot, you know? In the best way possible."

Cora's smile is warm, patient. "Want to talk about it?"

I take a deep breath, trying to sort through the jumble of thoughts in my head. "It's like... for so long, I felt stuck. Like life was moving on for everyone else, but I was trapped in this loop of grief and guilt. And now..."

"Now you're moving forward too," Cora finishes, squeezing my hand.

"Exactly," I breathe, amazed at how she always seems to understand. I pull her closer, needing to feel her warmth, her steadiness. "You know, I never thought I'd want this again. Let alone have it. A family. A future."

Cora's arms slide around my neck, her eyes shining. "And in December of all times."

A laugh escapes, the joy nearly splitting me open as I press my forehead to hers. "I love you, Cora. So damn much."

Her lips curve into a smile against mine. "I thought we weren't talking about that until tonight?"

I chuckle, the sound rumbling low in my chest. "Yeah, well, I've never been great at following the rules. Especially when it comes to you."

Cora's laugh is soft, her eyes dancing with joy. "I love you too, Jake. Every complicated, wonderful bit of you."

As we rejoin the others, my arm wrapped securely around Cora's waist, I feel a sense of peace settle over me. It's been one hell of a ride back, but with my girl, my family, all by my side, I know I can face whatever comes next.

39

Cora

I follow Mark and Arden backstage at Navy Pier, unsure what to expect. My heart quickens as we weave through the chaotic area. Roadies and techs rush by, shouts and snatches of music echoing around us. We turn a corner and see the door, "All Rhoades" printed across it in crisp black letters.

Stepping inside, my eyes instantly dart to Jake, who's tucked away in the far corner of the room, lost in his own melodic world. With eyes closed and headphones on, he mouths along to a mysterious tune while his fingers dance across an imaginary guitar. The sight of him, completely in his element, makes me hesitate. Will I be a distraction?

As if sensing my presence, Jake's eyes snap open, colliding with mine in an electric instant. The surrounding noise and chaos fade away, and I swear I hear a record scratch. His lips curve into a slow, heart-melting smile, and those mesmerizing blue hues steal my breath like a thief in the night.

Jake's arms are around me before I can even blink, his woodsy scent mingling with hair gel and cologne as he pulls me close. My heart skips a beat at the sight of him—all styled hair and pre-show jitters, yet still unmistakably my Jake.

"Hey, you," he murmurs, nuzzling my hair. "I wasn't sure they'd let you back here. Who'd you have to bribe?"

I can't help but giggle, my fingers tracing the nape of his neck. "We wanted to surprise you. Your brother might've been my partner in crime."

Jake's eyes find Owen, his grin as bright as any spotlight. "Best. Surprise. Ever."

"Glad you approve," Owen chuckles. "Now, lovebirds, curtain's in ten!"

I start to step back, but Jake's arms tighten around me. "Nuh-uh, you're not going anywhere. Stay right here with me."

His warmth envelops me, and I notice the faint melody coming from his discarded headphones. "Ooh, what's that? New song?"

He lets out a half-laugh that vibrates against me. "It is. Want a sneak preview?"

Before I can answer, he's slipping the headphones over my ears. His velvet voice fills my senses, and suddenly, I'm lost in a world of his creation.

Your lips on mine, a perfect fit...

The lyrics wash over me, each word a caress to my soul. Two fractured souls uniting... My heart swells as I realize—this is us. Our story, set to the most beautiful melody.

Shattered pieces fusing flawlessly...

Tears prick at my eyes as the song continues. How does he do that? Turn our journey into something so breathtakingly beautiful?

When the last notes fade, I'm speechless. Jake watches me, a mix of vulnerability and hope in his eyes.

"Jake, that was... wow," I manage, searching for words adequate enough to express what I'm feeling. "When did you write this?"

He smirks, pressing a soft kiss to my cheek. "That's for me to know and you to wonder about."

I pout playfully. "Tease. Come on, spill!"

His thumb traces my jawline, sending shivers down my spine. "Patience, sweetheart. All will be revealed in due time."

"You're impossible," I huff, but can't keep the smile from my face.

Jake's forehead rests against mine, his blue eyes twinkling with mischief. "Impossibly talented? Handsome maybe?"

I silence him with a kiss. When we part, I whisper, "Impossibly perfect for me."

His answering smile could outshine any stage light. As Owen calls for final preparations, Jake steals one last kiss.

"For luck," he winks.

I watch him saunter off, his new song still echoing in my mind. Two hearts finally home at last... Yes, I think. That's exactly what we are.

* * *

The stage energy fades as we make our way to Jake's car, the night air crisp with possibility. As we slide in, the atmosphere shifts from the electric buzz of the performance to something more intimate, just us two.

Streetlights dance across the windshield as we head towards Sadie's, casting a warm glow over Jake's profile. I can't help but trace gentle patterns on his palm, my heart still soaring from his electrifying show.

"So," Jake says, his boyish grin sending butterflies through my stomach, "how'd you like being my number one fangirl?"

I laugh, playfully swatting his arm. "Fangirl? I'll have you know I'm your biggest critic, Mr. Rock Star."

"Oh really?" His eyebrow arches in challenge. "And what's your professional opinion on tonight's performance?"

I pretend to consider, tapping my chin thoughtfully. "Well, the lead singer was a bit of a showoff..."

"Showoff? Ouch," Jake gasps mockingly.

"But," I continue, leaning closer, "I suppose he was pretty irresistible up there."

Jake's eyes darken, his gaze flickering between me and the road. "Irresistible, huh? Care to elaborate on that?"

I trail my fingers along his jawline, relishing the way his breath catches. "I could show you instead," I murmur.

Jake groans softly. "Babe, I'm trying to drive here."

My phone chimes, breaking the heated moment. Jake chuckles. "Looks like your fan club is calling. Go on, check your messages. It is your birthday, after all."

I scroll through the flood of birthday messages. Then I see it—Logan's name. My stomach knots.

He's never going to stop, is he?

Jake must sense my tension because his hand finds mine, squeezing gently. "Everything okay?"

I nod, pushing thoughts of Logan aside. "Yeah, just... a lot."

Jake's thumb traces soothing circles on my hand. "Well, the night's still young, birthday girl. And I've got one more surprise for you."

"Jake," I start to protest, but he silences me with a soft kiss to my knuckles.

"Trust me," he says, his eyes twinkling with mischief and love. "You'll like this one."

We pull into Sadie's parking lot, and Jake leads me toward the bar. But I stop when I hear my name called, already placing the voice.

Logan.

Jake pulls me close as Logan approaches, hands raised placatingly. "I'm not here to cause trouble," Logan says. "Just wanted to talk."

"Then talk," I say, my voice cool.

Logan's eyes flick to Jake's protective stance. "I wanted to apologize to both of you," he starts, peering up at me. "I'm letting you go, Cora. I just... I needed to see that this... that he is what you want."

I lean into Jake's embrace. "It is, Logan. Jake makes me happier than I've been in a long time."

Regret flashes across Logan's face, but he nods. "You deserve that, Cora. Someone who puts you first." He turns to Jake, a cynical smile tugging at his lips. "Take good care of her. She's one in a million."

Jake nods, his thumb finding the now-familiar scar on my wrist. "I know it better than you might think."

Logan takes a step back, shoving his hands in his pockets. "Well, I guess this is goodbye, then."

With a final, bittersweet smile, Logan turns and walks away, his silhouette fading into the night. Maybe for the first time, I see Logan as he truly is, behind the sparkling veneer. A man spoiled by privilege, ever-accustomed to female sympathy and getting his way regardless of cost. I wonder if that was always there, if I'd been so caught up in the idea of us to see it.

Then again, it doesn't matter. That chapter of my life is officially closed.

Jake's forehead drops to mine, empathy etched in taut lines around his eyes. "You okay, baby?"

"Yeah, I really am," I say, surprising myself with how true it feels.

Jake smiles softly. "Good. Now, about that birthday gift..."

I pull back slightly. "Right now? You're about to perform again."

He chuckles, reaching for my hand and gently tugging me toward the bar. "They won't start without me."

As we head down the hallway toward one of the offices, I hear Owen's voice bellowing behind us. "Fifteen minutes, Jake."

Jake isn't phased as he unlocks a small office, guiding me inside. "Thought it'd be nice to have some privacy for this," he says, closing the door behind him and pulling a wrapped package from his bag.

My heart races as I take it, feeling the weight of something more than just a gift. "Jake, what is this?"

"Open it," he urges softly, his hands fidgeting nervously. "I found it at my parents' house last week."

His parents' house?

As I tear away the paper, my breath catches. A worn, stripped journal. One I'd know anywhere. Memories from that night hit like lightning bolts, sharp and electric. Words that saved me when I needed it most. When I needed something to put my hope in. Believing someone could love me this deeply, this selflessly.

"Your notebook," I whisper, my voice trembling. "From five years ago. You just found it?"

Jake nods, his gaze intense. "I never knew..."

With shaking hands, I open the cover. There, in Jake's messy scrawl, is a dedication and benediction rolled into one. *I can love you like this.*

I turn page after page with building urgency, as the same message flashes. Promises meant for someone else, now mine.

I pause on the last page, scarcely daring to believe the note highlighted and circled on the paper: *This one was always about you, Cora.*

His starry-eyed angel.

I look up, finding Jake's eyes brimming with emotion. "It's always been you, Cora," he says, his voice rough. "Even when I didn't know it."

"Jake," I breathe, overwhelmed. Everything clicks into place—the accident, the songs, the coffee shop, Sadie's. All leading us here. Leading me to him.

He steps closer, cupping my face. "That day you walked into the coffee shop, it was like... waking up. You've always been the one to save me, Cora. To bring me back to life. And I should have seen it so much sooner."

Tears spill over as I clutch the journal to my chest. "I can't believe you kept this. That you found it."

Jake's thumb brushes away a tear. "I love you, Cora. I think I have since that first night at Sadie's. I just couldn't admit it then."

My heart soars. "I love you too, Jake. So much."

Our lips meet in a kiss that feels like coming home and setting off on a new adventure all at once. Jake's arms wrap around me, pulling me flush against him.

"You're everything I've ever wanted," I murmur against his lips. "Coffee shop Jake."

He chuckles, the sound vibrating through me. "And you're my starry-eyed angel. Always have been."

We lose ourselves in each other, making up for lost time with every touch, every sigh. It's only when a sharp knock interrupts us that we reluctantly part.

"Jake? You in there? We're starting!"

Jake groans, resting his forehead against mine. "To be continued?"

I smile, feeling lighter than I have in years. "Definitely. We've got all the time in the world now."

He steals one last kiss before opening the door. Owen's agitated look quickly morphs into amusement as he takes in the scene.

"Save it," Jake says, cutting off his brother's smirk. "We'll be right out."

Owen raises his hands in surrender, backing away.

Jake turns back to me, his eyes soft. "Happy birthday, babe. I'll be back soon. Promise." He presses a gentle kiss to my forehead before slipping out.

I lean against the wall, fanning my heated face. How am I supposed to walk out there and act normal after that?

Pulling myself mildly back together, I smooth my dress and make my way to the reserved area. Arden takes one look at me and bursts into laughter.

"Oh no," I groan. "Is it that obvious?"

Arden reaches over, fixing my hair with a sisterly touch. "Let's just say you're glowing, and it's not from the stage lights."

Behind me, the lights dim and the crowd erupts as All Rhoades take the stage.

I turn, seeing Jake, mic in hand and a grin on his face. "Welcome to New Year's Eve at Sadie's," he stars, his voice filling the room. "For those who don't know us, we're All Rhoades. We play at this fine establishment quite often. But tonight, we'll be your tour guide, welcoming you to the New Year. We'll start by taking you back in time with a song I'd like to dedicate to a very special birthday girl."

His eyes find mine across the space, and magically, it's like we're the only two people here. As the first notes of a familiar '90s ballad start, my cheeks flush. He's serenading me. Publicly declaring his love in front of all these people.

"You two are ridiculous," Arden murmurs, but her eyes are misty as she watches Jake sing.

I lean into her, overcome with gratitude. "Thank you," I whisper. "For everything."

She squeezes my hand. "Happy birthday, sis."

"Happy New Year's, mama-to-be," I reply, cherishing this moment together.

As midnight approaches, the band wraps up, and the screen turns to the live countdown.

Before the applause has even died down, Jake's off the stage, navigating through the parting crowd. He pulls me close, and I breathe him in, sweat-dampened shirt and all.

"You were amazing," I rasp, my fingers tracing patterns on his chest as reality and fantasy blur.

His eyes pin mine, intense and full of promise. "I meant every word for you up there."

Heaven help me, after a lifetime of empty words, the sincerity in his voice has my breath catching.

As the countdown begins around us, Jake's mouth grazes my jaw. *Fifteen.* "So, Cora Cooper, any New Year's resolutions?"

I laugh, my arms winding around his neck. "I'm thinking maybe it's time to start believing in happily ever afters again. You?"

Jake's smile is soft, his eyes never leaving mine. "You." His thumb brushes over the scar on my wrist. "To wake up to your smile every Christmas morning. To kiss you breathless at every new year."

My pulse crashes heavenly as he presses his forehead to mine, his ragged vow resonating through me.

"What are you saying, Jake?"

His nose nudges mine tenderly. "All your Decembers, Cora," he breathes. "Every single one, together, for the rest of our lives. How's that for a resolution?"

My answer is lost to the crush of his mouth, sealing heated promises as the voices around us grow louder.

Ten.

This was always where I was supposed to end up. Whether it was six years ago or now, here in my arms is everything I've wanted...my ever-after, all my future chapters, all my Decembers, the love I was supposed to find.

Six. Six years ago, I saw Jake for the first time, unconscious.

Five. Five years ago, we both saved one another without realizing it.

Four. Four years ago, we were both lonely and confused.

Three. Three years ago, I thought I found my forever love.

Two. Two years ago, I started to realize I was wrong.

One.

Now, we've found each other. And that was always our destiny.

* * *

BONUS CONTENT:

The day Jake met Cora was the same day Mark and Arden reunited. Read on for a preview of their introduction, and look for 'Rewriting the Rules' to discover more of their story six years prior.

Rewriting the Rules

Chapter 1

Arden

Now, December 13th

I stab listlessly at the salad I forced myself to grab, my stomach twisting with anxiety. I'm barely holding back panicked sobs, gruesome images flashing relentlessly—the first responder's somber tone telling me the devastating news, blood-smeared accident photos making bile rise in my throat, my vibrant little sister broken and unmoving when I first saw her in that hospital bed. A twenty-car pileup on the highway...where *I* should have been driving, not her.

I wrap both arms around my heaving ribs, trying desperately to gulp enough air and clamp down the hysterical screams clawing up my raw throat. Even the thought of choking down a single bite makes waves of nausea roll dangerously.

Cora's stable now. She's upstairs sleeping, I tell myself again. *The doctors think she'll fully recover in time.* A broken wrist, some cuts and bruises. She's one of the lucky ones, based on the cries I've heard echoing from the hallway all evening.

But none of it steadies the panic attack building as I sit here alone. Everything feels seconds from unraveling completely. I'm barely holding together, attempting to stop imagining all the tragic what-ifs that can still go wrong, trying to stop feeling so responsible for her pain.

The day was a mess, starting with breakfast, when I was reminded about my forced fate—moving to Florida after graduation to join our parents at their new condo. Last Christmas, the part of me who wanted to find a middle ground agreed. But with the final semester starting in a few weeks, I'm not as convinced. Was that what propelled me to shut down? To bring up the leadership final I needed to finish, with the hope Cora would volunteer to drive them to the airport instead of me? It worked. And now I'm here, wishing I'd never opened my stupid mouth. I should be up there in that hospital bed, not Cora.

I scan the cafeteria desperately, seeking any diversion from reliving today's trauma for the thousandth time. But my frantic gaze freezes on an achingly familiar face, sending an icy spear of betrayal through my already ravaged heart.

Because, sitting a mere six feet away, looking unfairly handsome as always, is none other than Mark Bell. The man who pushed me away without explanation and pretended I didn't exist for an entire year afterward.

That cocky playboy is the last person I want to see right now.

Bitterness churns as I recall our night together last December. I guess I should be careful asking for *any* distraction.

As I debate slipping away unnoticed, Mark shifts in his seat, eyes blowing wide as they catch mine. Alarm flashes across his stupidly perfect features.

Shit.

Not the place he expected to see me, obviously.

Panicked, I drop my gaze to the table, throat tightening. Maybe Mark doesn't even remember me. We were together all of five hours, and they clearly meant nothing to him. He'll just keep ignoring me, right?

Wrong.

I brace myself as his shoes appear next to me on the carpeted cafeteria floor, and I notice his large knuckles grip my table.

Thank you, universe! I can totally handle an awful trip down memory lane on top of everything else going wrong today. No problem.

"Arden Cooper?" Mark's gentle rumble hits like a body blow.

Put on your perfect veneer, girl. Don't let him see you vulnerable.

But it's no use. When I glance up, seeing the concern swimming in the chocolate depths of Mark's eyes, I can't prevent the tears that spring forth against my will. As much as I wish his genuine empathy didn't effortlessly shatter me, one comforting look has me breaking into the pieces I've barely held together all day.

"Arden, hey. What's going on? Are you okay?" His normal charismatic tone is replaced by something gentler, almost sweet. And I hate that I secretly want to wrap myself in it.

At Mark's gentle question, the last threads of my composure loosen completely.

"My sister...she was in a car crash earlier," I gasp between sobs.

Mark murmurs my name, tentatively reaching for my trembling hand. I cling desperately as the dam inside me crumbles. He was the solid comfort I unloaded my secrets and dreams to on a whim one night last year. And however foolish, his compassion reaches me like a lifeline amidst the trauma threatening to drown me.

I'm shaking as I describe the morning, the waiting room, seeing Cora so helpless. Mark's hand tightens on mine as I weep brokenly over how close I came to losing my baby sister. Her car was pinned between three others. The pictures of the mangled steel flashing on the news testify to what could have happened.

As if sensing my spiral towards hysterics, Mark opens both arms questioningly. Without thinking, I fall into his solid chest, clinging desperately to this near stranger's comfort because I have no one else. Our parents are stuck in Florida until tomorrow.

Eventually, my ragged sobs quiet to hitched breaths. Mark's hand rubs gentle circles on my back, murmuring comfort. I vaguely process coffee cups being dropped at our table, appreciative when Mark passes one to me without a word.

I cradle the warmth with clammy hands, exhaustion hitting fully as the adrenaline drops. Sipping the bold liquid, I feel marginally more human facing Mark's compassionate stare. Am I breaking down in front of him *again*?

"Sorry. I'm not usually so dramatic," I mumble embarrassingly.

"You don't seem like the dramatic type, Arden," Mark insists lightly. "So, please don't apologize. You've been through a lot today. No one can hold up forever alone." His dark eyes radiate only kindness—no judgment or alternative agenda. "I'm happy to sit here and talk—or stay quiet—as long as you need."

My natural instinct is to raise the guard I've prudently crafted for men like Mark Bell, to spit back some comment about how he couldn't make time for me before, and to flee before revealing any more vulnerabilities. But the quiet care in Mark's expression stops me. Instead, I slowly unburden what's been swirling inside my mind. The guilt consuming me because Cora took my place driving our parents to the airport. My worry over the surgery she'll now have tomorrow. The challenging morning after we said goodbye to our childhood home in the suburbs, and my parents left for their new place in Florida.

By the time I finish, the weight on my chest feels slightly lighter, like voicing my fears out loud released some of whatever power they had. Mark listens intently, interjecting only thoughtful questions, holding more emotional intelligence than I knew he had.

Actually, that's a lie.

He's proven he could listen, that he's more than just a pretty face.

I mean, isn't this how it happened last year at the party? He approached me, flirted, and then showed genuine concern. And like a girl who thought she'd found a diamond in the rough, I let him see the real me. Heck, Mark was the one who gave me the confidence to finally tell my parents I didn't want to go to law school. In one night, he'd infiltrated parts of my heart I didn't even know existed.

Then he vanished. He shattered those newly found pieces before they even had a chance to take root.

I take a long drink of coffee, desperate to shift the dynamic from trauma and tears. "What about you, Mark? Living it up post-graduation?"

A cloud passes over his expression before he shrugs. "Oh, you know...same old. Work, parties, bar, keeping the rotation moving."

His generic playboy answer seems trained, unwilling to let go of his guise and show the additional layers I know exist. I don't know what compelled me to offer my troubles to him freely, but I wish he felt comfortable doing the same.

I tentatively reach for his hand, struck by how natural the contact already feels despite our rocky history. "Mark, why are *you* at the hospital tonight?" I probe gently.

Pain flickers briefly in Mark's eyes. "My roommate was in an accident earlier, too," he admits softly. "Car caught fire. He barely got out in time." His haunted gaze shifts toward two men clutching coffee cups nearby. "Those two...they're his brothers."

Guilt spears through me. Here I spilled my pain selfishly, while he comforted me, despite his friend's crisis.

As I open my mouth to apologize again, Mark twists his fingers into mine, squeezing gently.

"Hey, you're fine. I'm glad to be here for you, Arden."

Did he just read my mind?

I stare, almost dumbfounded, as his dark eyes turn tender.

"After everything, it's the least I can do." He chews on his lip, dropping his gaze. "I, uh...maybe I could get your number? In case you ever wanted to talk more or..."

My number?

Heat rushes to my cheeks as vivid memories from our night together flood back unbidden: Lying tangled in his sheets, the warmth of his skin against mine, his husky voice as he tossed me his phone to enter my number, the searing press of his lips...

Don't go there, Arden!

I hastily shut down the treacherous thoughts before wishful thinking trumps logic.

Definitely time to rebuild those walls.

"It's probably still in there. Unless you deleted it," I answer with forced casualness.

"Yeah..." Mark glances up, rubbing his neck.

Is he thinking about that moment, too? The electric anticipation between us when I typed in my number? The unspoken promise of something more?

I hesitate, the crestfallen look on his face tugging at my heart despite my better judgment.

Softening slightly, I offer a tentative olive branch. "But really...thanks for coming over. I guess I didn't realize how much I needed that hug."

A hug. The words feel foreign on my tongue, too intimate, too revealing.

But Mark's genuine smile in response warms me in a way I'm not ready to acknowledge. "Then I'll give you a call. We could grab coffee sometime. Or, uh, if you ever wanted to give those pants back..."

My gaze drops to the flannel pajama pants I have on—his pants. The soft fabric suddenly feels like a brand against my skin.

Damn it.

"Maybe if you'd called last year, you could've gotten them back sooner," I deflect, my voice tight as I grapple for composure, reminding myself *why* I still had them. Mark ignored me as if his life depended on it.

Forcing a polite smile, I back away. "Anyway, I should head back upstairs. Take care of yourself, Mark."

As I turn to leave, Mark's hand gently catches my wrist. "Arden, wait." His eyes search mine, a flicker of regret passing over his face. "I know I messed up last year. But seeing you here, now...I don't want to make the same mistake twice."

I hesitate, my heart yearning to believe him despite the armor I've put back up. "I...I need to focus on Cora right now, Mark. But maybe, when things settle down, we could..." I trail off, unsure of what I'm even suggesting.

Mark nods, understanding. "I'll be here whenever you're ready." He releases my wrist, but the warmth of his touch lingers as I walk away, leaving a bittersweet ache of what could have been settling in my chest.

Chapter 2

Mark

One Year Prior, December 9th

The icy glare from the woman dressed as Black Widow flashes a clear warning—she's noticed my shameless flirting. Not that it took much effort on my part. Captivating female attention is a reflex sharpened from years of watching my parents' endless infidelities. One I exert without intention now.

Still, Little Miss Widow Maker over there scrutinizing me is...intriguing. Everything about her screams buttoned up, from her self-assured posture to her sexy, yet conservative, costume. She's not my usual ditzy, easy conquest. Something about the defiance sparkling in her eyes ignites my curiosity, drawing me to her.

I murmur a vague excuse about needing a drink to the sophomore girl draped over me. Detaching my forearm from her grip, I cross the room and casually brace myself against the wall next to the woman in black.

I flash my most charming smile, keeping my tone low. "There must be something wrong with my eyes, because I can't take them off you."

After a humorless laugh, she gives an exasperated sigh. "Because every girl dreams of cheesy pickup lines," she mutters dryly, dark, coffee eyes ticking up to mine. "Is it really that easy?"

"I got your attention with it, didn't I?" I counter, letting my gaze travel slowly down and back up every curve of her body. "Can I at least get a name for the lady monopolizing my thoughts tonight?"

Something flashes in her eyes—Satisfaction? Amusement?—before they narrow with a resigned huff. "Arden. I'm Arden Cooper."

"Arden," I repeat, savoring how her name rolls off my tongue like a forbidden treat. I offer my hand, letting my fingertips graze hers a moment longer than strictly necessary. "First time here? Think I'd remember a sexy, bubbly bombshell like you."

She rolls her eyes so hard I'm afraid they might get stuck in the back of her head. Taking a sip of her drink, she fights to keep a straight face, but the delicate pink blooming on her cheeks gives her away. She's digging this banter.

"Not my usual scene. But when I heard there was a Christmas costume party, I couldn't say no," she deadpans, lifting her cup in a mock salute.

"Glad you like it. It was my suggestion. Thought it might...inspire some creativity." I flash her my patented panty-melting grin, relishing the flicker of appreciation in her eyes before she blinks it away. "I'm Mark, by the way. But you probably already knew that."

She lets out a throaty laugh that hits me straight to the core. "Oh, I know who you are."

My reputation precedes me, as usual. But I'm not letting this sassy goddess off that easy. "And what exactly have you heard about me...Widow Maker?" I lean in, close enough to catch the faint scent of her perfume, an irresistible mix of vanilla and sin.

Arden arches a perfectly sculpted brow, her lips curving into a smirk. "Oh, I've heard plenty, Pirate Playboy. Enough to know that, if you're hoping to plunder some booty tonight, you'd be better off setting your sights on easier targets. Like that fairy princess over there, who's been undressing you with her eyes all evening. I'm sure she'd be more than happy to walk your plank."

I clutch my chest in mock offense, but I can't deny the sting of her rejection. This girl is proving to be a tougher nut to crack than I anticipated. "Ouch! Ye wound me, lass. And here I thought we were having a moment."

"A moment?" She scoffs, but there's a glimmer of amusement in her eyes. "Please. I'm just enjoying the free entertainment. Watching you work the room, laying on the charm thicker than your guy-liner...it's quite the spectacle." Her gaze rakes over me appreciatively, lingering just long enough to set my blood on fire. "Though I must admit, it looks rather exhausting, putting on that performance all night long."

A surprised laugh bursts from my chest. This cheeky little minx, calling me out on my bullshit while eye-fucking me like I'm the last piece of candy in the dish? Oh, it is *on*.

"Aye, 'tis a heavy burden, being this devilishly charming." I grin, letting my accent slip into a playful pirate brogue. "But fear not, me saucy—"

"Okay, that's enough of that," she cuts me off with a snort, but I catch the way her cheeks flush ever so slightly. "Don't you have some poor, unsuspecting damsel to go deflower?"

"Nah." I wave a hand dismissively. "I'd much rather continue this delightful chat with you. In fact, I can't think of anything better."

Arden bites back a smirk, her eyes glinting with a challenge. "You're incorrigible."

"And you're loving it," I shoot back, letting my gaze burn into hers. "What do you say we continue this conversation somewhere a bit more...intimate?"

Arden holds my stare before flashing a coy smile and leaning close enough that her breath feathers my ear. "In your dreams, Pirate Playboy."

She starts to pull away, but before she can make her grand exit, a drunken party-goer stumbles into her, sloshing their drink all over Arden's sexy black costume. She gasps, jumping back as the sticky liquid seeps into the fabric.

"Oh my god, I'm so sorry!" the drunk girl slurs, swaying on her feet. "I didn't see you there!"

Arden grits her teeth, clearly trying to maintain her composure. "It's fine," she says tightly, but I can see the frustration building.

Sensing an opportunity, I grab a few napkins from a nearby table. "Here, let me help you with that," I offer, dabbing at the damp spots on her costume.

She swats my hand away, her cheeks flushing an adorable shade of pink. "I've got it, thanks," she mutters, but I can see how her hands tremble slightly as she blots at the stain.

"C'mon, let's get you cleaned up," I insist, placing a gentle hand on the small of her back. "My room's just upstairs, private bathroom and all. I can even rustle up some dry clothes for you."

Arden's eyes narrow, flashing both suspicion and intrigue. "Oh really? I'm supposed to believe you're just some Good Samaritan?"

I shrug. "Can't a guy be chivalrous without ulterior motives?"

She snorts, rolling her eyes. "In my experience? Rarely."

"Well, allow me to change your mind." I flash her my most winning smile. "No funny business. Just trying to help that damsel in distress you mentioned."

Arden raises an eyebrow, a reluctant smile tugging at her lips. "I can handle myself just fine."

"Oh, I don't doubt that for a second," I chuckle. "Just come with me."

She hesitates for a moment, then sighs dramatically. "Fine. Lead the way, Pirate Playboy. But I'm warning you, any funny business and you'll regret it."

As we weave through the crowded room, a thrill of excitement hits at the thought of getting her alone in my room. Sure, I promised to behave, but a little harmless flirting never hurt anyone, right?

Once we reach my room, Arden beelines for the bathroom, shutting the door firmly in my face.

I smirk, shaking my head. Should've expected that.

After a few minutes, I knock gently. "Coast clear in there? I come bearing gifts." I crack the door, waving a pair of flannel pants and an oversized tee. "Thought you might want something comfier than that damp costume."

Arden eyes the clothes suspiciously. "Let me guess, your 'favorite' pajama pants?"

I grin, caught. "What can I say? I'm a sucker for the classics."

She rolls her eyes but snatches the clothes anyway. "Don't get any ideas about how to get these back."

"Wouldn't dream of it." Though my thoughts are already well underway.

I retreat to the bed, surprised by the nerves twisting in my stomach. Since when do I care about impressing a girl beyond getting her into bed? But there's something about Arden that makes me want to be...better, somehow. To be someone she might actually like.

Arden emerges a few minutes later, swimming in my clothes. The oversized shirt hangs loosely off one shoulder, and the pants are rolled up adorably at her ankles. Her dark hair tumbles around her face in messy waves, making her look less like a seductive temptress and more like a soft, rumpled dream I never want to wake up from.

Damn, I want her to like me...Actually like me.

I clear my throat, trying to keep my voice steady despite the way my heart's racing. "You know, as tragic as it is about your costume, I gotta say, this look? It works for you." I gesture vaguely at her outfit, my casual tone belying the heat I feel creeping up my neck. "You could pull off the casual girlfriend costume if anyone asks."

Casual girlfriend? WTF, Mark?

Arden snorts, tugging at the oversized shirt. "More like 'Just Rolled Out of Your Bed.'"

I can't help the grin that spreads across my face. "Is that an offer? Because I'm more than happy to help make that look more authentic."

A pillow flies at my head, which I catch with a laugh. Arden's trying to look stern, but I can see the smile she's fighting. "Keep dreaming, Romeo."

"Oh, trust me, I will," I wink, patting the space next to me on the bed. "But in the meantime, how about we make those dreams a reality? We could throw on a movie, wait out the chaos downstairs. Unless you're eager to show off those stylish new pants to the masses?"

Arden hesitates, and I can practically see the gears turning in her head. She's tempted, I know it.

"Wow, first your room, now your bed? Your game is strong tonight, Pirate Playboy. Do you ever quit?"

I hold up my hands in mock surrender. "Hey, I'm just being a good host. Two friends, hanging out, watching a movie." I pause, then add with a smirk, "Unless, of course, you ask nicely."

Arden raises an eyebrow skeptically. "Friends, huh? Is that what we're calling this now?"

I lean in, voice low and teasing. "Well, that depends. What would you like us to be, Arden?"

Arden's eyes widen slightly at my question, a flush creeping up her neck. She recovers quickly, though, crossing her arms with a challenging smirk. "I didn't come tonight for titles, just entertainment."

"Fair enough," I lean back, reaching for the remote. "Prepare to be entertained, then? I promise I'll keep my hands to myself...mostly."

Arden hesitates for a moment longer, then sighs dramatically. "Alright, Romeo. But I'm choosing the movie."

"Wouldn't have it any other way, Juliet," I grin, tossing her the remote.

My heart does a little flip as Arden settles onto the bed next to me, close enough that I can feel the warmth radiating off her skin.

As she settles onto the bed next to me, close enough that I can feel the heat radiating off her body, I struggle to keep my cool. She flips through the options, eventually settling on a horror flick.

"Horror? Didn't peg you for a scary movie fan," I tease, nudging her shoulder.

She shrugs, a mischievous glint in her eye. "What can I say? Your theme inspired me."

As the movie starts, I can't help but steal glances at her. Something about the way she looks in my clothes, all sweet and messy and adorably grumpy, makes my chest feel strangely tight.

I shake my head, trying to clear the unfamiliar sensation. *Focus, Mark.* You've got a girl in your bed. This is no time to be catching feelings.

But as Arden nestles closer, her head resting on my shoulder, I'm hit with a realization that knocks the wind out of me: I don't want this night to end. And that terrifies me more than any horror movie ever could.